EVERY
LOST
COUNTRY

ALSO BY STEVEN HEIGHTON

FICTION
Flight Paths of the Emperor
On earth as it is
The Shadow Boxer
Afterlands

POETRY
Stalin's Carnival
Foreign Ghosts: an utaniki
The Ecstasy of Skeptics
The Address Book
Patient Frame

ESSAYS
The Admen Move on Lhasa

ANTHOLOGIES
A Discord of Flags: Canadian Poets Write About the Gulf War
  (with Peter Ormshaw & Michael Redhill)
Musings: An Anthology of Greek-Canadian Literature
  (with main editor Tess Fragoulis, & Helen Tsiriotakis)

CHAPBOOKS / LETTERPRESS
Paper Lanterns: 25 Postcards from Asia
The Stages of J. Gordon Whitehead

EVERY
LOST
COUNTRY

STEVEN
HEIGHTON

ALFRED A. KNOPF CANADA

PUBLISHED BY ALFRED A. KNOPF CANADA

Copyright © 2010 Steven Heighton
Map copyright © 2010 Steven Heighton

www.randomhouse.ca

Library and Archives Canada Cataloguing in Publication

Heighton, Steven
    Every lost country / Steven Heighton.

ISBN 978-0-307-39739-3

I. Title.

PS8565.E451E93 2010   C813'.54   C2009-905244-X

Text design: Leah Springate

First Edition

Printed and bound in the United States of America

10 9 8 7 6 5 4 3 2 1

When the conquerors have come down from the mountains,
then we shall be able to go to them again, simply and quietly.

—EARL DENMAN, *Alone to Everest*

Where there are humans
you'll find flies,
also buddhas.
            —ISSA

The opening pages of this novel are based loosely on an incident that occurred in September 2006 in the Nangpa La, a high pass on the border of Nepal and the Tibet Autonomous Region of China. Through this pass and a number of others, an estimated 150,000 Tibetan refugees, including the 14th Dalai Lama, have fled into exile since 1959, when the People's Republic of China consolidated its hold on Tibet, which it invaded in 1950.

The rest of my story is wholly invented, as are all of the characters.

—S.H.

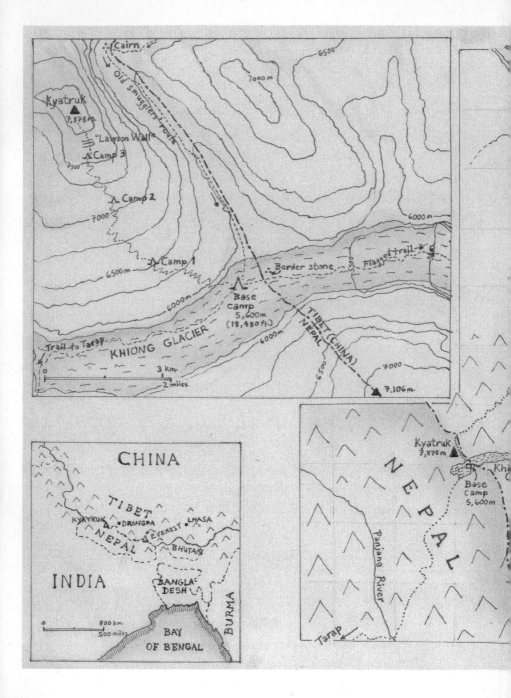

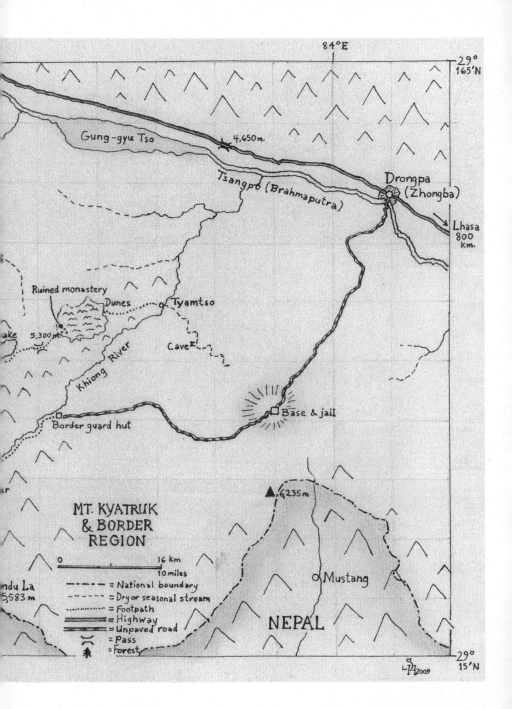

CONTENTS

ONE

BORDER STONE

AIR THIS THIN turns anyone into a mystic. Dulling the mind, it dulls distinctions, slurs the border between abstractions—right and wrong—or apparent opposites—dead and alive, past and present, you and him. The brain, rationing oxygen, quiets to a murmur, like a fine-print clause or codicil. You're at high altitude for the first time and this mental twilight is a surprise as rewarding as the scenery. This recess from judgement, sedation of the conscience. How your sleep here seems too shallow for the nightmares that await you at a certain depth. You and the rest of the party are basically drunk. Till now you've had to treat others for minor problems only, small cuts and contusions, headaches, insomnia, so this intoxication remains a luxury, not a medical challenge. Or a moral one.

To you, right and wrong are not abstractions.

Still, think of the freedom of those summit squads dreamily bypassing climbers fallen in the Death Zone—the strange luxury of that. What Lawson himself has done. You might have thought twice about joining his expedition as doctor, and bringing along your daughter, if you'd known his story when you signed the contract. But at this altitude your numbed mind has to wonder. Camp One. Put yourself in his boots if you can. Now say for certain what you'd have done, or will do.

September 20, 2006, 4:17 p.m.

SHE SEES THE TROUBLE COMING because she knows her father.

Sophie sits where she has sat for the last few afternoons, on the flat top of a concrete cylinder rebarred into the glacier, her backside in Nepal and her boots in China—Tibet. The seat of her favourite ripped jeans covers the line of Chinese characters inscribed in the concrete. Beside her stands a lightweight aluminum flagpole not much taller than she is and skewed some degrees off vertical. The breeze cooling her back can't stir the small Chinese flag, because monsoon winds or, more likely, mischievous Sherpas like Kaljang and Tashi have spooled and tangled the flag tightly to the pole. Come to think of it—and the notion pleases her on a number of grounds, playful, political—she is likely seated a dozen steps or more inside China now. Chinese border patrols have to hike up the glacier and adjust the markers from time to time. A week ago, she and her father and Kaljang and Amaris stood at the edge of base camp and watched the Chinese set up a device on a tripod and take readings and untangle and lower the flag and remove the flagstaff and pry out the marker and roll it laboriously upslope and core new holes in the ice and slot it in. Some of the men were in blue coveralls and black toques like a SWAT team, others in olive down vests over camouflage gear. They trudged from chore to chore and said little. They ignored their audience, though one of the men in camouflage, maybe eighteen or so,

4

waved shyly and blew kisses to her and Amaris. Amaris ignored him. Sophie waved back. Beside her, Kaljang's eyes narrowed merrily in his brown face and he showed his nicotine teeth. She snuck a glance at her father on her other side, but he too seemed tickled by the scene, rubbing his salt and pepper stubble, shaking his head affably. He seemed almost himself again up here.

The Chinese formed up in a crescent and saluted as they raised the repositioned flag. The red had faded to pink. "There," her father said. "They just reclaimed the thirty feet of territory the glacier pinched from them."

By four in the afternoon here the sun sets behind the Himalayas, but a quarter-hour later, the cold dusk already deepening, it finds a nock between two summits and reappears, spotlighting the pass and the valley and dyeing the glacier descending into China, so it resembles a vast, glowing channel of lava running down a volcanic slope. It happens a minute or two earlier each day. Yesterday a few others walked over from base camp to watch with Sophie, but today she's alone with her sketchbook/journal. Perfect. She was a romantic as a child—a keeper of padlock diaries, a lover of horses, fantasy novels, evenings in the dark of the covered porch on her papa's or mama's or *yiayia*'s lap, hearing the natter of rain on the roof shakes, the nicking of drops off the eaves into the garden—and at seventeen she retains enough of that lyrical spirit to choose sunset over the recreational flirtations of the Sherpas in base camp. Kaljang especially. He's cute, for sure, and to her surprise they like some of the same music, though on the whole she prefers to hang out with—tag along behind—Amaris McRae. She understands herself to have a bit of a crush on her. What girl wouldn't?

Now, as small figures, distinct in the sun's spotlight, inch toward her up the glacier, she thinks not only of her father but also of

Amaris. Amaris will want to be here, to see and film this . . . this what? It's no border patrol, even at this distance she can tell. She glances over her shoulder at the slopes of Kyatruk, where Amaris, with Wade Lawson and the rest of the summit team, should be back at Camp One after an acclimatization run and a night at Camp Two. The sun in her eyes shuts them hard. She turns back and looks down the glacier. She stands up. The figures, of varied sizes, children, adults, some in brilliant maroon garb, some in parkas, are in hurried, jerky motion, a few coming at a tottery jog. Clawing at the thin air as if pulling themselves up a fixed rope. She catches sight of other figures some distance behind them—the blue SWAT team and soldiers in camouflage gear. They're yelling, the cries coming small but emphatic, caroming off the valley's steep walls. Then another noise she can't identify—small popping sounds, like someone stepping on bubble wrap. She pulls back the hood of her fleece. A few of the soldiers are halting and falling to one knee, as if resting. More of that popping sound. An awful thought occurs to her. She turns around to base camp, gets a faceful of sun. Visoring her eyes with a hand, she opens her lips to call out. Her father, though—he will probably be first to respond.

Kaljang is slouching among the tents at the edge of camp, smoking a cigarette and watching her. It's becoming a minor annoyance, how she always seems to be on his GPS, but now she's relieved. He waves, flips back his hair and with the cigarette clamped in his lips he trots toward her on short bowlegs packed into tight jeans. Maybe he hears the faint shouting from below the pass—it's growing clearer, along with that other noise—or has he just read her anxious posture? "White people are easy to suss out," he said once in an untypically tentative way, and at first she guessed that he must have heard others, maybe British climbers, use "suss," and he wasn't sure he was using it right. Then it hit her—he felt awkward because he didn't mean *all* white people were easy to read, just Sophie.

She turns back and looks down. The amber light on the ice is shearing to one side. In the widening blue penumbra, one of the lead group has fallen, others stopping to help. Some glance back over their shoulders. She herself edges back from the border stone. Her father will be angry at her for not calling him, but he will hear the shots soon enough and he will come. Kaljang, winded, reaches her side, tosses his cigarette, takes a look down the glacier and clutches her arm through the fabric of her hooded fleece.

"Sophie. Come on."

"What? We have to do something."

He pulls her toward a crop of rockfall boulders, another of her sunset lookouts. When the expedition first arrived, Mingma Lama and his nephew Tashi strung ropes between the boulders and festooned them with white scarves and prayer flags in navy, white, scarlet, green, and yellow, and she and her father helped them. Mingma Lama said the flags and prayers would go down with the glacier into China, a gift to the Tibetans. The colours seem weirdly lurid now, hyper-bright. She tugs her arm free. She is taller, maybe even heavier than Kaljang, but he's always foisting his chivalry on her—helping her over obstacles, grinning as he grapples with her pack, trying to wrench it off her body and lug it himself—and this pushy helpfulness bothers her most when in fact she does require his strength and expertise.

"I think the one is shot," Kaljang says. "Tibetans."

"I know."

A housefly, by the sound of it, has just whizzed overhead. That's strange.

"I'm okay," she says.

He grips and pulls her more firmly and her legs lag, numb and clumsy, as if the tendons are severed. Again she yanks her arm free.

As if in refusing his help she might conjure away the situation that has caused her to need it. In air this thin the brain slows, so when things happen quickly, your thoughts straggle—the climbers tell her it's a prime danger up here, and far worse higher up.

"Here," he says. "Stay."

He tries to push her down behind the nearest boulder, whose grey face in the last of the sun radiates dry heat like a sauna stove. "Dr. Book!" he yells toward base camp.

"Don't call him yet! I need to think. We need to think what to do."

"Please, down."

Jigme and Lobsang are strolling toward them. They hiked down here from Camp One this morning. Jigme is in cargo shorts and a parka and wearing earbuds, wires running down to the MP3 player in his hand. Kaljang flaps his raised palm at them: go back! Jigme shrugs and they keep dawdling over. Kaljang plucks his two-way radio from its holster with a flourish of manly competence—courting her, even now—and crouches down beside her. She's unaware that she has crouched down. A sweet juniper whiff of sweat, tobacco. "Hi there?" he says into the radio. "It's Kaljang."

"Oh my God," she says, "how did *he* get here?" Wade Lawson stomping through base camp with what looks like a machinegun slung on a strap over his shoulder.

"Get the Dr. Book now," Kaljang says into the radio. "We need him."

One time when she was ten, her father charged out the front door as if on an emergency call. She'd called him, shouting from the front window to the kitchen where he was making spaghetti and meat sauce, drinking a glass of beer, humming off-key. She'd never seen him on an urgent call but she guessed that on his foreign postings—the long stretches when he was away—he must race around like this all the time.

Across the street, two high school thugs were performing the ritual preliminaries to an assault. Their victim was the street's most conspicuous target, a timid, chunky clarinet prodigy who always carried his instrument around. Matters had just reached the shoving stage—one attacker shoving from the front, the other from behind, the kid's head bobbling. Her father moved with an oddly stiff, lunging gait, slippers slapping the icy pavement, and she in the doorway, watching him go, hugging herself to contain the trembling. He wasn't a big man (now, at seventeen, she's as tall as he is, and even then he didn't seem paternally huge), though he was fit and gristly and had a focused gaze of the kind she associated with predators who could render prey catatonic with a glance. He was a karate expert, too, she told herself then, on the freezing porch, as he rushed toward the bullies. Had she told herself that? Anyway, it was something she believed back then, later discovering it wasn't true—he had one of the lesser belts, had only taken a couple of courses, years back, before medical school.

The bullies turned toward him and took a step back each. Her father, seen from behind, standing in the gutter, looked small, while they, big guys in inflated parkas, were elevated on the sidewalk above the curb.

"Hey, relax, man. We were just fooling around."

What her father said next she didn't hear. Short jets of white breath huffed up from him, like comic strip word balloons with brief expletives. Simon, the clarinet boy, recoiled his pudding face and rounded his eyes at her father, as if reconsidering the source of his peril. Her father stepped up on the curb. The bullies looked at their boots, wagged their hooded heads lamely and splayed their gloved hands as if dropping weapons on the snow. Then turned and slouched off.

And then? The radiance of the remembered crisis had overexposed what followed. Her father, she knew, would have comforted Simon, his hand on the boy's shoulder, head tilted as he looked him firmly in the eye—*You sure you're all right?*—and maybe chucked him under the chin.

Hours or days later, dinnertime, still scared and thrilled, she asked him what he'd said to those guys. Her mother set down her fork. Her brother, Pavlos, looked up from the broccoli floret he was trying to atomize with his stare. Her *yiayia*, who viewed domestic strife as a form of entertainment, slid her glance expectantly from face to face; her son-in-law might be an Anglo, not a Greek, but at the table he was seldom lost for words.

"Never mind," her mother said shortly, though her eyes flicked toward her husband with a wry, impromptu fondness. "Never mind what Papa said."

"Pass the wine, love," her father said.

"Papa should learn to be a bystander sometimes. Or call the police."

"There's no such thing," he said.

"As what?" Sophie asked.

Her mother filled her own glass, then *yiayia*'s.

"Bystanders." He said the word quietly, as if embarrassed to find it in his mouth.

With both hands Sophie took the bottle and poured her father some red wine, sorry for him, painfully proud, still unable to see how her mother might feel: that by making his care, his very life and limb, equally available to all, he deprived them of an exclusivity they had a right to expect.

3:05 p.m.

WADE LAWSON STANDS on the eastern lip of the level acre of snow and rock now known as Camp One. He stretches his cracked lips for the video camera. The camera's humble size still bothers him. Amaris has explained, but all the same. Kyatruk may not be the world's tallest mountain, but it's a handsome rock with a tantalizing history, one of the few worthy peaks still officially unclimbed, and Lawson feels that the IMAX treatment, or at least 35 mm widescreen, would do it better justice. It, along with him. Take the view behind him: two lines of lesser peaks framing a massive glaciated valley curving down to the Tibetan plateau, its dry, khaki plains sprawling outward with a clarity inconceivable at more banal altitudes. Scintillating sunlight. How can a camcorder hope to show the scope of that? Show the bigness of this whole venture. But that's how Amaris wants to do her "doc," she has told him, stressing words like *spontaneity* and *immediacy* and *intimacy*. "You're the expert," he keeps saying, though it isn't a phrase he ever feels comfortable using. In Lawson's experience, real experts are rare, and when you work with people you have to exert as much control as possible if you hope to have things work out in rough accord with your will.

All the same, she seems to know what she's doing, and she seems to be on his side. He wasn't sure at first. He still isn't—not always. In fact, he shunts back and forth between opposed certainties: one minute she's definitely "on side," and how could it be otherwise, given who he is and what he has been through and the intense time they are spending together, and the next minute he feels certain she's going to betray his trust and enrol in the regiment of his detractors . . . *and maybe she already has.* That would be the easier course for her, wouldn't it? As a sort of journalist?

Then again, she has a reputation for working against prevailing opinion.

"Right," she says in the drillmaster tone she uses when shooting, "I'm starting now."

"I thought you *were* filming," he says.

"With you grinning into the lens like something off a tour bus? You still don't get the idea, Wade. And it's not film, it's tape."

He enjoys her cordial rudeness. It's less cordial in the morning, but that will be the altitude. He knows how much she isn't sleeping.

"Take out the gum," she says.

Shy, deferent women (what he mistook her for at first, with her pageboy haircut, her reading glasses, her Asian face and small stature) are usually more attractive to him, but he's always prepared to adapt and this is a temporary arrangement. Their fondly hostile banter, he feels, is a fun and clever mode they are developing and it reminds him of a certain couple he saw once in a film, though he can't recall which film, or any details. If this repartee finds its way into Amaris's film, it might help show the world that he's not the humourless ego machine his critics make him out to be.

Maybe his attackers' problem is that they're not the directors of their own lives, so they hate the few people who are.

"Turn that way," Amaris says. "Toward base camp. Right. In profile. I just want a couple seconds here."

Proud of his profile, Lawson approves of Amaris's instruction. In his view, most men worry too much about the muscles of their torso, and especially the arms, to the neglect of their legs and also, yes, their *face*. In the case of the legs, this is no mere cosmetic point—not for a professional athlete. The face is another issue altogether. For one thing, it's the part of you that's always visible. Few factors affect appearance like the bone and muscle structure of the face. Heavy brows, a strong jawline with prominent, almost equine jaw muscles—these are secondary sexual characteristics, markers of virility. Years ago Lawson read in some magazine that men who chew gum have stronger, more dramatic jaw muscles. He'd taken up gum-chewing and over the years has left a trail of colourful chewed nuggets down the cordillera spine of the western hemisphere and high up in the Alps, the Caucasus, the Himalayas.

As Amaris films, he works his jaw slightly and gazes out over the valley. He doesn't forget himself for a moment, yet he isn't immune to the beauty. He has loved the high country since childhood, when, after his mother died, his father moved them from Vancouver to Nelson, B.C., to open a brake repair shop. Lawson and his big brother Clyde—passionate amateurs who improvised their equipment or went without, relying on strength and guts—summited Mount Gimli when he was just thirteen. He's still proud of that.

Something nabs his eye a long way down the valley, at the toe of the glacier by the turquoise thaw-water pond beyond the terminal moraine. At this distance—a few kilometres—he can make out nothing distinct, just specks of colour amid the grey scree fields and boulders around the tarn. Slight movement.

"All done?" he asks.

"For now."

He pats his windshell pocket for the binoculars.

"Tashi! My binoculars. In the tent."

"Sahib!"

Lawson shakes his head and grins. He feels that the young Sherpa's antiquated salute, while no doubt sincere in its desire to please and impress an admired leader, is also a touch satiric. The salute pleases him anyhow. He doubts that viewers of the documentary will catch the wink of artificiality. So he grins on, with leaderly tolerance, while in his gut a twinge of concern delves deeper. There should be no activity at the base of the glacier. The Chinese aren't due back to correct their border until after his expedition should be done and packed up and hiked out to Tarap. Few travellers or pilgrims, he has heard, still use this high and difficult pass. Lawson wonders if another expedition could be on its way up, from the Chinese side instead, but what are the odds? Kyatruk remains unclimbed not so much because of certain technical challenges above 7,000 metres, but because it's so remote, so *expensive*. He'd remortgaged his house and his failing climbing gym to underwrite this assault and it still wouldn't have happened if he hadn't convinced one of the regulars at the gym, along with his "nephew" Zeph, who works there, to enlist as paying climbers, and if Amaris hadn't landed two film grants. As for sponsors, the big players won't touch him now and he has landed just one, a credit renewal company called New Future that was attracted by the theme of the climb and of the film—"redemption"—and that seems to see Lawson, disgraced but still game, as a man their ruined clientele can relate to.

Now he gauges the possibility that a team of his rivals has launched an expedition as a direct challenge to him. A wild idea, but for a moment his scalding sense of grievance makes it plausible and also lends a grim gratification, like any mental screenplay of victimhood, yes, and vengeance—because now he sees that they'll be so far behind on their acclimatization, they can be no real threat. His little summit team will be ready to go in three or four days, if he and Mingma can get the fixed ropes in place by then. In fact, if he had to, he could probably summit within a day or two, solo, no ropes or oxygen, as he would much prefer. But he has to get both paying climbers safely to the top, along with Amaris—Amaris above all. Her and her little camera. Getting her up there past the Lawson Wall, as he already thinks of it—that'll be the challenge.

"The Chinese come back?" Tashi asks, bowing his head as he presents the binoculars with both hands, a fawning courtier. (Is that a slight smile?) Amaris has followed the young Sherpa to where Lawson stands. She flips her sunglasses up onto her toque and squints into the distance. Freckles on her small, sunburned nose. Her strong chin lends a hint of aggression to her girlish face, like a skeletal assertion of will and robust sexuality. Who'd have guessed?

Lawson slots the barrels into his eye sockets and scans the blurred landscape impatiently.

"What is it, Sahib?"

"Give me a second," he snaps.

"Oh . . . I see it now, Sahib."

Lawson figures this is a lie. He has concluded that the kid needs glasses. A fresh wave of grievance swells up in him. The best Sherpas are too expensive for him and the best climbers, or best *known* climbers, now shun him. Jake and Zeph are respectable rock climbers but lack high-altitude credentials. His head Sherpa is a drunk and the rest are raw teens. The team medic, cheerfully social, weirdly unserious, belongs to some outfit like Doctors Without Borders, so he's used to working for pocket change in war zones and sweltering African clinics but knows zero about high-altitude medicine. Plus he's brought along his daughter, with her nose ring and her snowboard—another mouth to feed.

"I see it too," Amaris says. "I'm getting my camera."

"Your camera?" Lawson says. "But this has nothing to do with the climb!"

The rustle of her parka as she walks away. He finds his target zone and focuses. A group of people, twenty-five or thirty, filing up a rough trail over the gravel of the moraine, nearing the toe of the glacier. They're dressed as variously as folk in a big city multicultural parade—some in bright parkas and jeans, others in layered purple robes (monks or nuns, he guesses), a few in heavy, weathered-looking coats he dimly recognizes as traditional Tibetan wear. On a man's shoulders, a bobbing toddler. Further niggles of motion catch his eye in the unfocused valley behind the group. He adjusts the lenses. A second, smaller group leaps to clarity: Chinese border guards and soldiers armed with automatic weapons. For a moment he wonders—hopes—could the armed men be some sort of escort—maybe for pilgrims? As if. He shakes his head. This air slows the brains of even the people most used to it. It's hard to estimate the space between the groups. Not far, though. The first Chinese trooper, or officer, has reached the shore of the tarn. Lawson refocuses on the Tibetans. He can feel the pulse in his temples and at the root of his tongue.

"Sahib?"

He doesn't care much about politics, but he's roughly aware of the situation in Tibet; one of the attractions of Kyatruk is that the border up here should be too remote for refugees. He can't look away. He's willing the Tibetans to hurry and escape, although escape, naturally, will bring them across the border and into his base camp, and possibly draw the Chinese with them. "Oh, fuck," he says under his breath—"why now?" And he sees, now, that it will probably be best for the Tibetans to surrender where they are, to go back with the soldiers, before anybody gets killed.

A brief, concise clattering beside him. He turns his head.

Amaris has set up her camcorder on the tripod and stands tensed behind the lens.

"They're Tibetans, I think," she says.

"Yeah." Lawson guesses she hasn't seen the Chinese yet. Her camcorder's zoom lens will lack the range of his high-power binoculars. Good thing.

"I'm going to have to go down to base camp," he announces. "You two stay here."

"I'm coming too," she says.

"Don't be ridiculous, Mari—you're exhausted."

"Wait!" she says, "there's something else . . . Oh, wait . . . I think it's those soldiers we saw last week. What would they . . . ?" Her voice dries up.

He juts his jaw as he lowers the binoculars. "Right. I better just go down and make sure everything's okay."

"*I'm* coming too," she tells him in her hard, argumentative tone, turning her face to him, the camera still running.

"You've got to rest, Mari. We'll be going back up to Camp Two in—"

"Wade, are you *serious*? You think I'm not going to go to base camp now and shoot what's happening down there? This is what I *do*."

"But this is not your story. Look, we've come halfway around the world . . ."

"It's a *story*, Wade!"

"What's that supposed to mean?"

"And stop shouting all the time!"

She flicks the camera off, unhitches it, roughly collapses the tripod.

"But the Tibetans," he says, trying to confine his voice, "they have children and baggage. They'll arrest them way before they get near base camp and you'll have made the trip down for nothing. It'll take, like, maybe two hours . . . if it's both of us."

"You saw those soldiers and you weren't even going to say."

"The view's better from up here, anyway. You'll get better shots from up here."

"Are you coming, Wade, or am I doing this alone?"

Lawson is good at altitude, as good as anyone he knows, has summited Makalu without oxygen—he knows it for a fact, even if the Others dispute it—but now he feels a keen need for bottled gas.

"Amaris. You are exhausted. You look exhausted. You haven't slept in days."

Tashi lets a chuckle slip, then channels it into a cough. The goggling sunglasses on his bony little face made him look like an anthropoid housefly. Lawson shoots him a glare. The kid looks down, turns on his heel and flits back toward the camp, where Mingma stands staring and Jake's face, with its bushy, pale moustache over beaver teeth, peeps out of a sagging tent.

"Dude," says Jake, "what's up?"

"If you push too hard," Lawson goes on, "I have to warn you, Mari, you can get really sick up here. You don't want to get sick up here."

"*You* don't want me to get sick up here," she says, and turns and stalks toward the trail.

"Well . . . of course I don't!"

She's marching with the tripod over her shoulder, a petite, purposeful form: coat-puffed body, boyish hips and thin legs in Lycra, nothing on her feet but yellow boot liners. The altitude is getting to her, all right—normally she's so organized and composed.

"Amaris, wait!" he calls with a quaver in his throat that distresses him very much. Deepening his voice he says, "At least get into your boots."

And he adds, in his mind, *I knew you'd fuck me over too.*

VOICE OVER, SCENE 4?, with slow pan upward from base camp to the peak, maybe with Dutch tilt?, then series of stills: Albert Murloe with Princeton rowing team, 1921/ a copy of a Murloe pamphlet/ unknown solo pilgrim with yak/ second slow pan upward, but of camp 1 and camp 2 part of slope:

Lawson claims he is drawn to Mt Kyatruk by the story of amateur climber Albert Murloe, the only other person known to have attempted the peak, who disappeared somewhere on its upper slopes in early September 1924.

A young American who flees Princeton in 1922 in the wake of an unspecified scandal, Murloe drifts through various towns and cities in Western Canada, including Lawson's own home base, Nelson, where he becomes an amateur mountaineer and also writes and hand-sells pamphlets endorsing his peculiar theories about health and stamina. Murloe's basic theory is that meats, fruits and vegetables in their natural, fresh condition "over-liquefy" the body, therefore "diluting and draining its strength through diuresis"—and that such foods should only be eaten in a preserved, dried state. ~~He writes, "Let a man subsist on nothing but such desiccated fare, he shall have the stamina and will-force of our remotest ancestors, that is to say, of ten modern, civilized, men.~~" It's an idea that will convince Murloe that he can achieve what others can't.

Like Maurice Wilson, Earl Denman, Aleister Crowley and other mystical amateurs of the early and mid-twentieth century, Murloe is drawn to the Himalayas for spiritual as much as physical reasons ~~or for reasons that exist in the place where the spiritual and physical overlap~~. In fact, his original plan is not to climb mountains at all, but to trek north from Dehradun, India, and then slip across the border into Tibet, at that time an independent country closed to foreigners. Disguised as a pilgrim, his face darkened by means of henna and walnut juice, he will then hike a thousand kilometres to the forbidden city of Lhasa, subsisting on jerky, raisins, prunes and seeds. But in Drongpa the Tibetans catch him and escort him under guard to a pass on the border of Nepal. There, struck by what he describes in a letter left with his guards as "the most sublime and lovely mountain in the world," he declares an *intention to climb Kyatruk, as the Tibetans tell him it is called, with only the clothes on his back and his now sparse store of dried food. His guards try to dissuade him, but Murloe is adamant, ~~and anyway the face of the mountain he means to climb is on the Nepali side of the border~~. The Tibetans, though they have no obligation to help Murloe, nevertheless lend him a sheepskin coat and set up camp on the glacier at the top of their side of the pass, near where Wade Lawson's base camp now sits. They expect Murloe to come down off the mountain in a day or two, and figure he will need assistance when he does. He never comes down. According to the guards, who later deliver his letter and their account to the regional governor in Drongpa, he is last seen climbing up the extensive snowfields high above the glacier, probably near Lawson's own camp 2.*

3:46 p.m.

HOW CAN THERE BE so little oxygen up here? Here, where there's so much sky, and air—huge blue volumes of space seeming so cleansed, fresh, ecstatic with energy . . . so *breathable*. She and Wade are pounding down the switchbacks worn into the dense Styrofoam slopes above base camp. Already this morning, all but sleepless, she spent two and a half grinding hours applying her brakes to descend the steep trail from Camp Two. Now every few switchbacks she needs to rest, bent double, hands braced on her quivering knees. Her lungs seem filled with vaporized glass: with each deep breath, she hacks until she half expects to leave a crimson froth on the snow.

This pace is unnatural but she will not ease up. Easing is not Amaris's way. She will not ease up, yet she's slowing down and Wade is close behind her, casually overtaking her. It's humiliating to work so hard and be overtaken. At Camp One, starting out, she vowed she would beat him down and half believed she could do it, could draw on her years of triathlon training, along with this spike of professional adrenaline (she keeps glancing over at the glacier to see how events are playing out, but she can't focus, her vision slurred, head trembling)—and her deepening dislike of Wade. Now, at a hook in the trail, he grazes past her, his elbow making the slightest contact with her breasts, and this contact is more insulting than either a rough jostle or a squeamishly complete avoidance would be. She knows, of course, that he's too crudely direct to *plan* so sly an affront. His breathing has a brusque, chuffing sound, like a man in a gym kicking a heavy bag. He slows to keep pace with her from the front, as if to be helpful.

"The Chinese might mistake you for a Tibetan," he booms.

"Very funny, Wade." Seconds pass before she can finish. "A Tibetan with a high-tech video cam?"

"Why not?"

"Nobody's brain works up here," she says in a breath.

"You're making a mistake."

"Like we've all got Alzheimer's."

"It's not too late to go back, Mari."

"*Amaris*," she says.

"It's not far."

She totters, rounding the next switchback, thrown off by the tripod on its strap over her shoulder, a green steel Manfrotto, indestructibly solid, a bit heavy for up here, but then with the Sherpas around she has rarely had to carry it anyway—though she has tried. She should have asked that Tashi or Mingma come down with them, but she set out in a huff. Wade, she knows, is aware of her struggle and is trying to capitalize on it to change her mind. "Here," he says, "let me take that for you." He says it as a command and she always declines commands. She hates what people assume about her from her size, coupled with her race. She sees it in their complacent looks; she speed-reads it in the lingo of their smallest gestures. How salesmen will spice up their pitches with a hint of smirky aggression. How barflies figure it's cool to hit on her harder and longer than on, say, a lofty, forbidding blonde. They assume (or so she assumes) that she is pliant, pushable, eager not to offend, gratified by the slimmest attention, and she relishes those little scenes when she debunks them.

Now she surrenders her Manfrotto, coughing hard, refusing to meet his eyes—or the machine-sleek facets of his aerodynamic shades. His black bodysuit, designed by himself, resembles a wet-suit, and this enrages her too. Her fuse has always been on the quick side; up here it's instantaneous.

"We should have roped up," he says, shaking his head tragically. "I had no idea you were this tired."

"Walk!" she tells him, too winded to shriek the word.

Having staged this scene of his own, he pelts away down the switchbacks as if to levy interest on her humiliation, or maybe to run off and pitch the Manfrotto in a crevasse. That pounding swagger—it's like he's trying to stamp indelible footprints into the mountain. Can't he see that whatever's happening down there could add to the story, *his* story? True, it might also be the key to another story. Maybe a better story. She doesn't know how much more time she can spend with Wade John Lawson. Even the sex is mediocre now, though she can admit that's largely because of her own fatigue, this dredging cough and a thumping headache like a nonstop hangover. Getting closer to him wouldn't be good for the film, anyway—or for her. Always best to be the one who feels less, who can scramble clear of the smoking crater when things implode.

At first the sex was very, very good—in the hotel in Kathmandu, the lodge in Pokhara, even in the tea houses as they trekked up through the Dolpo, her energy buzzing on the cool, crystal air and the sunshine and the glasses of sugary milk chai and the exercise her body felt born for. And the eye-popping visuals she was taping. Not that she ever much *liked* Wade. Yes, he has the Olympic body and is handsome in the older way she prefers, with prematurely grey hair that looks terrific against his coppered skin, and he sports a solid, rhinocerine self-esteem that's striking, almost touching, given his public fall and his private losses, and he remains the proud curator of his own personal hall of fame and either doesn't know or doesn't know *why* this antagonizes people. His unguarded cockiness in an age of canny PR makes Amaris feel almost reluctant now—an expert hunter training her sights on something lumbering and endangered, like a last mastodon.

Several of her films have focused on a difficult outsider. She believes it's only by chafing up against abrasive characters that you can agitate your fears and assumptions into the light of day, shed them and grow in useful directions. Most people—most of her acquaintances—instinctively seek out agreeable people as lovers and friends and business partners and creative collaborators, and who can blame them? Like the instinct for musical harmony, it's perfectly natural. Yet harmony is conservative and you can only surprise and change yourself by diving into discord. She believes that face-on encounters with dissonant people—what she herself tries to be when confronted by the presumptuous—might force her audience to question themselves and their ideas.

At any rate, making those films has changed *her*. As has her choice of some highly discordant lovers in the past decade. Each has left her more independent, stronger, smarter. So will Wade. She will not appear on screen, but her voiceover will casually refer to their involvement. Wade's wife has recently divorced him, so the reference shouldn't bother him. He'll probably love it. Wade the horse. As for how it makes her look, she tells herself to forget it. Being hated isn't what hurts your possibilities, the fear of being hated is what does. How he feels about her after the film's release means little to her. She knows he's twinning their mummy bags each night partly in hopes of exercising control over the story. Fair enough. As in real, unrecorded life—or the version of it she has arrived at—they're using each other. Well, love with no fine print or provisos is a sentiment with *wishful* splashed all over it.

These slopes lie in blue shadow but the hidden sun lasers light onto the pass and down the glacier. As she rests at a hook in the trail, she picks out the Tibetans, lit up distinctly, and the Chinese behind them. She hears a faint snapping she doesn't recognize and decides it must be gunfire. She thinks of taking out her Canon and trying for a hand-held pan, but with her lungs heaving and her heart thudding its way up her throat, she'll catch nothing with the zoom but a blur. There's someone by the border stone, wearing black. Sophie Book. The girl should get back from there. She's way too naive, too trusting. A faint maternal twinge helps push Amaris on, with her quaking knees, shrieking thigh muscles. Just a minute's rest and her sweat is cold. Up here in the stratosphere, almost, when the sun goes, the temperature skydives like on some outer planet. Wade says that for climbers, above 25,000 feet or so is the "Death Zone." To her, everything here is a death zone. She thought she'd love it, she was dying to hike up and climb and shoot, but there's nothing growing or dwelling here, like in Antarctica. She can see the beauty—the naturally polarized light, fresh nuances in the spectrum of whites and blues, these monumental forms—but it's the lifeless beauty of a tomb.

An interface of light and shadow bisects the glacier lengthwise, sweeps over it with time-lapse swiftness, muffles it in dusk, while the slope she's descending lights up again. The sun reappears straight in her eyes, a solar cymbal clash. Wade is down there, spidering through the rock debris at the edge of the glacier, her precious tripod over his shoulder. On the glacier now he lopes up the flagged trail into base camp, surprisingly close below.

More faint sounds of gunfire, hollering.

Her legs are themselves again, oddly revived.

As she trots among the dozen scattered tents of base camp, Lew Book, up ahead, ducks out of the larger "control tent" and strides off, pulling a sweater over his shaggy grey-flecked hair. Now Shiva Gurung flaps out of the tent, waving Book's medical kit and running after him. It's the first time Amaris has seen Book in 911 mode. Sometimes he's subdued, quietly serious, donning his glasses to examine a cut or a sprain, gauging his few words in a voice sounding disused, rusty and deep. More often he's the heart of the party. She has never known anyone to change so fast in the vicinity of food, drink, company. He's medium height, handsome in a weathered, rumpled way, pale green eyes, the whites very clear in his sundark face. He'll enter the tent taciturn but then, smelling dal or ramen, wrapping his hands around a mug of chai, sitting on a camp stool by the Primus stove, he'll unfold: cheeks flushing, hands and face unclamping as if in a photo sequence in retro order. Book aging backwards. Effusive vitality draws you in from the night, like a campfire or a packed cocktail lounge, and before long the Sherpas (always game for a party), the climbers, Shiva the Chef, Sophie Book and Amaris herself are all clubbed together in chatty rounds of stud poker or a two-board tournament of *bagh chal*. Even Wade will join in, though he always seems a touch distracted, as if trying to puzzle out just how he's been deflected from the obsessive work of his climb. Or is it that he's not the centre of attention here? Then again, neither is Book, who seems to moderate things, an instinctive impresario, so the limelight pivots round among the partiers—Book bantering inclusively, giving astute compliments, refilling mugs with coffee, milk chai, Nepali gin, once breaking out a bottle of decent Chianti he secretly packed up to base camp. She has seen how fast he'll spot the agitation in Wade, or the skeptic's edge in herself (she's a loner more by professional will than inclination, but it's a habit now and she starts to panic when spontaneous revelry tempts her from her work)—and he'll strive to draw them out, draw them in, as if sensing in their reticence a threat to the group's soaring mood. At first she figured he was a drunk, booze loosening his various valves as quick as a nitro tab under the tongue, but then a few times she watched him earlier in the day: Mingma Lama would pour gin into his own chai, but Book just stuck to chai. And still the circle leapt to life. At times Sophie would watch him with a mildly mortified, dubious look Amaris recalls from her own youth: the disillusionment of thinking a parent is donning a public face, as Amaris's adoptive parents did constantly. But though Amaris is always game to debunk a phony, what she senses here is that Book, the social, sensual Book, isn't faking. He thrives on groups. His own good mood is umbilically linked to the happiness of others.

It's the other Book, the high-minded humanitarian, she doesn't quite buy.

Ahead now, Shiva, in shorts and knee socks and a green Gurkha sweater, catches up to Book, gives him his kit and grips his other hand in the Nepali way as they stride together, almost running, toward the border. 4:26 p.m. *Nice shot*, a part of Amaris's mind reflects, while the larger part is hurrying after them, her hands unzipping her parka and the inside sack she wears at her navel like an external womb, to keep the camera secure and warm.

4:02 p.m.

LEW BOOK AND KALJANG SHERPA sit playing *bagh chal* on a folding card table in the so-called control tent. They sip milky chai spiked with Snow Leopard gin while smoking two-rupee cigarettes—something Kaljang is always doing and that Book does mostly when he's having a drink and when Sophie isn't around. Right now she'll be a few minutes' walk away, at the edge of base camp, on the border, where she likes to sit sketching or writing and listening to her music.

Beside the card table Shiva Gurung sits on a folding stool, watching their game avidly, as if Nepal's national honour hangs on the outcome. He's gripping the cracked handle of a skillet full of dry lentils, shaking them as if panning for gold. As the game nears its crisis—one tiger trapped, two goats eaten—his shaking takes on small tics and arrhythmias.

Kaljang flicks the bangs out of his droll eyes. "If tigers win this next match, I receive your daughter's hand in marriage."

"I doubt it," Book says cheerfully.

"Tigers are very hungry now."

"Sure, but the goats are unscrupulous."

Kaljang jumps a third goat and removes it from the board. "Does that mean similar to unsuccessful?" he deadpans.

"Resourceful," Book says. "No . . . cunning, full of tricks." He tops up the young man's mug with the eight ounce mickey. "Willing to do anything to win."

"Ah, but they're smaller, the goats—the gin affects them more!"

"Nah," Book says briskly—though he hesitates with his next move, sensing that somewhere on the board he is missing some tiny, crucial thing. (That's always what kills you.) "What's a cocktail spread out over a herd?" he says, stalling. "Just loosens them up. These goats are in the zone, Kal. These goats are on their game."

In *bagh chal* four tiger-shaped pieces try to "eat" their prey— twenty smaller pieces in the guise of goats—by jumping them checkers-style, while the goats try to neutralize the tigers by sur- rounding them. Book needs to pin down a second tiger, soon. At this altitude, thinking a few moves ahead is hard. If he loses a fourth goat, the game is all but lost. If he loses a fifth, it's over.

The rattle of lentils, louder now, is like a drum roll before an execution.

"Attention now!" Shiva tells Kaljang, who plucks up a tiger and pauses, exhaling smoke with cocky slowness, then raps it down decisively behind a stray goat on Book's side of the board—right under Book's nose. Book has been wholly focused on the main crisis on the other side of the board. How very like him. He shakes his head and groans.

"Oh dear—too bad!" exults Shiva. (Book has defeated Kaljang just once, Shiva twice, but the Nepalis collectively mourn, debate and recriminate each time it happens.) Shiva adds something cele- bratory in Nepali, then quits shaking the lentils to tweak out a few black pebbles that have worked their way to the edge of the pan.

"You can resign now, Doc," says Kaljang, suavely relighting Book's cigarette. "To spare the goats their final shame."

"You mean the tigers take prisoners?"

"Why should they not?"

"Besides, we might rally," Book says. "Never discount the goats." Squinting through the smoke of his cigarette, Book moves to block the threatening tiger. Shiva tops up his mug again. Book knows they oil him with gin partly in hopes that he'll retaliate with his comic Nepali—really a random salad of Hindi and Nepali. He's been posted in Nepal and India several times in the last few years and wherever he's posted he picks up local phrases and mannerisms, though he only really performs them while at table, drinking tea, coffee or booze, playing cards or telling jokes.

In July he was in Darjeeling, treating outcaste locals and exiled Tibetans, including several who'd recently fled their country, when he got the news about Sophie. It wasn't the first time she'd been in trouble with the law, though in the past it was after protests—against an arms fair, nuclear power, the closing of a women's shelter—and less serious. Book arranged to cut short his posting and return to Toronto, but not before he read a mass email about a climbing expedition seeking a base camp doctor. As Book flew home (if you could call it that: divorced now, growing distant from his daughter and son, he stayed in motels on his brief stints in town), it occurred to him that by taking the job and bringing Sophie back with him to Asia he could temporarily remove her from her troubles, her now ex-boyfriend and her manic texting and general stress, while allowing himself and the girl to reconnect. And they'd be in the mountains—an isolated base camp—where she could hike and sketch. He knew she was yearning to go to Asia and was passionate about the Tibetan cause and they'd be right on the border, so she could still feel politically engaged—which would matter to her, he knew. At the same time, she would be on a true retreat.

That Amaris McRae is up here with them is a bonus he didn't expect. He hasn't seen her films, but he knows that her last one, about the alleged hypocrisies of a demagogic documentary filmmaker in the States, got up a stir. Now she and Sophie are spending a bit of time together, and Amaris is even talking about using a few of Sophie's photos as stills in her film—a huge thrill for the girl. Amaris acts really different around Sophie. With Lawson, Book and the rest, she often speaks with a pre-emptive aggression, as if anticipating resistance or disrespect; with the girl, she's like a slightly tart but affectionate young aunt. And while Book can tell she's indifferent to Sophie's earnest politics, she acts tolerant enough—though she keeps challenging Book himself about his own work.

Book keeps his connection with Lawson civil but reserved. Not that the man will care. Book guesses he sees doctors on expeditions in the same way a ramrod colonel might see an army chaplain on a campaign: one extra gut to fill, but necessary for show and for the comfort of the weak.

"Your cause is hopeless, Doc," Kaljang says now. "Please resign."

Book sips his drink. "Still lots of goats on the hoof, Kal."

"The altitude is affecting them, I think."

"They're *mountain* goats."

Kaljang draws on the roach of his filterless cigarette and butts out on the table next to the game. Shiva has set the skillet in his lap and is following the endgame with bugged eyes: Kal advancing his cutthroat tiger to the kill.

The fifth goat falls.

"It's nature's way," Kaljang says, shaking his head in sham condolence, extending his right hand over the board.

"Nice work, Kal."

As the two shake hands, Shiva asks Book, "You play against me, now, before I make the dal?"

"Sure thing."

"And I be tigers?"

"Number me among the goats."

"I'll go check on Sophie," Kaljang says, standing, "now that we two are betrothed."

"Tell her I did my best to save her."

Shiva Gurung is a dark, sun-dried little man with broomstick limbs, who, as a porter, can carry what appears to be several times his own weight. Over a *bagh chal* board, unlike the impulsive Kal, he's a tentative, anxious plodder. The game starts slowly. The light is changing, the afternoon sun returning, transfusing the tent with its tranquil amber, the warm colour of bourbon. How lovely it makes the polished brass board and the small, shadowed tigers and goats! Shiva ponders his second move. Book stifles a yawn. He hears a sound. Distant echoes of a climbing axe smashing ice, he thinks, or rock. But no, he shouldn't be hearing sounds from the mountain—there's only snow at Camp One, and the climbers up there should be done for the day. He takes off his glasses, tilts his head. A voice crackles out of the handset radio holstered on Shiva's hip. Shiva drops the tiger he's holding, toppling two goats, and fumbles the radio to his face.

"Come in?"

Book hears every word Kaljang is saying to Shiva, Sophie's voice in the background, her words unclear, the tone shrill. More of those snapping sounds. Book is on his feet before Shiva signs off.

As he nears the border, his medical kit in one hand and Shiva holding the other, every stride changes the picture for the worse. Sophie is standing behind one of the prayer flag boulders, holding her cellphone camera over the top like a periscope. Kaljang's hand is on her nape, his elbow flexed high as he tries to force her to duck down. Lobsang peering around the side of the boulder, yelling what sounds like sports field encouragement, and Jigme squatting *on top* of the boulder, his little earphones still in place. And Lawson: between Book and the boulder party the man stands with Amaris's green tripod over his shoulder. He's staring down the glacier, mouth ajar, arms slack at his sides. The strap slides off his shoulder and the tripod falls next to his boots with a dull crump. Book speeds up, more or less dragging Shiva Gurung, who as usual refuses to liberate his hand.

A little mob of ragged Tibetans comes lurching up the glacier, as if wading against a current or fighting a monsoon. The lead group, adults and children, is maybe a hundred metres off, while a second, larger group lags behind, lugging some burden. Book can imagine. The faint firecracker din he heard in the control tent and over Shiva's radio goes suddenly louder, and louder still the sonic ricochet of those shots off the cliffs—a harsh, tearing sound, as if jet fighters were keening overhead. The men pursuing the fugitives are dropping to one knee to shoot, but they seem to be aiming high, muzzles angled steeply, warning shots, maybe because of the foreigners watching from the border. It's a body they're carrying, the slower Tibetans, two monks and two other men each holding a limb, while a man in a sheepskin coat bears in his arms what looks like a child. He's falling behind. The soldiers screaming.

"Wade!" Book calls as he walks behind Lawson, straight toward his daughter. "Let's go, take cover!" He doesn't look back to see if Lawson follows.

"Papa," she says—a form of the term she hasn't used in years.

"Your hand," he tells her. "Get it down."

Kaljang has given up on Sophie and is gripping Jigme by the back of his parka to drag him off the top of the boulder.

"I *have* to," she says.

"You have to keep down."

"Someone has to record this!"—and her blue eyes flare at him, earnest as a small child's—long-lashed eyes so embedded in her face that even when she wears no eyeliner they look kohled, just as the hair falling across them is so black it seems dyed. Her mother's eyes, her mother's hair. A cramp in his throat stops his words. He kisses her cheek. Detaching himself from Shiva, he steps back the way he has come, to one side of the boulder, exposing himself, as if the best way to protect her is to offer a better target. Lawson is still out there, in his own exposed spot, though now he's hunkered down. And now, as Book gapes, Lawson swivels on his haunches, turns his back on the action and holds a small camera out in front of him, getting shots of himself with the chase on the glacier in the background. Amaris is approaching blindly from the edge of base camp, her video camera at her face, feeling with her boots over the rough, dirty ice. No more firing. A thud as Jigme and Kaljang tumble to the ice together amid half-hysterical laughter.

"Come on," Book whispers, watching the fugitives, "almost there." He locks eyes with a teenage boy in blue work pants and a fleece-lined jean jacket, who looks back at him with a drained but dogged gaze, mouth panting, as if Book were the marshal at the finish line of a marathon. Beside the kid, a nun with a red parka over long, wine-red robes and flashing white sneakers. She is young and running and seems to have strength in reserve. They've almost reached the border stone, the tangled Chinese flag, but he can't let them stop there because the true border now lies slightly beyond and he believes the soldiers will chase them at least that far. He starts toward them. In his heart, that familiar mix of indignation at an obvious wrong and the reluctance, even resentment, of a good-natured man who hates conflict but can't seem to avoid it.

A hoarse cry, a crashing volley of gunfire. By his ear a fizzing sound like a beer can being opened. He's unaware of ducking but he's hunched low over his legs—frozen in place. The young nun lies on the snow a few body lengths short of the border stone and her red parka and her robes seem to be melting off her and expanding over the snow. An old man in a sashed sheepskin coat stoops toward her, slowly, as if puzzled or wondering if he can help; then he grips his chest and crumples. The volley of shots has not stopped the Tibetans but stampeded them. The lead group spills toward and across the border, passing Book on either side as if he were invisible. He smells them—buttery sweat and woodsmoke and the acrid ketones of hunger, fear. He has glanced back to check on his daughter, but now he can't move forward, as he must, to reach the nun who lies weltering in a slurry of crimson snow and the old man with his face pressed into her lower back. The slower Tibetans stand or sit just short of the border, their hands in the air, the blue SWAT team moving among them. The four fugitives carrying the body have sagged onto the glacier with their burden. The man cradling the child is on his knees, quaking with soundless sobs. Others crying loudly, wailing. A young monk in robes and a parka haunches down beside the father, talking to him. Five men in camouflage gear, down vests and earflap caps, led by a doughy, tired-looking man with horn-rimmed glasses and a pistol, tramp past their prisoners and toward the border stone and Lewis Book.

He has heard about paralysis under fire. He never has faced direct, aimed fire, though he has been in dangerous locations often enough, twice under bombardment. But never at high altitude. Is this what's happening here? Strange that while paralyzed with fear on a Himalayan glacier, where someone you love more than your own substance could also be in danger and where others you want to help might be dying, a part of you is capable of feeling mundane embarrassment, as if you just spilled a tumbler of Scotch on the emcee at a gala fundraiser in Toronto. Then the thought leaps through his bizarrely clear mind that Sophie and the others will be watching the Tibetans, not him.

"Papa, don't move!" he hears her call, and it springs him back into motion, as stiff in the legs as if he were hatching from a body cast. Glancing back at her—her raccooned eyes staring over the boulder, cellphone still in position—he yells, "Stay where you are!" with extra force on the *stay*, as if to suggest that immobility, like his own just now, is a wise and necessary tactic. He turns and hurries downslope toward the fallen Tibetans as the officer and soldiers trudge up to meet him. By the border stone he veers a few degrees so as not to collide with the Chinese, but the officer, his thick eyebrows crimped to a scowl above his glasses, swerves to block him. The man lowers his pistol and raises the other hand, the palm glazed with sweat. Book points at the fallen Tibetans. "I'm going to help them." With a slight bow he steps to one side, like a partner in some mannered dance or game. The officer moves to block him and again Book slips around him and the man explodes, barking some high, shrill phrase, shaking the pistol next to Book's ear. Book walks past, staring straight ahead. Someone calls out in Chinese behind them and the officer quits yelling mid-sentence and starts away, back up the glacier. Book glances back. He wonders if the Chinese will actually approach the prayer flag boulders, or base camp itself, but the men and the officer halt a few strides short of Amaris, who is still taping. Beside her, Lawson frames big, hyperbolic hand gestures as he roars at the Chinese in fractured English. *We no understand you! Here is border!* A soldier pointing at Amaris, the officer shouting again, clawing at the air in front of his face, a clear signal, Lower your camera. Behind her the escaped Tibetans are being ushered deeper into Nepal—into base camp—by Lobsang, Shiva, Jigme. Sophie is still by the boulders with Kaljang, watching Book.

"Go into base camp," he shouts at her. "Now!"

She hesitates, then begins to run after the others.

He turns and runs down to the bodies in the snow. Kneels and shoves a hand down the neck of his sweater and draws his glasses from his shirt pocket. Triage on the glacier. The nun has fallen face down, her arms tangled under her. Blood no longer pumps from the entry wound just below her nape—bright arterial blood, darkening into her parka and the snow. He has seen bullet wounds before. He slips two fingers under her chin for a jugular pulse and there's nothing, as he feared. His fingers emerge bloody.

He turns to the old man in the rank sheepskin coat. His back, where Book expected to see an entry wound, is unmarked. There are rips in the coat but no holes or blood. Book eases him over. The man's heavy head rolls from the small of the nun's back onto the backs of her knees. A sunned face the colour of walnut oil— no loss of colour. A little blood on the hair but apparently not from any wound of his. Book makes a decision and tugs the man's body clear of the nun, the back of the coat snagging on gravel in the glacier. He braces the man's head with one hand as it slumps off the nun's body. The grey-streaked hair parted in the middle, plaited at the back. He breathes into the man's open mouth, thrusts with both hands ten times on the sternum and breathes into him again, deciding to give extra breaths in the rotation because of the air's thinness. The man's mouth has a sharp, starved odour, like scorched toast. Faint smell of caries. After a fifth round of chest compressions. Book detects a faint jugular pulse. He's dimly aware of the captured Tibetans and the Chinese SWAT team watching him work. Sophie should be in the camp by now. Dizzy, he keeps breathing. When he looks up from another round of it, the officer and men are marching back down, Amaris McRae between two of them: a small Chinese-Canadian woman in athletic gear gripped by Chinese soldiers who now look much larger and, coming downhill toward Book, more menacing than before. The puffy officer in the horn-rims holds Amaris's camcorder in one hand, his pistol in the other. From the top of the pass, at the edge of base camp, Sophie watches with Kaljang and Lawson, who is gesticulating and stamping his boot like a fool, yelling down at Book, ordering him to come back. It's too late. Book can't read his daughter's expression from here. *The camp*, he thinks. *Go back to the camp.* Yet he is proud. He has to stay and augment the old man's slender breathing. Above him, the officer says in a hoarse, mechanical way, as if reading words from a language primer, "You also will come with us."

TWO

SOLO ROUTES

"Summit," Barry says, looking at me and smoothing a finger down each side of his moustache. "There's no best way to get to Summit, Mrs Kane."
—RAYMOND CARVER,
"So Much Water So Close to Home"

In the time of the later Crusades, while Christian armies slogged through the Holy Land waging sacred war—converting or slaughtering the inhabitants, capturing cities or being repulsed—a Muslim army, similarly inspired, marched east from what is now Iraq, across deserts and mountains, converting or slaughtering the inhabitants, capturing cities, until finally they neared the forbidden city of Lhasa. One barrier remained: the Nyenchen Thanghla Shan, an immense escarpment bulking up out of the plateau northwest of the city. The army would have to cross this barrier via a pass almost 7,000 metres high. Thousands of men, mounted and on foot, their chain mail, helmets and lance heads flashing in the hot equinoctial sunlight, clanked upward hour after hour.

As the air grew colder and thinner, the men began to struggle. Some lagged behind or slumped by the wayside. Officers forced them back to their feet and drove them on. On the evening of the second day, the skies clotted with cloud. Snow began to fall, at first lightly, and the army bivouacked up in the clouds, an east wind ravening over the pass. In the scorching cold, in silk pavilions or lightweight cotton tents, the trembling army lay sleepless, except for those troops that Death was quietly recruiting as night deepened with the storm. In the morning, snow thick on the ground, the reduced army tried to march on—there could be no turning back—square into the wind, sure that the storm must yield by the will of God. It worsened. The men and horses stiffened and slowed like a host of clockwork toys

*winding down. By evening, still short of the pass, all movement
ceased among the multitude. For hours along the trail the army in
its armour stood or lay, frozen in place, as if waiting for the order to
push on: infantry and cavalry vanishing under the mounting,
drifting snow.*

*The small force of Tibetan defenders awaiting the invaders at
the pass had fled down to the plateau during the storm. Some days
later—their yak teams breaking trail like bovine snowploughs—
they plodded back to the summit and over the top and there they
found the frozen army, the snows receding to disclose the dead. The
Tibetans stripped the men of their armour and weapons and the
horses of their tack and caparisons and loaded these treasures,
along with lances, scimitars, regimental standards and helmets
inscribed in Arabic, onto their yaks and returned to Lhasa. For
centuries afterward, at every Tibetan New Year until the Chinese
invasion, a thousand men and horses decked out in medieval
armour and ornate fittings paraded through the streets of Lhasa:
the frozen army revived.*

THEY WON'T STOP ME, he thinks.

Eight p.m. and he should be 2500 feet up Kyatruk in the tandem mummy bag with Amaris, trying to convince her it's important they get some sleep, while she, oddly energized, post-sex, scribbles in her notebook with one of those gel-point pens that keep bursting and nosebleeding everywhere. But she's gone, frog-marched down into China along with the doctor, and Lawson is fighting to keep his expedition alive.

For several years the words *they* and *them* have been a growing part of his private vocabulary, *they* being the many people or forces that by accident or, more often, out of grievance and envy attempt to screw him. And now this. Seriously, though, who'd have given odds? He's taken ruinous risks to buy himself this last chance, this shot at reinstatement, and look at him. Awash in Buddhist nuns and elders. Lawson seldom thinks about God and he certainly never prays—he can't see much difference between praying and panhandling, a kind of spiritual dole, and he still believes in himself too much to beg—but if he did believe in God, and Satan, he'd have to conclude they were against him now.

He's not one for mobs, and his sizable Control Tent now feels about as roomy as a Nepali bus. Humid, dense smells of unshowered bodies, wet sheepskin, propane, with sharper notes of cheap Chinese tobacco and MSG from the cooking ramen. (At Camp One the air will be stratospherically clear and pure and the moon will be rising out of the glacier like a disk of pristine ice, super-naturally bright. Jake and Zeph and Tashi are still up there, lucky bunch—he told them to stay put, so they could all resume their summit preparations tomorrow.) He might be flailing his arms in frustration now, stamping, hammering his fist, even pitching stuff, but you can hardly shift your weight in here without stepping on a Tibetan. Shiva has turned down the stove where he's cooking ramen and boiling pot after pot of water, but the tent is still swel-tery. The fourteen refugees—a nun, a monk, two small boys, several old folks and others of various ages and uncertain back-ground—are crammed onto the stools around the satellite tele-phone table or sitting cross-legged on the tent floor. Two are stretched out, asleep. A few of the women murmur, a child weeps softly, the others eat and drink and stare and say nothing.

Mingma Lama is here—he rushed down from Camp One, against instructions, soon after Lawson and Amaris. His eyes seem small and inflamed, his face shrivelled with strain. He's helping Kaljang and the silent Lawson to allot painkillers from Book's supplies and treat some of the Tibetans for horrific blisters and cuts and welts and sunburn. Lobsang is picking his way among the crowd with a fast-emptying bag of ginger snaps—the third and last bag, in fact. Jigme, earbuds still in place, sits nodding to rap tunes and playing *bagh chal* with a teenage Tibetan in a fleece-lined jean jacket buttoned to the collar despite the heat. The kid is chain-smoking and that breaks the rules in here but Lawson will let it go. Sophie helping Shiva at the stove and serving mugs of chai and bowls of steaming ramen with a focused gravity that might touch Lawson more if his thoughts weren't swarming off at panicked angles. He can see she's been crying, who can blame her, her father gone, her mother unreachable so far, but she's holding up. Her eyeliner is rubbed and smeary, as if after a beating—black-eyed. Not a bad kid. She's a bit concave, slouchy in that teenage way Lawson just doesn't get, but she isn't sullen and she strikes him as pretty motivated.

He wedges down in front of a skittish boy whose toes look to have been fed into a wood-chipper. On either side a Tibetan woman sits, one still young, probably the mother, one older, maybe a grandmother, hump-backed, with sallow teeth and eyes. They wear garish cardigans over long striped aprons. As they slurp tea, dark faces moist from the steam, the women watch Lawson with vacated stares, as if resigned to whatever he might do next, doctor the kid, torture him. Lawson has seen that look on the faces of tired, spooked novice climbers, especially after an accident on a peak.

"Ming. Tell this kid I need to put some antibiotic cream on his stinky feet."

Mingma nods, frowns, says something in a hoarse, halting voice, clearly picking his words with care and maybe some uncertainty. According to Kaljang, the Sherpa tongue is a close cousin of Tibetan but is no exact fit; it can't help that Mingma had been tipping a mickey of Snow Leopard gin into his chai since getting down to base camp—the only place where Lawson has given up controlling the man's intake. But Mingma's words seem to relax the boy. Lawson, scrunching his nostrils, salves and gauzes the small outer toes and the boy makes no sound—that famous Himalayan stoicism, Lawson assumes, that he already respects so much in the Sherpas.

The younger woman says something to him in a tremory voice. Despite her condition, he sees now, she's attractive: wide-set eyes, dramatic cheekbones, heavy turquoise pendants hung from tiny earlobes.

"Don't mention it," he says.

"No," says Mingma, "she *asks* you for something, Wade Lawson. More noodles for the boy. Chai for her mother."

"Right," says Lawson, standing. His throat and chest reconstrict. He feels crowded again. A crowd squatting on his chest. "Right—another round," he says with an attempted smile, but his voice is husky and betrays the latest hairpin swerve in his mood. Sophie's gaze leaps to him. But what does she know. He has nothing against these people—he wishes them all the luck in the world, which unfortunately doesn't seem like very much these days—but he has to get them out of here.

As if talking over a direct challenge, shouting it down, he says loudly, "Thing is, we've left ourselves no margin for error."

The crowd looking up at him, paying full attention, as if they understand.

"Of course they have to keep eating and drinking, whatever they want, for tonight, but . . . we've left ourselves no damn margin here. Zero." Food, he's thinking. Fuel. Time. Luckily, the Tibetans will *have* to leave tomorrow, according to Mingma— they need to get down to a lower elevation, for the air and the milder nights, there aren't nearly enough extra sleeping bags to go around.

Mingma crouches to examine the livid, cantaloupe-sized knee of the monk, who has rucked up his maroon skirts to expose it. "Yes," says Mingma, "we are not quipped out to care for them here. As I am said, we must guide them down to Tarap."

"Right." (Lawson is caught.) "I guess we can spare Jigme. And maybe Shiva. And enough food to get them to the villages."

Mingma looks up from the monk's knee. "But, Wade Lawson— it's not enough. It's two days to the first village, maybe longer for these condition. And then to Tarap. We need to carry the food for them. They are too weak."

"Who's we? How many is we?"

"And the children need to be carry part of the way, maybe more."

"How *many* of you, Ming?"

The satellite phone starts bleating.

"All of us would be the best. We all go together to Tarap."

Kaljang grabs the phone. Kathmandu again, probably.

"I can't do that, Ming. We can't all go. I have paying climbers up there." He jabs a finger toward the upper mountain and the shadow of his hand on the tent wall is a bucking pistol. If he'd had one of those this afternoon, he thinks, he wouldn't have let them take Amaris and his doctor without a fight. He comes from a hunting family and he can shoot.

"I've promised to get my paying climbers to the top. And my sponsor's flag."

Sophie seems to roll her eyes.

"It's your mother," Kaljang says.

"*My* mother?" Lawson asks.

The girl clatters the empty mugs on the table and grips the receiver. Kaljang plants a comforting hand on her shoulder, averting his face with affected discretion. She twists herself clear, tilts her face away, clamps the phone closer.

"Mama?"

Lawson nods toward Sophie, lowers his voice: "And what if the Chinese bring her dad back up here tomorrow, with Mari? They probably will. They'll have to. This is like some . . . international kidnapping. The Chinese don't want this, right? With the Olympics coming? They'll probably send them right back up tomorrow, before the media gets involved, and Soph should be here."

"Why are you talking about the *Olympics?*" she blurts, not bothering to cover the mouthpiece—then goes back to talking, whispering to her mother. Tears starting, her voice half cramping. "It's crazy, Mama. I can't believe any of this."

"Listen, everyone," Lawson calls. Everyone already is. "I've spoken to the Nepalis in Kathmandu and *they're* not asking us to kill this climb. They're sending Gurkhas up to Tarap, to meet these people halfway. It's all good. It's going to work."

"Yes, you told this," Mingma says with a puzzled frown.

"I *cannot*"—Lawson karate-chops his palm—"kill this climb!"

"I can leave, maybe, my nephew," Mingma says.

"Tashi? One Sherpa?"

"And Shiva, maybe."

"I need Sherpas!"

"I'll climb," Kaljang says softly, as if not wanting Sophie to overhear. "I really want to climb."

Mingma speaks sharply to Kaljang in Sherpa, then tells Lawson, "Anyway, we come back from Tarap, six days, maybe five, then, maybe, okay, all climb. If the doctor—"

"Too late. You'd have to reacclimatize and by the time you do we'll be stuck for food and it'll be too late in the year. And my permit will expire." *The one I'll still be paying for when the last Himalayan glacier melts.* "And who'll be here to run base camp and take the phone? Kal's my base camp guy. We'll be swamped with calls, any minute. Don't you want to—"

"We'd be okay without acclimatizing," says Kaljang, a novice with no high-altitude experience. "I would."

"Forget it," Lawson snaps—though in fact Kaljang has given him an idea. "I can't be losing anyone on this climb. That would be the end."

"It's why you need doctor," Mingma says. "And the doctor is gone!"

"I told you, he'll be back."

"Maybe not soon," Mingma says softly, glancing at the girl.

"I need you to leave me three Sherpas."

"But there is only me and the four."

"I know, damn it! But I hired you and you work for me and you can't just tell me you're all packing it in and leaving, because the fact is . . . because you work for *me*."

The man ponders him, as if Lawson were a gaping crevasse.

"We have a *contract*, Ming—all the Sherpas do."

"Pardon me, Wade Lawson, but I am *sirdar* and my Sherpas pursue me."

"Break your contract and I'll see that other climbers hear about it."

"But, what do climbers say if they know we don't help these? This is an urgency!"

"We are helping! Plus, there's your drinking"—the words thrust their way out of Lawson, though in fact he likes Ming and thinks he functions pretty well, considering—"not a great recommendation."

One of the sleeping Tibetans, a man in a ripped orange parka, has wakened and propped himself on his elbow. The others, Sherpas included, glance back and forth between the arguing men. Mingma gently drapes the monk's robe over the hideous knee. He stands and speaks with a sort of cornered dignity: "I am *sirdar* on so many climbs, Wade Lawson, and the Sherpas pursue my orders. Kaljang, too. Tomorrow morn, we guide these down to Tarap. My nephew I do leave you, and Shiva. Miss Book can choose what to do for her own. You may choose if you want us to return from Tarap, okay. You may choose if you want to make a climb on your own, okay, but I think a wrong idea."

Eyes on Lawson. The Tibetans, he senses, know what is going on. This bolted attention seems to call for a dramatic response, but for a moment he feels outmanoeuvred, beaten—a feeling he once thought himself immune to.

Then, in a flash, he works out a new route.

"With or without Sherpas," he says, "this climb will continue. Tomorrow, after you leave. But someone needs to be here at base camp. Two people, at least. I mean—forget about *me*— what if more Tibetans make it over the pass? Plus . . . plus, I need people on the phone here, twenty-four hours a day. The media, Ming, they'll be all over this by the middle of tonight, and we need to get this story out to the world—don't we? And Shiv's English . . ."

Mingma stalls, mouth open under his small moustache. "It's true," he says, "about the phone. But, I wish *you* would stay in base camp, Wade Lawson . . ."

"I've come twelve thousand miles."

No sound but the stove's gassy hiss.

"Ming—I need Kal as well as Tash."

The man nods, barely. "I guess Kaljang's English . . . maybe best."

"By far."

"I guess . . . I leave him and Tashi, then."

"Okay!" Lawson says briskly. "I can accept that."

Sophie, softly on the phone: "*I can't believe he's trying to go on with it after what's happened.*"

Someone has given the girl a cigarette. Lawson will let that one go too.

The moment Sophie stretches out in her mummy bag she knows it's no use trying to lie still and do nothing, let alone sleep. She will have to go after him.

The moon is up, a few days past full, her small tent suffused with blue light as if she has pitched camp under a halogen street lamp. On the glacier it will be bright enough to read, or write in a journal, as she knows well, having done it a couple of times, before being chased back to the nest of her tent by icy breezes blowing up the glacier or over the shoulder of Kyatruk. But this night is windless. Ideal conditions to cross the border and follow the trail down the glacier. The guards and soldiers and their captives and her father and Amaris will not have gone far. When she lost sight of them, far down the glacier, it was already dusk. Her father looked back once, from a distance that would have made it hard, she thinks, for him to see her. She couldn't read his face but she knew he was looking for her, and he seemed to slow and stop, as if to take a more focused look, and the bizarrely tall soldier on his right, holding his arm, said something and her father ignored him and kept searching till a soldier seized his other arm and tugged hard. Just then—when she should have been watching most carefully, she thinks, or taking photos—her sight fogged up with tears that felt scalding to her unblinking eyes in that cold air. *Forget about me*, she should have yelled—a phrase she has heard someone else use tonight—Wade Lawson? *Forget about me, I'll be okay. Just don't do anything crazy.*

She guesses the soldiers and captives will have camped by the lake at the bottom of the glacier. Even if they've gone a bit farther, they'll be bedded down by whatever track or road leads to the soldiers' base, and she can catch them easily if she follows the marked trail down the glacier. She doesn't trust her father. She knows her father. All her instincts urge that this situation, already serious, could quickly worsen. Her presence might keep him from acting reckless, and also restrain the soldiers, because she's still a child, technically, and most adults can be trusted not to hurt children, can't they? And when *was* it, she wonders, that she started worrying more about her father than he worries about her? It's not fair. A moment like that must come eventually for every child and parent, but for her and him it's forty years too soon. So she tells herself. Then recalls that she's in Asia with him because of his concern about her, what was happening at home.

She feels the tent floor for her cellphone and flashlight. Heat-seeking drafts of cold air invade the down bag as she gropes, wondering why she can't just leave things in the same place and hearing her mother's calmly exasperated voice. She sits up and pulls on a Shetland sweater—a shapeless, pilled thing of her father's but warmer than anything of her own—over the hooded fleece she wears at night. Then her parka.

She has already downloaded the video footage from her cellphone onto her laptop, but now she studies it again while burning two copies on CD. The laptop, like the cellphone, could use a recharge at the control tent, and because of the air up here it keeps revving strenuously, but there is enough power and she knows this blurred, jolty footage is important. She can picture it on news sites, on YouTube—an important recording of an atrocity, something to help the Tibetan cause. Not that she can upload it from here, where there's no satellite dish. She wishes it was better and she blames herself again for not bringing her digital camera to the border stone, but how could she have known? She'd taken enough sunset views. She pauses the image she was waiting for: her father crouched down during that gunfire, the woman in the red parka lying on the glacier a little beyond him, guards and soldiers approaching. The image makes it look like her father has been hit and is bent double over a wound—maybe about to collapse, like the old Tibetan man standing a few feet from the shot woman. Sophie's heart accelerates, as if it needs to. What she has been wondering: is it possible her father actually *has* been hit, in the side or arm? True, after some seconds—here, watch him—he straightens and darts a look back and shouts something unclear on the audio, although she recalls it as *Stay there!*, and he tramps down toward the captured Tibetans before the frame jiggles (Lobsang, jostling her) and he's lost to view, her lens framing the nearer Tibetans and Amaris, who's filming . . . but maybe he was just putting on a strong facade. Hiding the hurt. That would be so like him.

She stuffs her daypack with a plastic water bottle and crackers and sunglasses and her toilet kit and a T-shirt and extra underwear and a half-roll of toilet paper—"white man's prayer flag," Kaljang and Tashi call it—then pauses a few seconds before adding her journal and the small box of tampons and pads. Including them means admitting that she might be gone for more than a couple of days. All right. Her hand hovers over the pile of paperbacks, some of her choosing, others part of the deal she made with her father when he pre-empted her first semester of grade twelve and brought her to Asia. She likes some of this required reading a lot, some a lot less. In the *Tagore Reader* she found lines she wrote in her journal, though she would be horrified if anyone else, parents, friends, ever read them there. *When the patter of rain at night brought dreams from the dreamland, and mother's voice in the evening gave meaning to the stars.*

She takes two of her own books, *Persepolis* and *Beloved*, and one of his, small and challenging, *Beyond Postmodern Physics*.

Kaljang is slumped asleep at the table when she ducks into the control tent, a microclimate of hot, humid air rife with stinks that are almost welcome at this moment because they signify life, the human crowd. Both satellite phones lie on the table by Kaljang's elbows and beside the right one is a sheet of paper on which numbered lines are written in large, bold caps, with lots of strident underlining. Even if she hadn't seen Wade's handwriting before— SMOKING DISALLOWED IN CONTROL TENT!!—she would have known it was his. By Kaljang's head, a mugful of cold-looking tea, two ballpoint pens and a foolscap notepad showing one scrawled line. A battery lamp hangs from the tent-peak above him. Over his folded hands, his head is wrenched sideways in handsome profile, lips squashed against the sleeve of his fleece. A hank of blue-black hair (shiny but somehow never greasy) lies over his upturned eye as if carefully arranged to block the light. Past the table's end, where the medical supplies are spread out, Mingma Lama lies on his back on the floor, no pad under him, no sleeping bag, his brown, mummied hands crossed over his chest. His face under the lamp is weirdly shiny and perfectly still, like the face of a frozen body being thawed.

The propane stove murmurs and in dim corners of the tent the refugees sleep, the children in down bags the Sherpas rounded up for them, the adults furled up in their coats. None of them stirs. Sophie would have expected snoring, long sighs—symptoms of heavy, emptied slumber—but these people sleep in silence, as if it's a habit of secrecy they've cultivated while in flight.

She has prepared herself to speak to Kaljang, explain things, but now she realizes it never would have worked, he would not have let her go. Finding him asleep like this is best. She slips over to the table. On top of the foolscap pad she sets the CD-ROMs. S.B.'S VID OF ATTACK, she has labelled them. She knows that Kal will ensure they go down with Mingma to Tarap. He looks beautiful here, asleep by the phones, both more boyish and more adult than usual. A boy simply sleeping, a man weighed down with exhausting duties. It's a weight that will get heavier with her departure, because Wade, she senses, was hoping she would handle

EVERY LOST COUNTRY ~ 57

most of the phone traffic, once it gets going, and probably planned to have Kaljang porter stuff up to Camps One and Two. Now she guesses Kaljang will be on the phones twenty-four hours a day. She wishes she could kiss him goodbye, on the cheek, and as she looks at him she shivers with tenderness, a strange sensation that makes her feel older than her age. They've necked a couple of times—Kaljang darting his tongue with wonder across her front braces—once behind the boulders and once on the easy slope north of base camp, when they tried snowboarding together on her board, him squeezed beside her, and laughed themselves helpless and wiped out, but she stopped him after a certain point, when he tried to rush it.

Like her father, Sophie will not be rushed.

She slips out of the tent into the still, searing cold and walks with crunching steps toward the edge of camp and behind her the satellite phone goes off—awful in this silence, like an alarm detonating in a store as you leave, pockets filled with pinched stuff. There's no second ring, just Kaljang's startled "Hello?" And from just beyond the control tent the sound of a smaller tent zippering open—Wade Lawson, she thinks, and speeds up.

If this moon were the sun, its angle in the sky would mean the day was getting late, fewer hours of light left than she'd thought or would wish. Around her the Himalayas heave up into space and jab at the dense froth of the stars. The glacier glows beneath her as if radioactive. She crosses the border. In the place where the nun and the old man fell, a sprawling stain, darker than Sophie's passing shadow.

Anger is almost as good as exertion when it comes to keeping warm. For a long time now she has been pursuing her father in her thoughts, or pretending his absences don't matter because his work is so important and she shouldn't be selfish, then chasing him mentally anyway, afraid he won't make it back. The last few years, of course, she has pretended not to care. Now she actually has travelled to the other side of the planet and he has slipped away again. That he is affectionate, fun and kind, never smothering when he's with her . . . hard to say if that makes things better or worse.

Every hundred steps or so a pennant marks the trail: a triangle of red cloth on a waist-high aluminum rod. Her steps echo faintly off the granite walls cupping the wide glacier. There's the growl of an avalanche or a rockslide high up in the peaks, where snow-fields absorb the moon's light and emit a dim, focused glow, as if in meditation. If not for her steps echoing, the solitude and immensity might be terrifying as well as beautiful. It is terrifying. She slips the earbuds under the rim of her hood and turns on the cell-phone MP3 player, loud enough to help her walk but not so loud that she won't hear if something comes up behind her—though there's nothing out here, of course, according to her father and everyone else. Nothing but human adults.

Not much of a comfort there.

If she could have snowboarded down. It makes her grin, the notion. Impossible with the surface so hard, grainy with embedded gravel. What a strange thing a grin is out here. Mark Lanegan has the sexiest voice possible, but she turns the music down further, knowing the charge in her MP3 player won't last more than a couple more hours.

The downward pitch eases, the marked trail detouring around a blue-lipped slash in the ice, a metre wide in places. There's a swath of something leading to the edge of it, dark like the blood up by the border stone. For a moment she stares at the swath, unsure whether to approach the crevasse, while Mark Lanegan sings about a wedding gown in a husky, unmarried-sounding way. She turns off the song. From deep in the glacier, an echo of trickling water. Her spine is ice, as if the night has found a way inside. Her pulse high in her throat. She won't approach the crevasse, though it pulls at her, seems to want her down there too. Before her father started leaving for longer periods and returning subdued and distracted, her parents as a duo created a warm, lively feeling at home, a chaotic harmony that made her eventual collisions with adult cruelty and conflict a shock. She'd thought fighting was what kids, like herself and her brother, did. Adults were too mature for that, too composed. Even during the trial separation her parents were civil to each other—no, more than that, they were kind. It's scary now to think that maybe there are no adults.

She looks into the distance. On the surface of the lake, at the toe of the glacier, the mirrored moon floats. How fast she seems to be losing it. No sign of firelight or lamplight, but they must be camped down there somewhere, no one would be out marching in this cold in the middle of the night. A thrill at her own daring flares through her, and the thought of how proud her father will be, under his anger.

She looks back up the glacier toward base camp, out of sight over the top of the pass. The lobe of the glacier is vast and dimly phosphorescing. She can't imagine climbing back.

She crawls and seat-slides down off the ice where it tapers, steeply and suddenly, to a crust above a slope of gravel. From under this terminal ledge, a gargling of water that now sluices out into the light, flashing in a veil of icy vapour, cascading down and away. Small floes on the lake below circle in the current. Here the air is less bitter, but it still burns her nostrils and throat as she pants. Amaris has a parka, her father only a thick fisherman's sweater, no toque. Sophie's boots on the switchbacks down the slope are clumsy with the cold and her hurry. The moon approaching a silhouetted ridge. It's almost four a.m. and she can look a

long way down the unglaciated part of the valley, which curves to
the east in a way you can't see from the top of the pass—an
immense, perfectly U-shaped groove that the shrunken glacier
used to fill, though it looks like it might have been formed by a
sphere the size of the moon rumbling down out of the
mountains.

From far off, a sound, a dog's bark, maybe—she hopes. She
stops and stands, trying to quiet her breathing. The sound comes
again and this time, as she feared, it's a shot. Of the stream flowing out of the lake and down the valley as far as she can see, the
moon makes a braid of trembling light. No other light in view.

The moon has almost set and still they're on the move, a ghost-lit
procession filing down the scoured, treeless valley along the river.
From ahead and behind, the whine of the SWAT team's all-terrain
vehicles, driving at a crawl. They'd reached the vehicles an hour's
trek below the glacier, where the boulder fields ended. From there
the guards had driven, while the soldiers, who must have ridden
up with them yesterday, kept walking, half-speed, on either side
of the trail. The shuffle and crunching of boots on gravel, the
clink of weapons, coughs appearing as puffs of breath silvered
by the moon. The captives stagger along. The small girl on her
father's shoulders pitches in sleep. The Chinese are stumbling too.
A freakishly tall one, who looks like an Asian Abraham Lincoln,
face caved and mournful, has dropped his assault rifle, maybe
dozing as he walks. In a popular film, a Tibetan, or Book or
Amaris, would have pounced on the rifle and known how to use
it and shot down or held off the soldiers and led the captives back
up the glacier to freedom. Instead, they all pause and stand numbly
as the soldier picks up his rifle and the officer marches back and

rants up at him, the soldier absorbing the tirade with a look of sad yet dignified submission.

Each step takes Book farther from his daughter and from safety, yet he half wishes they could speed up, so he could generate some heat. A Tibetan kid dressed like a Blood or a Crip—baseball cap, dark parka over a hooded sweatshirt, droopy jeans with a wallet chain, hulking court shoes—has politely, silently offered Book a thin blanket, which he has accepted, caping it over his shoulders and knotting it at the throat. His bare ears still burn and throb. His hand, just covered by the blanket, grips his medical kit.

A young nun and a much older layman are wounded and Book has treated them briefly, up on the glacier, just out of sight of the pass, when the officer called a halt. It was a place where the trail skirted a crevasse. In the near-dark Book worked by penlight—Amaris holding it—cleansing the tidy through-wound in the man's side and applying antibiotic cream and gauze, then treating the stout calf of the nun, whose tibia must be smashed: on either side of it, tattered exit wounds, about a dozen small holes. As Book flushed the wounds and tweezed out whatever lead or bone fragments he could find, the SWAT team, their submachineguns slung around to their backs, dragged away the bodies of the dead nun, the man who'd been carried up the glacier and was now being carried back down, dead, and the old man Book had tried to revive. The Tibetans were pointing, chattering. They began shouting. Book and Amaris looked up from their little operating theatre. "Oh *fuck*," Amaris said, more quietly than he'd ever heard her speak. Two guards were heaving, flopping the nun's body like a rolled carpet into the crevasse. "What are you doing?" Book called out, but the Tibetan clamour washed over his voice. The penlight, aiming straight into Book's face, shook in Amaris's hand. Two other guards had the second body. The kid in the baseball cap and parka stomped toward the crevasse, shaking his fist, but a soldier, looking more Tibetan than Chinese, stuck the bayoneted tip of his rifle in front of the kid's nose. The bayonet looked puny and lethal. "Stop!" Book and Amaris said together, Amaris standing with the penlight pointed at her feet, Book holding a sterile pad in one hand, bloody tweezers in the other. The second body went down. No sound as it fell and came to rest somewhere inside the glacier, ten feet below or hundreds.

The puffy officer stepped between the Chinese and the Tibetans, holding his small pistol by his hip. His grim face, fitted with horn-rimmed lenses, swivelled slowly like a surveillance cam, passing over the Tibetans, Book, Amaris. At Amaris he stopped. He frowned as if trying to place her. He said something. He said it again. Amaris glanced fiercely at Book as if he, the international medic, ought to speak Mandarin. "Just help me," Book told her and knelt again by the silent nun's leg, Amaris crouching, taking a breath, aiming the penlight. The officer stood frozen. Book glanced at Amaris. She'd pieced herself together. He was rigging a splint with one of the aluminum rods that flagged the trail, bending it back and forth until it snapped, then binding the shorter length in place with medical tape over the gauze. The nun's face was tight, but she let out no sound, only clutched the hem of her robes hard as if she thought Book might try lifting them higher. An old woman's wailing kited over the din as the SWAT team (Book sensed the action as much as saw it) tumbled the old man's corpse into the crevasse.

The officer, turning away, muttered, "We could bear them no farther."

"But far enough," Book heard himself say, "that it's almost dark and you're out of camera range."

The officer stopped in his tracks, his back still turned; after a moment, he walked on. Amaris watched Book's face tensely and said nothing.

Now the wounded nun in her robes and purple knit cap hobbles in front of Book. He has mimed an offer of help, but she has chosen to crutch herself on the shoulder of an elder nun, a short, burly woman whose tonsured head is bare. Both nuns wear cheap sneakers. The wounded man, in a sheepskin coat and a roguish fedora, walks behind Book. Book turns to check on him, and this man, this casualty, *grins* in his patchy beard. At times he grunts and stumbles and Book takes his hand, but on the whole he seems unnaturally strong. Amaris walks behind the man. Her pretty, impatient face, usually churning with strong opinion and emotion, is immobile now, swept blank. Briefly her eyes flare at Book, as if he could assure her that this moment isn't real. In a crisis, people always assume a doctor's competence extends far beyond medical matters.

In fact, Book has no idea what to do.

"You all right?" he calls back.

She won't answer him, or she can't.

"Hang in there," he says, shamming an upbeat tone, "we'll be all right."

"Is this where we high-five, Lew?"

"What?"

"You shouldn't have crossed that border," she says hoarsely.

"Amaris, it's not like . . . it wasn't like multiple choice up there."

"Borders are there for a *reason*, Lew."

"And if they'd crossed to our side before getting shot," he says, "that would have been ideal."

She says something under her breath, *do-gooders*, he thinks he hears, though it's hard to tell—it sounds like she's mumbling in her sleep. She's too exhausted to keep arguing, he sees. Normally she loves to argue, unlike himself.

He calls out loudly, "Okay—we need to stop soon!" The words, especially that jaunty *okay!*, sound absurd out here, useless, though the officer, somewhere up ahead, does speak a little English. But he doesn't respond. Instead, a young soldier trots up and walks alongside Book. In the moonlight Book can make out the browner face and blazing red cheeks of a Tibetan, or perhaps a Mongol—the one who aimed the bayonet at the hip hop kid, back up on the glacier. He's compact in a sporty way, a small, dynamic package. Despite the cold, his gloves dangle by strings from his cuffs. A thumb hooked under the strap of his rifle, his free hand bringing a cigarette to his mouth for flashy drags, he seems like a kid who has just enlisted, proudly playing soldier.

He pins up his fleecy earflap on Book's side.

"You will smoke?"

Book nods. Any heat source is welcome now. The man, or boy, passes him his cigarette. Book puffs, coughs for a moment, takes another drag, hands it back. Against his will he says, "Thanks."

"Do not mention it, friend." The man speaks stiffly, like an extraterrestrial impostor.

"You know English," Book says.

"A little."

"We have to stop. I need to tend the wounded, and these others need rest. The wounded need water. Tea. Tell your officer. Am I speaking too fast?"

"I think so."

Book slows down. "Why are we not camping? Some of these Tibetans . . ."

"Camping?"

"Stopping for the night."

"Too dangerous!" the soldier says in a jovial tone, passing him what's left of the cigarette. Book half turns and hands it on to the wounded man, who receives it like something edible. Amaris has fallen farther back.

"Dangerous because," the soldier says, pronouncing it *be-cows*, "in the dark, without the tent, the Splittists might try to evade back up to our border."

"None of these people could make it back up the glacier tonight," Book says. "Or tomorrow."

"I think you are right."

"So talk to your officer."

"Okay, I go right now." He doesn't. Still springing along, he cups his hands in front of his mouth and lights another cigarette with a plastic lighter. "Permit me to introduce myself. My name is Palden Jangbu."

"So you are Tibetan."

"You may call me Pal. And you . . . ?"

"Canadian."

"I mean your name, please to meet you."

"Lewis Book. Look, we have to stop now. Please talk to your—"

"Your name is Book?" Palden has a look of tickled curiosity. He's around twenty or so, maybe a bit older—the moonlight makes it hard to estimate.

"Yes."

A fit, nimble elf with an assault rifle.

"I am pleased to have a chance to practise my English. More smoking?"

"No."

"Does the camera woman speak English either, I hope?"

"I don't think she speaks anything else."

"But she is Han Chinese, as anyone can see. Lieutenant Zhao will speak to her, if ever we should stop."

"She's from Canada."

"I don't think so. Lieutenant Zhao thinks not so, either."

Book steps from the path and trots up beside the limping, wincing nun and points toward the river. "We rest here," he says and halts, gently gripping the arm of the wounded man as the man walks up, his colouring lurid now, especially in contrast with the robust glow of Palden's face. Palden has stopped and tossed down his cigarette. One of the captive men stoops to retrieve it. Palden frowns thoughtfully.

"But Lewis Book—it's not time to stop."

"Do you want more of these people to die?"

"Not far to the base now, Lewis."

"Maybe that's not a fair thing to ask you," Book says.

"Pardon me?"

"What is it?" Amaris calls.

"It's for safety of us all," says Palden. "We must . . . oh, dear."

The Tibetans, maybe thinking an order has been given, are falling out and flopping along the path. Palden shouts something and Lieutenant Zhao hurries back toward them. Though he's pudgy, he picks his way through the sprawled refugees on concise, almost dainty feet. His small mouth sucks in around a cigarette. He flings it away. Curtly he addresses Palden, who salutes and launches an amiable reply, but the lieutenant cuts him off and turns to Book—Book digging out his glasses, kneeling beside the wounded man, who is cross-legged on the ground and now sags back with a pneumatic groan.

The lieutenant's moonlight shadow obscures Book's view of the wound.

"Amaris, the light. Something's wrong."

She crouches on the other side of the man, fumbling to get her mittens off. "Fuck. *Fuck* it." The older nun helps the injured nun down onto the ground and then sits beside her and glares up at Lieutenant Zhao, her flat face and bulging eyes taking the full, last light of the moon. She speaks angrily, pointing to her mouth. The moon, behind Zhao, blacks out his face. Ignoring the old nun, he tells Book, "You are not yet to stop."

"We have to," Book says. "Even for an hour. I have to treat these people. And everyone needs water and tea." He looks down as Amaris snaps on the penlight: the man's sheepskin coat over his belly is darkly saturated, glistening.

"Didn't you say it looked all right?" she asks.

"It did. Then he walked for hours."

He wants to slice open the man's coat but knows a homemade coat like this, even bloodstained, is too precious. He starts untoggling the front. From above him, a sound like a deadbolt snapping clear and he looks up: Zhao holding his automatic pistol high above his own head. The muzzle flare and ripping blast go together, far too loud for a weapon so small. Amaris gasps and the penlight wavers, steadies. Zhao waits a few seconds, then fires again. The Tibetan child screams and screams.

"We are *not* yet to stop."

Book's ears reverb with the shots and the shunting of his pulse as he strains to make out Zhao's face.

"Look at this," Book tells Zhao. "Can you see this?"

Zhao, lowering the pistol, leans slightly closer.

"He'll die," Book says.

He makes out Zhao's eyes behind the glasses. They're skimming back and forth between the wounded man's torso and . . . not Book's face, but Amaris's.

"We may stop here, then," Zhao says at last. "Not long. And the Sergeant Jangbu"—he nods toward Palden—"he will assist with the small torch." Then he points at Amaris and snaps some phrase in what must be Mandarin. She stares back at him, then glances at Book.

"This woman I will talk to."

The officer with his pistol leads her off the trail, away from the party, toward the river. Her breath tightens and so do her muscles, which feel used up, worthless, and she's furious at her body for this defection after how many years of punctual gym time, swimming, sweating on the treadmill, the Stairmaster, the elliptical, in the Nautilus room. If the fight-or-flight response is meant to help you survive, why does adrenaline make you feel so shaky and scared? Then she thinks: calm down, it's all right, you have a passport, a Canadian passport, not on you (as the officer knows—his men conducted a quick search up on the glacier), but back up at the camp, yes.

The officer points at a low boulder beside the river and says something in a growl, like a Kurosawa samurai. The voice doesn't go with the puffy face, the silly earflap cap, the chunky horn-rims. She sits on the rock saddletop. Its cold comes up through her tights. Still, the air is milder here and bears notes of moisture, the wet, sweet smell of the river. Up the bank, the old Tibetan nun and the kid in the baseball cap and baggy parka fill clattery cook pots with water. Another kid, in a toque and parka, like a gangmate of the first kid, stands smoking. A few steps from Amaris the officer hunkers over his small combat boots, dipping something in the shallows. Moonlight glazes the icy stones and pulses on the rippling current of the channel. It's a night full of photons in dancing animation and her eyes, even now, are framing it—by this stage in her life it's less a habit than a molecular instinct— panning, zooming in. It calms her now as it always does.

The officer stands and comes toward her, holding a dribbling mug. He hands it to her with a grunt and a few words that might be English, though the river is a white-noise machine and neutralizes sound. She pours the water straight down her throat. The officer takes back the plastic mug and goes and repeats the process, though this time when he stands and returns, he doesn't hand it to her, as she is so hoping, but arranges himself on a second rock, facing her. He studies the mug's lip, as if for crumbs or lipstick, then drinks. Over the mug, he eyes her through his glasses. He shifts on the boulder uncomfortably, sits straighter. He has realized he has taken the lower rock. His knees are forced up toward his chest, like a pudgy adult wedged into a schoolchild's chair. She hunches down further to accommodate him, but her face is still higher than his.

He says something.

"I'm sorry," she says, "I really don't understand. I don't know Mandarin. I don't even know if that *is* Mandarin."

He repeats it, further roughening his voice, while trying to inch his spine upward. As for Amaris, if she hunches any lower, her chin will be in her lap. Usually she does the opposite—tries to stand taller, sit straighter.

"I'm not Chinese," she says. "I'm sorry. I speak English, okay? You speak English. Please speak English to me."

"So you are not Chinese," he says, "according to you."

Hearing English she feels safer, in spite of his tone and his face—haggard, unhappy, like a customs officer on a long nightshift.

"My biological parents were Chinese," she says. "I never knew them."

"Biological parents? I do not understand. Surely there is no other kind."

"I was adopted, when I was a baby."

"I see." He nods, as if accepting the explanation—then he lets off another burst of Chinese while his impassive, pouched eyes gauge her from behind the lenses. It's awful to feel you need help. She swallows the salty clot in her throat. Not in front of him she won't.

"My birth parents died in Vietnam," she says firmly—"Vietnamese Chinese. I left with other refugees. I mean, I was taken along—okay? When I was a baby."

"Ah," says the officer, leaning forward, "you were a refugee? You have sympathy for the refugees?"

"Yes. I mean—yes, I was. But listen—"

"And your parents, they were on the imperialist side in the Vietnam War?"

"I have no idea," she lies. "They lived in Saigon."

"I think you speak Chinese. Tell me your name."

"Amaris McRae."

"Your true name."

"I was *adopted*," she says, "in Vancouver—in Canada! By a Canadian couple!"

He drains the mug. Without freeing her gaze, he clips the mug onto a carabiner hung from his belt, next to the holster. He digs a packet from the leg pouch of his trousers and tips out a cigarette and a brass lighter. His stubby hands work nimbly at his mouth. He drags on the cigarette the way someone dying of thirst might suck water through a straw.

"We reach the border"—he puffs forcibly from the side of his mouth—"and there we find a Chinese refugee woman ready with a video camera? This is too much of a, a . . ."

"Coincidence," she says quietly.

"Yes."

"It's *not* a coincidence—I mean, yes, it's a coincidence! I was shooting the climb. It's a climbing party. Your men saw us up at the border, maybe ten days ago, just after we arrived. Weren't you there?" (She knows he was. She never forgets a face.) "You must have seen me too."

"I took careful note."

"I need water. And I need to pee." He isn't about to offer her a smoke. A stone's throw behind him the Tibetans, cross-legged in a circle on the ground, are passing around the water pots. The moon is an interrogator's lamp, though it's about to set.

He says, "Your presence was fine timing for the Tibet Splittists' behalf! May is the main climbing season in the Himalaya, not in September."

"But it's the cheap season—Wade said that—September."

"And in the Khiong Pass, nobody climbs in any month. Who is this Wade?"

"He's leader of the expedition. I think you must—"

"He is Tibetan, this leader?"

"Who—*Wade*?"

"Or a foreign sympathizer, I think!" the man says, bunching forward over his knees.

She feels herself smile at the thought. Then, God help her, she begins chuckling. Tibetan faces, guzzling water, pivot toward her. Book is hunched over the bleeding man in a nimbus of blue light—a spooky blue, like the glow of a soul leaving the body—but suddenly she's helpless, delirious with fatigue and disbelief. Wade, a sympathizer! A *Tibetan*! The officer in his earflaps and horn-rims watches her, appalled. Her lapse is some grave indiscretion.

"Wade Lawson," she gets out, pulling herself together, "he's just a . . . he's a mountain climber. He just wanted a mountain no one had climbed."

"Then why you not *climbing* it!" the man cries, his English slipping now. "Why all waiting on the border! You, and a physician, and the Sherpas to help out!"

"We came down from Camp One," she says. "We saw what was happening and we came down."

"From up high? This is not likely. None of this is likely. I think you must be some spy and sympathizer with the Splittists and Dalai Lama! There are so many of you now."

"Look, this is—you have this so wrong! If you think I drive around at home in a VW van with a Free Tibet sticker on the tail . . ." *Like my adoptive parents*, she thinks.

"All of you would like to infame the Chinese government and the people! And many of you want to make motion pictures, like you!"

"Where's my Canon?" she says. "My camera?"

"We have confiscated it."

"It had better be safe."

"Tell me your name."

"A*maris* Mc*Rae*," she enunciates, as if repeating herself to a defective voice-recognition system. "The last name is Scottish— my father is Scottish-Canadian. My mother is *Jewish*. Oh my God! Look, get on the phone, get on the Internet. You must have that at your base. You can get all the information you want on me."

"Maybe false information!"

"Thousands of hits' worth? Plus, I have a website!" A link to the site, www.amarisfilm.com, blips across her mind's eye. Absurd. This is all absurd—she's bragging about her web presence to a tinpot interrogator who's looking smaller and smaller on his toadstool of a stone, his voice getting ever higher, as if he's sublimating away through his cigarette. He is armed, and there may be danger here, but not for her and Book. She feels for the Tibetans but can't help feeling relieved for herself—she's a citizen of a First World democracy, has a solid presence in that powerful world, and it's absurd to be afraid.

Scowling, he says, "I can't understand this, 'hits'?"

"You can't just go around *abducting* people," she says. "I'm a citizen of Canada. So is Dr. Book. There are international laws . . . and I never even crossed the border up there!"

The truth of the phrase, the unfairness of her predicament.

"You carry no passports," he says.

"When will we get to a phone?"

"And the laws here are *Chinese*."

"What about when the media gets onto this? Do you have any idea what's going to happen when—"

"From a rich country, you think, from North America, you are special!" Again he tries to sit highest, but Amaris is no longer slouching. In fact, she's sitting as tall as she can. Abruptly he gets to his feet and fillips his cigarette into the river. The eastern skyline has sliced the moon into semi-eclipse.

"Let me have my camera back," she says, "and there won't be any trouble. People will see . . . I mean . . . the media will show that you're giving me the freedom to . . ."

His face stops her. His right hand isn't by his holster but, almost worse, behind his back, as if he's trying to keep from reaching for his gun. He no longer seems laughable. A pulse of fear demotes her to childhood; she's being intimidated by the birth father she never met, who may, she knows, have questioned prisoners, among other things, for the Americans in Vietnam.

"We march again now," the officer says, and adds some brusque, conclusive phrase in Chinese.

~

The moon is gone but new light is broaching from the east. Five
a.m. by her watch. She drags along in a trance of exhaustion.
Along the valley walls, life finally appears, dwarf pines and a few
thatches of low, spindly trees with yellow leaves. They pass a rock
pile streamered with strings of ancient-looking prayer flags—rags
of coloured fabric meant to spread the hymns of peace inscribed
on them, Sophie has told her; like a secret broadcast via the winds.
Nice idea. The winds, she sees, eventually tear them to shreds.

She walks behind Book, both of them just off the trail where
the lame nun hobbles with the older nun, and the wounded man,
his eyes shut in a wince, jounces on a stretcher the Chinese must
have brought up with them. The Tibetans and Book and Amaris
keep trading places around the stretcher. Amaris glares frankly at
the lively soldier and his giant comrade, who don't offer to take a
turn, though the giant does keep glancing over ruefully, as if he's
sympathetic and might be willing. The lively one, a Tibetan (she
overheard him and Book talking before), keeps nattering at Book,
who says little in reply. There's something wrong with Book's
feet. Instead of walking with a normal roll, heel to toe, he plants
his boots flat on the ground in a stilted movie-monster plod. Old
leather hiking boots, scuffed uppers, eroded heels. She's too tired
to ask what's wrong. It's a myth that suffering makes you more
compassionate and helpful; past a certain point, it just confines
you to the small, private country of your pain.

To either side the mountains fall away and the valley widens as
it curves east, opening onto a desert, low knolls and dunes and
sprawling flats and the glacial river carving down into a ravine
and out of sight. Closer, where the valley and desert meet, there's
a low cinderblock hut, like a bunker from some forgotten war—
the Chinese base, finally, it must be, though it looks too cramped
for everyone to stop and rest in, even if this light shows clearly

how small the refugee band is: the two nuns, the grey-haired father and his little daughter, the wounded man, the two young guys who look like extras from *The Wire*, four young monks and a tiny old woman—a widow since only last night. Amaris doesn't include herself and Book in the roll call. As if they can't possibly be present. As if she's watching all this through a lens.

As they near the hut, the buzzing ATVs, one with the officer standing on the back, scutter ahead and park beside two military trucks. A red sun blisters out of the horizon and the grey concrete of the hut turns to adobe and the desert goes maroon, like the surface of Mars. The head border guard confers with the officer while the other guards file into the hut. The officer, pointing at his wrist, waves off some suggestion. The guard leader salutes, turns, walks inside after his men. Now the Tibetan soldier jogs past Amaris, and as he heads for the parked trucks, it hits her with a wallop—they aren't stopping here, they're going farther. "Lew!" she begins. His back is turned, shoulders slumped under the grey poncho of the blanket, his boots slung around his neck by the laces. He's barefoot in the cold gravel, the hems of his blue jeans turned up as if to keep them off his heels, where the skin is flayed and seeping. The line of captives starts to move. The nearest truck—a troop carrier, its box roofed in with canvas, open at the back—gives a throat-clearing sound as it starts. Surely Book will demand some kind of medical stop before they go on. He's a doctor, they'll have to listen. But he squats and grips one pole of the stretcher and stands and shuffles ahead, shoeless and caped in his blanket like a street person, as if he's too cowed or tired to speak up. The second truck shudders and roars. The river is fifty metres off, behind the hut, and there she spots what she's looking for, a concrete outhouse nestled in a thicket of small trees. She has to go before getting into that truck. The thought of it slamming over ruts and potholes for who knows how long with her bladder like this . . . and how can she be so *thirsty* and her bladder so full?

A soldier slaps down the tailgate of the first truck. Book and the teenager in the baseball cap crawl up and pull the stretchered man inside, others pushing from the back. Now soldiers start driving or hauling prisoners aboard, though the two nuns and the man with the daughter remain by the tailgate, arguing with a soldier who has a cruelly handsome, hard-angled face, a brushcut hairline starting not an inch above his eyebrows. The father speaks angrily and turns and squats his daughter down and lifts her skirts and the soldier grabs the girl's braids and tugs her upright, then unslings his rifle and holds it across his chest, jutting his face into the father's face as if about to butt him. The girl howling. This is outrageous; Amaris looks for the Chinese officer. He's emerging from behind the hut, smoking, his walk still graceful, his face deathly pale. She walks toward him, trembling. He raises his open hand and jabs a finger at the trucks. "Go back now!"

On one of his dusty boots, droplets gleam in the sloping light.

"I need to go too," she says. "We all do. Please! And your men are acting—"

"We are going, just now."

"No, I mean we need to *go*."

He looks fiercely baffled.

"The toilet," she says.

"Get aboard the truck now! There is no time!"

"The child has to pee too. So does the nun."

"It isn't far."

He clasps her left arm and, like someone leading in a Latin dance, pivots her cleanly so she is facing the trucks, as he is. The smoke of his cigarette in her eyes. As he walks her toward the trucks, his clutch is firm but doesn't hurt; he has chosen not to hurt her, or she's hurting too much elsewhere to notice. Most of the Tibetans are aboard now, though the nuns are still outside arguing with the handsome, hard-faced soldier, who smacks his rifle butt on the lowered tailgate and makes a gargoyle face at them. Amaris is not climbing up there. She shivers. Cold sweat prickles from her pores. She jerks her arm free and in one motion peels her tights and her panties down and squats in the gravel. Her parka covers her, mostly. The officer snaps something in Chinese, then, "What are you doing!"

She won't look up. She stares at his small, sprinkled boots and the gravel around them. Each tiny stone and its shadow. Her thighs shake. Tears squeeze into her eyes. She can't pee. There's more commotion around the back of the truck, the older nun ignoring the shouting soldier as she helps her wounded friend to squat down, bracing her from behind like a midwife. From under the young nun's robes, urine flows and pools, smoking in the cold. The kid in the baseball cap and parka—unzipped, his necklaces dangling—slides off the open tailgate and stands, back turned, by the trembling tailpipe. His stream is audible. The soldier starts toward him but now the Tibetan father is climbing out of the truck, half blocking the soldier, who shoves him and barks words. The father ignores him and lifts his daughter down. Into the back of the truck the soldier yells; the Chinese giant, his face doleful and scared, ducks and crawls out to help him. It's too late—the other teenager and three of the monks clamber out after the giant, followed by a third soldier, blushing and very young, who doesn't seem to scold the monks but to plead and reason with them. He eyes Amaris shyly. The eyes of the monks deftly avoid her. The officer stalks toward the truck, hesitates, a hand twitching to his holster and then retreating behind him so that his fist is glued to the small of his back. The truck goes on emptying. The fourth monk helps the old widow down. Only Book and the wounded man are still in there, out of sight. Everywhere urine flows triumphantly. Those fountain sounds, the feel of rebellious, communal release, loosen her at last, and with searing relief, as if her exhaustion and fear and loneliness are draining away too, she lets go.

Wade Lawson is not twenty minutes up the switchback trail to Camp One when he spots a figure descending toward him and Shiva. He stops, lifts his sunglasses, lowers them again. Zeph, maybe? Jake? Surely not Tashi. Tash wouldn't disobey him. Nor would Zeph, he tells himself—though Zeph might just forget.

"Shiv, can you see who that is?"

He turns to check on the tiny porter, dwarfed in Book's parka, hunched and huffing under a colossal pack. In a panting voice the man says, "Mr. Lawson" (*Larson*, it comes out), "I think it is Jake. Or else, it is Zeph. Or, perhaps, Tashi Sherpa."

Lawson closes his eyes, tries to get his wind. His own pack is overloaded too—he doesn't want to make another run down to base camp, if possible—and he slept maybe an hour last night. Still, starting up this trail, getting out of earshot of the jangling satphones, he felt almost cheerful. Base camp was like Namche Bazaar on a festival day, with Ming and Jigme and the refugees milling around, cooking and eating, eating, *eating*, preparing to set out. As Lawson made his escape, he savoured the quiet that grew around him and the warm, dorsal embrace of his backpack, which always seems to complete him, a second, solidifying torso, a good burden firming him to the earth. . . . Now he watches that other climber's zipping descent of the switchbacks. It *is* Zeph. Lawson's dream is dissolving. He sweeps his gaze down the glacier. No sign of the Chinese returning with Amaris and his doctor, though he counts

on that happening with all his will—they *have* to return, by afternoon, so Amaris, if she's not too exhausted, can come up to Camp
One tomorrow and still climb with him and make the film.

Speaking with Sophie's mother at six this morning was the
worst. She'd been trying to get through, she said, for two hours.
Lawson was carefully shaving, sipping black coffee, mentally jot-
ting a list of stuff for Shiva to porter up to Camp One, when Kal
signalled him. *Who?* he mouthed. "Mrs. Book!" Kal basically
shouted, not bothering to cover the mouthpiece. Lawson had been
on and off the phones for a couple of hours already. News services, mostly. He'd hoped to avoid Sophie's mother. He'd figured
that she and Kal had nailed down a rapport last night, so she'd be
happy to speak only with Kal now—and, of course, with her
daughter. He set down his personal mirror and razor and took the
receiver and smothered the mouthpiece. "Tell her I'll go get
Sophie for her. I'll go wake her up now."

"I said *I* would do so," Kal whispered, now that whispering was
irrelevant—he looked rattled, as if wakened from a climber's
nightmare—"but she says, for now please let the girl sleep."

"Let her sleep and she'll sleep till eleven. And she'll need to
spell you off soon."

"Her mother says she'll call back in two hours. She says, now
she must talk to you."

"Is this Mrs. Book?" Lawson deepened his thinning voice,
trying to sound calm.

"Dr. Nika Stefakis," she said after the satellite delay, which
always made it sound as if people hadn't quite heard you.

"Pardon? Is this Sophie's mother?"

Delay. "Yes, but my name is not Book."

"What . . . ? Oh . . . okay. Listen, I'm really sorry about your
husband . . ."

"We are divorced."

"Right, I knew that."

"Kaljang Sherpa tells me there is still no sign of them." Soft but firm, quietly urgent, like the voice of a woman instructing a lover on a rendezvous. Slight accent. A husky voice. He drew himself up as if she were eyeing him from across a bar.

"Right, but the Chinese should have them back here soon. I'd guess by this aft. The guys who took them must be in deep, uh . . . in deep trouble with their own people."

"Their embassy says they still haven't any information, but will try to issue a statement today."

"Which means heads are rolling as we speak."

Delay. "Is it true you will be climbing back up the mountain now?"

"Uh, that's correct, but Kal, Ming, Jigme and your daughter will remain here."

Longer delay. As if she's scanning the Internet for breaking news. "Aren't some of those names you mention leaving? To take the refugees down to the city?"

"Well, uh . . . not to the city, no. I mean, they will be taking them over to Tarap, yeah—but then returning, right away. And I doubt they'll be ready to go till . . . well, it's hard to say. They might not even end up leaving till tomorrow."

"And *then* it will be only Kaljang and my daughter in the camp?"

"Your husband will be here by then. Lew, I mean. And Amaris McRae, the filmmaker."

"I know who Amaris McRae is. You seem sure they will be back."

"I'd stake my name on it," he said, grinning bitterly. "And listen, Nika"—he lowered his voice—"don't worry about Kaljang and Sophie on their own. Kal's a good guy."

"What . . . ? That isn't what I meant."

"You sure you wouldn't like to speak to her? I can go wake her up right now."

"It's you I want to talk to."

And Lawson, just like that, had had enough. The strain of being personable while somebody tweaks, needles, prods away at you—how did others endure it, in offices, public positions, day in, day out?

"Okay, look—I am sorry your husband crossed that border, but it was a *border*."

"From what I understand, he had to."

"But you *don't* understand. It wasn't his business."

Delay. "I know Lewis. When people are in trouble, there isn't a border."

"This climb and the people on it are his business—he gave his word. He signed a contract! What if people die on this expedition because he's not here to help? I mean, look, now even your . . . he's not even here now for your daughter."

"*Your* expedition," he caught (they were cutting across each other's delayed sentences now), "and you'll need to hold off until Lewis and Ms. McRae return!"

"At this point, putting it off is cancelling it."

"For a day? What difference could that make? You did say they'd be back today."

And Lawson saw the truth of it: he was far from sure. It could be two days, hell, it could be *five* days, by which time Amaris would be in no shape to climb and film anything. And a part of him had known this truth since the moment of her capture and had factored it into his panicked planning.

"I mean, it's hard to say how far the Chinese base is. It could take a bit longer."

"So you were lying to me."

"Look, I'm not down in the big city, like you! Things are never clear-cut above 20,000 feet and you people down there with your cellphones and Blackberries don't get it."

Delay. "Sophana and Pavlos and I . . . we want Lewis back safe. That's all."

A plaque of bitterness narrowed Lawson's throat. He couldn't swallow for a moment. What kind of divorce was this, anyway? As if his own ex would ever say something like that about him.

"This is a *climbing* expedition, ma'am, not a rescue mission. If men like your ex-husband go around violating international laws and crossing lines, they've got to accept the outcome, just like I do every time I rope up to climb." He rapped his disposable razor on the table like a tiny gavel. "If I end up alone up there and dying, you think I expect anyone to dice away their lives coming up to save me?"

"Yes, your past actions show how you feel about mountain rescues."

"So the media's starting to rehash its lies?"

"I'll be calling back in two hours to speak to my daughter."

He has noticed before that when you piss people off they suddenly wheel out possessives like *my daughter*, *my son*, *my husband*, as if refusing to acknowledge your first-name connection with their loved ones. Closing ranks against you—what people always do to you, especially in an establishment like the climbing world if you're from the rougher side of Main and you keep doing things your own way, and *succeeding*.

He'll summit Kyatruk for himself—to hell with the media and the climbing world and everybody else.

Now he and Shiva slog on upward as Zeph descends. Lawson thinks of radioing up to Tash or Jake to ask them what the fuck's going on, give them hell for letting Zeph go, but they're going to collide with the kid soon enough. Despite the big pack Zeph seems to be lugging, he has found a loping rhythm, quick on the hairpins, zippering down.

"Hey, Uncle Wade! Hi, Shiv!" he calls in a raw, excited voice when he's still minutes above them. Lawson plants himself across the path in a relatively flat spot, Shiva behind him. He breathes from the belly, regains his wind. At last Zeph rounds the hook in the trail. He's rangy, six foot two, and standing upslope with his high pack he seems to tower above Lawson, the sun just to his left like a gleaming buckler. Blinding. Lawson thinks of ploughing a shortcut up the steep snowface and reaching the trail just above the hook, behind and above Zeph, but decides that blocking the route down is the stronger position. Not that strength is needed here. Delicacy is needed here and Lawson knows himself to be clumsy in kid gloves. Zeph, though physically impressive, is weirdly sensitive, once almost crying after making a gaffe and getting corrected while learning to belay, because Jake, he said, might have gotten hurt. Lawson's brother, Clyde, went too easy on the kid, folded too often to the hippie whims of the older woman he met and married, to the whole town's surprise, when Zeph was ten. Zeph is short for Zephyr. His blood father had become a guru or a druid in some kind of solar cult and disappeared when Zeph was five. His mother, Coriander, was the most stunning woman Lawson had ever seen, even with her armpits unshaved on her wedding day. Still is the most beautiful now, as a forty-six-year-old widow. Lawson can almost grasp how Clyde, of all men, could have turned vegetarian for her—though Lawson could never stand how the marriage bevelled his brother's edges, ate away at his drive, his *will*, especially for climbing. That lack was what killed him in the end. So Lawson maintains. Nevertheless, he feels a duty to his brother's family, and for four years has employed Zeph at his climbing gym and coached him as well.

"Hey, Zeph, what's going on? The peak is thataway."

Zeph lifts his sunglasses onto his slacker toque as he always does when talking to you, even when the sun off the snow is dangerously bright, like now. Lawson readies for expressive eye contact. "Uncle Wade, I . . . just couldn't sleep last night."

"You and me both, Zeph. The altitude's a bitch. You're in good shape, though. You look ready to go."

"I was thinking stuff over . . ."

"At night? Thinking stuff over at night's a bad idea!" Lawson shows his front teeth while pulverizing a lump of gum with his molars. "Night changes everything, Zeph. Makes everything worse. But it's a great day for climbing—look around! Why would you be heading down?"

"Yeah, it's awesome. But I was like . . . thinking maybe I should help them?" Brown eyes soft as a fawn's, pink cheeks, blond beard and platinum curls coiling out the edges of his toque. "The, uh, refugees."

"The Tibetans are fine, Zeph! They have plenty of help. And they'll be leaving any minute."

"Yeah, I can see them down there, but, you know. I can catch up to them, and . . ."

"Is it partly about the film?"

"The . . . what?"

"Because I still think Amaris is going to make it back and join us for the climb."

"Film? No, no, it's not the film, I mean . . . God! I don't care if I'm in a film or not! We don't even, like, own a TV."

"We won't wait for you, Zeph—you understand that? We can't. You go down to Tarap with them and your climb is over."

"I know, Uncle Wade."

"The Tibetans will be fine, I promise you!" As he says the words he believes them with all his heart. "They don't need you. We need you! You're part of the team."

"That's what Jake said."

"Jake's right."

"But I'm still, like—"

"Damn it, Zeph, *I* need you!" The truth of the words, this sickening admission, almost doubles him over, ripping its way up and out of him, an urgent peristalsis. If he summits alone again, who will ever believe him? And it's not just that. Zeph's eyes wander slightly as if trying to peek past the wraparound shades that Lawson calls, half in jest, his re-entry shields. With his instinct for gestures of power, Lawson sweeps them off his face, squints against the sun.

"Just turn around, Zeph, and we'll go back up together now."

"Uncle Wade . . . I'm sorry, I just can't. I have to go down there and help. I know Ming and Jigme could use the help. I talked to Ming on the two-way, and I just—"

"Ming *asked* you to come down?"

"No, no way, man, nothing like that! It was, like, my decision?"

Since when do you make decisions? thinks Lawson. Zeph has dithered and shirked and hedged for as long as Lawson has known him. Still lives at home. It kills Lawson that this towering twenty-six-year-old child is defying him.

"Couldn't live with myself if I didn't help," Zeph says.

"But you'll have to live with giving up this mountain!"

"I sort of feel like, you know . . . their mountain is realer?"

Lawson works his soles deeper into the trail. "Your own life is the realest thing you'll ever have, Zeph, and this is your chance to do something with it! Goddamn it, I feel like I've been trying to drag you uphill into your real life for years now while you smoke up with your snowboard pals and philosophize and write reggae songs."

"I won't be asking for my money back or anything. I know I'm, like—"

"Good. Because you won't see a dime of it. I covered most of your costs anyway."

"Uncle Wade—"

"And you're finished at the gym, you understand?" *The gym is finished.*

"I'm really sorry, Uncle Wade . . . this is, like, the hardest choice I ever made in my life."

"And you can find another coach."

"Okay, like—fuck, I'm sorry!" He looks down at his boots—Finnmarks, a recent gift from Lawson. "But I better go now," he says.

How are they going to manage this? This trail is not made for two-way traffic, and Lawson is no mood to make room. But Zeph has sensed the impasse. In a halting, self-effacing way, he draws his ice axe and sidesteps down off the trail, shortcutting down the snowface to meet the next switchback. He keeps his axe in cane position, as Lawson taught him on Mount Gimli a few months ago, to dig in if he slips.

"Let's go," Lawson tells Shiva with a glance back, half surprised to find the porter still with him.

Lawson may be livid at Zeph, but as the steepening slope cuts into his rage and siphons it away as manic fuel, he feels a touch sick about his words. Over the summer he and Zeph worked hard to get ready for this climb. Zeph the neph, as the kid calls himself around his step-uncle, is the nearest thing Lawson has to family now. At first when Zeph said he wanted to come on this expedition, Lawson balked, afraid the kid lacked the necessary fibre and focus, and also leery of a mishap—of losing Coriander's *son* as well as her husband. But then he sniffed out a narrative rightness—a deeper note of redemption—in getting his brother's stepson up an unclimbed mountain and down safe. And think what that would mean to Zeph himself! Clyde had been sixteen when he led Lawson up Mount Gimli and thirty-nine when he died in Lawson's arms on Mount Logan, four years back. *Come on, Cly. Keep going. You can do it.* By that time, anyone who didn't know the brothers would have assumed Wade was the elder. He'd certainly become the better climber—a famous climber, a leader of climbs—so in the end he was held responsible for the death.

Lawson's baby son, too, died in his arms. Lawson opts to believe that. The boy spent all of three, four minutes in the world. The obstetrician was a dashing, pompous young city type on a locum in Nelson who'd never troubled to conceal his unhappiness about the placement and kept calling Lawson "Dwayne" and Jennifer "you," and when he said, at the critical moment, *You will need to leave immediately, Dwayne, so we can handle this,* Lawson looked him in the middle of the brow, as his father had taught him, and said, slowly, *My place is right here.* It had worked. It always did. But remaining with Jenn for the birth had not made it a *birth.* Poor little climber, tangled in his own ropes. The feeble life signs had tapered, fought back for a moment, then faded forever. The cyan face and purple lips of hypoxia, a condition Lawson knew well from high-altitude climbing. A tiny, toy oxygen mask. By the time Jenn, and then Lawson, held the boy, he was gone, officially, though he was not yet cold, not yet fully (so Lawson maintained) dead.

Media types like to refer to Jenn "leaving Lawson" in terms of his "disgrace"—after his brother's death on Mount Logan, after his disputed solo climb of Makalu, where he'd also "failed to save" a dying man, a Swiss soloist he had passed on his descent (advanced pulmonary edema at 26,000 feet: what was he to do, a fireman's carry down ice cliffs?)—because that made a neater story and it thrilled the public to see a man slip and tumble all the way to the bottom, shattering every bone, every dream, just as it had thrilled them before to see him struggle and grit his way to the top, stand there in photogenic glamour and wave the flag, *their* flag, for them. . . . But Lawson opts to believe it was the stillbirth (as the hospital insisted on calling it) of Wade Lawson Jr. that killed the marriage. How for eighteen months the ashes remained in a silly turtle-shaped urn that Jenn had selected, waiting to be buried or scattered in an alpine meadow, but he and Jenn kept deferring the moment, just as, having tried to start over by moving into a bigger house he had planned and built for them—two-storey, vertical pine log, on a south-facing slope above Nelson—most of their stuff had remained packed in boxes. So for the final months until Jenn left, those rooms had never stopped echoing. She wouldn't admit it was about the baby. She denied it was about his public disgrace. She said it was him, damn it, just him.

At that point he'd started planning this climb.

Shiva lags far behind by the time Lawson, an hour later, pounds into Camp One. Jake rolls toward him, lanky, loose-jointed, like a bit player in a western. He has a wedgelike face: sloped, balding forehead, long sharp nose, bushy moustache over an overbite that keeps his mouth pried open in an apparent smile.

"Apologies, dude," he says with that beaverish smile that isn't one. "I tried to keep him up here."

"Yeah. Well. This might work better in the end."

Lawson does feel better roped to Jake Kravchuk than to Zeph. He *gets* Jake. Jake's a guy's guy—a beer drinker, not a pothead. He has guts and doesn't complain. True, he lacks Zeph's rock climbing finesse and power, but Lawson feels, now, that up on the Lawson Wall Jake will be a sounder bet.

Kaljang's voice scratches out of Lawson's handset radio. Lawson has been expecting this for a while—for Kal to patch through a call from someone who insists on speaking to the expedition leader, even though it's around nine p.m. Vancouver time.

"Come in?"

"It's that climbing website," Kaljang says. "They want to speak to you. And your corporate sponsors, they want you to call back to them. Over."

"You're not coming in too clear, Kal." This is the truth. "Over."

"But first," Kal says, "I have to inform you with some news. Over."

"Bad news, right?"

"I am not sure. But I think, probably, terrible."

Over. It's over.

"Sophie's not present," Kal says, "in the base camp."

"What?"

"——gone. Her mother called again and I couldn't find her. Over."

"Kal, wait a minute, she wanders off all the time, she could be anywhere."

"Pardon? Come in?"

Lawson repeats himself.

"No," Kaljang says, "I know her places. Zeph and me now just looked everywhere. And she has taken her things. I think that she has chased her dad down the glacier trail. Over."

"Jesus," Lawson whispers.

"Come in? Maybe I should go in hot pursuit?"

"No! Absolutely not! Look. Tell the Himalaya dot net people I've got to get organized up here—we'll call them in an hour.

And don't mention anything about Sophie yet. Not till we're sure she's crossed the border."

"——late. Her mother knows. She is so upset. She'll call back, too, and she calls back the embassy, quite soon. They've just informed the Beijing authorities, too. Oh . . . and Zeph has already been answering some questions of the climbing website. Over."

Glancing down the glacier Lawson spits his gum into the snow, where it disappears, a dimple of shadow left on the surface.

They've been in the truck for some time, accelerating over straight reaches of the gravel road, slowing to thump and smash over rutted stretches. The dusty air is warmer than at base camp and this enclosure smells of cigarettes and gasoline and the barny odours of wet sheepskin, urine and blood. Whenever the ride roughens, Book stoops low over the wounded man, digging his hands under the limp shoulders to cradle him over the corrugated steel floor, trying to absorb the road with his arms and keep the wound from reopening. The man's face is tallowy and his eyes are closed. He's balding, the hair closely shorn. Every few minutes a bad bump jolts a groan out of him. Book is being helped by the kid in the parka and baseball cap, who has introduced himself by saying "Norbu" while pointing at his own face, the bony cheeks a relief map in acne, downy hair on the chin and above his lip. RED BULL, his cap reads. He points at Book's patient now and says, "Lhundup Boshay."

Book gives his own name—straining his voice over the engine, the crunching of the tires, the Talking Heads throbbing from up front in the cab, "Take Me to the River"—then adds, "Can you speak any English . . . Chinese?"

Norbu spits out something that sounds like "Motherfucker."

"What . . . pardon?"

The kid shrugs politely. Book looks around, then clears his throat and calls out, "My patient needs water—please." At the end of each facing bench, by the open back of the truck, their guards sit: the young guy with the low hairline and virile, almost muscular face, and the emaciated giant, his head stooped under the sloping roof-canvas in a way that looks as much apologetic as practical. Both men grip their assault rifles tightly. A gap on the bench separates each guard from a row of captives, crowded up to where the truckbed meets the cab. There, a small window allows a glimpse of Palden Jangbu driving, Lieutenant Zhao apparently dozing beside him.

"*Water*," Book repeats to the guards, pointing at the patient, and he mimes taking a drink. In fact his patient needs blood, pints of it. A few moments later the sheepish giant leans and, with a superhuman reach, proffers a tin flask. The other guard scowls out the back, smoking murderously. When Book says *shei shei*—one of the few bits of Mandarin he recalls from a posting in a flooded part of Jiangsu, in 1994—the giant nods slightly and turns away.

Book braces Lhundup Boshay's head with one hand. With the other, he holds the flask and drips water between the seamed, swollen lips, which suckle at the rim. "Come on. Come on." The ride is rougher now, Palden accelerating as he turns up his music again. Book glances out the back of the truck: the second, empty truck falling behind in a smog of dust, and above the dust, a disembodied mirage of white peaks. The adventurer that Lawson loves to talk about must have caught his first glimpse of Kyatruk from around here—that high pyramid, titanium white, thrusting above the glacier and the lesser peaks, with a long cirrus of snow blowing east off its summit like a phantom windsock. The night after they all reached base camp, Lawson gave a lecture in the control tent: "Murloe and the Mountain." He turned out to be an engaging speaker, his ego taking a step back behind his boyish enthusiasm for the story. (Book was only distracted by the name "Murloe," which kept reminding him of good red wine.)

You can see now why Murloe and Lawson both succumbed to the mountain's spell. It's hypnotic, unearthly. The longer you stare, the more it seems a refuge above all human borders and distinctions and this constant dialogue of violence. Up there, he'd hoped, he and Sophie could step away from trouble and karma for a while.

At least the girl herself is still safe up there.

"How far do you think they're taking us?" Amaris asks from behind him, where she's wedged between the injured nun and the man with the sleeping girl nested on his lap.

"I think Drongpa," he says. "It's the closest city. There'll be a hospital there, and we should be able to call the embassy. But this road . . . I don't know. I'd have thought we'd go along the river."

"Well, I'll be giving them an earful," she cuts in, as if letting him finish might make his doubts a reality. "This captain, or whatever, is going to wish . . ."

"Zhao—he's a lieutenant. Listen, that was brave of you, squatting there . . ."

"I didn't have a choice."

"Courage usually comes down to that," he says. "But what I mean is—"

"It's just my bladder, Lew, not some noble choice! I thought you'd call for a medical stop there."

"There wasn't time, we've got to get this man to an ICU. But what I mean is—you need to be a bit more careful."

"Well, it's not like they're going to shoot us, Lew! This Zhao probably still hopes I'll turn out to be some Mata Hari, but I've got him thinking now. And you're *white*."

"But they won't hesitate to shoot at these folks, and we're with them."

"For now."

"You should close your eyes, Amaris. You must have walked eighteen hours in the last twenty-four. I was just lounging at base camp till sunset."

"I'm fine, thanks."

"Do you want another hit of Diamox? We're still up pretty high here."

"I'm *fine*."

The nuns are talking over each other—no, praying, chanting the same words, but out of sync. The widow weeping, the hard-faced guard hectoring the giant one, Norbu muttering to his friend in the parka and toque and now grimly tapping fists with him. Music thudding. An anxious cacophony.

"Why did you have to *do* this, Lew? Cross that border?"

He isn't sure if she has forgotten that she made her point last night or is in documentary mode, pursuing an answer. Before he can speak, she adds, "My job is to *record* things, not get taken hostage. That footage could have made a big difference to this . . . this whole crisis. Now it's gone."

"Would your footage have made a difference to *him?*"

"As if we can save everyone!"

"But I have to act as if maybe I can."

"Right, I knew it, you're one of those messiah types who want to parachute in and rescue everyone and get credit, and half the time you just—it just makes the trouble worse. Like my adoptive parents, always interfering in every . . ." Untypically she loses her course, seems unsure. The Tibetans and the guards are all watching.

He says, "Maybe you're right about the border."

"Why are you *agreeing* with me, Lew—don't you ever want to fight?"

"For one thing, the media's going to focus on the lost filmmaker and humanitarian doctor from Toronto, instead of on these people."

No reply. "Psycho Killer" is on. He and Nika used to dance to these songs back when they were in medical school. How simple life seemed before he realized he owed something back to the world. (He gropes in his kit for the blood pressure cuff.) Book is a bon vivant infected with conscience; if he could forget that he's urgently needed, in any number of places, he might still, even now, dance and eat and drink and sing and socialize and make love forever without ennui, unlike some of his colleagues—sombre introverts who, if they couldn't find enough victims to save, would have to invent them. Book would rather be mixing drinks for his patients, dealing cards. We were made to get along, to be together, and it's a truth that's medically attested: love and dance and connection strengthen every bodily system, while isolation, rage and sadness poison them with cortisol.

How well he knows both opposing states. He must be saturated with poison after his years of crisis postings, especially the last dozen. He wonders whether the old, social him is now anything more than a role he occasionally reprises, hamming it up, trying to keep the manic encores rolling and hold the other stuff at bay.

He billows Lhundup's coat out around the shoulder and applies the Velcro cuff. Through his stethoscope he strains to hear and count over the road's roar. Blood pressure still low, though it hasn't dropped further. He removes the cuff, points at the patient's waist and says, "Norbu?" Norbu aims the penlight as Book lifts the crusted blanket. Book nods, relieved the clamp is holding, though he doubts there's enough blood left in the man for another serious hemorrhage. The truck gears down. They're climbing now. Behind them a tricolour vista: burnt earth, white mountains, blue sky. Above the desert a high pitch of the Kyatruk glacier glows, maybe thirty miles away but seeming much closer. The truck levels out and crunches to a stop. They seem to be on a barren hill. Debris like tumbleweed scurries across the road. Amaris twitches and her eyes shoot open.

"Hi!"—it's Palden, clanking open the tailgate—"we arrive at the base, Lewis!"

"Where's Drongpa?" Book asks, almost shouting, the music still throbbing out of the cab. "Is this it?"

"It's the base!"

"Drongpa?"

"Pardon me? No Drongpa here!"

The guards clomp down, the scrawny giant flopping with fatigue.

"We need a hospital," Book says. "Where's the lieutenant?"

"It's not possible today. Tomorrow, maybe possible. Let's get off, please!"

The Tibetans filing out. Amaris takes one of the young nun's arms over her shoulder and, teamed with the older nun, helps her down off the tailgate.

"Don't worry," says Palden in his earflap cap, with his imp's rictus, "we have a doctor!"

"Here at the base?"

"Yes, of course! It's yourself!"

The sun has been up for some time. Sophie's hood is back off her head, her parka hangs open and she holds her daypack limply over her shoulder by one strap. The downhill grade barely keeps her feet clumping along. Ahead, at the trail's end, where this valley opens onto the desert plain, a concrete building. It doesn't look big enough, but they must be in there, all of them. Smoke twines up from the chimney pipe. Beyond the building and the parked ATVs—which she heard in the night whenever the wind died down—the plain looks too wide to cross, though a shadowy road, hardly distinct from the desert floor, snakes to the east.

"Finally," she breathes.

As she draws close, she wonders if she should announce herself and approach with hands clasped on top of her head, like in a movie. The low window facing her is barred with four rusty iron slats. Maybe everyone is asleep, jammed together like the refugees on the floor of the control tent—though a guard or two must be awake. She lobs a greeting ahead of her, softly, "Hi," like a pebble tossed at a window. It sounds pathetic. "Hello?" she tries. She can see inside now, dimly. Two men asleep on cots along the far wall, dark blue tunics and black toques hooked on the wall above. A small barrel stove.

She leans close to the window. Just two more men asleep beneath it, to either side. That's it.

She squats down under the window and lowers her face into her hands and tries to think. If there were anything in her stomach, she would throw it up.

No feeling in her legs as she walks past the ATVs, not even trying for silence now, boots flapping a slow, defeated beat, fuck it, fuck it. She stands at the start, or end, of the road. And what the fuck now. He always used to be close by when things went wrong or she felt weak. Her head droops, her torso begins shaking as if jerked by electric shocks. Once he told her that a bad shock can make the muscles clench so powerfully they shatter bone, and that's how this feels. Her ribs are cracking. *I'm going to kill him when I find him.*

A voice calls out and she turns around, her vision blurry. She swabs her eyes with her sleeve. In the doorway there's a guard in a white undershirt and blue trousers, barefoot. She returns his stare. He ducks back inside. She spins and runs up the road, her pack jouncing on one shoulder, then she veers left across the gravel moonscape toward the ravine that she saw from back up on the trail, the river cutting down into the desert floor. She could still go back, ask him for help, she'd been about to approach the guards, possibly, she thinks, it's no longer clear, but here she is, just running. The voice hollers. She glances back. He now wears his blue tunic, as if he felt it was important to be officially dressed for whatever comes next. He holds his small machinegun aimed at the ground. He yells again. Her legs are light, flying, and the river isn't far. She always could run. She and her father trotting in the ravines along the Don River for half an hour, longer, with Bones, the collie cross she'd loved in an earlier, perfect life. An engine yowls behind her like a waking chainsaw. At the ravine's lip she hardly slows. It could be a cliff edge for all she can see, but she runs straight over it and steeply down a gravel slope in a few giant, sliding steps, like running down a dune. Her small pack flies loose and she lets it go.

The bank at the bottom is a narrow flood plain and she runs along it, along the churning river, outpacing the current. This urge to run and this running fill her mind and banish all other thought. She is pure, panicked flight. No sounds of pursuit over the gush of the current and the blood thudding in her skull—then the air behind her fills with a whine. She looks back: an ATV edging over the ravine's lip like a large, awkward predator, trying to pick its way down. The hungry eyes of its headlights. The engine surges, the machine bucks forward. She keeps watching, baffled, her legs still pumping beneath her as if part of a separate animal. The guard seems to be performing some gymnastic feat, handstanding on the handlebars of the machine as it thumps diagonally down the ravine's face, now tipping sideways, the man's grasp coming free, one hand and the other and he's tumbling midair as the machine flips and rolls. It seems the two must somehow reunite, magically completing the stunt, the driver deftly back in the saddle, but he falls out of sight behind the machine, which somersaults twice to a clunking halt, upright on the riverbank, a wheel in the shallows.

At last she stops running, stands breathing. Behind the machine, in the shallows, a hand flutters, as if beckoning her. The animal in her aches to sprint on, but it's not an option. It's like her father is watching—expecting her to do what's required, no matter how much it scares her. She approaches. The guard lies face down at the edge of the river, just past the ATV, his head cranked against his shoulder at an ugly angle. The little machinegun lies beside him. In a sort of trance she kneels numbly at his side, weirdly resigned. It's inevitable, this latest outcome, as if she has toppled into a dream and is spiralling from one level of horror to the next. A bit of the guard's face is visible, the rest squashed into the damp sand. He's maybe twenty years old. He has bed-head and bare, little boy feet, the toes turned inward. Luckily, his visible eye is closed. She feels for a jugular pulse, as her father has taught her, and her hand shakes. Before yesterday she'd never seen a dead body. Now she is touching one.

She checks the skyline above the ravine. It seems unlikely but may be possible that the others, in a hard sleep, didn't wake.

He could have fired at her, but he didn't fire.

Her green day pack lies at the base of the slope, flopped over and dusty. The zipper has come wide open. She peers into the pack vaguely, casts a look around her feet, zips the pack closed.

Inscriptions in magic marker criss-cross the fabric: LOVE YOU
TONS SOPH!! EAT LOCALY, LOVE GLOBALY. END THE HUMAN WAR!
Scott's rock star signature, a flashy squiggle followed by an
ECG flatline. Friends' names, phone numbers. None of this
helps her now. She stares for a few seconds at the ATV, careful
to avoid the guard's body with her eyes, then turns and runs on
downstream.

The banks of the ravine grow higher, the river cutting deeper,
and she runs in shadow with the morning sunlight on the opposite side. Her side of the ravine at times plunges straight into the
river on a bend and she needs to make her way along a scanty
path, maybe a goat track, worked into the steep face. If they do
follow her, it will have to be on foot. On the far side of these
traverses, more riverbank, small beaches with sand like fine-
ground pepper, which she takes care not to step on.

Even in this shade the air is mild and she's soaked under her
sweater and open parka. The sweater's humid wool exhales a faint
smell like turmeric, woodsmoke—her father's smell, childhood,
those windless October ravines in Toronto. She eases to a jog, then
a fast walk. The river is slowing, widening. The banks of the
ravine are maybe twenty metres high and thatched now with clinging stands of small poplars turning yellow. A following breeze
trembles the leaves. There's a faint but definite trail now, and on
the far side of the river the same.

She glances back: she's leaving no prints. As for the crumbly
gravel bank she ran down, the guards have surely gone down
before, and the rolling ATV should have scrambled her tracks. She
hopes so. Being captured was actually her intention, and getting
arrested is not, to her, a terrifying unknown, but she wants to be
rounded up with her father and Amaris and the others, not alone
in a hut with the surviving guards.

The impulse to grab her cellphone whenever she wants to reach someone has been fading slowly in the weeks since they set out from Kathmandu, but now she feels another twang of it. It still seems unlikely that there could be places right off the dial, where even 911 doesn't work. Years ago, on a family trip in the Yukon, her father or mother had set the car radio to scan and she'd watched it loop through all the numbers and cycle round again, AM, FM, searching for a lone signal to hook onto. There are still such places. Being isolated from all her contacts would have seemed unsurvivable just three months ago, before things started to fall apart for her. Now, in some ways, it feels better to be off the dial. Just not out here, right now.

On the edge of a crescent beach she drops to one knee and strips off her parka and sweater and fleece hoodie. Her T-shirt is wet through. She manages to cram the parka and hoodie into the pack, but the sweater won't fit. She knots its arms around her waist. She finishes her water and refills the plastic bottle from the shallows and walks deeper into Tibet, the lost country she has wanted so much to see.

You get what you want, but never in the way you want it.

Across the river, the north side of the ravine, or valley now, is much wider and has patches of cropped grass and stands of tall poplars fully leafed, gold and green. Its riverside path looks more defined, almost a minor road. The whole north side and its high, far-off embankment are flooded with laser-pure sunlight. Between groomed-looking stands of trees, a stone hut. No smoke from the chimney, but in a lull of the wind she does smell smoke. Past the second woodlot, a field of yellow grass that must be some kind of grain and beyond it another field terraced above the first. Beyond that, stone buildings, fumes from a chimney, a dog standing in a doorway with its ears pricked, looking toward her. A pen with horses, necks stretched over the fence. She's a long way across the fields and the river but they watch her, as if unused to seeing movement over here on the shadow side of the valley.

As far ahead as she can see, there's no bridge to the north side and the river is a long stone's throw across, deep and strongly flowing. More farms appear. In the fields of the next one, several men and women, faces dark under their hats, are cutting grain, light flashing off the scalloping scythes. She stands watching. It's such a relief to see these calmly working figures; she wants to wave or call out, yet they seem barely real. It's like the river's far bank is a computerized set where digital figments perform in a historical film. Gleaners from a distant time.

She closes her eyes as if to clear them and leaves them shut a few seconds. A strange parade crosses the inner screen of her eyelids—cartoon faces, lava lamp blobs, fluttering hands, like when you first lie down and shut your eyes after being up all night. In June she and Scott and a few friends ate hash in the form of zucchini cake and she didn't like those intensified visions—though she didn't admit it to her friends. She's a vivid dreamer as it is. She opens her eyes. One of the gleaners, a woman in a headscarf and long black skirts, stands among the flattened stalks, a hand peaked above her eyes. Sophie lifts her own hand in a tentative wave, slowly lets it fall, as if to say, *Yes, this is odd, isn't it. And I don't know what to do about it either.*

She walks on while the Tibetans stand watching. Beyond those terraced fields, an orchard where women and children pick fruit— apples, pears. She is seeing things with hyperacute clarity, as if her eyes had a zoom lens. The high slope of the ravine on her right still keeps her in shadow. She walks on, dizzy, weak and excited. Across the river, beyond the orchard, a larger pen where yaks are grazing and a man sits straddling a fence, smoking. He doesn't look over. She doesn't wave. She can see some distance downriver. The country on the north side seems to get ever greener and lusher, riotous with life—the damp and dense green smells of it!— but no sign of a bridge. Maybe there is no bridge, maybe no one from the rich side of the river ever needs to cross. More orchards, a big dog cantering among the trees where a woman stands on a stool picking apricots and dropping them into her apron.

Fruit, the idea of food, should make Sophie's mouth water, but in this growing warmth all she can think of is sleep.

A patch of stunted poplars grows between her trail and the wall of the valley, and here the wall is not so steep, so that sunlight is pushing toward her across the river and will soon light up her path. Sunrise near noon. She enters the tiny forest. The trees are maybe twice her height, little more. Rippling leaves of bright yellow, the rusty dead ones at her toes rustling in their layers. November smells, as if she's back home with Scott, searching the woods for a good place—a kiss, a feel, is sweetly scorching in the cold—hearing the busy viaduct and the parkway, those soothing urban rivers.

At the back of the wood she finds a spot, dead leaves over white pepper sand, and pulls on her father's sweater and lies down. A shuddering wrings her to her core and when it dies out she begins to sob. She pulls the parka over her body. As she closes her eyes, that Halloween parade of faces appears again, along with a dimmer face, turned away as if in shyness or mourning. Her eyes spring open. The dead guard. She is hiding in a clump of trees by a glacial river in Tibet and she has no map or food and she is being hunted, maybe, by vengeful twenty-year-olds with submachineguns—not the metro police. *I'm sorry I wasn't here, love, but I'm here now.* Her father, six weeks back. Her father telling her again that he wanted to get her out of here, meaning North America. *For years I've wanted to.* Before her parents had split up, he'd wanted them all to live in Central America, or India, or Peru, or move with him among his safer postings, get a true education, he said. But Sophie had her school, her friends and guitar and blog and cartoon, Pavlos had his team sports and sullen rages, Yiayia would rather live with them than with her son in Sherbrooke, and Sophie's mother had a research position, her colleagues, her home. Her husband had apparently lost his mind, she said. Even Sophie, who adored him, could see that he'd grown impractical. Sixteen months ago her parents had separated—which simply meant that when her father returned, ill and skinny, from Sumatra after the tsunami, he'd checked into the Lakeshore Motel and come to "visit" the next day. She guessed he was to blame, after all. That's what he said himself. So each departure since then made her blame him all over again, yet his returns made her forgive, so that her mother, lacking the benefit of this dramatic pattern—departure, absence, return— bore the eventual brunt of Sophie's deeper blame, and ensuing actions. Her dad rehydrating infants in Darjeeling while the cops rapped unsoftly at the door and asked for Sophana Book. Scott's parents calling in a fury. They believed Sophie had led their son astray and it turned out that Scott had urged them, along with the cops, to think so.

"Your papa should be back in town any minute," her mother had said, wryly, no sign of grievance, as Sophie noted with some hope. (Her mother's accent thickened whenever she spoke of family, as opposed to professional matters, when it all but vanished.) "Whenever someone is in trouble on the other side of the world, he hops onto a plane."

And he did.

As she lies in the plum-yellow shadows a sentence unrolls in her mind: *In my youth he sheltered me, and I'll protect him now.*

Something memorized in grade school, the other side of the world. The rest seems gone. *The other side of the river.* Her heart is slowing down at last, it hardly seems to beat. Sloping sunlight, the day's first hit on this shore, filters down through the candling leaves to warm her eyelids.

Take Me from the Wilderness

In the spring of 1898, the Canadian doctor Susie Rijnhart, née Carson, and her husband, Petrus, a Dutch missionary, embarked on a journey across the Tibetan plateau toward the forbidden city of Lhasa, where they hoped to establish a Christian mission and medical post. They brought with them their eleven-month-old son Charlie, three native porters, a number of ponies for riding and for carrying supplies, and their dog. The young couple had already carried out several years of medical and missionary work on the Tibetan-Chinese frontier, so they had the advantage of speaking the language and understanding the customs of the country. They even dressed Tibetan-style for their journey. Still, in setting out to reach Lhasa, they were trying to accomplish what no other Westerners had ever done.

Over the course of the summer they managed to cover a thousand kilometres across desert and through marshes and over passes where at times the trail was forlornly defined by the bones, recent or ancient, of travellers and their animals. They crossed into a lawless province and before long the bandits then common in the region stole some of their ponies. Two of their porters deserted them. Then, in August, their son, seemingly healthy as he rode in his father's arms, fell into a sleep from which his mother could not revive him. He lay pale and still. In her own words, she "loosened baby's garments, chafed his wrists, performed artificial respiration, though feeling almost certain that nothing would avail." Possibly Charlie died of some kind of altitude sickness. She and her husband, trying and failing to get through the hymn "Take Me from the Wilderness," wept, along with their porter Rahim, over the body of this child that Dr. Rijnhart had called "[our] little flower blooming on the bleak and barren Dang La."

They pushed on toward Lhasa, broken-hearted but still set on their missionary intervention, continuing to dispense evangelical tracts written in Tibetan but now meeting stronger opposition— sometimes the official opposition of regional governors and their troops, sometimes the random harassment of outlaws. In early autumn, having sent Rahim home on one of the ponies, they were attacked by a band of these men and lost their dog and all but one of their remaining ponies. They fled and camped in a snowstorm on the banks of the Tsa Chu—the sourcewaters of the Mekong River— hoping to cross the next day and reach an encampment they could see in the distance so as to buy more ponies and supplies. The next morning Petrus Rijnhart waded into the river. When he was halfway out, at the edge of the deep channel where he would have to swim, his wife saw him glance upstream—her own view in that direction was blocked by rocky outcrops—and then stop and slog back toward her. When he reached the shore, he yelled something that she did not hear and then started walking upstream, vanishing beyond the outcrops. It was the last she ever saw of him.

Dr. Rijnhart walked down to the shore and looked upstream and saw another encampment not far off on her own side of the river. No sign of her husband, who she assumed must already be inside one of the tents, negotiating. However, when he failed to return by the next morning she realized the truth: he must have walked straight into an encampment of outlaws—perhaps the same ones who'd attacked them a few days earlier—and was now surely dead. The doctor could only flee eastward, two months later reaching a mission post in the same Tibetan frontier region from which she and her lost family had set out some six months before.

In 1901 the doctor published a book about her experiences in Tibet. A few years later, in China, she married another missionary, and in 1907, pregnant and ill, she returned to Canada, where she died eight weeks after giving birth to another son.

"Here is your nice clean single cell, doctor."

Palden Jangbu holds Book's bicep gently and, with the other hand, sweepingly indicates the tiny cell, like a concierge showing off a VIP suite. His assault rifle is over his shoulder, a cigarette drooping from his mouth. It seems to have gone out.

"Thanks," Book says, "but I have to be in the end cell. With your compatriots."

"But Lewis, they are not patriots, they are Splittists!" He speaks sincerely, patiently. "They wish to bring Tibet back into the, the primitive age—before the liberation."

"I need to be with the wounded man and the nun."

"We can take you there whenever there is a need! It is very full up."

"They need me now."

"You are not used to it, I am thinking."

"Palden—"

"And this cell is so nice."

He sounds hurt on the cell's behalf. Book exhales and glances past him. A few dim, bare light bulbs hang by their wires from the hallway ceiling, showing the concrete floors and walls and ceilings and the bars of the cells and the steel door at the head of the hallway, all painted a bilious green. Book's boots, with bloodied socks scrunched up inside them, hang by their laces over his shoulders.

"Please," he says, the word a rumble low in his throat.

Palden sags his head, brings out his lighter, cups his hands over his mouth and rasps, "Okay, Lewis," in a cloud of smoke. He takes Book's arm and draws him toward the last of the five cells that line one side of the hallway. Each cell has a back wall, side walls and, facing onto the hallway, a row of floor-to-ceiling stanchions with a barred door set into it, like a jail cell in a western.

"Lew . . . ?" Book glances back. All he can see of Amaris is her small, tanned fists gripping the bars of her cell—the first of the five—near the head of the hallway and the side passage leading out to the yard through which they were just herded in. "I can join you in that cell too," she calls thinly. "If you need the help."

She might be lonely—or is she just offering out of a sense that she should? She doesn't strike him as the lonely type, or the type for oughts and shoulds. But who can say. She's frank with her opinions, her feelings show graphically on her face, but that doesn't mean there aren't lots of other things she walls up inside. He calls back, "I think two of us would overcrowd them. Stay put, get some rest while you can."

Ahead, the giant soldier stands in front of the last cell with a medieval-looking ring of keys, gently rattling the door to check that it's locked. Behind him the soldier with the hard, muscled face holds his rifle poised. An odd ruckus resounds from the cell. At Palden's nod, the giant inserts a key and swings open the barred door to let Book go in.

This cell is a bit wider than the first four, though still far too small for its occupants. Yet it's a scene of celebration, as if Book has stumbled on a wedding in the corridors of a death camp. In fact it's a reunion: the father, his daughter and a very pregnant woman, whom Book hasn't seen before, cling together. The little girl, held high between them, hinges them with her arms in a swaying, shuddering family hug. Beside them, the old nun and the wounded one press their brows to the brow of a plump, rosy young nun—a little Buddha in maroon and saffron robes with a chunky necklace, shaved head and milk-bottle glasses held on with a strap. Despite the chill, her right shoulder is bare in the traditional way.

The nuns and young monks have already moved to opposite sides of the cell. Three of the monks sit in a row on one of the fold-down cots, while the family and the other refugees occupy the cell's cramped floor. Norbu and his friend in the toque seem to eye the row of monks as if staring down a rival gang. The old widow with the skein of grey braids, her face wrinkled and dark as a Navaho elder's, sits on a blanket with a smokeless pipe chomped in her gums. At the back, Lhundup Boshay lies on a second cot. One of the monks kneels beside him. In the cell's corner, a reeking, rim-spattered hole in the floor.

Palden Jangbu steps into the cell after Book and announces something in loud Tibetan, his tone businesslike and brusque. Faces swing toward that voice. Book wonders now if Palden could be a bit slow. The lighting is poor, but how can he be unaware of the hatred seething around him? The widow's grief seems hardened to rage. The monks and the two youths now seem allied in their animosity, like rival gangs turning on a lone cop.

Palden shifts blithely to English: "Oh, Lewis! I just informed the Splittists that you will be staying here in the cell also. Also I said that we will give you all tea and a nice snack, by and by, before so long."

"Palden, I told you—we need water, now! And I need to see the lieutenant."

"Of course, Lewis. Thank you!" He pivots crisply and strides out amid further murmuring. The giant soldier relocks the door and shambles away.

Book nods to the pregnant woman—beautiful wide-set eyes, a space between her front teeth, scores of long braids draping over a mauve cardigan—and then to the plump young nun in her thick glasses.

"Welcome!" she tells him with vigour.

"*Tashi delek*," he says, going to the wounded man's side.

"My name is Choden—Choden Lhamu."

"Lewis Book."

"Do you speak our language, then?" she asks, with an odd, melodious lilt he tries to place. Though the magnifying lenses blur her eyes, their warmth and focus is such that they give an impression of limpid clarity. She looks unnaturally well for someone who has been jailed, he guesses, for several days.

"Just a few words, I'm afraid."

"I can speak some English," she says. "I studied back in Lhasa, with an engineer?"

That accent. He feels his cracked lips stretching into a smile.

"We had to keep the tutorials on the sly. He was a fellow from Waterford? Please see to your patient and we'll chat when the tea comes."

"Patients, actually."

"Of course—her name is Pema Dolkar." Choden nods toward the wounded nun. "The elder one we call Ani Dolma."

"Thanks," he says. "And that would be the Irish Waterford?"

"It would."

He examines the dressing over Lhundup's wound. From among her mother's skirts, the child watches Book work, while her father speaks, gesturing emphatically, apparently telling his wife and Choden Lhamu their story. The joyous tone of just minutes ago has vanished. The wedding has become a wake. The capture, the dumping of the bodies in the crevasse—Book can almost follow the narrative via the lifts and falls and stresses of the man's qua-very tenor. Now even Choden looks troubled. Norbu supplies an incensed outburst and one of the monks seems to counter it, softly, as if trying to calm him down.

Book finds his stethoscope and blood pressure cuff. He sees that there's a blanket under Lhundup's back; somebody, maybe the pregnant woman, has given up her cot.

Somehow the man's blood pressure is holding.

"Choden . . . how long have you been here?"

"About two days." Her brogue is thicker on some words, while on others she sounds more like Palden. Calmly, as if recounting a distant event, she says, "We were all trekking up the valley toward the ice, with the soldiers coming, when Lasya began having her pains. She seemed sure to be having an early birth. It was getting higher and colder, and we were after drop-ping most of our bags and packs, so we might trek faster. She decided that she must walk down and surrender to the guards, and I returned with her, to help her. She wanted Sonam—this is her husband, Sonam Goba?—to go on, to be sure of getting their daughter to the frontier, and perhaps Lasya would be able to join them soon, in the future. We did hope that our surrender would slow the pursuit. So down we go and surrender and a pleasant guard brings us down to the guard post and two soldiers come for us in a truck and drive us here."

"Not to the hospital?"

"Luckily the pains did stop."

"Her water didn't break, then."

Choden's enlarged eyes go blank, but then she nods. "No—her water didn't break then."

"And there's been no, uh, no cramping since?"

"There hasn't."

Book nods toward the seated monks. "Shouldn't she have the cot there? The bed?"

"I agree with you, and the monks would too, I think, but Lasya is from a small town, very traditional. Oh, and the beds are too narrow for her now, she complains."

Lasya and her family are watching. Choden nods—bows, really—toward the old widow with the pipe. "She, Dechen Nima, feels likewise."

Book bows his head to the widow, trying to convey his sympathies.

"By the way," Choden says solemnly, "may I offer you some socks, Lewis?"

Faces turn toward the door: the parade-square tromp of Palden's boots returning. He appears through the bars, jingling the ring of keys, singing the pulsing refrain of "Psycho Killer" under his breath: *fa fa fa faaaaa fa*. The hunched giant follows, bearing a tray with two large tin pots, stacks of nesting cups and a heap of grey, brick-like things.

"Water and oolong tea," Palden calls out as the heavy door grates open, "and the PLA ration bars. Very good!"

"They really are quite tasty," Choden says. "Really sweet."

Norbu's lips are spliced tight and his acne is livid; he's scowling at Choden as if she is some kind of collaborator. Book hears a faint grunt and turns to Lhundup, whose narrow eyes have opened to stare fixedly at Palden. The sclera is not bloodshot but clear as the white of a poached egg. Lhundup whispers something and Norbu looks over and nods fiercely. Besides that, there's a silence more ominous than the muttering before.

"We still need a hospital, Palden. Are we—"

"Yes, Lieutenant Zhao says he will speak to you shortly." Palden won't quite meet Book's eyes. "Just please you rest for the moment."

The clang of the door closing and locking, and he's gone.

"The others don't care for him," Choden says with no sign of personal grievance. "He's Tibetan, you know."

Book nods, his mouth watering.

"I don't know why he would join against his people," she says. "Even if he felt the old Tibet wasn't perfectly fair, the present Dalai Lama is so modern. Alas, Palden isn't the only one. Please, you'll have my tea. I've had several cups during my stay."

"I'll save it for him, thanks."

The family, the old widow, Norbu and his friend are all cross-legged on the floor as if in a nomad's yurt, the women filling the mugs, the child passing them around. Book gets Choden to brace Lhundup's balding head as Book holds a mug so the man can sip tea and swallow antibiotics and codeine. He brings more Clindamycin and codeine to Pema Dolkar, who nods thanks, smiles weakly and swallows the four pills at once, as if she takes pills every day. Through Choden he asks Pema to lie on the cot and rest; later he will check the splint and change the dressing. He returns to Lhundup. He takes his own mug and guzzles the tepid, wonderful tea, wishing only that it were spiked with a finger of Mingma's drastic Nepali gin. He gnaws at something resembling a slab of dirty rock salt. A taste of peanuts and sickly sweet condensed milk. The texture of sandstone. Marvellous.

He closes his eyes as he chews.

Some curious lapse or lurch in time's passage: the quiet in the cell has thickened, the air humidified, and many of the refugees are asleep, the girl lost among Sonam's sheepskin coat and Lasya's skirts, Lasya curled on a blanket facing them, Norbu and his friend lying back to back. Two monks are managing to share a cot, the other two stiffly supine on the floor beneath. The old nun, Dolma, lies beneath the cot on which Pema sleeps, while Choden Lhamu sits against the wall, seeming to meditate behind her glasses—though after a moment her eyes hatch open brilliantly: "Sure, Lew, go ahead and rest a little. I shall watch him for you."

He winces a smile. "Thanks, just a few minutes. Wake me when the officer comes."

He sits back against the cot with his legs crossed under him; there isn't enough room in the centre of the floor to straighten them out. He pulls on his blood-brittle socks. The back of his head is touching Lhundup's thigh. He'll know if anything changes. Sleep seeps into him as if through a saline drip, and through him also a sadness circulates, sadness flecked with dread. Up at base camp it had been going so well—he and Sophie were having fun, on their own and together. Now he has vanished into another crisis. Her warm, noisy girlhood, maybe it has come to seem to her like an elaborate hoax, the upbeat trailer before a sombre film. He did crisis postings then, too, but would return for longer and be relieved when he did. Those loving scrums on the arrivals level at Pearson; on long road trips, the customary songs, the ritual repartee. A family is its own small country and culture and he has been displaced from his, just a marginal participant in its constant, necessary renewal.

He seemed to cope well enough in the aftermath of Bosnia, where he'd once counted spinal columns—all that remained after a shelling—or Rwanda, where he'd dashed in off the bloody street, not having noticed his latest soaker, and left crimson shoeprints in the clinic corridors. But each posting marked him until a part of him was indelibly soiled, a ghost that leaves bloody shoeprints everywhere it goes. Meanwhile his own world felt less and less like a refuge: an alien culture of complacency, ingratitude, the petulant expectation of ever-increasing comfort and plenty. It grew harder to spend time with oblivious friends, except at loud, frenetic social events, infused with booze. And then Nika, of all people—she too slipped gradually out of reach. Now it's only over here among the doctorless that he still feels he matters, belongs. He returns "home" now only for the children, and there too there's a distance, though you expect that eventually, even with your own kids, who belong less to this wounded adult world, you hope, than to the world to come.

Well, let it come.

Before she sinks below the level of dreams, into that hard, paralytic state akin to coma, Sophie dreams she is sitting on her feet by the river, conversing with a small eddy by her knees, where a greenish froth like frogspawn revolves on the surface with the trapped, eternal current. It's the dead border guard and they are speaking in a tongue that's neither English nor Mandarin nor anything else she can name. There's no face or human feature on the eddy, it's just a part of the river, yet it has a voice, cool and fluent—a soft, hypnotic monotone—and Sophie is moved by the words, which she understands somehow. She and the dead guard are speaking the language of all waters. He is sad but resigned to this latest karmic mutation, he doesn't blame her at all, and she promises to return to the shore and talk to him again after nightfall.

For some minutes Amaris has been awake and staring through the bars of her cell at the green-painted steel door at the head of the hallway. Faint coughing, shuffling from behind it. It's like a bulkhead door in *The Battleship Potemkin*, but with a lateral slit in the steel at eye height, and that's where she keeps her gaze, unable to tell if anyone is staring back. She sits cross-legged on the fold-down cot, still in her parka and with the cell's one blanket shawled around her. The blanket, pocked with cigarette burns that look like bullet holes, smells faintly of urine, tobacco, jasmine. A heavy stench wells from the hole in the floor with chilly drafts. She has sloshed a full bucket of rusty water down the hole, to no effect. Still, she's breathing in as deeply as she can, exhaling slowly, fixing her eyes on the door.

It cracks inward. She draws herself up, lets the blanket fall, folds her jumpy hands in her lap. *You're on.*

Zhao emerges in an officer's peak hat, a green tunic with small epaulets, a black belt and holster. Behind him the door eases shut with a hydraulic sigh. He flicks down his cigarette and pivots his toe on it slowly, neatly—all his motions have a weary grace—then walks past the side corridor leading outdoors and stops in front of her cell.

"You are not asleep, Miss McRae." Under the horn-rimmed glasses his eyes are puffy and his doughy, morose face looks water-logged, too large for his rounded shoulders. "Is this private cell not comfortable?"

"You can't expect me to be sleeping peacefully."

"How you sleep is not vital. Only that you sleep enough so that we may talk."

She says, "Have you ever slept behind bars?"

His gaze holds steady, but his right hand slips behind his back.

"I've just learned something about it," she says. "Even when you're asleep, you never forget where you are—that you're trapped. It colours everything, even your dreams. If you want to talk to me, if you want to hear what I have to say, you'll have to let me out of here."

"I have been waiting to talk to you."

"*I've* been waiting for you to wake up, so I can use the telephone. Or the Internet." Calm is impossible now, but men can be fooled; she taps her triathlon watch, keeping a fix on his eyes, her heart gunning. "I mean, it's twelve thirty. I expect you've had some calls about us by now."

"We have been having some minor . . . disabilities with our satellite connection. I have no idea why. And it is three p.m., not twelve thirty. I see that the sergeant did not take your watch."

"Three p.m.?"

"The Tibet Autonomous Region is on Beijing time. So is all of China for this matter."

"What about your land line? I saw telephone poles out there."

"Before the telephone, we must speak with each *other*." He talks softly, almost intimately, his mouth close to the bars as if to avoid disturbing the others down the hallway. How she would love to scream now, to see him flinch and retreat, his grim face fragmenting. "First, though, I shall speak with the doctor. But tell me, Miss McRae—what do you know about his daughter, Sophana, or Sophie?"

"Sophie! So you have had calls. When did she call?"

"I am posing the questions. Please soften your voice."

"It wasn't a question. I'm saying . . . I'm trying to tell you that the outside world is on to you now, so you should realize it's time to—"

"These threats, Amaris McRae, they are a waste of our time!" He can handle the paired r's in "Amaris McRae" with no Charlie Chan fumbling, but he says the names with a slight sneer and he's straining to keep his voice down. "You may answer my questions here, or you may answer in Lhasa. Or perhaps both. I think, both. We must conduct a proper investigation. I've not yet had time to study most of the tape in your camera."

"You're being careful, I hope—you know how to use it?"

His thick brows converge above his glasses. "I am not some kind of . . . barbarian."

She holds herself in.

"I've not always lived in this wilderness," he says. "And as you're indifferent to a private cell, I shall ask the sergeant to place you in the main one, where the doctor chose to go. You will find it crowded."

"Look, I *offered* to join him in there, to help him!" If there's anything to ignite Amaris, it's a moral critique, direct or implied. "He insisted I'd be in the way in there."

"You were not more tempted to show solidarity for the Splittists, like him?"

"I'm not even sure I know what a Splittist is."

"A rebel. A dissident."

"I prefer rogues to rebels."

"Pardon?"

"I find rude minds more interesting than high minds. They're less phony—less judgemental. Have a look at one of my shorts, online, and you'll"—for a moment Zhao recoils, blushing heavily, and she almost laughs—"one of my *films*, online, and you'll see what I mean. Have a look at the tape in that camera!"

"Amaris!" she hears Book call warningly. Zhao's head snaps toward the voice. Somehow he wrings more of a scowl out of his face. He turns and walks back toward the steel door, a hand fisted at the base of his spine. His soft torso sways with anger; his boots on the concrete step primly, soundless as slippers.

The steel door closes behind him.

"Amaris . . . are you all right?"

"Fine."

"You have to stop baiting the man!"

She opens her mouth to yell back, fresh fury rearing—Book, after all, is the reason she's stuck in this open toilet of a cell—but she doesn't. (At the back of her mind, something nibbles away:

they might have seized her for filming the attack even if Book hadn't crossed the border.) She draws a breath, holds it deep. Her adoptive parents were professional activists, or so she came to think of them, who would issue constant little corrections and ethical lessons and parables, as well as "invitations" to demonstrations and marches. Their oceanview house bristled with joss stick bouquets fuming in casually syncretic shrines—Buddhist, Hindu, Wiccan, whatever—and posters of Che Guevara and Nelson Mandela and, yes, the Dalai Lama. Her older stepsister's room, populated with portly little buddhas, exuded fogs of sandalwood and patchouli. She papered the walls of her own seedy bedroom with anti-idols: Patti Smith toppling off stage, Harvey Keitel in *Mean Streets*, Kurt Cobain wearing kohl, John Singleton filming *Boyz n the Hood*. Phil and Naomi, her first-name parents, tenderly lectured her on the hollow glamour of nihilism, its longterm karmic costs. The break came when she was home for reading week in '92 and refused to sign a petition against the latest bombing of Iraq, not because she was *for* the bombing but because she had developed an anaphylaxis to worthy causes and knew it would hurt them.

But think of them now! At home in North Vancouver, one eye on Newsworld or CNN, scouring the web, blogging, granting telephone and TV interviews like the old pros they are, they will be less alarmed than beaming, teary with pride at her involvement—and alongside a doctor without borders, the kind of engaged helper they would have loved for *her* to become! *Mar has definitely experimented a lot over the years, but we've always known she was willing to step up when it really counted. We are so proud of her!* Their fists shooting up in a suburban power salute. *Free Tibet!*

She has to smile at the irony: the publicity will do wonders for her films, which are utterly apolitical—except in the way they sometimes point out hypocrisies in the politically involved.

She calls out to Book, "So did you hear all that?"

"A bit. I woke a few minutes ago." He sounds bothered by this admission, tired. He speaks softly, though a number of the Tibetans are clearly awake now, talking among themselves.

"I think Sophie must have called here," she says.

"I thought I heard you say her name . . . you really think she called?"

"I think she must have." And she adds, "She must be worried sick about you."

No response. Of course, what could he possibly say back? He probably thinks she's baiting *him* now, though in fact she's thinking of how she would feel if her own dad were in trouble like this.

Her parents are ridiculous, but she loves them.

"How's the wounded man, Lew? The nun?"

"Holding their own, somehow." Pause. "I have to get back to them right now—please be careful, okay?"

Still sitting on the cot, she sips cold dregs from the mug of tea dispensed a few hours ago with this rock-hard parody of an energy bar. When she shifts position, air wafting from under the collar of her parka brings a vinegary smell, the acrid sweat of stress. When this is over, she thinks, and it will be over soon, Amaris, what will you do, girl, when this is over? A steaming, leisurely, scented bath, bergamot or rose, followed by a slow, languorous shaving of the calves, though she barely ever needs to, the creamy glide and faint burn of the razor, the silken salve of the almond oil after. Then dressing up. Mexican turquoise earrings and impractical shoes—slingbacks in the same semi-precious hue. A teal clutch. Her favourite summer dress (officially it's fall now, but in Toronto it's still summer: big cities generate their own dome of weather)—a wispy A-line with a halter neck, espresso-brown on her golden shoulders. Going out with a friend (she has many, none really close) or on a date with a man with an intriguingly louche grin, stubble with a touch of grey, imperfect teeth, maybe to Rodney's for oysters with squeezed lime and wasabi and thick-crusted Italian bread, fresh greens. She can taste the greens, the rocket and radicchio, the acid tang of the dressing, lemon juice, burnt sesame oil! With ice-cold beer. Or a classic martini, gin, desert dry, two olives.

Sex with somebody new. No encasing commitment; no derailing pain.

A metallic clatter and she opens her eyes: the woozy wardroom green of everything. That bulkhead door swings in and Palden snaps into the hallway as if striding up the runway of a fashion show. His cheeks and eyes shine. He sports a dark green beret, navy sweater, camouflage pants tucked into polished boots. He has strapped on a new weapon, a tiny snub-nosed machinegun that looks like it should squirt water. His giant sidekick follows with a ring of keys. "Hello, Amaris!" Palden hails her as he passes. "I see that you are meditating like a nun!"

Palden's hold on Book's arm is friendly. His other hand clasps the grip of the little machinegun, its muzzle next to Book's spleen. "I am happy for this chance to practise my English," he repeats, leading Book through the steel door at the head of the hallway and up a narrow corridor lit by a bare bulb. Book, after years of postings, is bored of asking people where they learned their English—there are always more interesting things to ask—but now he takes his jailer's cue. Delighted, Palden answers, "Oh, after high school I was a bellhop in the Lhasa Howard Johnson, then tourist guide in the Potala Feudal Palace, for groups of

American and British tourists. But always I longed to enrol in the People's Army, to be part of such an important thing—and here I am!"

To think this affable fanatic may have killed one or more of his own people yesterday.

They enter a large, stuffy room with a window giving onto the fenced yard. It's a small window and the high desert's focused light burns in as if through a magnifying lens. Beneath the window, a barrel stove with a kettle on top, socks slung on a line above. There are cots along the wall and on one of them a man in a white T-shirt and camouflage pants sleeps, turned away, his brushcut skull knobbed and ridged. Above him, a large map of Tibet barbed with stick pins like a voodoo effigy. Another soldier slumps in a chair, his thumbs prodding at a small object that cheeps in his hands. It looks like a Tamagotchi. A third soldier sits at a desk by a door on the far side of the room. He looks too small and junior for his cigarette—it's the boy who blew a kiss to Sophie when the Chinese were up on the glacier, rectifying their border. The huge telephone in front of him blurts and the boy smiles shyly at Book and nods and picks it up.

Palden leads Book past the boy, opens a door and extends his hand as he must have done a thousand times while showing hotel guests into their suites. "Through here, please," he says, adding in a stage whisper, "Hope it goes well, Lewis! Please be helpful, please. Be seeing you . . ."

The cubicle is smoky, windowless, lit by a pair of buzzing fluorescent tubes. Zhao sits very straight behind an old hulk of a tin desk, stubbing out a cigarette. His thick black hair is side-parted and combed. He looks older without his glasses, the pouchy little eyes red and raw.

"Sit down, doctor."

Book has readied himself to be firm but civil. He knows his own temper in the face of injustice; he knows antagonizing Zhao could deepen this emergency, for everyone.

"Thanks, I'm fine. We need to be fast here."

"Sit down and it will go faster."

Book sits on a plastic folding chair that wobbles under him. It has been placed by the door—which is slightly open—some distance from Zhao. On Zhao's desk are his glasses, a thick laptop computer, a black hardbound sketch- or ledger-book, and a push-button telephone, one message-light pulsing.

"I won't waste our time, doctor. I know you will want to return to your patients. Would you care to take a cigarette?" He half stands and leans and holds out the packet. Empty. Book senses that this tease is not deliberate. The overhead light deepens the morbid sacs under the man's eyes.

"What I need is a washroom," Book says. "To wash my hands, for one thing. And we need to get those patients to a hospital."

Zhao sags back into his chair. "You may use my own WC when we are finished. This interview need not occupy more than a few minutes. Please simply tell me the truth of what you were engaged at, up on the border."

"I work with InterMed—it's a crisis response outfit based in Canada—but right now I'm a doctor for a climbing expedition—base camp staff. And I brought along my daughter. You've been in touch with my daughter—with base camp?"

"We'll speak of this shortly. First, though, your colleague, Miss McRae, she has urged me to investigate her work via the Internet." He nods toward the open laptop screen. "This has taken somewhat longer because of satellite problems—but now, what do I discover? That the subject of her very last documentary is a strong sympathizer with the Dalai Lama!"

"But, lieutenant, that's not a rare . . . Were those sympathies the point of the film?"

"I have not yet succeeded in downloading it."

"I've never heard her mention the Dalai Lama. She doesn't make political films—I'm sure of it—she told me that. She's making one about a climber now."

"Yes, Wade John Lawson. Who has worked with Sherpas on several expeditions on our frontier. Who are ethnic Tibetans and who support the Splittist cause!"

Book, breathing, eyes the man. "I need to go back, lieutenant. I have a patient in critical condition. Please just tell me—"

"We shall finish here first."

"—have you talked to her? My daughter?"

"In a *moment*, doctor. If you will only help me, I will see that you and the needy ones are taken to Drongpa in a moment, soon!"

"It might be too late—we need blood, we need drugs."

"Of course, the longer you delay . . ."

"So ride with me to the hospital."

"It's impossible, doctor."

"I'll talk to you at the hospital!"

"I need your help *now*. And you will give it!"

"Then there's that woman—she could go into labour any time—is this how you always treat prisoners?"

Zhao's fist hammers the desk and he drills home his words like rivets in a wall: "Of *course* I cannot leave my post now! We must talk *here*! I need this information *now*!"

He stops himself. Glances at the throbbing red light on his phone. His fist loosens—stumpy, orange-stained digits now tapping the desk. The hand drops out of sight. He resumes in a more composed tone: "Doctor . . . how can I help suspecting your own feelings about the Dalai Lama and the Splittist cause? Consider that when I insert your name into the, into the search engine, I discover that you were once posted in China, and perhaps understand more Mandarin than you pretend. Then I find that you are based most recently in *Darjeeling*, one of the chief centres of Tibetan exile activity! And then, there you are, present at the foot of a mountain where no expedition ever climbs, waiting for these Splittists to cross the border! You see why I deduce you to be a sympathizer?"

Behind Zhao, a bookcase stuffed with Chinese volumes and a few dozen English paperbacks, literate thrillers, names like Le Carré and Ambler and Forsyth.

"I sympathize with these ones," Book says.

"But with the Splittist cause . . ."

"InterMed is a non-partisan NGO, lieutenant. We don't care who our—"

"With the Dalai Lama!"

"Look, I just happened to be on the border when you started killing Tibetans! My daughter—"

"You say you're not on their side, then?"

"Whoever's bleeding—that's whose side I'm on."

Beyond the door, a kettle's whistle rises.

"Doctor, I warn you, I have further proofs, all of them indicating deliberate intervention. Just as your people have always sought to do in our affairs—interfere!—force upon us opium, or treaties, or religion, or governments, as though we lack the right or the ability to arrange for ourselves!"

Book looks down at his bloodied socks on the floor. A man without shoes is at a disadvantage. In fact, he agrees with Zhao's last point; he nods slowly, strains to his feet. "Lieutenant—my patients."

"Sit down. You are hurting them by not confessing to me."

"If I had no family, I'd lie and tell you whatever you want, to get those people out of here. But my daughter is waiting at base camp."

"Ah. I've read also about your son, Pavlos."

"Read about him?" Book sinks back onto the chair, more in exhaustion than compliance. "What, on the Internet?"

"In a moment."

Book's eyes veer to that black-bound book. The kettle's steady falsetto screaming.

"What *is* that on your desk?"

"I learned to speak your language while I was in prison, doctor. I had several years to dedicate to study. I was there as one of a group of junior officers purged"—his two-syllable phrasing makes it sound like *perjured*—"after the Tiananmen incident. For being too . . . too patient with the protestors. No, *lenient*, that's the word."

"Lenient."

"At Tiananmen there were many different moments, doctor. Do not suppose your truthful news channels furnished you with all of them."

"But you weren't lenient yesterday."

"Then why are almost all of the Splittists alive?"

"Would they be alive if we hadn't been there watching?"

"Yes, of course, alive! We are not murderers—we are enacting the laws!"

"Or if Amaris and I weren't here now?"

"This is not the first time that Splittists have tried to defect by your route—as you must know. As you must know, last occasion, not one was harmed!"

"Did they promote you for that, or punish you?"

Pondering Book with swollen eyes, Zhao looks almost bereaved. The kettle's piercing scream finally dies.

"After the prison sentence, I was inducted again into the PLA. In due course I became a sergeant, then a lieutenant, and for five years I am posted here. For us, Tibet is a, what is the term, a hardship posting. Very much. Such postings are an experience you know of, I understand . . ."

Both phone lights are flashing now in a syncopated pattern.

"I too have a family, Dr. Book. A wife and one son, twenty-two years old. They reside in Beijing. I see them once a year. I was once a tai chi instructor for our troops, in Beijing, but here . . . here, my few men would rather play the electronic games, and MP3. Yet I believe I may finally be transferred from Tibet, because of this work I have just done, especially if I can, if I may say, finish the job. The evidence plainly proves that you and Miss McRae are guilty of interfering and abetting the Splittists, but a confession is final proof. Without it, without such proof, my position here could become . . . awkward. In exchange, I would ensure that your daughter is kept perfectly safe."

"My daughter? What are you . . ."

Zhao lifts the black book with both hands.

"Half an hour ago Corporal Hua returned from the guard post with this. It seems to be your daughter's diary. I have read only a few pages, but already I have found out so much."

Through the roar of hot blood in his ears Book hears the spine crack as Zhao opens the journal and turns it face out. The words, seen from where Book leans on the lip of his chair, are blurred, but the page's pattern—blocks of tight cursive alternating with sketches and cartoons—is like a voiceprint. He makes out the sketch of the Chinese adjusting their border, simple line figures around a bright red flag—she showed him that one just days ago.

Book extends a hand. It's visibly trembling. Zhao closes the journal.

"No, doctor."

"Where is she."

"Held at the guard post. We assume she infiltrated across the border soon after you were arrested. I am willing to have her brought here at once, if you will make a full confession. Her position there . . . she is not being harmed, of course, but her position there is somewhat awkward, as one of the guards was killed when they attempted to capture her, and his fellows are unhappy. I think it would be better to have her here."

"Killed?" Book says numbly. "No. What do you mean?"

"An accident. His name was Li Bo. He was nineteen years old." A silence, then Zhao puts on his horn-rims, flips pages and turns the journal back toward Book. "Now—in this diary, beside one of the most recent entries, I find this, what is the term, this small label which you will recognize . . ."

FREE TIBET, a glossy decal, the Dalai Lama's grinning face superimposed like a sun on the Tibetan flag. Above it, in pencil, Sophie has cross-hatched a mountain range.

"Will you not respond at all, doctor?"

"The Sherpas," he gets out, "they gave her that. She's just a kid and she was hanging out with them. She takes on all sorts of causes, but she's not . . . Give that back, it's not yours to read!" Unconsciously he is rising and hears something and glances over his shoulder. The Tamagotchi player stands with a submachinegun in the widened opening of the door.

"In the accompanying entry, she writes—although I cannot make out some words—that she likes to sit on the Chinese side of the border at the sunsets, but that *she knows it's not really China, it is Tibet.*"

No, he thinks. Something's off here. He shakes his head—more a shudder. It's as hard to think clearly when you're shocked and tired and scared as when you're breathless at 21,000 feet, the highest point he and Sophie hiked to from base camp.

"And an entry from, ah, three days ago mentions that she has been in some trouble with authorities in Toronto. And that she has strong sympathies for 'the persecuted.' And where, I ask myself, where must she learn such ideas? My son is very much like myself."

"It's not always like that in Canada."

. . . attempted to capture her . . .

"No!" says Book, the cogs finally clinching. "Wait—you'd have brought her here if you had her, not made a driver go all the way up to the guard post and back for her journal."

Zhao's eyes dart down and to the side.

"You'd have wanted to question her yourself, now!"

Zhao shakes the empty cigarette pack, tosses it back on the desk. The man is more than depleted. He too is addled, frightened.

"Doctor—"

"Why isn't she here, though? Has something happened? How was the soldier—"

"Enough, doctor!" he cries, raising his hand. "Yes. No, perhaps we have not captured her, not yet, but we will have her, very soon. The border security guards are tracking her down the River Khiong at this moment. She dropped the diary near to the guard post."

"I can help," Book says—"help you find her. Let me join the search. I know her, I know the sort of places she'd hide in. I can get her to give herself up without . . . creating more trouble for you. Please! You don't want a child hurt on your watch."

A Western child, he means. Book is playing the white card and is too helpless for shame. In *bagh chal*, the goats beat the tigers any way they can.

"But doctor—you have the wounded here, and we shall catch her very soon."

"If I help you, will you go join those guards and see she isn't hurt?"

"Help me, doctor?"

"Give you what you want. Your confession."

"Well . . . perhaps. Perhaps I could. Yes. I or Sergeant Jangbu."

"You. Right now."

"And you would make a full admission, on video?"

"On *video*?"

Zhao's lips curve in a small, chilling smile. "I do own a digital camera, doctor, but I feel that using Miss McRae's superior device would be a, a poetic justice."

Silence. Book finally says, "Palden would have to take me and the wounded ones and the pregnant woman to the hospital immediately."

"Very well, then. When we are done. You were all to be moved this evening anyway, tomorrow at the latest." Zhao lifts one eyebrow slightly, drolly. "This is not some Guantanamo, doctor."

"And the second I've handed over their care, Palden will drive me to wherever Sophie is, and we're not to be separated afterward, not till the embassy deals with this."

"I will do my utmost."

"You realize when I 'confess,' I'll state clearly that my daughter and Ms. McRae are completely innocent?"

Zhao's right hand darts down and behind his chair back, as if he's crossing fingers against his promises. "I must give this point more reflection."

"Not if you want your video."

For moments neither man blinks, then Zhao looks up at something behind Book—probably the soldier in the doorway. Finally, audibly, Zhao deflates. "Very well, doctor. But the world will draw its own deductions about such 'innocence'—as it will do if you try to withdraw your confession when you are eventually released to your country, whenever that should be."

Book nods. "Then I'll do it as soon as we've got them to hospital and you've taken me to her."

"What?" Zhao's heavy eyebrows rise. The scrape of a drawer and he lifts Amaris's camera into view. "Doctor, you mistake yourself. You will have to make this confession now, at once!"

"Now? No, after."

"Or nothing happens."

Book is silent. He can feel the seconds, minutes, melting away. "You lied to me a minute ago," he says. "How can I . . ."

"I had not yet given my word. I now give my word."

Sophana's feet leaving tracks on the earth, her light, coltish stride beginning to slow as she peers back over her shoulder. He meets her brown eyes and she seems to call out to him but there is no sound. *Papa.*

Book bows his head. "Turn it on, then. You'll have your fake confession."

"Nevertheless, doctor, I know you are guilty."

"Maybe," he says under his breath, "but not in the way you think."

On the walk back to the cell with Palden and the Chinese giant, Book's silence makes Palden even chattier. They pass Amaris's cell. She sits up, trying to read Book's face with her intensely homing eyes. He gives her a tight, coping smile. She won't be fooled. He's shattered, sick at heart. They pass on down the hallway and the giant unlocks the door of the main cell. "Ah!" Palden says, "I now remember—I made a Canadian friend when I worked at the Howard Johnson!"

"I'll check Lhundup first."

"Oh, sure."

"Then we bring him out to the truck."

"His name was René," Palden says, "and in Montreal he works as a, a . . ." Distracted, trying to find the word, Palden follows Book a step or two inside the cell. It's a fatal lapse. The assault comes without warning. Norbu and his gang friend spring out of the dim corner beside the door, the whites of their widened eyes identically fierce and clear. Book is between them and Palden so that he's jostled backward, and something, the gun's muzzle, jabs into his spine. He twists clear, regains balance. Old Dechen, who'd seemed asleep on the floor, has lunged with a weird reptilian litheness to lock her arms around Palden's knees while Norbu and his friend tackle him. Palden's last phrase—"*as a clown!*"—ends in a gasp as he falls. The child's father, Sonam— till now a quiet, kind-faced older man—charges out through the cell door at the giant soldier, who drops the key ring and raises both hands, yelling in a deep, shocked voice as Sonam, and now one of the young monks, launch into him. The soldier is tall but he's unarmed, thin, ungainly, and Tibetans, as Book saw in Darjeeling, are very strong. They buckle the giant back into the wall of the corridor, his cap flying off, head thunking. Norbu is up now, gripping Palden's submachinegun and trying to wrench it off his body by the strap. His kneeling friend pins Palden's arms. The strap jerks loose. Norbu has the gun. A second monk joins the attack, shedding his maroon parka to expose his robes, his right shoulder bare. The two other monks stand paralyzed as if in argument with themselves. Lhundup, despite his wound, has raised himself onto his elbow and is urging on the attackers in a hoarse whisper.

"Lew!" Amaris calls, "what the hell's going on down there?"

Choden stands in the doorway above the figures grappling on the floor and chants some phrase with quiet intensity. She might be urging them to stop their attack or to escalate it—but now clearly she's trying to block Norbu, to keep him from going out into the hallway with the gun. She raises her palms. Her magnified eyes plead. Norbu jabbers into her face in a strained, staccato voice, gripping the little gun across his belly.

Book pulls back on the hood of the kid attacking Palden, who is on the floor, covering his face with his hands as his assailants strike down with short, clubbing blows. The monk's bare shoulder flexes. Palden's head bounces on the concrete, his beret gone. Dechen, shrieking oaths in a cracked voice, slaps at Palden's legs and crotch with the tin teapot. Norbu has shoved past Choden and now plants himself outside the cell, his shoes braced wide, his cap brim askew, aiming the little toy of a weapon up the hallway.

"Norbu!" Book yells. "Amaris, down on the floor!"

Book has dragged Norbu's friend up and off Palden, but the kid pivots, his eyes raw and blind, and shoves Book, who reels backward, trying not to fall over Lasya and the child—though now he sees Lasya crouching in the back corner by the hole in the floor, hugging the sobbing child tight to her belly. Norbu's friend turns and dives back onto Palden, who is no longer trying to parry the blows but just covering up, curled fetal. Book has to leave him there. He skids past Choden, out into the hall. He reaches for Norbu, who's fumbling to cock the gun. The steel door at the head of the hall, some thirty steps off, opens and Zhao and the hard-faced man and the Tamagotchi player spill through. "Stop!" Book cries, but too late—the weapon juddering in Norbu's hands shouts him down and the bangs echo, overlap in a shattering crash. Up the hallway the three figures vibrate and blur as if caught in a seismic tremor. A light bulb detonates. Sparks carom and incandesce off the heavy steel door. Shots come back in reply and one sizzles past Book's ear. Norbu has moved away from him, out of reach. The monk crouching by the unconscious giant slams backward. The giant's long torso jolts as a red gash appears in his arm. His eyes spring open and he's staring at Book in the dazed, stricken manner of a child waking in a strange place. "Amaris, stay down!" Book yells, though the gunfire is stopping now, echoes waning, no one left at the head of the hallway to fire back at Norbu.

"Lewis . . . please!" he hears Palden whisper from the cell behind him. He doesn't know where to begin.

Amaris looks up from the cot where she has been curled, her fingers meshed over her skull. Her ears still thunder. Three bodies sprawl on the concrete around the heavy steel door, which has closed itself on its pneumatic hinge. Zhao lies limply on his side, totally still except for his small eyes, which dart and swivel, for a moment meeting hers. The wound in the side of his chest looks like a Remembrance Day poppy. His pistol lies on the concrete a few steps from him and beside it his horn-rims sit, upright, undamaged, as if neatly set there. The handsome, muscular guy is slumped on the floor against the bloodied wall with his legs stretched out, his eyes staring blandly, his white T-shirt buttoned across the chest with a line of holes that look too small and neat to have killed him. A third soldier lies prone, his small machinegun half under his torso, his head not far from Amaris's cell. Around his body the blood pools quickly, in appalling silence, a thin rill of it now flowing across the concrete toward Amaris.

She stares unblinking, unbreathing, half expecting an instant replay, over and over and over, like when the twin towers disintegrated and collapsed. These days, how can you believe what you see, or half see, only once?

"Lew? Are you . . . ?"

She hardly hears her own croaky voice over the roaring in her ears.

"You all right?" Book calls faintly.

She won't lower her feet to the floor because of that probing flow of blood. It will move toward her feet, follow her, wherever she walks, she can feel it must. A nosing lamprey of blood. Now it's inside the cell, swimming through and around the bars, and there it pools for a moment, stops its advance, then continues.

The pimply kid in the baseball cap prowls up the hallway past her cell, training his little machinegun on the fallen Chinese. An image from TV news, low-res black-and-white video, high school shootings. He's trailed by a young monk with wet, gaping eyes, who has the key ring and opens Amaris's cell door and tells her something in a shrivelled voice. She gets to her feet but then sags back down, paraplegic. Norbu is standing over Zhao, with his court shoes set wide. *No*, she thinks. *No more shooting*. "Norbu!" Book's voice comes snapping up the hallway and now he's rushing past her cell, his eyes bright and bulging in anger, or fear, or anger and fear, yes, both. His right arm extended. "Norbu, please!"

No way. None of this.

Norbu's gang brother appears and he's tugging a machinegun, not gently, out from under the bleeding soldier. The man's underside is drenched dark. She winces her eyes shut, stands, opens her eyes. She floats toward her open cell door and over the stream of blood and out into the hallway. Mouths are moving but she can't hear and there's moaning but it's far away. Her eyes are fogged. Maybe it's the dust and smoke. The cellblock could be a dim subway after a bombing, figures shuffling into the hallway with

zombie faces, the old woman and two monks struggling to bear
Lhundup on a blanket, the squat nun helping the wounded one to
hobble. There's a caustic, throat-clawing smell. At the hallway's
dead end, by the cell where Book and the Tibetans were, a chip
of concrete seems to fall in slow motion from a star-shaped hole,
and a monk lies with his arms straight out, another monk kneeling beside him. The giant soldier sits gripping his own arm, rock-
ing fast and moaning.

Now Book stands between Zhao and Norbu, who clearly wants
to finish Zhao off. The other kid, toting a machinegun slung on a
bloody strap, peers through the slit in the steel door and she hears
herself calling, as if he might understand, *Careful . . . there must be
one more in there! . . . maybe more.* Her voice resounds in a hollow
way. A nun she doesn't recognize, bare shoulder, thick glasses, is
there now with Book and Norbu. Her fresh face, as she listens and
moves her lips, looks calmly concerned, a young guidance coun-
sellor summoned to a school office to deal with a small problem.
To Amaris this looks like the end of the world. There's a loud rattling as if someone has just flung stones against the other side of
the steel door. Norbu's friend ducks low, looks over, calls out.

Book is kneeling by Zhao, pulling on his glasses.

"Amaris!" she hears clearly, "my kit and the blanket. In the cell."

She nods vaguely, turns and drifts down the hallway. In the last
cell, where a few dazed refugees mill around, gathering things,
she sees Palden nestled on the floor, whimpering. Nobody else
seems to notice. There is blood. She can't shake off this bloody
dream. She gets the blanket and the black vinyl kit and floats back
up the hallway. Book's reaching hand is steady, yet his head trembles. He's grey, his lips impacted. He grabs the kit, snaps it open.
"He'll live, if I can keep Norbu off him. But we're completely
screwed. I can't believe they did this."

I think we need to leave right now, Lew.

She isn't sure if she says this.

A painful blast of light—Norbu has opened the side door that gives onto the fenced yard through which they entered. In an Irish accent that completes the sense that this is all a trance or dream, the nun is saying, "I'd stay with you, Lewis, to help out, but we'll have hurt ones with us also, and Lasya, too. I'm afraid you'll have to come."

"We have to bring Palden," he says.

"Sure, but Norbu and the rest—I'm afraid they'll hurt Palden. Hurt him worse."

Book nods at Zhao and whispers, "If I can do some work here, he'll make it till help comes. And the giant's going to survive. But Palden, he'll be a dead man for letting this happen. What genius came up with this plan?"

"No plan," the nun says quickly—"there was a—a debate while you spoke with the officer. Norbu and his chum Sangye and one of the monks and old Dechen all wanted to attack, to take Palden's gun. The rest of us argued, but we couldn't stop them. Then even Sonam and another monk helped, when the moment came."

He shakes his head. "Here, take the swab."

"It's like this now in Tibet. Some won't listen to the Dalai Lama's teachings. We fear, the violent ones will have their way."

"The syringe now—the needle."

"They say if His Holiness is in another country, how can He understand?"

Refugees are filing toward the exit: the two nuns, the father with his sobbing daughter in the crook of his arm, a very pregnant woman Amaris doesn't know, then the old woman and the straining monks bearing Lhundup. Norbu shouts from the side door and the nun with the glasses remarks, "He says we ought to hurry, Lewis."

"I *know*." There's something in Book's voice—as if he's aware of some other reason for haste beyond the obvious. His hands work fast, injecting what might be local anaesthetic, filling the pulpy wound with antibiotic gel, unrolling gauze. Zhao is now on his back, seeming dead except for his eyes, which gaze up at Book with unblinking attention, as if he's committing the face to memory. Over Zhao's body, Book spreads the blanket Norbu gave him last night and says, "*Dui bu qi*"—I'm sorry—a bit of simple Mandarin Amaris does know.

"You're apologizing," she says, not questioning, just noting this latest surreal detail.

"For leaving him like this," Book says.

They exit into the desert's incendiary sunlight and flinch and raise their hands blindly as if coming under fire. Somebody sneezes repeatedly. She and Book shoulder Palden's limp arms on either side. His gruesome head lolls and the toes of his boots drag in the gravel. The nun with the glasses walks with them, glancing around, ready to translate, it seems, or to defend their decision to bring Palden. Ahead, the others clump up at the swing gate in the high safety fence topped with a helix of razor wire. Beyond the gate, the two trucks. Beyond the trucks, the earth falling away. This hilltop commands a panorama of the high desert and the Kyatruk massif floating huge and white to the southwest.

Norbu and his friend stand between the refugees and the base—a long cinderblock bungalow crowned with a gleaming white satellite dish. There's a tinkle of breaking glass. From the base's small window, now shattered, comes a terse, tentative spray of shots. Norbu and the other man fire back wildly, pockmarks appearing in the concrete around the window, where a shadow ducks out of sight. Norbu yells over his shoulder and his voice cracks like a pubescent boy's. In the small, panicked crowd pushing up against the gate, a monk is fumbling, the big key ring in his hand. Norbu's friend dekes in among the standing and lying Tibetans. Amaris expects him to blast the padlock with his machinegun but instead he takes a pistol—it must be Zhao's—out of his baggy jeans and holds it sideways, gangsta style, and fires until it clicks empty. He drops it and pushes the gate and it swings out on its wheel. The three monks lift Lhundup. Amaris and Book and Palden follow the nun and the others through the open gate, Palden's head drooping toward Amaris's shoulder, her face. A smell of salt blood drying on his scalp. He's mumbling, "Leave me, please . . . leave Palden, please . . . ."

"You'll be okay," she says, as if she could know, as if, out here, her assurances mean anything.

Book has his free hand up, shielding his eyes, scanning the desert falling away to the west. The first truck's tailgate claps down. Two monks scramble up, turning and extending hands to help load the others aboard. A spatter of gunshots and everyone ducks and freezes, then continues with the boarding, faster. The nun with the glasses, nodding toward Palden, addresses the other Tibetans. Norbu is backing toward them, hunched down, still aiming his puny, deadly gun at the base, but now he scowls a glance over his shoulder at Palden, Book, Amaris, and yells words at the nun with the glasses. She answers briefly, calmly. More head-splitting gunfire—the other gang kid shooting out the tires of the second truck—and Amaris is ducked low, trembling, almost dropping Palden, whose body is now moving strangely, jerking downward as if something has leapt on his back.

"In his pockets," she hears Book, "it must be!"

A monk straightens up—he has been digging in Palden's pockets—and says something to the nun with the glasses. "Nothing there," she translates—"no key."

"Palden—wake up! Where's the ignition key?"

Palden shakes his bloody head. "Inside the base, I think, please."

"Let's get him on the truck."

"But, Lewis," the nun says, "if there isn't a key . . ."

"Help me talk to Norbu. Can he drive? Amaris, can you?"

"I can try. I haven't driven stick in years."

"You'll only have to steer, and brake. It's downhill from here. Toward the river—the Khiong." He points in the direction of the late-afternoon sun. "From there we can try to hike back up to the glacier."

"I'm not sure about Norbu," the nun says, "but I'm quite a good driver myself."

5:40 p.m., 6,800 metres. Lawson follows Tashi, Jake and Shiva up the thirty-five-degree slope between Camp One and Camp Two. The men, roped together a few body lengths apart, carry heavy packs—rope, food, fuel, oxygen canisters—on what should be the last supply run up this stretch. Lawson carries the lion's share. If all goes well, they'll get these loads up to Camp Three tomorrow, and then he and Tashi will finish preparing the fixed ropes on the Lawson Wall. By the day after, if this weather holds, they'll push for the summit.

This stretch is essentially a gruelling stair climb, at least for the others. Lawson doesn't find it all that tough. A crampon slog on hard-packed snow. He's in caboose position so he'll have time to dig in and help anchor the team with his ice axe if somebody slips—and because if he were out front, he knows, he would want to forge ahead too hard, thoughts of capturing this peak making him forget there are climbers behind him who want to stop every thirty steps or so and lean over their ice axes and pant. Tashi, a chain-smoker, is the most unathletic Sherpa that Lawson has ever seen, and his daydreamy pace is perfect for Jake, as well as for little Shiva, who shouldn't be up here anyway.

Jennifer used to tell Lawson that on their forest hikes with Reinhold, their malamute, he, Lawson, would forget her presence and stop conversing, start to "brood," accelerate till he was ten strides ahead of her or farther if she didn't labour to keep pace. Until she called him back, called him out of himself. He wasn't aware of doing it until she started to complain. *I wish you lived in the world sometimes, Way.* And she had a point. In a sense, he *doesn't* live in the world—the truest part of him resides up here, in the high troposphere, lives for these tense, striving hours and this particular integrity of light.

Maybe the real reason the marriage died was that he could never persuade her to climb with him.

These frequent stops give him leisure to skim the vast, expanding views of desert rolling to the northeast, views he would normally be savouring. From up here you can see as far as a large lake, some eighty kilometres off, near Drongpa, a city he has seen on the map and that now manifests as a darkening, like a cancer on the landscape, under a sickly yellow dome of smog. He has no idea where Amaris and the doctor and now Sophie might be. Kaljang hasn't radioed for three hours, Lawson having asked him not to patch through any calls until they reach camp—unless Sophie and the others should reappear.

At the edge of Camp Two, a few hundred steps above, the bright blue tent that he shared just last night with Amaris can be seen. Some hours higher is Camp Three, a snow cave hidden in

Kyatruk's steepening flank. Above it loom the ice cliffs of the Lawson Wall. Then the peak, at 25,998 feet—a figure that seems to thumb its nose at Lawson. He prefers to round up. Or give the elevation in metres. He feels suddenly *tired*, leaning on his ice axe like some codger with a cane—last night's many sleepless hours. Picture a pack of coyotes harrying a bull moose, darting in as the bull slows, nipping, needling away with those high, yapping calls.

He won't be going back down, as Kal asked him to. Going down wouldn't bring the girl back. He doesn't believe in hollow gestures. None of this is his fault. The girl has gone and done the same idiotic thing as her old man, and on Book's shoulders be it. He should have known what she might do. If he was a good father wouldn't he know her that well? He shouldn't have risked bringing her up here. He knew the dangers. Etcetera, etcetera . . . Yet something in Lawson still sits wrong. Lawson, who hates looking inward, who can gaze down between his knees while soloing a wall at 20,000 feet and feel merely thrilled, yet can't take a hard look into himself without suffering vertigo, even nausea.

But now he does look deeper. Like scanning a ragged, foreign landscape with dusty binoculars. There. It's his lost son, briefly embraced, and what Lawson was able to feel for that flayed-looking creature without even having known him—so that now he can't help pondering what it must be like to love a child you've known and loved for years.

Kaljang's voice comes crackling from the radio. Shiva glances back down expectantly at Lawson. If Lawson answers the call, the rest stop will last longer. As the other two also look back—Jake in his big moustache and aviator shades, Tashi in those ludicrous goggles—Lawson lifts a hand and nods, *Hang on*.

"Lawson here. Is it Sophie and the others? Over."

"Pardon? Oh . . . no Sophie yet . . . " (Lawson hears the words as *Soviet* and for some moments stands gaping at the snow, scintillas of evening gold now showing among the glittering blues and whites. Then it clicks.) "Sorry not to wait until you're up at the camp," Kaljang says, "but it seems too important. You see, strange news has come about Sophie. Now I have Sophie's mother again on the phone, and on the other phone it's from your embassy in Beijing. Which one do you want to take first? Over."

Lawson lets out air. "Give me the guy in the embassy."

"Uh, it's a woman, Wade Lawson. . . . Go ahead."

The voice comes through, more or less. At these removes, communication is a bit like playing broken telephone in a swarming schoolyard.

"*Allo?* Is it Wade Lawson here?" French-Canadian accent, a nasal voice scraped raw as if with overuse, though that might be the reception.

"Lawson, yeah. I can't hear you very well."

"Lysiane Girard at the Canadian embassy in Beijing. *Allo?* You *can* hear me very well? I am assistant to the *chargé d'affaires* here, and, ah . . ." Static mangles the rest.

"*Can't* hear you. Look, we have to keep this short, I'm on an exposed slope above 22,000 ft and we're running out of sunlight. Can you tell me what's up with, uh, with Ms. McRae, Dr. Book and the girl?"

"Well, yes—no. It isn't clear. I was hoping to ask *you* some questions about exactly what it was that—what passed when the, the—"

"The thing is, I don't *know*. Oh, you mean at the *border?*"

"—encountered the Chinese party, at the frontier. Pardon? Did you say . . . ?"

"I'll tell you when we get up to camp—the full story. Or Kal,

Kaljang, he can fill you in right now. But just tell me what's happening with my team members, okay? They all right?"

"Pardon? Are they . . . ? Oh, all right. We're receiving different messages. The Chinese say they're trying to"—long moments of snarling static—"and *running*. A guard was hurt or even killed pursuing her, this morning. They may have captured her already, but ah—ah—sorry, I was speaking Mandarin for an hour just now—"

"Pursuing *Sophie*?"

"Ms. Book, yes. It's not clear. You know we've been attempting to reach you for some hours?"

"What isn't clear? Killed how?" His heart is going like a trip-hammer. A moment ago he was still wondering if Amaris might somehow make it back up here for the climb; now he's alarmed on Sophie's behalf—and on his own, yes, should the girl get hurt—and even concerned about Amaris, who until this moment has struck him as too tough and smart to get into real trouble.

"Conflicting reports," the voice says crisply, the line suddenly so clear it's as if the woman is standing beside him. "One official, he thinks she is now in custody, another, that she's still in flight. They are being very civil, but not clear with us, you know. Maybe they don't want to be clear, it's possible, but I think maybe they're not sure themselves."

"What about Mari—Ms. McRae?" The climbers stare down at him, Tashi digging in his parka pocket for the cigarettes he carries loose there. "And the doctor."

"Excuse me? You're very unclear. You mention a copter . . . helicopter? Ah, wait, you wanted to say—"

"McRae. And Book."

"—I said, yes, something is going on at the base. We aren't sure what."

146 ~ STEVEN HEIGHTON

"What base?"

"Where they were taken today, about, ah"—another harsh squall of static—"the frontier. We've been working————— speak to them."

"You've spoken to them? Oh, you mean you've been——"

"Our contacts at the Chinese government aren't sure, but we've had a report that some or all of the prisoners escaped. We've tried to——but——"

"Escaped," he repeats quietly. "Fuck me."

"Pardon?"

"Hello?"

"It's all right, Mr. Lawson, you're clear again. We've been— —————tact the base directly, but we're not————"

"*Attacked* the base? Who?"

"Pardon? Ah, no—*contact*. And are . . . are you there? We . . ." The remote voice repeats a word that's probably *hello*, but the second vowel keeps getting cropped off so it sounds like *help*, or *hell*. He glances up at the three faces studying him, then down the slope toward Camp One and his miniature, toy-tent base camp, a vertical mile below. Those lower zones are flooded with dusk. Soon he and his team will also lose the sun, and when its pursuing shadow, bleeding upslope, sweeps over them like the sea over Pharaoh's legions in *The Ten Commandments*, the temperature will drop fast. Tashi now drags on a cigarette as if it's the tube of an oxygen bottle, Shiva sways under the weight of his pack. This delay could get dangerous, with his team so bushed. He shouldn't have answered his handset. Communicate with the world down there and things just get worse. Amaris and Book will not be returning in time—that's clear now. It's just him and the mountain. Him and his remaining team and Murloe, wherever he is, and the mountain.

Lawson's legions.

"Lisette?" he all but bellows. "I'm going to have to go. We'll talk again, I'm sure. Can you hear me? Yes? Just keep me posted. Sorry about this mess you're dealing with." *If you only knew how sorry.* "What's that? Yeah, of course. Okay. Okay. . . . Kal? Kaljang? Do you copy? Look, I can't talk to Sophie's mom now. No. We'll be at Camp Two in twenty minutes and I'll try to respond then. Once we're set up and secure. Okay? Over."

Kaljang says, "But I'm worried about Sophie, even more so."

"Me too, Kal. Not much we can do, though. The embassy is on it now."

No answer. The pulmonary crackle of static.

"And Kal?" Lawson turns his back on the team, shielding his mouth with his gloved hand. "You said you wanted to climb higher, right? And Shiv really shouldn't go above Camp Two. Camp One, even. So I'm going to send him down tomorrow morning. You can come up to Camp Two and take his load from there. You can come right to the top, if you want. If you feel strong. We really have to get some people to the top now. For the others' sake. Hello?"

"But Shiva," says Kaljang—"he can't handle the phones so well."

Exactly. "He'll be all right, Kal. We'll give him instructions. Kal, you read me?"

Silence, though not a very long one, considering what the decision must mean to the kid.

"I'm sorry, Wade Lawson, but I can't do this. I want to do this, but no."

"Kal—"

"I think, for Sophie's safety, maybe for the others too, I should be here."

"But, Kal . . . it's not like you're a paramedic or something."

"No, on the sat phones, I mean. It may be important."

A familiar rage radiates through Lawson, but it eases before his body can fully respond and circulate further adrenaline—the last thing he needs right now. He draws a long breath, puffs it through his lips, a sort of respiratory shrug. Kal's words are not so surprising after all. Lawson finds he's already accepting them, helpless, as he turns back and grins tersely at the others and waves them on. And with this acceptance, he dimly perceives, he has completed a long transformation: from a man who believed that the world could not rebuff his will to one who *expects* to be baulked at every hook in the trail. Like that bull moose, besieged by puny predators, scratched and nibbled to the point of collapse. So be it. And screw them all. He still has his will, and the world of predators is a long way below.

AIR THIS THIN TURNS ANYONE into a mystic. You can see why Murloe and Lawson succumbed to the mountain's spell. It looks, even now, like a sanctuary above all borders and distinctions and this constant dialogue of violence—the sort of place where Sophie should have been safe, the sort of place (you think now, recalling what you know of the country) that Tibet itself tried to be. Centuries ago, when Buddhism first arrived here, it converted a nation of warriors into one of monks and nuns and farmers, united by the Buddhist impulse to relieve suffering and avoid seeding it for the future through unmindful action and reaction. So Tibet became its own unique, isolated experiment, a nation trying to dissolve the ancient chain of reactive consequence going back, an eye for an eye for an eye, to a time before countries or even tribes. For centuries Tibet's mountain palisades helped insulate the experiment, but the world finally crashed in: feudal mandarins from the east, capitalist materialism from the west, Maoist fundamentalism from the east again. You can't help regretting the experiment's disruption. For years you've been treating and burying the victims of other failed experiments, political and religious; it would have been nice to see how this one— flawed, halting, but overseen now by a modern, open-minded leader—might have gone. An experiment not based on the notion that future utopias can be floated on seas of blood, or houses of worship built with enemies' bones, or happiness mass-produced through material advancement.

You've always felt an affinity for these Buddhists, in part because their faith replaces gods and temples with the human brain and heart, but also because your own work, field surgery above all, is a sort of Buddhist practice, demanding calmness in crisis, a mind fixed on the pulsing moment, an awareness that mental wobbling into past failures or future fears can mean disaster. And maybe this is more than just affinity. Maybe now, with Sophana lost in Tibet, you are finally being made to take sides. Maybe, in a way, you've found your country at the very moment the country itself—occupied, hemorrhaging exiles through its passes, its young people turning to violence, its banished leader approaching death—ceases to exist.

And yet to belong to such a place means belonging to something beyond countries and tribes—beyond belonging itself. Such a place, you think, can't really cease to exist.

A COLD, BONY MOON, a few days past full, shines down through the still leaves of the poplars. It's in the same place in the sky where the sun was when she fell asleep. Disorienting transition. She remembers her phone. Its ringing just now woke her, unless she was dreaming. She yanks back her fleece hood and with the other hand gropes inside her parka. The phone hasn't played its ring tune, the theme from *The Prisoner*, since they were in Pokhara almost three weeks back, and it shouldn't work here, but she fumbles it open, certain he has somehow found her, found a way of reaching her. Of course he has. He always will. "Papa! Hello?"

Silence, then a sharp deedling, repeated three times: the battery dying.

She stares at the lightless power gauge, her tight breaths clouding. The earth may be going greenhouse, the glaciers melting, but the universe, according to what she has been reading, is getting colder. Still, it's milder here than it was last night coming down out of the mountains. Smells of Canadian fall, like a windless night in October—the sharp, toasted odour of dead leaves.

Going by the moon, it must be eight or nine. She has slept since around noon, her throat so painfully dry it feels like a strep infection, her chilled body hangover stiff. She feels in her daypack and after some groping finds the bottle and uncaps it and chugs down half the cold water. Exhaling, she stares at her pack. Shoves her hand back in and pulls out the plastic flashlight, aims it down into the pack, though the moon's light is more than enough. She upends the pack, spilling its contents onto the dappled, moon-blue imprint her curled body made, like a fetal ultrasound, in the sand. The wasabi rice crackers have worked loose from the packet and lie strewn among her things. A zip-lock bag of gorp she'd forgotten about. Half a dozen pens and pencils. She shakes and searches the daypack a second and third time. No journal.

She picks up a cracker and without brushing off the grit she slides it into her mouth and grinds slowly as she looks at her pathetic possessions. Her eyes blur with tears. From inside her head, the crashing sound of her chewing seems fatally loud. They'll definitely be after her. Her journal left behind like a killer's calling card, not far from the guard's body where her pack flew off and came open. She wonders if her father could know by now, and will he think she drowned in the river—she's a poor swimmer—and there's a twist of grim pleasure in the thought. He'll never know how often, during his dangerous absences, she has had to picture *him* dead.

Her throat too dry to swallow, she washes the cracker down with her last drops of water.

She squats in the sand for a fast, vigilant pee, then gathers her stuff, dons the parka and pads through the miniature forest toward the river's sound. She picks her way between wind clusters of leaves, but steps on a few. Their small, tinny rattle seems so loud.

At the edge of the grove she looks up and down the riverside track as far as she can. Across the river, on higher, terraced ground, a fresh-mown field, sheaves of grain looking like tiny, stylized mountains in the moonlight. They weren't there yet when she entered the grove. From somewhere the clank of an animal bell and a dog's answering bark. Soft yellow light from a window across the river, maybe a hundred metres upstream.

She dips across the path to the river and hunkers in wet sand to fill her water bottle, then starts downstream at a brisk, cautious walk. But soon, unable to resist the instinct, she runs. There has to be a bridge. *Where there's a will, there'll be a trail*—her father used to say that when they were out jogging with Bones in the ravines and wanted to find a shortcut home, and it always turned out to be true.

Water slops in her belly as she runs and it's as if both thighs are charley horsed. After a while—she can't say how long; none of this seems to be happening in real time, the real world—she slows to a walk. As the liquid-full feeling eases, hunger comes. Hunger is not the word. This is a clawing, scraping vacancy that shrieks to be filled. And she keeps going. She has read of Native bands in the Yukon whose girls had to go into isolation in the mountains, fasting, surviving, and the romantic in her has envied that rite of passage, the sort of challenge she thought only boys in those tribes ever got to face.

Sooner or later you get what you envy.

Just before a full turn in the river, where the steep embankment blocks her view of the next stretch, she veers off the trail. At the embankment's foot she crouches among thorny, small-leafed scrub. She zippers her pack open quietly. The loss of the journal sickens her nearly as much as the thought of being pursued and beyond help. Those pages contain her urgent last few months encrypted in poems and cartoons and quotations and drawings, a feverish self-portrait in process.

She's chewing gorp (raisins, tamari almonds, peanuts, pumpkin seeds, banana chips and Smarties) when she gets a waft of something bad. She peers into the mesh of moonlight and shadow in the bushes behind her. Luminous squares of toilet paper around a dark heap of something. She seals the bag of gorp and closes her daypack and stays down, listening, scrunching up her nostrils. A few moments and she hears voices, barely hears them. A murmur diluted by the river's rich drone. She might be dreaming it. And the dream returns—she and the dead guard whispering in the river's language. But this is real, a soft swell of conversation from downstream, around that bend in the trail.

The guards—they must have passed the tiny grove when she

was sleeping. Somehow she'll have to get around them now. There's no way she's turning back, retreating upstream, uphill, who knows how far back. Her bridge is ahead. It must be.

The embankment here is like the Scarborough Bluffs, and she should backtrack before climbing something like this, find a better spot, but she's too tired and sore and starving—that word her father won't let her use casually—to think it through. She starts up on all fours, diagonally to the right, away from the hidden camp. Sandstone, gravel, jutting shelves of harder rock. Her hiking boots have good treads and she has bouldered a little with Zeph and Kaljang up at base camp. At first, fear seems to levitate her, as if she's bounding free of gravity up the inside of a lunar crater. Then she's stopped by a smooth, vertical face, as high as the brick wall of her school. She edges laterally along the base of it, feet on a narrow shelf of loose stone, her arms spread wide and forehead pressed to the rock. With the skewed, stubborn logic of panic, she feels there must be a way up, since she won't be able to find her way back down. No question of down now. She jars a rock loose and freezes, hearing it slide and thump and clack to the bottom. She's higher than she thought. She forces herself on, traversing, close to crying, *I hate you, I hate you*, speeding up now, reckless, get this over with, because he deserves that, whatever happens. And finds herself leaning forward as the slope tilts away from her, easing off. She looks up. Different rock, a sedimentary face, all cracks and ledges that the moonlight tags for her like rungs. Okay. She rests for a moment, embracing the slope, trying to slow her heart down as it pumps against the cliff. Then she drives for the top. The grade lessens even more and her relief sucks a sigh from her, the top within a few minutes' steady clamber. And her dead phone revives. Those warning bleats again. Even from inside her pocket, with what must be the last of the charge, that sound seems to gouge the moonlit quiet like a car alarm. She stalls, frozen to the rock like a gecko, then jerks upward again, tearing at the slope, going for the top. Cheap useless stupid fucking phone. Sophie all but running up a steep, narrow gully of scree, panting hoarsely, sagging back with each step almost as far as she advances, avalanches of stones behind.

She falls over the top and lies there for some seconds, then rolls clear. Pulls out her cellphone and smashes it against the ground three times, one for each of those betraying beeps. She gets up and hurls it inland as far as she can and she's sobbing as it flies, not just her music but her photo gallery, her family, her friends and the ex-friends she'd lost by being so obsessive about Scott, a last undeleted picture of him, another piece of her gone.

The second she pitches it away she regrets it. She wants to go looking for it among the zillion cellphone-sized rocks on this desert plain, but there's no time.

The plain is flat, featureless, rising slowly toward the east, where a few small lights cap a distant height of land. She thinks of running toward those lights but can't tell how far they are, or what they are. She looks back to the southwest—the wide gorge of the river narrowing as it winds back up to the foot of the mountains. A high strip of glacier glowing blue as a Bunsen flame under the moon. She knows she has come some distance from there, yet it seems so close, the peaks still huge and eerily black-lit in their snow.

In a downstream direction she runs along the top of the embankment, though far enough in from the edge that she and her shadow are clear of it. Just past the bend in the river, she creeps over to the edge and peeks down. In the gorge below, a campfire burns by the trail. A man—from up here he's a brimmed cap over a foreshortened body—stands by the fire yelling into something. A response crackles back. The other guard or guards must be back around the curve now, searching where she just was. The small bayonet stuck on the man's machinegun shines in the moonlight. That bayonet scares her more than the gun, yet her memory of the haunting dream has reduced, if not her fear, then her aversion to the Chinese, who she has hated with a convinced, confirmed hatred since the massacre up on the glacier. Now, looking down, it's as if she's spying on a different kind of search party—sad searchers looking not for her but for the young guard, as if his body has been washed downstream.

She runs on. Clear of the guards' fire she runs along the edge of the embankment, so she can see the river and, on the far side, a few lamplit windows. After some time, up ahead and far below, a bridge finally appears, its hanging span traced by the moon like a blueprint. She stops and stands panting. Her will insists on the bridge but her mind disputes it—the unlikely geometry of its arc out here in the wilderness and how it leads across to a snug cluster of huts, buttery light from the slits of windows, smoke rising. She has never seen anything so inviting. She longs to climb down into the gorge, but the embankment is even higher here and there must be a better way down, ahead.

Where there's a will, there'll be a trail.

She's a little past the bridge when her path falls away into a small ravine intersecting the gorge at right angles, cutting into it from the southeast. She scrambles down the side of the ravine to a dry streambed that must be a snowmelt torrent every spring. It's a steep, short walk down the streambed into the gorge. Now, at a cautious lope, she approaches the bridge, which is just upriver. She peers farther upriver, watching for the guards, but she has come several kilometres and probably not in the direction they think.

Stone steps polished with years of use climb to the top of a white plastered cairn. From there, the bridge's hanging span falls away to a point just above the river, then rises to a second cairn on the far bank. For handrails there are two ropes strung with prayer flags. A flimsy walkway of footboards hanging below. Walking her hands along the ropes, she totters down the boards to where the current flashes just under her feet and there she freezes—the bridge jiggling wildly—then draws a breath and climbs on upward.

Ahead on the landing there's motion, a large dog rising out of the shadows with its ears pricked. Sophie stops and tenses for the barking spree. The dog lowers its boxlike, hyena's head and prowls slowly toward her down the footboards. From its thorax, a warning rumble. The hackling mohawk of fur on its spine is moonlit grey.

Sophie stops on the trembling bridge but doesn't withdraw, because there's no way to back up fast and no way she's not crossing. The dog, this mythical guardian, pauses and weighs her with its eyes red like in a botched photo. She whispers to it as she edges forward. If you've owned and adored a dog you're not easily scared by them. She is scared, but not enough to turn back toward the guards. Again the bridge quivers with her steps. The dog's deep, abdominal growling thins to a whine and it looks at its paws on the footboards. Sophie sees what's happening. She shimmies the bridge hard, see-sawing with her feet, pulling in on the ropes with her hands. Everything wobbles. The dog retreats a few steps, turns tail and trots back up to the landing, where it rounds on her, reinflating itself. It's granting her the bridge, but no more. Sophie is going to have to do that thing she hates most—that the people she most admires never seem to do. The pathetic melodramatics of it. Hard to imagine Amaris or her father or mother ever doing it, and she hates how people see kids of her age as needy, indecisive. "Hello," she calls softly, then much louder, "Hello!" She's trying not to say the actual word, *help*.

Rich, fatty lumps and strands of meat in a salt broth thickened with some kind of flour and spiced with chilies. She's on her second large clay bowlful. She has vowed she will never be the sort of vegetarian who makes exceptions to avoid upsetting or inconveniencing meat-eating adults, but her rescuers have offered this stew and she can't get enough of it. And the tea, butter tea, with its grossly rancid odour but a greasy, salty taste she seems to crave. Every time she looks up from this endless meal (a bowl of stewed vegetables has just appeared, onions and maybe cabbage with mustard and a savoury spice she doesn't know), the large room holds more villagers, young and old. They are pushing in through the low doorway and spreading neatly around her in the lamplight, as if they have their own customary places on the woven rug, the packed clay floor—as if they often gather here to stare and stare at mute visitors exhibited on milking stools and lavishly fed. Some of them talk among themselves and giggle or laugh loudly, some point at Sophie's clothing or nose ring, most of them beam when she smiles her thanks with her lips closed, resolutely chewing. The older folks nod back while sticking their tongues way out and down like campy rock stars—some sort of local greeting? Their eyes crinkle warmly.

Except for the rainbow stripes of the women's aprons, most of the clothing around her is dark, brown or black, which along with her fatigue and shock deepens this scene's narcotic strangeness and makes the black-haired faces seem to float in the gloom like flickering bronze masks, the eye slots shadowed by the beams of a hanging storm lamp and smaller lamps here and there, wicks in clay bowls full of melted butter—she saw them back in Nepal, in Tarap, a stone village full of Tibetans. . . . An ancient woman with a milky walleye and a string of beads like Yiayia's *kombolói* sits cross-legged, mumbling a chant through her gums and twirling what looks like an antique percussion instrument—Sophie knows it's a prayer wheel—as if trying to appease or ward off the foreigner.

More villagers cram in, their eyes bright with curiosity in faces still slack and blank with sleep, like people waking and rushing to view some interesting emergency. It must be near midnight. This food is ballast and Sophie's sense of hallucination starts to fade. Her host, who looks a bit like Johnny Depp—mid-length hair parted in the middle, earring, bladelike cheekbones, a skimpy goatee and teeth that look like they've been tended by a Hollywood dentist—sits with his pretty, pregnant wife on a cot between a fireplace and an altar where a butter lamp glows in front of clay Buddhas and a pack of cigarettes, fruit, a small photograph of the Dalai Lama. Already villagers have flung sentences at her with the words *Dalai Lama* eagerly stressed, pointing at the altar photo or making framing gestures with hands and fingers. She knows images of the Dalai Lama are banned here.

When Tenzin, her movie star host, first led her back here from the bridge, there were three small children asleep on the cot where he and Karma, his wife, now sit. As Sophie entered, they leapt up, surrounding her, chattering, then ran out the door barefoot and returned, in what seemed like moments, trailing more children and grown-ups, too. There are at least twenty kids here now, popping out from between the shoulders or through the legs of the adults to peer at Sophie. Karma and two of the girls are serving tea. Tenzin frowns pensively at Sophie and occasionally addresses her, as if hoping that as the meal revives her, her comprehension of

Tibetan will improve.

"Picture please, Dalai Lama?" A schoolboy, maybe ten, stands beside her, his sooty, snotty face slightly above hers. He eyes her with a smirk, as if he has just said something jeering instead of polite and pious. With both hands he presents a glass containing a creamy grey liquid. A clay bowl has appeared with green plums, a yellow apple, an apricot.

"You speak English?" she asks the boy. He cackles and looks over his shoulders and jabbers something to his friends or parents or to the village in general.

"You have to tell them the guards might come. The Chinese."

The boy grins with gaps where the eye teeth should be and he backs away. Still, Sophie thinks, she hopes, Tenzin understands her. At the bridge he shooed away the dog with a stern hiss, a lazy kick—Sophie was too dazed and tired to object—and as the dog grovelled away ahead of them down the cairn steps and along a lane between flagstone walls, past other rumbling mastiffs, Sophie kept pointing upriver toward the guards' camp and babbling, *The Chinese, Chinese guards! Soldiers!* Tenzin eyed her obliquely, seeming to listen, and she'd tapped her watchless wrist and showed two fingers, hoping he would grasp that she knew they were a couple of hours away at most.

The drink has a fermented smell and a gluey thickness, and suddenly she feels full, way beyond full, but doesn't want to rebuff this kindness. The first sip tingles in her mouth like orange juice gone sour. *Chang*: her father and Mingma drank it in Tarap, her father describing it as mildly alcoholic—not a bad description of himself, she'd thought, a bit reproachfully. He said she could try a small mug. She sniffed it and passed. Tenzin rises with a tin jug in hand and tops up the glass she has barely drunk from and speaks to her again in Tibetan. As if alcohol might loosen her up enough to speak. He points at her glass and seems to ask something, his voice a hospitable growl.

"Yes," she lies, "it's good," and she drinks deeper, smiles. A small girl darts in and pokes at her braces and dashes back to her laughing friends. There's someone behind Sophie. Hands in her hair. She turns far enough to see a woman in a small stetson, kneeling on the rug, starting to braid her hair in tiny plaits. The woman's kneeling makes Sophie uncomfortable. *Please*, she wants to say, but the woman clucks her tongue and juts her solid chin and Sophie turns back toward the crowd, who laugh as if the scolding, the braiding, are part of a familiar comic routine. But the feel of those rhythmic tugs at the scalp, firm yet gentle, make Sophie's throat ache. Her *yiayia* still braids her hair sometimes. It seems months since Sophie has been touched, not just twenty-four hours or so since Kaljang's goodnight embrace outside her tent: *Don't fear about it, Sophie. We'll get your father back. Don't cry.*

"Picture please, Dalai Lama?" the sooty boy repeats. Grateful for the distraction, she glances down, digs into the daypack at her feet and brings out a pen and the quantum physics book. Opens it to one of the blank endpapers and draws. The boy zips back to her side and peeks over her shoulder, as does the braiding woman, and now others as well, jostling in to see. With light, relaxed lines, she frames the Dalai Lama's high round forehead, narrow eyes crinkling with merriment behind shaded glasses, small, mischievous mouth, his robes and bare shoulder. It's a crappy ballpoint but the sketch, somewhere between caricature and gesture drawing, is recognizable. Likenesses have always been easy for her. There are gasps as the face takes form. The crowd jams in closer and the smell is dense—peppery sweat, butter and, oddly, sulphur—not bad smells at the moment, but it's hard to get a breath, like being locked in a closet crammed with wool and fur coats.

She deckles the page out of the paperback's spine and gives it
to the boy and there's delighted laughter and what sounds like wild
acclaim. Small hands grab at the drawing the boy holds to his chest.
She should draw another but she's starting to feel ill, stifled, her
stomach bloated. The braiding woman and Tenzin must sense her
distress, because now they're pulling, shooing people back from
her. Tenzin leans over and talks into her face. There's a question
in his words. *Yes*, she nods, hoping it's the right answer. *Yes, I
think I need to use the toilet. Yes, I think I need to sleep.*

The gathering breaks up quickly, parents herding children
away, old men and women sticking out their tongues with a smile
and backing out the low doorway. Karma, who's about Amaris's
size except for her belly, leads Sophie into a back room where a
butter lamp glows before a shrine across from a low, wooden-
frame bed. Karma speaks slowly for a few seconds, pointing in
various directions and then indicating a clay pot at the foot of the
bed. Backing out of the small room, she bows and smiles warmly,
pulling shut a crooked door that leaves a foot of space between
the top and the lintel.

Sophie curls in a ball on a caved mattress that smells like bran
and straw. The room teeters as if she has drunk too much *chang*,
not half a glass. The pillow has a faintly scalpy, rancid smell and
the blankets are musky. Tenzin and Karma's bed. Sophie will get
up and thank them but insist that they sleep in their own room.
And she'll find the toilet. Her stomach is tossing, bloated. Last
night with her first real hunger pangs she did feel some concern,
but also satisfaction, thinking the one thing she might gain from
this crisis was a slight loss of weight. She's hardly bulimic but
now wonders if she should stick her finger down her throat. The
thought of how her bingeing and vomiting in a poor Asian village would upset her father now seems a strong endorsement of

the act. But not in that chamber pot. She has to find the toilet. She thinks the thought again, more insistently, like the last thoughts of a girl sinking in a river, trying not to drown but tiring of the fight. Yes, I must stroke for the surface. I really must swim for the surface.

For days after she and Scott Tyler crossed their own line, she had dreams like the ones that now kick-start her from heavy sleep, dreading the arrival of cops, guards, a SWAT team. In the five days until that knock at the door, she'd felt either defiantly proud (she hadn't just sat around ranting about injustice, she'd *acted*) or horrified, disbelieving. *If only they don't arrest us. If only we hadn't done it. If only we'd done it better.* The usual monsoon of her moods, but with a real crisis to feed off. Unwelcome thoughts of their "action" would hit her at random times—when she was in physics class, or helping Yiayia out of the bathtub, or drawing a cartoon for the school's online paper—and they would leave her flushed and winded, as if thrusting their way up into awareness from a place of tight confinement.

It had been his idea, a *big* idea, and she was crazy about him and didn't want to lose him, and like the others in their group she'd agreed at first, passionately, not thinking much past the moment's enthusiasm. It's fun and easy to commit to some bold thing when the date seems far away. So they made what-if plans, and then, step by step, refined them, and then, as the distant date somehow swooped toward them, uneasily firmed them up. The others started murmuring second thoughts. In the end, they backed out quietly, one by one, but Sophie couldn't seem to, not with Scott insisting he'd act alone if he had to, and her own self daring her on, and also—yes—the distant echo of her father's voice "joking" about lefties who talked a good fight and never fought so much as a cold.

And so, drunk on the romance of their righteous daring, they'd stumbled onward the whole way and now here they stood, alone and incredulous. He looked terrified and finally it struck her— *he'd been terrified all along.* He'd been waiting for *her* to call it off, to talk him out of it, so he could remain the fearless one who *would* have acted, who only backed off because his girlfriend begged him to and he didn't want to scare her. They were lurking in the alley between Café Amorgos and a boarded-up coin laundry, Scott wiping his upper lip, checking the time on his cellphone every thirty seconds until she wanted to shriek in his ear. She'd never seen him like this. His breath smelled rotten. Her heart kicking upward into her throat. For a moment their eyes met and his glance seemed to recoil and implode and she knew that all she had to say was *Let's get out of here* and he would nod in relief and they'd be gone.

She bit back the words, partly in fury at him, and, strangely, at her father, as if *he* had put her up to this. She glanced around the corner of the café—the patio was closed for repaving, one of the reasons they'd chosen the spot—and west up Danforth. Alex Diflakis would be lumbering along any minute. He was a talker and proud of the afternoon job he'd held since he was fifteen. He'd been heard calling himself the Human Brinks Truck, which had convinced Scott that he must mule thousands of dollars from his uncle's diner to the credit union at four every day. Enough of the kids knew his schedule that it was a miracle he hadn't been robbed. When somebody asked what would happen if he ever was robbed, Alex said insurance would cover it. Scott felt that if they got lucky they might land "four or five K," enough to save the homeless shelter and kitchen on Church Street, whose government funding had been cut and, now dependent on donors, was on the verge of closing. The moral math seemed sound. Basically, they'd be brokering a transfer payment from an insurance firm to an endangered soup kitchen.

Alex Diflakis was a big guy and had been since grade seven, but nervous accents yellowed his bragging chatter, which he delivered in a high, throttled voice. His slabby face was always sweating. Scott, who was skinny but fit and had a cocky, cold stare, said Alex would fall apart when confronted—at least by their full group, the six of them. Now Alex came hulking up Danforth in massive skateboarder shorts and basketball shoes, his pale moon-face and black curls haloed by the sun behind him. Sophie and Scott avoided each other's eyes as they turned their backs to the street and pulled on tight ski masks. She struggled with hers, swearing under her breath, then realized the trouble: she was shaking her head in disbelief as she tried to work the thing on.

They ducked behind a small PVC Dumpster as an old Greek in a fisherman's cap tapped past the mouth of the alley with his cane. Alex would be next. There was still time to bow out, stay hidden, just let him pass. They rose and lurched like zombies out of the alley and grabbed him, Scott on the outside, Sophie inside. Drew him back into the alley as if hustling him offstage in a comic skit, Alex limp now, flopping, all of them talking over each other like clumsy actors. *This way, here. We just want what's in your, uh, your daypack.* "What?" *The bag. The money.* "Wait!" *We'll let you go if, uh . . .*

"But I don't have a daypack!"

"Hurry," Scott said. "What? Just—just the bag there."

"It's a *satchel*," Alex said miserably.

"Just give us the money!"

"I can't, like, just hand it over."

"We've got knives!" Scott lied.

"But I'd have to pay it back!" he said in a choked falsetto. "Like, hundreds of dollars."

"*Hundreds?*" Scott said.

"You don't have *insurance?*" Sophie said, and Alex's bovine eyes rolled toward her, as if he was shocked to hear a girl speaking behind the ski mask.

"Don't move," Scott said, "or I'll use the knife! Give us the— just that bag there."

At the mouth of the alley the old Greek reappeared. He grinned, as if not quite getting what was happening. Or finding it funny. Across the wide street a man in a red-streaked apron stood with his hands on his hips, looking both ways, checking the traffic.

"*Now*, Alex!" Scott hissed, poking a finger into his kidney.

"You *know* me?" Alex sounded almost gratified. The big man in the apron was coming, dodging cars and taxis, yelling, either at the honking traffic or at them. Alex peered down, saw Scott's poking finger and wrenched his body clear. In the same motion he swung the satchel strap over his head and let the bag fall, then staggered backward, while Sophie and Scott also backed away and now turned to run—Alex and Scott and Sophie all fleeing the fallen bag like a suddenly ticking bomb. She glanced back as the man in the bloody apron thumped past Alex and the bag and kept after them, roaring that he was on their asses, they better run for it, *poustithes*, he was coming for them. Though the bag was still lying there untouched, Alex was shouting, "No problem! I only keep a bit of it in there anyhow!"

~

Choden leans far forward, her squinting eyes, behind the strap-on glasses, just above the steering wheel, her plump hands gripping the top of the wheel as if it's a ledge she's peering over. Despite her tense posture, her voice is calm. She and Amaris, side by side in the cab, are trading names and a few details (Choden used to drive the supply truck between her nunnery and a large old town a long way from here, and she always liked that). Her composure must be infectious—or maybe Amaris has run dry of adrenaline. *Maybe you're in shock*. Maybe this new feeling, almost like calm, like a calm dream, is what shock is for.

In neutral, the troop carrier rattles downhill over a tussocky gravel slope. The grade so far is gentle. The speedometer's quivering needle shows between twenty and twenty-five kilometres per hour. Below and ahead to the west, running perpendicular to their route, there's a seam of shadow—a valley or gorge—and on the other side, bare hills budding into snowless peaks that rise to meet Lawson's high pyramid and the other ice giants. The gorge, Amaris sees, must be a lower part of the river valley they followed last night—God, only last night!—and if you trace the shadow of the gorge back, you can see where it must feed down out of the high peaks. Maybe Book is right and they'll be able to get down to the river and from there try to hike back up to the border.

Through the slot window behind her head, Amaris looks down into the shadowy back of the truck and finds Book huddled over Palden and Lhundup. The small girl's father (his name is Sonam—Choden has told her all the names) kneels beside Book, helping. Norbu has completed his transformation from paramedic into paramilitary—he and his friend Sangye sit armed at the ends of the facing benches, where the Chinese guards sat before. She can't tell if they're trembling all over, or if it's the truck, or her own trembling.

She can no longer pretend she isn't also a fugitive, drawn back into the plight of her birth parents in Vietnam—as if this outcome, like certain cancers, were a genetic destiny, despite her years of ignoring it, of playing down the relevance of events that happened once in a distant land. (Like her friends, she has never seen any future in history and tries to live free of it.) Behind her sunglasses she shuts her eyes, but instant video of the slaughter at the base starts replaying. *You should never have come back to Asia.*

She opens her eyes. "Why did you leave your nunnery, Choden?"

Choden says nothing at first, and when she does speak, her English is wonky, halting. "Ah, well . . . it's these three of us, Dolma and Pema and myself? We took the bus for Lhasa, a small pilgrimage to Jokhang Temple, but also there to join a protest against, ah, all these Chinese immigrants, overfilling Tibet? And so we did. We did these both. After that, it's a . . . it's a longer story. Now might be not the place to tell you."

"Sorry," Amaris says. "I shouldn't have asked."

"Ah . . . we've a bit of a drop down yet, but I'm afraid we're sure to meet flat places before long. Please open the, the box there and fetch us a map."

Sand grinds in the latch of the glove compartment. Amaris finds a flashlight and candles and matches and a pack of cigarettes and brings a sheaf of maps onto her lap. She takes her reading glasses out of the belly pack for her camera—loose now, like an emptied womb—and it hits her again. You're not meant to give a shit about possessions at a time like this, but that video camera was more than a possession.

They're speeding up, a hot wind jetting in. Maps fly loose and crackle open. Choden pumps the brake like somebody driving on snow. The slope looks no steeper but the speedometer needle shivers toward thirty-five. "Tamp harder!" Amaris says, and Choden says evenly, "Pardon me?" but in fact she is braking harder, the truck skidding with each pressure. The base of the slope shudders up toward them: a flat expanse the colour of sulphur, like the bed of a dry spring. Choden calls out in Tibetan, maybe warning the others in the back. As they hit bottom and level out, the cab bounces and the whole frame shakes but then goes silent as they glide smoothly over the webbed clay. They slow down and roll to a stop near the far edge of the clay bed. Beyond the rim of it, the ground falls away again, more gently.

"I suppose we'll need a push," Choden says softly. Then, in a firm voice, she calls something out her window. She wrinkles her nose. "Once we let the brakes rest."

"These maps are in Chinese," Amaris says. "Can you read them?"

"I can, sure."

"Why don't you navigate, then. I can steer."

"I'd be grateful for a switch now, Amaris—my nerves are a little like those brakes."

They change places. The tailgate claps down. In the side mirror Amaris sees two robed monks brace themselves around the wheel-well and push, while Choden calls back to them. At the edge of the next downslope they give a heave and leap back on board and the truck rattles on.

Amaris steers them straight into the sun. Late afternoon has turned the cab into a solar oven. Sweat needles and blurs her eyes, but she keeps her wet hands on the wheel, glancing at the odometer as it slowly clicks over, more distance between them and the

base. The slope is gentle at first but gradually it steepens and she
has to work the brakes until she can smell them starting to burn.
After each burst of pumping, the truck reaccelerates. She's using
the hand brake now too. It's starting to feel stripped. Beside her
on the bench seat Choden somehow dozes, the map open in her
lap and her limp hands on it, fluttering with the truck's bounces.
They're going to lose control, Amaris can feel it, like a child on
a bicycle wobbling downhill. "Wake up now!" she says, but the
grade is starting to ease off and she steers them down and finally
lands them on another flat stretch of cracked yellow earth, a smell
of sulphur gusting in. They slow and roll to a halt and she
breathes—then hears the tailgate drop down and sees, in the
mirror, the monks bracing themselves to push again. "No!" she
calls out. "The brakes are dead!" But they only push harder, as if
thinking she's urging them on. She tries to stop them with what's
left of the brakes, but the monks grunt and keep shoving, forcing
the truck toward the far side, the next downslope. "Choden . . . !"
The nun's eyes are already open; after a moment she says, "Ah."
With no special urgency she leans out her window and calls back
in Tibetan. A monk replies and the truck creaks to a stop, close
enough to give a glimpse over the edge—the next downslope
steeper, too steep.

　　Amaris lets her soaked forehead sink to rest on the wheel.
"Thanks," Choden tells her, seemingly unfazed by this latest close
call. It's the sort of casual, good-natured fatalism that's been exas-
perating Amaris since she arrived in Kathmandu. She can't find
it charming, as Book seems to—not right now. An adult's job is
to control whatever's controllable, especially out here, where less
and less is.

~

Book tumbles out with the others and stands by a cairn of large, flat stones marking the outlet where this dry spring must once have spilled over into the gully that starts below it and loops down into the distance. It must meet the river gorge somewhere ahead. Each piled stone is engraved like a clay tablet with a sort of embellished cuneiform. Prayers. It should be some comfort to know that others once came this way and marked their passage with prayers, but it doesn't help now. It doesn't help to be reminded that something that once flowed can stop flowing. Sophie is down there somewhere, captured or on the run.

Amaris looks like she's trying not to faint. He grips her arm and says, "Can I have that map?"

"What . . . ? Oh, here."

"Your sunglasses."

"What about them?"

Gently he lifts them off, peers into her black coffee eyes. "Okay. Sit for a minute, in the shade here"—the eastern side of the cairn—"head down between your knees."

She sits, her bum resting on the parka wrapped around her waist. He dries his palm and sets it on her brow. "Christ, how hot was it up in that cab?"

"Yeah, it was." She sounds sedated. "You're still barefoot, Lew."

"Just keep your head down, okay? I'll be back in a minute."

"Okay. I'm okay."

The others have unloaded Lhundup. Sangye stands guard over the slumped Palden, as if that's necessary. Book joins Sonam, Norbu and the monks around the truck and in silence they push it toward the edge of the dry spring. As they heave the front wheels over the raised edge, they cry out, Book and the others, even the monks, all voicing the same raw, involuntary howl, like ice age hunters driving game over a cliff. The truck clatters and thumps away down the slope. After a few seconds it goes slapstick, catching air as it pitches over ruts and stones and then, farcically fast, tips and grates to a stop near the bottom.

They carry Lhundup back to the cairn, where Amaris waits. Book, Norbu and Choden examine the map, Choden translating. Her face is very flushed. She and Amaris, like Lhundup, will need water soon. Norbu might be willing to make do with somebody's blood; his nostrils quiver and he shuns eye contact with Choden and Book. On the map, the Chinese base is marked clearly, and the gully leading down from this dry spring seems to correspond with a dotted line running west to intersect the Khiong River at a village called Tyamtso. The map's scale makes the direct distance just ten or fifteen kilometres, but he, Choden and Norbu seem to agree that walking directly, up on the open plain, is not an option. They'll have to follow the winding gully.

"Let's go," Book says. "We need to hurry, please."

Over her shoulder Choden carries something like a long, furled Torah scroll: one of the stretchers they found under the truck benches. Book, two monks, and Palden Jangbu, with his punchdrunk eyes and turban of gauze, bear Lhundup on the other stretcher, down into the deepening kiln of the gully. Norbu walks beside Palden with the submachinegun. Amaris, still woozy, offers to help with the stretcher, but Book says, "We were shaded in the back— you were driving. You've got to take it easy now." The young nun jerks along with the older one's help, the rest of the party trailing.

The grade is gentle and the footing is gravel and firm sand; it would be an easy hike down if they weren't so burdened, parched and exhausted. The gully walls are about two men high and the streambed twenty steps across. After some time, a monk takes over for Book with the stretcher. Moments later there's a heavy throbbing in the air. The child seems to fall or be swung off

Sonam's shoulders, then Sonam and the child are down and the pregnant Lasya drops beside them. The others, reacting much faster than Book and Amaris, are down, too, lying in matching windrows along the gully walls like casualties in a shelled trench. Amaris looks dreamily skyward. Book tackles her and lies next to her on the hot sand of the streambed, his arm over her shoulders, holding her prone.

A khaki helicopter skims over the gully a few hundred metres upstream.

"Oh," she says vaguely, "shit. They see us, you think?"

His hand on her brow. "They may not be looking for just us."

"What . . . ? What's happening, Lew? Am I dying or something?" She shudders, chuckles with what seems a kind of giddy amusement. "Come on, Doc, give it to me straight." Her teeth are small and the smile is too gummy, the bared gums vulnerably pink, and it's touching to see them, her only imperfect, unguarded feature.

"You're dehydrated—feverish. But it's not heat stroke. We'll lose the sun soon, then we'll get down to the river. I want you to go on the stretcher for a bit."

"No way."

"I figured you'd say that. Look, just for a bit, so you—"

"Not if *she* isn't."

"Lasya, you mean? Or Pema, with the leg? Or—"

"Take your pick," she says. "Why don't we all rest here?"

"We *have* to get down to the river." He starts to rise but Norbu hisses at him and Choden signals him to stay down. Now Palden, prone between Norbu and Sangye, gives Book a strange, intense look that seems to mix suspicion and entreaty. Book tells her, "The Chinese think you and I are collaborators, for one thing. Especially now."

"Because we broke out?"

"That too." He'll explain about his "confession" when she's less dazed. Now, eyeing the Tibetans strewn around them, he says, "I can't understand why they don't just *let* these people leave if they want to. It's like the Himalayas are a Berlin Wall now."

The sky starts to pulsate and roar and the copter reappears, again buzzing across the gully, though this time downstream of them. It vanishes and the roaring recedes, approaches, recedes again but hovers not far off in the sky. They lie low. The sun nods out of view. The roaring gradually fades. Dusk rolls down the gully like a flash flood and he feels her trembling in the chill.

The party slumps onward. Book's own pain deepens, diversifies. His bare heels and soles burn, but he doesn't think of slowing—he's going on love and adrenaline, a sick surging of dread in his belly and chest. But an hour goes by and it's dark, no sign of the river, the others staggering. They'll have to stop.

By flashlight Choden finds a cave, five feet up in the north wall of the gully. Everyone easily fits inside, though all except the child have to crouch. A gap in the cave's roof—the desert floor—has been closed over with flattened oil tins layered like shingles. Choden shines the flashlight toward the back: a firepit full of ash, an old shrine, an oxidized copper Buddha, the stubs of incense sticks.

Book says, "Are we near a monastery? Choden, is this . . . ?"

She hunches toward him and Amaris, rattling something in her hand. He aims his penlight: bullet shells green with verdigris. In her soft brogue she says, "I guess it was a place where Tibetan resisters would hide away, some years ago. Or, perhaps, both a hermit's retreat and a fighter's hideaway. Some of the resisters were monks, you see. They tried to drive the Chinese out, but nothing became of it but so much dying. My father, he was a resister, too, and he was imprisoned awhile, before I was born."

Amaris mutters something—maybe *sorry*—and from the marsupial pack on her belly she brings out matches, candles and cigarettes she must have found in the truck. By the flashlight's sweeping, she picks out a spot on the floor and sinks down, wrapping her parka around her. "Think I'll rest here a bit," she says, slurring, and Book says quickly, "Right, good—rest. But just a few hours. But you need to rest."

"What . . . ?"

"Just sleep. It's okay."

He watches as she tugs off her boots, leaving the warm liners on her feet, and ranks the boots carefully beside her. Then she removes her watch, feeds the strap through the buckle, secures it, and places it on the cave floor, its face toward her face. All this though she's almost asleep. He knows better than to try to sleep himself. He'll be awake until he finds Sophana, and it's torture, torture by triage, not to go on *now*, down to the river alone, but he has Lhundup to see to, also Palden, Pema, Lasya, even Amaris. Still—if he loses Lhundup in the night, God knows how he'll decide whether to stay or go after Sophie.

Amaris wakes from dreams of frantically pumping a failing brake while a voiceover puns *failing break-up!* and somehow she knows it's the death of her engagement, at the end of film school, followed by the early abortion that Emil, her ex-fiancé, never knew about. In the midst of a true heartbreak, the truer sufferings of people in desperate countries seem far less real than your own. Now she is actually involved in the sort of graphic crisis you glimpse on news channels back home, and maybe that's why she just dreamed of Emil—she's nostalgic for the smaller, surmountable disasters of her life up until now.

She rolls onto her side, looks at what should be a hallucination. A candle flickers in the ash of the firepit and dark shapes lie or sit around it: Norbu and Sangye shakily smoking, old Dechen smoking her pipe. A second candle lights up the ruined shrine and, on the walls above it, faded paintings of robed, seated figures and a cartoonish blue ogre with a sword. Choden and the older nun and two monks prostrate themselves in front of the shrine, fingers steepled under their chanting lips. Sonam and Lasya lie on their sides, facing each other, with the sleeping child between them. They're whispering in an anxious tone. It's hard to watch. Amaris hates scenes that feel apt to break her open.

A few steps away, this side of the firepit, Book sits beside the sleeping Lhundup in a shaft of moonlight (a small aperture has been opened in the fuel-tin roof). He's in his black-rimmed glasses, studying the map, his sweater cuffs pulled down over his fingers. His cigarette smoke twines up the moonbeam as if it's a ventilation shaft. Stethoscope around his neck, tousled hair, those sideburns— he looks like a haggard intern pulling an all-nighter. His eyes close as he takes a drag. He lets out a gruff sigh, more like a groan, but still it reminds her of the other, sensual Lew, which reminds her of base camp, hot chai and her cozy tent, which links back to home, her neat office, the enclosing ritual of her routines.

"How you feeling?" he asks softly.

Terrified, she thinks, but says only, "I can't stop thinking of water. That river."

"We'll go there now—the moon's up. I was going to wake you. Your fever's gone."

"How do you know?"

"I just felt." He passes her his cigarette. She draws in the bad tobacco and, too sore to move, lies looking up at him. For a moment their gazes mesh.

"I thought doctors prefer Camels, Lew."

His faint smile is pained; it hits her that he might have lost his patient and she asks, "Is he okay?"

"Still here. Tough as a post."

"What're you finding on the map?"

"Trying to figure out where Sophie could be."

"What . . . ? She's at base camp, isn't she?"

He takes off his glasses. In the back of the cave now Choden and Norbu are whispering.

"What the hell is going on, Lew?"

"Zhao told me she's being tracked along the river. By those border guards."

"*What?*"

"Down where we're headed now."

"Oh my God—she came after you?"

He pulls off his stethoscope, stuffs it in his kit, barely nods. The cave hums with that whispering, chanting.

"Fuck, Lew, I'm sorry. I hope . . . but hang on—"

"Me too."

"Hang on a minute—don't worry," she says, thinking *Unarmed child, zero threat, they'll be careful, they'll treat her gently.*

Then something very different occurs to her.

"Wait a minute. Is this why we're going this way? Through this desert?"

"What do you mean?" he says, almost snaps. "What other . . . this is the only possible way to go. Choden and Norbu felt the same."

"Do they know about Sophie?"

"I didn't want to complicate things."

She sits up, her professional instincts zinging. Pain and fear throughout her body sharpen those instincts, if not her wits:

"And if . . . if the best possible route hadn't matched your own needs? What would you have done then?"

Pause. "I really don't know."

"Wait," she says, "hang on."

"It's always triage," he says softly.

"Would we even be *here*, Lew? I mean, is *this* why we broke out of jail and gunned down Zhao and those soldiers and probably screwed ourselves completely—so you could look for your daughter?"

"What?"

"I mean, Sophie's probably safe now anyway! The Chinese wouldn't hurt her."

"How do you know that?"

"They wouldn't have hurt *us*, either! Oh my *God*, I'm right, that's what happened, isn't it? You've got all of us . . . you keep getting us into deeper and deeper shit!"

"Keep your voice down. The first I knew of it, they were jumping Palden. I was as surprised as you."

"You must have joined the fight, though, once it started, right?"

"Maybe I was wrong about your fever," he says coldly.

That counterpoint of throaty chanting—like the ashram cassettes her adoptive sister used to play—sounds more and more absurd, ironic. As if prayers can draw a different result from the air. Maybe Zhao was right about Book, she thinks, maybe he really *was* up there to help the Tibetans . . . and at that moment he adds, "Of course I didn't help them attack Palden—I'd just cut a deal with Zhao, to keep Sophie safe—and the rest of us."

"A what?"

Softly, tersely, he describes his video confession and she listens and grinds the cigarette butt into the cave floor and says finally, "So . . . now we're wanted as self-confessed spooks and pro-Tibet agents as well as, as murderers and invaders?"

"I said you and Sophie had nothing to do with it."

"And they're going to buy that."

If nothing else, if they make it back alive, she'll dig a film out of this, with their desert ordeal as the frame. Book and his back chapters. His encrypted truths. She's seen it before, how altruists always have an angle, how the high-minded end up sparking more pain and carnage than all the "bad boys" of the world.

"Lew, are you saying they'll *believe* that Sophie and me . . . ?"

"I'm saying it's the wrong time to ask me."

"And you—I mean, I'm really starting to wonder here, Lew—how can I be sure your confession was actually *fake?*"

"Fuck," he whispers, "we're all losing it, already. I feel ready to kill and you're already getting . . ." He rakes a hand through his messy hair, folds up the map.

"What?"

"Nothing. Let's go."

"It was a simple question," she prods, though at the same time it hits her, the other her, fully: the girl might still be out there, somewhere. They really do have to move.

They climb down through the mouth of the cave into the bitter cold of a desert night and for some hours they walk in silence. The moon subsides. Cassiopeia blazes down with a cold, stabbing clarity and that radiant W seems to taunt them all with its reminder of the big questions, now reduced, for Book, to Why did she leave, what was she thinking, when did she do it, where is she now? Andromeda's galactic fog—first cloud to appear in the sky for days—glows more clearly than he's ever seen it. Two million light years off, it was the remotest thing anyone saw from the earth before the first telescope, as he'd explained once to his children, both crowding his lap in the Muskoka chair on the battered dock in the Thirty Thousand Islands. Early fall. Pavlos, that hyperkinetic young animal, could listen only in spasms as Book charted the skies, but the girl tuned in with her usual intense, silent stamina. (The warmth of his children in the cold of the universe, the burning sweetness of neat bourbon.) She never forgot a star once he'd told her, while Book himself was now losing some of the details he'd once had by heart. *Follow the arc to Arcturus.* At least she would not be totally lost, with these skies as her map. *Then speed on to Spica.*

The last star goes out like a coal and the dawn's thin light infiltrates the gully. Their route swithers downward. The first, faint sounds of the river waft up to them.

You never know what love is going to require of you; you just hope you'll be equal to the crisis.

In the morning, up on the flat roof, in hot sunlight and the cold air that x-rays her breaths silver against a violet sky, Sophie has her intermission in paradise. When she woke, Karma, carrying what looked like a bundle of towels, led her to a stone outhouse (two holes in a dirt floor) as cold as a freezer, scattered with dormant flies, then up a path between mown fields along a steaming, sulphurous creek to an oasis: a small depression bowered by nut and apricot trees and luxuriant shrubs, maybe rhododendrons, where a blue-green pool smouldered with a faint sulphur stench. Brimstone in paradise. Karma pointed, instructing, but Sophie was already stripping down. After the past two nights, and the three weeks before that, her desire for hot water easily trounced her shyness (she finds herself *big*—not fat, she's actually thin, but tall and muscled, jockish in a way she dislikes). She slid in up to her

mouth and heard her own long, erotic sigh without embarrassment. Currents in the spring bubbled like jets in a Jacuzzi. For
blissful seconds she lay perfectly still until she realized that the
pregnant Karma was soaping and scrubbing her clothes and bloodied socks on the stones where the spring brimmed over into the
creek. "Stop," Sophie said weakly, "please don't!" Karma grinned
over, showing a gorgeous silver tooth Sophie would die to have,
and said something cheerfully dismissive.

They strolled back down along the creek, Karma insisting on
carrying the washed clothes and Sophie's hiking shoes. Sophie
now wore a tight blouse and a black, sleeveless wraparound dress,
sashed at the waist. *Chuba*, Karma called it. Karma's own black
chuba hung to her anklcs, Sophie's to mid-calf; Karma kept looking her up and down and chuckling.

Now Sophie sits alone on the roof with a meal of warm flatbread and sweet almonds and a clay bowl of creamy, salty yogurt
and butter tea and a single, perfect apricot. Last night she bolted
pieces of fruit compulsively, but this one fruit she eats slowly, tast-
ing, with all of her nerves and cells, the tart and tender, lush flesh.
Sensing she'll never forget this apricot. This tiny amber world.

Around her up here, the flat roofs of other smartly whitewashed mudbrick houses, spicy smoke like incense rising. The
rhythmic clang of a yak's bell as a girl leads it by the nose ring
up the lone street. Prayer flags on its horns. It jangles past. It
seems to wear furry black jodhpurs. She sees the bridge, the
river's other, sunless side and the high embankment split by the
gully that she walked down last night. It's not a long bridge, a
wide river, but she feels (as she always feels things: with conclusive intensity) that she has crossed over into another world, a
safer place. She guesses the guards must have turned back, thinking she has retreated upriver.

For some moments, clean and warm and fed and safe, things feel so close to perfect she forgets how far from perfect they are. Those few moments, then the change. Across the river a dog barks frantically, and others dogs, closer by, respond. She spits the apricot stone into the bowl. She can't see motion on the bridge or on the far shore, but the barking amplifies. She swallows the last piece of bread. The tea's dregs have a sour, cheesy aftertaste. She's crawling toward the hole in the roof when the chapped, dirty face of one of Karma's sons pops up. He beckons dramatically. She follows him down the ladder onto the second floor, then down a stairway—it's hardly more than a ladder—into the main room, where Karma, shouldering Sophie's daypack, frowns, speaks softly, opens the door. The boy grips Sophie's hand as Karma leads them into a street full of barking dogs. There's Tenzin, towering over a squat older man and speaking urgently, pointing up the street. For a flash he meets Sophie's glance, looks away, continues as if he hasn't seen her.

She and the child follow Karma past the outhouse and along the creek, between pyramids of reaped grain, to the hot spring with its curtain of shrubs and dense trees clustered with fruit. She hears the voices of women and children, bathing or washing clothes. She figures this is where she'll be hiding, but Karma gives her her daypack and points onward and tells the boy something. He tugs Sophie's hand and runs with her across a sweep of stubble toward a brilliant yellow field with a few high sunflowers poking up out of it. The valley wall, the far border of this garden world, rises beyond the field. The boy is small but quick. Both of them barefoot. (Sophie and Scott, after the "robbery," scrambled down into the ravine, where they separated, according to plan, no Bonnie and Clyde kiss when they split up. She didn't want to kiss him. She never did kiss or even see him again after that—there was just the indirect Judas kiss of his betrayal. A much deeper sort of jilting. Betrayal doesn't just rattle your faith in yourself, in your looks, or even in love, but also in human nature.)

Hand in hand, she and this boy, no more than ten, whose name she forgets, whose village she has led armed men into, crash into the field and run. The flowers raking her face smell mustardy. At last he stops, takes her hand in both of his and yanks downward. She crouches. His brown eyes are huge, very round for a Tibetan. He instructs her slowly and firmly, his impish, filthy face gone tragic, as if something awful has already happened. Maybe it has. And he's gone, rustling off through the stalks, throwing up the black soles of his feet.

She rises onto her toes, her eyes just clear of the tops of the mustard blooms. The few huge sunflowers seem to watch the village with her, like surveillance gadgets in *The Prisoner*. The bridge and the street of yowling dogs are hidden by the backs of houses. Her clothes, which were drying on the rocks near the outhouse, have vanished. She crouches down. The earth is cold. The seed pods smell bitter. One thing leads to another. A chain-smoking sequence of events has brought her here—errors, including her own.

The sun rises and the walkers' long shadows, stretching ahead of them down the gully, look gawky and starved. Hunched with cold they shamble on, except for Book, who's forcing the pace the nearer they get to the river—its static sound channelled up to them through the gully—and Choden, beside him, holding the other front grip of Lhundup's stretcher. She still looks rosy and fresh behind her bulky glasses, while Lhundup has gone from middle to old age in just hours, his voice high and trembling, the lines around his mouth and eyes deeply carved. Yet the sclera remain eerily clear and his blood pressure is stable. Book has told Choden he's astonished that Lhundup has hung on—something he'd never say around a patient, even an unconscious one, who might understand—and Choden replied, "Did you know, Lewis, his name means 'miraculous'?'"

Now he asks her, "What was the long chant . . . the one you did three times last night?"

"Ah, you noticed it was the same! It's the Diamond Sutra. What did you think?"

Pause. "I'm not sure how I would have got through the night without it."

"I know," she says quietly. "You must be concerned about your daughter."

He looks at her incredulously. "What . . . how did you . . . ?"

"You and Amaris were discussing it. I couldn't help but overhear. I hope . . ."

"I thought you were arguing with Norbu."

"We were, but overhearing other conversations isn't hard after years at a girl's school, then the nunnery. I think your daughter would understand this. I hope to be meeting her soon."

"I'll see that you do," he says.

As his fear for her grows, she's growing backward in his mind, ever younger. He helped to deliver her sixteen years eleven and a half months ago. Nika was fierce and stubborn and at times grimly funny and Book was in awe of his wife and never more deeply in love. At times she raged and called him unrepeatable things in Greek and he had accepted that, seeing her anger as a reservoir of strength for the final phase.

As for Amaris, now, if her anger, even her wild suspicions, help get her through this, he'll accept that too. Her sleep and their argument have rallied her. Now she and Palden take over from the monks who were holding the back grips of the stretcher. Palden is chatty again, like a bullied nerd on a field trip, sticking close to the teachers, babbling nervously. He's recalling his days as a tour guide and asking Book about his travels. Book answers monosyllabically. At times Norbu, plodding alongside, snarls at Palden, who then briefly shuts up. Book realizes that one of the words Norbu has been repeating doesn't just sound like "motherfucker," it is "motherfucker."

Norbu seems taller, his acne fading, as if the cellblock coup and his new rank in the party have matured him, physically. But his sleepless eyes are the electrified, unreachable eyes of a fanatic. Choden has been telling Book about him and the others. Norbu, Sangye and their friends got into trouble in Lhasa after roughing up a Chinese policeman in a hip-hop dance club. (Choden mouths "hip-hop" and "club" with plosive stress and a small, dimpled smile, as if tickled by the pop in the words.) "When two more policemen came to arrest them, they roughed them up too, a little worse. The authorities won't stand for such a loss of face. They came in force and arrested all of them, except for Norbu and Sangye, who fled. And Lhundup—Norbu's uncle—he came with them, as a guide and guardian. The boys never had gone out of the city, you see." After a pause filled with their shuffling, she adds, "I do keep asking, leave the guns behind, but they'll not hear of it."

"They don't have the firepower to get us out of the trouble they've got us in."

"Do weapons really get people out of trouble, Lewis?"

"My father and I used to argue," he says. "He thought sending in troops to kill the bad guys first would help more than sending in doctors like me to treat their victims after."

"But then, aren't there more victims on both sides?"

"I've seen it, yeah. Still, there've been times I half wished I was armed."

Glancing back at Norbu, she says, "He blames the Chinese for all his trouble, but I think perhaps your popular medias are as much to blame."

"Also too, the colonialism!" Palden blurts, and Norbu jabs him with the gun snout.

"Blame the filmmakers," Amaris says. "Everyone else does."

Choden seems delighted with this, the first thing Amaris has said in hours. Now, her smile dimming, Choden explains that Dechen and her slain husband were trying to reach their children and grandchildren, who fled over the pass near Everest two years ago to live in the Kathmandu Valley. Sonam and Lasya wanted their daughter, and the child to come, to be educated in Tibetan. The monks are novices hoping to be ordained as full monks in Dharamsala, and the nuns are trying to reach a nunnery recently founded by the Dalai Lama, where for the first time they can earn their *geshe*, a religious doctorate, and where Choden hopes to become a mural painter. After a pause, as if trying to decide whether to finish, she adds quickly, "The group of us got jailed after a nun's protest in Lhasa. After release, we just fled." Before Book can respond, she swerves away: "Lewis, when you were in Darjeeling, what were people saying about His Holiness?"

"Actually he visited, in July, but I didn't see him."

Her brow crimps up and she looks half scandalized, her widened eyes exaggerated by her lenses. "You didn't see him!"

"Some of my patients did. I was there because of the cholera outbreak."

"But even if you were sick! Do you not admire him?"

"No, no, I was *busy*, night and day. I think he'd understand. My Tibetan patients said he seemed really well." Book's patients all seemed better for having seen him, too: the Dalai Lama as divine placebo. Now Choden's plump, dimpled face glows in the same way his patients' faces glowed then, and she seems content to bask in her thoughts, and that's a relief—it's harder and harder to listen and reply, keep the tremor out of his voice. His feet feel shredded. His stretcher arm burns. The static of the river grows louder and it makes his mouth water until fear dries it again. Sophana could be anywhere. They're all walking faster, Pema and Dolma lurching as if in a three-legged race. Breezes smelling of life and growth flow up through the gully and now sounds ride up with the breeze: the barking of dogs, maybe men's shouting.

Some minutes later they round another turn and the strong-flowing river is just below them, a sparkling mirage of millions of gallons of sweet, cold water. To the left, upriver, a rope bridge droops across to a village of whitewashed huts. From behind Book, a child's sparrowlike cry of joy and now Sonam, with his daughter riding piggyback, jounces past and down the dry wash toward the river. Sangye jogs with them, his submachinegun slung loose and swinging. Lhundup whispers something and Choden answers in a reassuring tone. Book resists the urge to run with the stretcher down this last pitch—in fact, to set the stretcher down right now and go drink and drink.

The village dogs howl and yammer. Norbu points toward the village, calling ahead to Sangye, who turns and gives some hand signal. Book squints, trying to focus on the people moving in the one, wide street that recedes from the bridge. No sign of Sophie. He spots the two Chinese at the same moment Amaris says, "Shit, those guards!" One of them stands shouting among the villagers while the other comes running back toward the bridge, vanishing behind the pier for a few seconds and then emerging on top, standing with his legs braced and a submachinegun at his hip.

Sangye hunches but lopes on down the dry wash toward the bridge. "Everyone down!" Book says. They set the stretcher on the sand and he, Palden and Choden crouch beside it, but the others—the monks and the limping nuns, Dechen, Lasya with her hands braced around her belly, Amaris—have already pushed past, following Sonam and the child downslope toward the water. Sangye fires a burst at the guard on the bridge. The reports are tinny, toylike. The guard fires back. Norbu, standing a few feet from Book, squeezes off a louder burst. Book glances at Palden, kneeling on the far side of the stretcher, his blackened eyes darting between the river and Norbu's unprotected back, and Book springs into motion, grunting with the strain. He's tackling his own patient and as he takes Palden down he cradles the swathed, concussed head to protect it.

"Lewis . . . please!"

"Just stay down. He'll kill you if you try anything."

"But, Lewis," he whispers, seeming honestly perplexed, "whose side are you with?"

"I wish you'd all stop asking me that!"

"Norbu!" Choden calls—then words in Tibetan. Norbu has started down the dry wash, firing a few rounds with every stride, the spent shells raining. A dozen steps and he halts and kneels and sights along the snub barrel. The guard on the bridge fires again and little geysers of sand spatter up behind Sangye as he dashes over the flood flats and stops and from the beach shoots up and across at the fumbling, reloading guard. All through this, the others are rushing down to the water—they're veering downriver, away from the gunfire, but otherwise ignoring it.

Sonam and the child are on all fours in the shallows. The monks now beside them. Amaris. Upriver, Sangye stands suicidally exposed, he and the guard maybe forty metres apart, shooting and missing, splinters from the footboards and mortar of the pier flying, sand and water splattering. Norbu firing too. In the wide street beyond the bridge, small figures scurry and plunge for cover. The other guard has vanished. "Stop!" Book hollers. "Goddamn it, enough!" Now Choden leaps up and runs downslope in her swirling robes. She puts her hand on Norbu's shoulder and he pivots, rising, to straight-arm her in the chest and spit out words and turn away, back toward the bridge. She falls backward into the slope. Book gets off Palden and runs down at Norbu, who's loading what must be his last clip and blasting away as if in a video arcade. Book is almost on him when Sangye, on the beach, sags to his knees and flops face down. A moment later the guard on the bridge pitches backward. Book's momentum carries him through Norbu and he and the kid tumble together, Book on top, and slide a few feet down the slope. Norbu's baseball cap twists free. His sweat-drenched face cranes around at Book, fear and then shock in the red, steroidal eyes. Pure adrenaline. He's incredibly strong. "*Mutterfugger! Mutterfugger!*" Book struggles to keep him and the gun pinned down.

When the shooting starts in the village and its echoes spread through the valley, Sophie is crouched low in the mustard and she freezes there, unable to rise and look. It's hard to remain still while your heart is bolting and impossible to think clearly, but two thoughts arrive to rattle through her brain: he would be disappointed that she would cower down here while her helpers, her saviours, are being massacred, which must be happening, they must be refusing to tell the border guards where she's hiding—and at the same time he'd *want* her to stay concealed, not endanger herself. Would want her to survive. This second thought seems an even stronger argument for action. She raises her head through the mustard blooms. The shooting goes on. Up on the far bank of the ravine, where she came down last night, small figures are moving, flashes of purple—monks or nuns— and others with them. Pilgrims and travellers must be coming to the village. Maybe for some reason the guards are firing up at them instead? Now she sees that one of the travellers is firing *down* toward the village.

She runs back out through the bitter field on painful bare feet, her legs numb as if she has been sitting on them for hours. She runs past the sulphur spring, now deserted. Maybe it will help if she appears in the street—the white girl. Then she remembers she's dressed like a villager. But she has to help somehow. She has made this thing happen.

The shooting finally dies out. She approaches the back of the village. Her view of the ravine's far bank is blocked by houses. She runs up a cold, ammoniac alley of dirty whitewashed stone, scattering a clutch of chickens, who flee past her. She comes out into the village. In mid-street a villager lies on her back, others crouched around her. It's a woman in a pink blouse and black *chuba*—not Karma. Karma stands in the doorway of her house and she's barricading her peeking children inside. Under the shuttered window, Tenzin sits on the back of a Chinese guard whose face is squashed into the dirt, where Tenzin holds it firmly. A young guy and an old man sit on the guard's lower back and legs. A brown mastiff lies writhing nearby, trying to get up. Its hind legs seem stapled to the dirt. Villagers slowly emerge from the houses and look warily up and down the street.

At the head of the street, on the cairn-like landing of the bridge, her father is kneeling over another guard—she can see the blue cap on the man's head—doing chest compressions so violently it's like he's finishing off the loser in a street fight. Amaris and a nun stand behind him on the swaying bridge, gripping the hand ropes. Downstream on the other side, Tibetans kneel on the beach, drinking from the river.

Sophie stands trembling, trying to take things in.

Her father totters to his feet, slowly shaking his head. He still hasn't seen her. The boy who led her into the mustard field runs up to her—he has slipped past Karma's barricade—and takes her hand, and now Sophie leads him quickly up the street, past the knot of villagers helping the hurt woman to sit up, past the silent, flopping dog. At any other time, she would stop to help. Her father hobbles barefoot down the stairs of the landing and toward her, squinting in her direction. He stops. The medical kit falls from his hand. Behind him there's a brushcut nun in thick glasses, along with Amaris, whose face is a tight, frozen mask, like she's had a stroke, but now her mouth opens, she whips off her sunglasses and cries, "Lew—it's her!" Sophie tugs her hand free of the boy's grip and runs toward her father. There's blood on his sweater and his hanging hands. His green eyes are soft with tears, something she has never seen before, tear tracks scoring down through the grime on his dark face, which looks a dozen years older, and he's scolding her in a raw voice but she can't hear him because she's shrieking, "What the fuck were you doing, Papa, why did you *do* that, why did you leave me up there, I just, I just, I fucking *hate* it when—why do you just *forget* about me all the time!" And she slaps his cheek as he yells that he told her to stay up there, stay up there, it's goddamn lucky she's even . . . his voice collapses, then he repeats, "I *told* you, just *stay*!" She slaps at him again but pulls the blow short, then punches his chest with a loose-clumped fist while reaching for him with her other hand, trying to embrace him while he reaches for her, too, and she punches him again and tries to keep scolding and her voice crumples and she's left sobbing limply in his arms.

THREE

❖

WHAT LOVE REQUIRES

Think this way of the fugitive world:
A star at dawn, a bubble in a stream,
A flash of light in the summer clouds,
A phantom, a failing candle and a dream.
                    —from *The Diamond Sutra*

Whoever loves being alone must be either
a beast or a God.
                    —PLATO

In 1959, thousands of Tibetan monks forswore their pacifist vows to fight the People's Liberation Army, which had been occupying Tibet for almost a decade. One group of monks—the survivors of a PLA siege of their monastery, situated on a hilltop in western Tibet where an army base now stands—retreated down a dry streambed and hid in a cave where a Tantric monk of regional renown had once fasted and prayed. For some months the fugitives emerged by night to raid Chinese camps and ambush their patrols, as the physical-spiritual discipline they'd developed in the monastery was quickly, almost seamlessly, rededicated into habits of guerrilla stealth and aggression—a border that proved easy to cross. The monks were effective fighters. Yet in the evenings they still meditated, chanted and prayed.

In September 1960, with a PLA company closing in on their hideout, the surviving monks fled west down the streambed toward the River Khiong. Reaching it, they crossed one of the oldest rope bridges in Tibet into the village of Tyamtso, where they seemed a wondrous sight with their bullet bandoliers and shouldered rifles and bloodstains, in the form of darker spots of the monastic purple, showing on their over-robes. The villagers gave them food and blankets and directions and a guide so that they could flee and try to cross over the Kyatruk Pass into Nepal, from which they might continue to make raids.

Once the six monks and their guide and his yak had climbed out of the valley, the villagers gathered around the pier of the rope bridge. Two of the strongest men, carrying axes across their chests, filed up the steps with a slow, stately demeanour, like executioners mounting a dais in preparation for a royal beheading. Some grand and awful, necessary act. They stood on the pier with their heads bowed, seeming to bear on their shoulders the weight of history and collective fate. On receiving the signal, they swung their axes at the heavy ropes that generations of hands had held to cross the bridge into Tyamtso. At first they chopped hesitantly, as if hoping the order might still be stayed and the victim spared, but after a few strokes they set their jaws and attacked the bridge with a strange new fervour—great, walloping blows—severing the two ropes at the same instant. Groans and cries rose from the small crowd. Yet the bridge hadn't fallen: the footboards were not only slung from the hand ropes, they were also secured to the pier—not strongly enough that someone could still have crossed the bridge, but enough that the hanging arc still held. So now the men hacked through these final ligatures. A helix of tangled rope, footboards and prayer flags folded into the river and washed downstream a short way until stopping, still fastened to the pier on the other side, the footboards bobbing, red prayer flags rippling in the shallows like eddies of blood.

So the villagers kept the approaching Chinese from crossing the river and capturing the monks. Eventually, when PLA reinforcements arrived with inflatable boats and got across the Khiong into the valley, they burned the unharvested barley and millet and mustard fields, and a firing squad shot three village elders for helping the monks to escape.

In the winter of 1961, the villagers set about rebuilding their bridge, receiving, to their surprise, some help, along with emergency rice rations, from a PLA military unit stationed nearby.

When Tibetan resistance in the region ended and the Chinese unit finally withdrew, the villagers again festooned the hand ropes of the bridge with prayer flags.

September 22, 3:49 p.m.

THE ONE THING HE FEELS lucky about is that this mild, clear weather is holding. And that up here on the Lawson Wall, where he and Tashi are completing their setup of the fixed ropes, he's not at leisure to answer his radio. In fact, he has asked Kal not to patch through any calls until dusk, when they should be back down at Camp Three.

This system of ropes is now all but superfluous. The master plan was for Lawson to free-solo the wall (he still means to do it) by attacking a gorgeous, near-vertical stretch about fifty metres west of the fixed system, while Amaris, edging her way up the ropes, filmed his climb. Jake was to go ahead of her, Zephyr to trail her, to lend a hand if necessary. Tash and Mingma were also to be on the ropes, with Ming, the *sirdar*, going first.

But Lawson's solo wasn't meant to be a mere vanity video—a way of proving himself, yet again, to the world. He really does want to climb Kyatruk *purely*, the way Murloe must have, if he ever got this far, which frankly now seems impossible: the wall's striated limestone is flaky in patches, and in shaded spots it's slick with verglas, a thin, treacherous glazing of ice over rock. The conditions facing Murloe might have been different, but even on a perfect day this cliff could take a few rounds out of an expert, let alone an impetuous amateur like Murloe. Amateurs are always impetuous. Or else, terrified into timidity. Both extremes will kill you.

Now it's possible that only Tashi will use the fixed ropes, and only because Lawson will insist, so that Tashi can get some photos of Lawson's solo. Jake Kravchuk is a maybe, at best, after his fall at noon. It wasn't a terrible fall but at this altitude, with everyone visibly deteriorating, it might be enough to end his climb. He was insisting on helping attach the ropes, instead of resting at Camp Three as Lawson suggested, and then he asked if he could lead one pitch and Lawson foolishly agreed, gratified, maybe *nostalgic*, to see somebody on this expedition show some guts and will-fire. . . . Lawson's old man had served in World War Two, seeing action in Italy and "taking a wound" (Lawson now guesses it couldn't have been a very bad one, since he had no visible scars and nothing like a limp). When he'd brought his sons to Nelson in the early '80s, Joe Lawson had looked around and scratched his red, sun-freckled crown and told Clyde and Wade that something peculiar was happening to men. They were all going AWOL. Down some hole into history. But being an optimist, if a somewhat grouchy one, Joe Lawson felt that this unaccountable desertion presented an opportunity—a gap to be filled by the few. Real men on the hoof would soon be as hard to find as honest real estate brokers and he told his boys to remember that. Wade Lawson carved it on his heart. Taking commerce at university—he was the first Lawson to attend university—his confident talk, exotic ruggedness and post-weekend climbing tans made him stand out. He grew accustomed to deference. He failed to realize that his classmates' interest in him was basically anthropological. Mouthy little drinking pals he had to bodyguard, girlfriends who thought him too rough-edged (he now assures himself) to bring home to their folks, which he would have liked, frankly, since he himself had become, for lack of a tougher term, orphaned, the old man having rolled his Cherokee off a mining road on the way down from the hunt camp on Sheep Creek.

Everything has come out wrong. The soft men of the world have slipped their keyboard-pecking hands onto all the important levers and Lawson's own approach just seems to put folks off. He wonders what his old man would have made of some of the mild young guys who come to the Lawson Climbing Gym with waxed or lasered bodies—and now even shaved armpits.

Jake was thirty feet above, laboriously hammering in a piton, and Lawson, on his belay stance, didn't like the look of Jake's left foothold. A puny nub, black-iced with verglas. Jake seemed to have all his weight on the front-point and two toe-points of his crampon. Lawson spat out his gum and was opening his mouth to call up when Jake's cramponed boot slipped, spasmodically kicking. He was coming off. He made no cry. Lawson tucked into the wall while yelling down at Tashi, *"Below!"* As if plunging down an elevator shaft, Jake fell straight, feet first, past a chocked anchor lodged in a crack, then bounced to a stop two body lengths above Lawson, who was wrenched upward, scraped into the rock. Jake groaned something through his oxygen mask and lay dangling against the wall, not even reaching out to secure himself or place his feet.

"Jake? Don't trust the protection—get yourself on the wall. Jake!"

He responded in slow motion, gloves weakly pawing.

"And *try* to be more fucking *careful*, okay?" The words welled out of Lawson. A stint of hard breathing, then he managed to add, "Anyway, uh . . . that pin looks solid. Good job on that. You hurt?"

"Maybe." Jake had lifted his mask but his voice still seemed muffled. "Right knee's starting to throb. Couldn't feel it for a second there. Suit's torn over the knee. There's blood."

"Okay. Listen up. You're going to have to rappel down, get back to camp. Uh, Tash can go down with you . . . if you need the help."

"I can get down all right."

That's the stuff. "You sure?" Lawson was already reaching for his radio to call Shiva, at Camp Three, to come to the bottom of the wall and wait for Jake, walk him back to the camp and boil water and clean his knee and get a baggie of snow on it. "You're the doctor now, Shiv," he said into the handset, shaking his head in disgust. "Over."

That was two hours back. Now the job is done, Lawson driving two pitons into a perfect crack on the ledge above the wall. Finishing, his head awhirl as if cartoon birds and stars are orbiting it, he stares up at the peak of Kyatruk, some thousand vertical feet higher, a spume of snow jetstreaming off the tip. What a magnificent rock. *His* rock. From here it's a forty-five-degree slog up the summit pyramid to the top, though not a safe or easy slog, since the last approach is along an arête—a razor ridge of probably unstable, corniced snow, especially dangerous in winds or whiteout conditions.

He needs just one more day of good weather. Just one. In fact, a few lens-shaped clouds are sailing in from the north—quite a number, in fact—but he thinks maybe he can see more clear weather in the offing beyond them. Clear skies or blue clouds, it's hard to tell. (His mind suspends further speculation.) He stares at the ledge where he has just fixed the rope to the anchoring pitons and clipped in. There's something odd. He lifts his goggles and squints through the glare. Reminds himself to keep breathing. For some seconds he has been staring at an animal hide, partly snowed and frozen into the ledge.

Tashi calls up to him, "Lawson Sahib?"

"Just a minute!" And he whispers, "Jesus, look at this."

"Sahib! I think maybe we go down quite soon. All will be dust soon."

Dusk, he means. It's true. Lawson half turns and glances down the mountain. Tashi's bulbous goggles, far too large for his bony little face, peer up like those novelty-shop glasses with goofy eyeballs on the lenses.

"There's something up here," Lawson calls. "Like an animal. Dead."

"An animal, Sahib? A bird? Is it a *gorak* bird?"

"No, I mean . . . uhh. Like a goat hide . . . it's . . ." It's Murloe, obviously. That heavy sheepskin coat his Tibetan guards gave him. It must be. *I've found him.*

"I think, Sahib, maybe you need to be gassed a little?" Tashi looks up with his merry, gap-toothed leer, the wall plummeting away below him. "Me also, of course! We all need the gasses up here! I think tomorrow, for the final climb, we must all be—"

"*Shut* up, Tash," Lawson calls down as he gets his knee onto the ledge and crawls toward what looks like the sheepskin-coated back of a man—Albert Murloe—who has curled up, his face into the slope, exhausted or maybe injured after his heroic amateur climb. *The Murloe Wall,* Lawson hears himself think: its true, earned title. Unbelievable. The poor bastard did it.

Lawson removes his overmitt and reaches with his gloved hand, gingerly touching the bleached hide. It crumbles like the shell of a songbird's egg. Lawson recoils, shuddering, as spindrift snow sifts from the hole like sawdust from a dummy. A lump of something appears beneath, almost poking through the hole, and for some lurching pulse-beats Lawson sees it as a blackened, ossified heart. Then he realizes it's part of the mountain—just rock. He prods gently at the parchment sheepskin and more of the rock juts through. There's nothing under this skin but rock and snow. This is just Murloe's coat. As if he slept here under the sheepskin, then went on up the mountain without it, to save weight. Or discarded the coat in a hypothermic delirium and maybe *didn't* continue upward—maybe just turned and walked the other way, off the top of the Murloe Wall, by accident or to cut short his pain.

"How is the surprising animal up there, Sahib?" Tashi's high voice niggles at him and finally it's clear, maybe because Lawson feels so raw, stunned and oddly moved by his discovery: the young Sherpa is definitely taunting him. But . . . why this raw emotion? As usual, he recoils from looking deeper. He refocuses on his anger at Tashi Sherpa, the leering sidekick. Flippant court clown. One more thing Lawson could do without. Trembling, he snaps three photos with his digital camera—it emits worrisome brittle clicks—then checks his descender and gets ready to rappel down.

When they reach Camp Three, Shiva teeters out of the snow cave. Before Lawson can speak, Shiva says that Jake Kravchuk is now at rest. Lawson stares at the small man's puffy, puzzled face; he looks like he's both drunk and baffled to find himself so. "That is . . . he is exceedingly well, Sahib!" He has picked up the *sahib* thing from Tashi. There's more news from the embassy and Shiva pants it out like a messenger who has just run up the mountain: Dr. Book, Ms. McRae and the Tibetans have indeed escaped from the army base near Drongpa, perhaps with help from "forces of Tibetan terrorists" (Shiva can't clarify whether the embassy believes this to be true, or the Chinese believe it to be true, or simply claim it). He concludes by saying that several more people are now murdered, and the Book daughter is still loose.

To climb above 7,000 metres is to enter a dreamlike world where it takes stern focus to keep your reason belayed and safe. This bulletin might be the latest sequence in a prolonged anxiety dream. As if Lawson has only to focus his mind and slap himself awake and it will vaporize; as if Shiva has emerged like a genie out of the mountainside and might be dispelled by force of will.

He sends Shiva and Tash back into the cave, but Shiva remains for some moments, ominously wobbling, before at last going, leaving Lawson to his seething thoughts. The view into Nepal— layered ranges of giant peaks islanded by moats of mist filling the two-mile-deep valleys, sunset red—stuns his mind into momentary silence, the kind he usually experiences only on hard solos, when he seems attuned to some higher guidance, when past and future shear away to either side like the walls of Kyatruk's razor ridge—the living moment, a mere atom thick—and there's nothing but him and the rock.

Over ramen and energy bars, the last in their supply, Lawson talks over the climb, and his discovery, with the others. Jake wants to try summiting despite the gash in his swollen eggplant of a knee, which Lawson has crudely covered with gauze and surgical tape from the first-aid kit. Jake's determination is impressive. With bottled gas and the fixed ropes, he probably can make it, yet Lawson feels an uncharacteristic, almost maternal, caution. Gruffly he says, "We'll look at the knee at dawn and decide then." Then he adds, reflexively, "But you should be able to do it—hell, looks like Murloe got up the wall without ropes or even *equipment*!"

"Thanks for putting it that way," Jake says in a muted voice. His red eyes are beady and his long rodent's nose protrudes, sunburned purple, over the lip of the mummy bag. His blond, thinning hair looks electrified.

"I just meant . . ." Lawson stops. It's hardly worth trying to explain that he's not putting Jake down, he's simply amazed and gripped by his predecessor's achievement.

"You believe he did climb on, to the tip top, Sahib?" Tashi looks serious now.

"Possibly. It has to be considered. But on the whole, I really doubt it. The wall would have beat out of him whatever he had left. He'd have been eating snow by now. Freezing to death. Totally alone. I mean . . . Jesus, who's ever been more alone than that? And still, he, uhh . . ." His aching throat contracts and stops his words. His eyes smart. The same thing occurred after the still-birth—missing night after night of sleep, he grew prone to these embarrassing losses of control. To a softening of the will. Unhelpful sentimentality. Is *that* what's making him so uneasy about Shiv's condition? The porter is curled in his mummy bag, confused and lethargic, so Tashi has had to take over stirring the snow in the melting pot. It's probably simple altitude sickness but Lawson finds himself fretting about cerebral edema. He has applied Shiv's oxygen mask for him, like a passenger helping a child in one of those pre-flight videos. Shiv is going to have to go down very soon. But who the hell can take him? The surviving team has to push for the summit, tomorrow.

Lawson's radio bleeps again. He doesn't know what he can tell anyone that Kaljang or Shiva hasn't told them already, except one thing: what he just discovered up on the wall. Snow squeaking under his knees, Lawson crawls out into the polar night and unholsters the handset. A crimson moon floats up over the eastern deserts, where some surreal crisis is now playing out.

He stands up. "Come in, Kal."

"Wade Lawson, it's you at last! I have another call from the magazine *Rock and Ice*. Over."

"All right. Patch them through. Tell them I have some exciting news for them."

"Pardon? Oh—okay. And I think they have, uh, exciting

new things to be telling you also. They do want a comment from you . . ."

"Really?" He's shivering. "Is it about Book and Amaris?"

"It is! Over."

"Well, what the hell *is* it, Kal? Kal? Come in!"

"——not very certain, but the embassy has heard this also. There's a, uh, a video of Dr. Book. Maybe. It's not very clear——"

"What—the video? You've *seen* this video?"

Tashi's moonlit face appears at the mouth of the cave. Lawson turns away, tucks the handset closer to his mouth. The distant lights of Drongpa, pulsing.

"I mean, maybe just rumours," Kal says. "But they do think there's a video, of Sophie's father, telling the Chinese people he was a, what is the word, an agent, for Tibetan rebels. And maybe Sophie and Amaris also. They must have forced him to say so, of course. Over."

"But has anyone *seen* this thing?"

"No, nobody yet. Just rumours."

Relax, Lawson instructs himself, but his brain, starved for nutrients, oxygen and rest, clumsily swarms over the possibilities. He gazes toward Drongpa. Thought: Book was recently treating Tibetans in India. Was always greeting and thanking the Sherpas *in their own language, or something like it*. His daughter made a show of refusing to refer to the land across the border as China. *It was always Tibet*. Yes. But wait. Slow it down. High-altitude paranoia he knows all about—has confronted, point blank.

He makes himself breathe slower, his chest in a vise. One thing he knows: if the video exists, then Book's admission, forced or genuine, will be instant Hot News and further overshadow this expedition. *Unless Lawson can interest the media in something else*. Murloe was no Mallory, but all the same, this discovery of a trace of someone who climbed a remote, difficult peak in the freest style possible will definitely rivet the climbing media, and might intrigue the larger world, too.

"Patch it through now, Kal. And I'll talk to any others, till eight tonight. After that, you patch through *nada*, okay? We need to get a few hours rest. You can explain that I'll be . . . I'll be getting up at midnight"—he more or less overhears himself say this last phrase—"to help a sick porter down to Camp Two, where you'll be meeting me at, uhh, around two a.m. Which means you'll have to start up the mountain around eight—eight at the latest, okay? Sorry, Kal, but Shiv has to come down. You and him'll rest at Camp Two, then go down to base camp at dawn. Bring some Decadron up for him too. Over."

"What about you, Wade?"

Through Lawson's chest and belly, warmth is spreading like a pleasant hemorrhage. He's doing the right thing and he knows it. It's a human sensation, the least lonely thing he has felt since the few calm moments of connection after he and Amaris last had sex. Yet as the feeling spreads, it's not unlike nausea, or even the pain in frozen extremities as your blood and life flow back in. Meanwhile a corner of his mind applauds itself for this worthy new plan—which only *he* is still strong enough to carry out—and for thus risking the final success of the climb. (Maybe this will silence his detractors.) "I'll have to start back up again right away. We're going up the wall tomorrow. Then try to summit. We really can't wait any longer. And you can quote me on that."

"Roger, but first"—Kal clears his throat—"uh, I should mention the new weather report."

September 22, 4:05 p.m.

THE FUGITIVES SIT IN A CRAMMED, smoky, tavern-loud room, guzzling butter tea and *chang* and attacking bowls of peppery, oniony stew and stuffed dumplings as big as kaiser rolls and stacks of flatbread and a basket of apricots. Their cheeks burn with the heat of the room, the tea, the food and the amazing warmth of their welcome. If Amaris could film and screen this moment, no viewer back home could imagine the context—what had been happening just hours before this scene, what sort of emergencies might soon follow. (She tries not to think about it.) Sangye and a village woman are wounded, a Chinese guard is dead, another captured, and more guards and soldiers will surely be on their way here. But for now a feast has broken out, as if the fugitives, even Sophie and Book and Amaris, are long-lost family— emigrants who've returned to an ancestral village for a reunion.

Someone is weighing down Amaris's plate with two more of the soft, hot dumplings full of spicy meat. Book has just come in from seeing his patients—all of them stable, he says, Lhundup starting to improve with water, tea and food—and he plops down beside Sophie with a reprieved sigh, puts a hand on her nape and kneads the muscles there. Amaris, whose whole body is a pulled muscle, would love to be in Sophie's place. The girl doesn't resist but doesn't respond, punishing Book a little more, conserving her leverage, and he seems fine with that, his face and body loosening in that graphic, time-lapse transformation Amaris must try to capture when she gets back to her equipment: voilà, the other Lew, the one she likes and *buys*, draining a small glass of the sour barley *chang* and licking it from his lips, baring that rakish gap between his front teeth, accepting a fill-up and a dish of dumplings, and he's laughing now, weak with relief, responding to something Amaris herself has said—who knows what, she's too light-headed to remember—and he tips his head back, laughing, so for a moment she glimpses the tongue behind his teeth. Next he does a corny trick for Sonam and Lasya's daughter and the grubby village children, meshing his hands and sliding them apart, seeming to remove his index finger. The kids shriek with delight. He displays his hands now and the kids study them and gravely discuss the phenomenon and repeat a word that must mean "again!" Book does it again. His long-lashed eyes are brilliant, on the verge, she thinks, of tears, while Sophie, lovely in her Tibetan dress and braids, has a glow in her face, a slender, tempered smile, as if she's seen him do this for kids a zillion times but will humour him under the circumstances.

The monks and nuns eat with fantastic appetites, like clergy everywhere. Lasya has fallen asleep over her huge belly. Amaris hasn't felt so enmeshed in a social moment in years—so touched by the cheerful, sincere generosity of hosts, these people with their now-endangered village. It's as if they expect nothing better. She knows Buddhists advise living in the present, and maybe this is the secret: to live in crisis, in a primitive region, so you have no choice but to exist moment to moment and party every chance you get. Much of the clothing here is black, like in the town of exiles they passed through en route to base camp, as if the Tibetans are a scattered tribe in constant mourning, so used to it, in fact, that it deepens instead of dampens their celebrations. This *chang* is blurring Amaris. It's wonderful to lose yourself, to melt into the carnival heat of this living scene, without that fear you get at an urban party, where guests are all calculating status—the fear of dropping your ego and going naked, human, susceptible.

"You like the beer?" Book asks unclearly, his mouth full.

"Is that what this is?"

"You tried the ones," he says, "with ginger and garlic?"

"What—*beer?* Oh, you mean one of the *mumus*—"

"It's *momos*, actually," says Choden, and she and Amaris giggle.

"I just hope they can spare all this food," says Sophie, reaching for more.

"Oh, the harvest is going just fine, eat your hearts out!" says Choden.

With his hands and a few words of English and Tibetan, Book is trying to communicate with their gorgeous hosts, Tenzin, a rangy, earringed brigand of a man, and Karma, his pregnant wife. Book's Tibetan seems feeble—a few halting phrases that crack up his audience—though Amaris still has her suspicions about him and his involvements. For now, though, forget it. The facts will emerge, one way or another, and for now they have to work together, escape together. So let it go—no editing, critiquing or outing—for a change. (Her shortened fuse at high altitude has been deepening her worry that she's getting bitter too young. At film school her temper was a sort of gimmick, a facade of brittle charm: the small Asian woman with the big, husky voice who took no shit. Now it's a mode entrenched by time and habit and it's starting to push people away.)

Norbu is the only one who's resisting the party. He sits on a stool outside the open door, brushing flies from his face. She watched him and Tenzin argue, earlier—clearly Tenzin won't allow him into the house with his gun and Norbu won't enter without it. Sullen, glowering in at Choden, Book and Amaris, he cradles the small weapon out there as if shielding a new Christmas toy from other children. He's collected more ammunition from the dead guard and from the captured one, who's being held, along with Palden, in the bedroom where Sophie said she slept last night.

Amaris overhears Sophie say to Book, "*What?* No way. I can't believe you'd . . ."

"What?" Amaris jumps in, afraid of anything that might disrupt or dispel the moment's glow. Too late. In a low, throaty voice Book is saying that when they flee onward, he should probably stay here to care for his patients, along with Lasya, who could go into labour any time, and Palden, who can't be trusted to come with them any farther.

"But Lew," she says, "you said yourself the Chinese will be here by tomorrow at the latest—right?" (He nods.) "So, they'll just arrest you and separate you from your patients anyway—after what happened at the base. And the Chinese will *have* doctors with them now, don't you think?" He listens with his rumpled head tipped slightly, his gaze flicking between her mouth and her eyes. "I mean, you wanted us all to come this way, and okay, you were right, we did, we all came here together, and now—you can't just desert on us."

"I don't think *desert*'s the word," he says. "It's not like I'm going to—"

"I mean it's no time to play hero again."

"Hero's got nothing to do with it."

"The old man," Choden cuts in firmly, surprisingly, "the one sitting with the wounded now? He has done the Tibetan medicine all his life, Lewis. As for Lasya, she'll not agree to be separated from her family again. They mean to escape as a family."

"I understand that."

"Do you?" Sophie says.

"So you're needed with us, Lew—with Lasya." Amaris strains

for a note of diplomacy and it's hard for her, even now. "I mean, more of us might still get, you know. Hurt."

"You come with us," Sophie says, "or I stay and get captured with you."

Book turns his head to her. Sophie's deep-set eyes, shadowed as if with tear-smudged kohl, now make her seem older—a brave young widow at a funeral, serious, wise, unwavering. Amaris sees she's got him. Book looks down, then swings his gaze to Amaris and nods. "I guess you're right." But there's something more in his expression, a slight softening of the pupils, an easing of the tight muscles around his mouth. He's *relieved*—he really didn't want to stay behind and be parted from Sophie again.

"And as long as we're free," he adds, as if to nail the justification in his own mind, "I guess they can't really harm the village. Since they can't be sure of capturing us before we reach the border and report what's happening."

If I just had a camera, thinks Amaris, to document all this. It's the least I could do for these people.

"I better get back to them. Palden's always glad to see me." He stands and leans and kisses the part in Sophie's hair. She won't look up from the page where she's producing her latest image of the Dalai Lama for the villagers. Her pen, her hand, her face frozen over the page.

He's gone. The circle of sundark faces around them, still urging more food and drink on them, watching Sophie sketch, is thinning out. Norbu and the young monks have slipped away too. Amaris asks Choden what's happening and the nun speaks to Karma, then explains: people are going to the bridge. The lookouts may have seen something in the distance. "Alas, we have little more time here," she adds. "Karma Chophel says we should finish the food while her husband loads supplies, and leave with him in the hour.

He knows an old trail used by the resisters, years ago, and before them the smugglers. It goes back up to the border crossing at Mount Kyatruk, but on a route that's more snaky"—her accent makes it doubtful, the word might be *sneaky*—"and he thinks it best that we walk by night."

Some minutes later, as Amaris and the others, bellies filled, sit dozing over the *chang*, wild cries electroshock them awake. Amaris gasps and meets Sophie's gaze. Sophie leaps up and goes for the door and Amaris jumps to intercept her, grabbing the larger girl's arm—"Sophie, wait!"—and then pushing out ahead of her. Karma, head bowed stolidly, keeps stirring a brick of tea into a kettle. None of the others react, either, as if they've been expecting the cries and know what Amaris will see when she steps out the door with Sophie on her heels: villagers teeming like gall wasps over the bridge pier, the arc of an axe and the quick, darting glimmer of knives. For a moment she thinks the villagers are fighting hand to hand with soldiers, then it hits her.

At 5:30, as they set out, the monks and nuns touch brows with the villagers and murmur blessings and Sophie tearfully hugs them all goodbye, as if she has spent the whole summer here. Book and then Amaris embrace the villagers and she echoes the phrase Book keeps using, "*Thu-je che!*" The villagers, young and old, beam and giggle as she mangles it. "Thank you!" she keeps adding, sure they must understand. But Karma, last in line, is suddenly impatient. She lifts her brows, juts her chin toward the mountains and speaks curtly. Time to go now. Hurry now.

In the sloping light they file out over the stubble fields and start up the far wall of the valley. They're still climbing when they hear the soldiers arrive—a dozen ATVs snarling down the dry wash across the river and pulling up on the beach, where a tideline of prayer flags lie strewn. Men, tiny at this distance, dismount and seem to gape up at the white pier or down at the river, where the remains of the severed bridge lie tangled, twitching in the shallows like the bones of some huge slaughtered thing.

They hike over a cracked gravel plateau where tumbleweeds roll toward and past them. Though they've gained Sophie, Tenzin and a large black yak panniered with supplies, the group is smaller, having lost Sangye, Lhundup, Palden and Pema. So besides the additions, the group now consists of Choden, Book, Amaris, Norbu, the nun Dolma, the three young monks, the widow Dechen, and Sonam, Lasya and Diki—fourteen people and a yak.

It's been days since they've seen more than wisps of cloud in these desert skies or over the mountains, but now, above Kyatruk, maybe thirty kilometres to the west, thick shoals of cumulus are massing. The sun has set behind the mountains, but its light still shines on the towering clouds, changing them by degrees from golden to resin to henna-red. Kyatruk's peak-pyramid darkens to a silhouette. Amaris wonders if Wade might be up near the peak right now; if so, he'd better be on his way down. Still, she would feel safer up there, on his controlled, artificial adventure, than she does down here as a refugee.

Stars appear and keep appearing, thousands of them, and for another hour they droop along over the dirt or scrunch across gravel, gradually uphill. It doesn't feel gradual. The food and drink and the villagers' warmth have helped Amaris recoup some strength and solidity, but she's coming apart again. Up ahead, the Tibetan family walks, the squat child chugging along between her parents, arms splayed out to hold their hands. Between them and Amaris, Book and Sophie walk side by side, hands clasped. They're like a smaller Tibetan family—he in an earflap cap, sheepskin coat and ornamental-looking black felt boots (gifts from the villagers, who didn't appear to have much to spare), Sophie with her hoodie and parka over the Tibetan dress and a turquoise necklace—another gift. Amaris still wears polypropylene layers and her state-of-the-art parka and toque, the lone remaining North American, a racial irony that should be more amusing, but in these clothes, and seeing Book and his daughter paired off, she just feels excluded—*more* alone now, as if the past few hours of connection were a cruel tease. Did her parents, refugees in their last hours, ever feel this alone, tired, scared? As usual, she bolts the crawl-space door on further speculation.

Tenzin, their new guide or leader, leaves his yak at the head of the line and strides back among the others in his olive gumboots, a cigarette in his mouth. He hands around a leather skin of water and jabs a long finger ahead toward the mountains, speaking in a lispy, excited tenor that doesn't fit his sexy outlaw's face. He asks Sonam something, then hefts Diki onto his shoulders and lopes back toward the head of the line and transfers the child onto the yak's back. The animal halts, peers over its shoulder through thick sheepdog bangs, showing the prayer flags and white scarves on its horns. Tenzin ropes the child on by the waist and claps the yak's woolly rump. Sonam and Lasya walk on either side, each reaching up to take one of Diki's hands, a picture from a folk tale or Bible story.

Beside Amaris, Choden appears, padding silently in her red sneakers. "Are you all right?" she asks in that soft, disorienting accent.

"I think it's true what they say—you get used to anything."

"You're feeling a tad stronger, then?"

"No, I mean it feels normal to feel tired and scared shitless. Sorry, I shouldn't have said that."

Choden's eyes, just visible through starlit lenses, now vanish as they do when she smiles. "Oh, I think it's an interesting way of putting it."

"No, I mean because you're . . . you know."

"My English tutor, Jim Garrity, he'd say 'shite'. It isn't a bad word here. Just part of the life, really."

They're almost whispering, Amaris muting her voice not only because they're on the run but also because the starry sky, this stupendous special effect, imposes quiet.

She asks, "Will Palden be all right back there?"

"Sure he will. Until the Chinese come. Tenzin Lodi is quite respected in the village—his father was a famous resister—and he told the others not to hurt him. Now, the Chinese may be harder on Palden because of what happened up at the jail. Then again, they do love having Tibetans in the PLA, and they mayn't want to lose him. By the way—we know your descent is Han, and you ought to be a little wary of Norbu."

"Shouldn't we *all* be?"

"He seems to mistrust you."

"One day I'm spying for the Dalai Lama," she says, "next day for China." After a pause, she pushes on, quietly, "You know about Lew's confession yet?"

"Sure—he explained when I was helping with the wounded. It was a good idea of his, I think, but then Norbu turned to violence."

"So, you're sure there's nothing in it?"

"In violence, you mean?"

"No, in his . . . in what he, uh . . . it doesn't matter for now."

"His *confession?* I doubt so. The man's eyes don't have a lying look, do they? Oh, and about Norbu—please don't take it to mind. He's young, just twenty."

"God, I didn't think he was that . . . grown-up."

"Oh, I don't think so either," the nun says, almost sharply. "There aren't so many grown-ups anywhere, when you think of it."

"Outside the nunnery, you mean," Amaris says with a hint of her old edge. "Among the unenlightened, like me."

"No, I do mean anywhere."

Ahead at the base of the Himalayas there's a mirage, a small copy of the mountains, slopes and rifts and peaks starlit ghostly white like a dim hologram floating far below the original. At first she thinks it's a range of snowdrifts, then realizes, dunes. She's talking again, not looking at Choden but at the far dunes and, silhouetted against them, the small child swaying up on the yak's back. "My parents were refugees too. For a few days. In Vietnam, after Saigon fell. I was adopted by a family in Canada, as a baby."

"Ah. You never knew those first parents?"

"Nobody knew anything about them, at first. My adoptive parents thought I was the child of peasants, probably from a bombed village. Napalmed. Or that's the story they settled on. That's how it happens—first you're probably the child of bombed peasants, then the probably gets dropped and everyone forgets. The village got promoted to a heroic Vietcong hideout attacked by the marines—Lieutenant Calley types. Then some information leaked out. Some people got out of Vietnam in the mid-eighties. I was about twelve then. Turns out my parents had been ethnic Chinese, which was no big deal, no issue at all, but they'd also been involved with the South Vietnam military. Wasn't clear how, but I guess it didn't involve uniforms. Maybe they were in propaganda. Or they were agents of some kind. Interrogators, even. I hope not. Maybe they were just liaisons, with the Americans. It's not important now. I really don't care anymore, and I'm not flying to Vietnam like some of my friends *still* urge me, to pick up my parents' scent and make a, a self-involved documentary . . . award-winning film . . . daughter returns to find her dead parents, her lost roots, herself, whatever."

She pauses for air, light-headed, the plateau slowly climbing. It's like trying to talk while pushing yourself on the treadmill. Breath blossoms around her.

"But I wonder now. I mean, what was it like for them? Just for the time it took till the end. We were with a big group, I guess, in a motorcade of Jeeps, cars and taxis. It would have been really hot. The road was muddy, it got jammed up with bombed trucks and cars, and we got stuck. Okay—probably I wasn't there with them. I mean, I just *wasn't*. The kids had all been sent ahead, a few hours or a day ahead, and they, the kids, they made it out to the coast. Big orange school bus full of orphans-to-be, little faces pressed to the windows—that's how I used to picture it. But in my mind, I wasn't on that bus. I saw myself with my *parents*, in a stretch limo—a limousine—with a rosewood bar, and I'm older, not a baby and there's root beer and peanuts for me, and comic books, and a chauffeur in an officer's cap. Beats the real story, or what's left of it—my parents and the others trying to catch up and the road's totally blocked. All of them looking at their watches, yelling out windows, trying to ram their way through. Knowing we're up the road and we'll be going aboard—we—I see a little sister beside me too—and sailing out, any time."

Amaris snorts softly, as if in mild disdain.

"Your kids slipping away and you're gridlocked while MiGs strafe the road."

The stars are closer up here, by three or four kilometres, but they seem light years closer, the entire sky a Milky Way.

"Sorry—God—I hate when this happens."

"You mean when you tell about your . . ."

"It's not because of *them*—it's me—I just feel so weak. I mean, no one gets worked up like this except for themselves, really. That's what it comes down to."

"But you seem quite calm, Amaris. It *is* a sad story."

"You're really nice," she says. Then, after a few seconds: "Phil and Naomi—my adoptive parents?—I don't think they ever quite forgave me for being the spawn of the dark side. Allies of the imperialists. It *embarrassed* them, some way they couldn't admit to. Me, I don't take sides now. I couldn't care less. In this corner, wearing black pyjamas, a mob of homicidal idealists . . . in this corner, a puppet regime of crooks, pushers, profiteers. It's all bullshit—politics, opinions. Phil and Naomi started watching me, the bad seed, for any sign of reactionary instincts. Any break from the party line. When I was, like, *twelve*. They didn't even notice they were doing it, these people who thought they were so enlightened, so rational! What's funnier is the profs I dated, the wine and cheese radicals who got all ethically stressed when they heard about my pedigree. Because that's when I used to 'share my story,' as they say. Just like you're supposed to."

The white dunes are nearing. Choden seems a bit lost, nodding vaguely, her dimpled smile taped on. Amaris says nothing of her ex-fiancé, with his love of agitprop and political montage, who kept doubling back to her story, sure she needed to return to Vietnam, to "work out the karma" of her loss and of her parents' presumably evil careers. How she broke it off two days before the wedding. Hardest thing she'd ever done, till then. But afterwards it got easier to do stuff the community recoiled from and she came to wear her ostracism like a badge.

No. (Is something a lie if you don't say it out loud? Say it to yourself, at least.) She'd delivered herself to him unconditionally, made a hostage of her whole being, surrendered her irony and her toughness and her cutting, unhappy smile, hoarding nothing in reserve, so when the engagement died she seemed to lose her better self along with Emil; she was orphaned, as if for the first time. Drunkenly, piously in love, she'd told herself that marriage would be her new nation and she'd swear out citizenship for life and raise her hand to recite the oath and learn the anthem by heart so she could sing it way better than the lazy, longtime citizens who always fudged the words and hardly even moved their lips. She would put her hand over her heart and *sing*. Then abruptly it all collapsed—there was an earlier love he'd thought he was over and now he realized, of course, he was not—so that he, in the end, broke it off as much as she did.

No. For once in your life, be honest about love.

He, Emil, broke it off, against her pathetic pleas, and their shared little myth of a country dissolved and vanished from the map of her future, and it's unbearable, now, to recall such naive faith. That you can belong to any country but the private one you create for yourself.

Cold consolation: she'd vowed to out-achieve him and she has.

As they walk, Choden's bare hand finds Amaris's gloved one and after a moment seems to transmit warmth right through the fabric. It does help. It helps a lot. They're side by side but it's as if the nun is ahead and guiding, half towing her up the grade of this dead plain toward the base of those dunes, now silvered by a rising moon. She's glad the two of them are at the back of the line. This generous connection aches like loss.

Book and Sophie are nearing the top of the steep range of dunes, feet sliding back with each step almost as far as the step has gained, when he hears faintly, over the shunt of his pulse and his redlining breaths, a choppy drone. The Tibetans in their ripped layers and cheap sneakers are stopping, turning to look back, their faces lit up. Book and Sophie turn too. The moon is high and its light makes a rutted Martian plain of the hours of hardpan they've just crossed, while in the skies over Tyamtso a smaller, white-hot light descends like a landing module. As it disappears now, swallowed by the distant valley, the stuttering of the rotor grows louder, amplified by the valley's bowl. A brilliant dome of light glows in the sky above it, like a stadium lit up for a night game.

One by one, the fugitives turn their faces back toward the slope and struggle on.

Descending the long backslope they enter another world, a vast, chiaroscuro desert of rolling dunes white as snowdrifts in the moonlight. It's cold enough for snow, too, though Book is roasting in his sheepskin coat, which he peels back off his torso so it droops from the waist sash in the style of Tenzin, Sonam and Lasya. The yak plods stolidly with the child on its back, her parents beside it. Book catches up and asks Lasya how she feels— Choden translating—and then notices, half-hidden among the panniers, a saddle scabbard with the stock of a rifle showing. He shakes his head. In Tyamtso, Norbu urged Tenzin, Sonam, Book and then, in desperation, the monks to carry Sangye's machine-gun, or one or more of the captured guns; the kindly-faced Sonam unhappily agreed, but Tenzin spoke in a low, forceful voice to Norbu and the extra guns were left behind, to be turned over, along with Palden and the captured guard, to the Chinese. Good decision, Book felt. Better to show the Chinese—and before long the world—that the refugees were little threat. Though Norbu has clung to his own gun, and now Tenzin has brought a rifle.

Choden tells him that Lasya is feeling quite strong and there's still no cramping.

His last moments with the wounded in Tyamtso were rushed—he thought the noise of the villagers destroying their bridge was the sound of fighting, till Choden came in to explain. Lhundup's diastolic reading was up to 64, almost normal, and there was strength in his grip as he grabbed Book's sleeve and urged him, in Choden's words, to flee with the others at once. The old village doctor had already changed the dressings over Pema's wounds and fractures with foxed gauze and weakly adhesive surgical tape that might date back to the time of the Tibetan resistance. The result looked messy, far from antiseptic, and Book redid it under the pretext of checking for more lead and bone fragments. He left the nun four codeine tablets and careful instructions. The village woman, shot through her stout thigh with no vascular or bone damage, had already checked herself out of this ad hoc ward—the front room of Karma's parents' house—and Sangye was sitting up on his cot, breathing shallowly, wincing with each sip as he drank rancid butter tea. A bullet had cracked one rib and deflected clear; a second bullet had pierced him just under the left clavicle, missing the lung but grazing the bone and likely causing a hairline fracture, Book couldn't be certain without an x-ray. He left the kid a half-course of Clindamycin—almost all that remained—and the last of the codeine and more instructions, which Choden relayed to the old Tibetan. The Chinese doctors would have to complete the course of drugs and they would act professionally, Book felt sure—and not only because the authorities would now want to minimize Tibetan losses, with the world tuning in. Finally Norbu twitched into the room and Book raised his hand, then signalled firmly *Leave the weapon out there.* The kid growled something but complied and came back in and put his forehead to

Sangye's in the traditional Tibetan greeting or goodbye, while their hands described some kind of gang salute and held a long fist tap.

Another hour and old Dechen replaces Diki on the yak. While Book and Choden confer again with Lasya, Sophie takes Diki's hand and the child peers up and gabbles at her in her Alvin and the Chipmunks voice. Sophie, as if understanding, nods down with a fondly amused look on her beautiful face, which Book can actually *see* for a change, her hair back in braids and the hood of her sweatshirt off. For a moment he glimpses his daughter as a young mother and his heart seizes. She always was compulsively maternal. As a small child, if no doll was at hand, she would nurture almost anything. Once he found her in the garage, humming lullabies to a dirty oil filter he'd just removed from Nika's Opel.

He takes her free, mittened hand.

"I think Diki's asking me when we're going to stop," she says, and he guesses she herself wants to know when, but doesn't want to seem weak by asking.

"I'm not sure, love. Tenzin has a place in mind. Maybe a couple more hours. The villagers, they'll send the soldiers the wrong way, but we've got to keep moving."

Her hand, at first grudging, gets a better hold.

"Papa, your patients back there—they'll be okay, right? Without you?"

"I'm pretty sure of it."

He might not be so confident in other circumstances, but these are Tibetans and something toughens them. It's their expectations, or lack of them, he believes. Unfortunately he has almost exhausted his antibiotics and codeine; out here, in an emergency, there won't be enough left for any of the fugitives, including Sophana.

"I still feel sick about that dog," she says.

He nods slowly, looks straight ahead. "I know."

"So . . . did it die? I looked for it before we left . . ."

"A bullet severed its spine, love. I'm sorry."

"And that killed it?"

"Not directly, but it's dead now. Out of its pain."

"But if its spine was cut, there wouldn't *be* any pain, right?"

The kid's ultrasound is always on, full scan.

"It was shot in the lungs, too," he says.

No response. In this sand, not even a sound of footfalls. He feels certain she's working things through and will keep pressing him, asking how it actually died, who actually finished it off. The dog was a bitch, maybe eight or nine. Her fawn pelt was threadbare, foam-flecked purple lips drawn back from a panting yellow smile, bloodshot sclera exposed as she rolled a panicky eye toward Book. She'd had several litters by the look of her. Book's first interest in medicine was veterinary, on his parents' farm, where from the age of ten he would help care for the sick animals—and would have to finish them off (his father insisted) when they couldn't be helped. *The other half of caring for them*, his father would say.

"Do you ever wonder if she'll take you back now, after this?"

"What—your mother?"

"Of *course* my mother," she shoots back with that rhetorical Greek syntax she unconsciously defaults to in argument.

"You know she's not like that," he says. "If she makes up her mind, there's no unmaking it."

"But you have to keep trying, Papa! Or start again—especially after this."

He has known the girl feels this way, deeply, and yet she has never said so, not once. Still, this talk had to happen sooner or later. He looks around to make sure Amaris and Choden aren't close enough to overhear. They are, though. He says, under his breath, "Sophie—love—listen. Your mother has always been the one for me, okay? But I can't convince her of that. Or, no—she knows it—it's just that it's beside the point now."

"*Beside* the point?"

"I was gone too often. And at times when she really needed me there. You know that, Sophie—I mean, if anyone understands, I know it's you."

"But she even said—she told me she told you—it didn't have to *be* like this, but you wouldn't meet the conditions! After the police came we were talking about it and she told me and she didn't mean to but she did."

Diki watches them with a curious, concerned frown, like a child hearing her parents fight for the first time.

"We need to keep our strength up, love. They'll be coming after us tomorrow. Maybe they won't wait that long. I need to get you home. We'll talk about this later."

"For fuck's sake, there might not *be* a later!"

"Don't talk that way!"

She rips her hand free. "We're being chased through a desert by, like, helicopter gunships and soldiers who'll be shooting to kill and you're worried about my *language*?"

"I don't care about your language! I mean don't talk nonsense. There'll *be* a later." As if she were still young enough to lie to, he adds, "And there's no way they're going to be shooting to kill." She rolls her eyes at him, as if locked in a trivial, routine dispute back home—he's a bully for not letting her stay out an extra hour with friends. For her, everything has an ultimacy, so when things really do go ultimate, like now, she has no higher gear of expression to shift to. And yet she is right. There might not be a later.

He says, "Your mother told me I had to stop leaving, period. No more crisis postings overseas. She wanted me to work in admin, or with patients in the city if I still had to do outreach work. Street health clinics. Emerg, in Scarborough, with all the gang shootings. She said there's a refugee crisis at home—in the Corridor, in the housing projects—and she was *right*, damn it, I knew she was, but I couldn't do it, I couldn't stop leaving right then. It was just when—"

"You blew a chance to bring us back together because you wanted to keep going over*seas?*"

"It was just after the tsunami. I'd promised her, but they were frantic for doctors on Bangkaru, paramedics, nurse pracs, anyone. They had nobody. And if I hadn't gone right then, I'd still be wondering how many fewer might have died. Maybe none, maybe dozens, or more—I don't know. Family's important, Sophie, but it's not everything. It can't be. And that choice—it was murder, the worst. She shouldn't have done it. It's the one thing about her, damn it, all the tidy deadlines, the firm agendas, the conditions . . . I shouldn't be saying this."

"She says you've done enough for the world. She respects you for it but she thinks it's, like, someone else's shift now—you should be back with us."

"With *us?* What do you mean—has she—you mean she's—"

"Before it kills you."

"You mean with *all* of you?" Book's heart seems to fill, dilating warmly, the way a collapsed lung might feel being reinflated. "She says this *now?* No . . . she must mean . . ."

"I don't know! I don't know—I guess she means just, like, back in town, to see Pavvy and me every week?—but maybe she's going to feel different now."

He nods and tries to look encouraged, to look encouraging, to *feel* it. Whatever it takes to get them both through this. Anyway, it is time to go back, to remain close for a while, if not to go actually, improbably, home. They've become one of those centrifugal modern families: Sophie in her room with her cellphone, texting back and forth with her boyfriend about crazy, half-baked holdups, Nika charting stats in her lab, Pavlos the angry little soccer star booting goal after goal, alone on a field, Yiayia in her black weeds watching Oprah, Book in a blood-spattered field tent eight time zones away.

She asks him more about his video "confession" and he's relieved that she's on another scent, maybe picturing her mother and brother and grimly muttering *yiayia* viewing the clip as it plays and replays on the various networks. Ruefully she smiles— "She'll be wondering how we turned into such a bunch of criminals"—and he shams a chuckle to sustain the new course of her mood. The thought of his own brief fame, or shame, or however it's playing out at home, doesn't excite or trouble him. From up here on the roof of the world, with the blood of the dead and the wounded in his hair and under his nails, that other place seems even more inscrutably foreign and virtual.

An hour deeper into the small hours. The waning moon has passed overhead and leads the party westward. Dechen rides sidesaddle on the yak, her glowing pipe augmenting a witch's profile: hooked nose, crumpled mouth, pointy chin. Norbu hunches against the cold with his parka hood up over his baseball cap, machinegun hidden on the far side of him. His jeans keep getting baggier, droopier. The kid has left his best friend and his uncle behind, and Choden isn't sure but she thinks his parents must both be dead—so she has told Book, adding, "Alas, Lewis—Lhasa is a city of such things." (With Palden for the last time, shining the penlight into his eyes, Book asked if his family would be wondering about him, and Palden said he had a big family but they never saw or talked to him anymore—never, since he'd enrolled in the

PLA. In a glum, almost sulky monotone, as if hurt now at being left behind, he added, "Be seeing you soon, I hope, Lewis.")

They come over a gap between high dunes. Below them, half filled with sand, there's a sprawl of roofless ruins, and just past them the sands end and another stretch of moonlit hardpan rises toward a ridge of bare, snowless peaks and the higher Himalayas beyond. Though Kyatruk is the highest peak in the area, from here it's hidden. A paradox of perspective: how the high peaks you see from fifty miles away vanish behind the lower ones as you near, so getting a view of a mountain is like getting a clear vision of a life—you have to pull away from it before its shape starts to emerge from behind all the concealing layers.

The ruins look ancient, as if a forgotten city has been all but swallowed by the dunes. Choden kneels in the sand in front of a truncated wall and studies the patchy remnants of a mural lit up by the moon. The lenses of her glasses are an inch from the wall. These ruins, she explains, were once a monastery, likely destroyed during the resistance, in '59 or a year or two later. "It's very fine work!" she says, "part of a very large painting." Her tone is buoyant, as if the rest of the mural is safely buried and will soon be uncovered and restored, not abandoned to the bleaching sun and the sandblasting winds. Amaris crouches next to her and makes out two doughy elephants wrestling, human figures riding a sturgeon-like fish across a lake, a couple embracing in a pagoda. The dense detail is wonderful, both whimsical and baroque; she thinks of Hieronymus Bosch and then, oddly, Peter Greenaway.

The remains of two walls meet at right angles to break the cold wind breathing down out of the mountains and in that corner Tenzin, a cigarette in his lips, hitches the yak by its nose ring. An exhaust of white breath chuffs from its muzzle as Tenzin unloads it. While Choden and Book sit with Lasya—Book murmuring questions as he palpates her huge, taut, moon-pale belly, she gnawing her lip between answers—Amaris, Sophie, Sonam and the monks help Tenzin to roof in a shelter, using a ragged square of tough canvas that a yacht-sized sail could be cut out of. With stones pulled from the rotten mortar, they weigh down two sides of the canvas sheet along the top of the right-angled walls. Tenzin props a stretcher pole in the sand to hold up the sheet's fourth, unsupported corner. Near the pole, just under cover of the sheet, he starts a small fire with twigs he takes out of the panniers, some clear liquid from a small bottle, and dry loaves of yak dung.

Choden tells Sophie, "The fire is really just for the tea. Really our heater is Zapa." She nods toward the back of the shelter, where the yak stoically munches hay from a small mound that Tenzin has set out. Its withers are just below the level of the sagging canvas; its decorated horns would poke into it if its head weren't lowered. Choden urges Amaris and Sophie to find a spot in the sand close to Zapa, for warmth, but the big animal scares them. What if it panics in the night and stampedes? Or when it pees, shits? Choden seems tickled by their fears and instantly imparts them to the other fugitives, who guffaw in chorus, as if she has just nailed a killer punchline. Sonam, Lasya and Diki soon establish themselves in the gloom almost beneath the yak's belly and now the other Tibetans settle in around them. Amaris, Sophie, Book and Choden find spots closer to the fire, while Norbu chainsmokes and paces back and forth in front of the shelter, his gait stiff and twitchy, as if he's on crystal meth.

"Sleep now," Choden tells them, and Amaris sees Book break from what he's doing—shining the penlight into his messy doctor's bag, searching—and stare up at Choden with a zoned, blank look, then shake himself, run a hand through his mussed hair, like a night driver trying to stay awake. "Right—thanks," he rasps.

"Please," says Choden. "I'll be sure to wake you all when the tea is ready."

"I'm okay," Amaris lies—though a moment later she's stretching out beside Sophie, who's already curled in a ball, motionless: baby fat still on her sunburnt cheeks, those plump, chapped, open lips. Soft snoring. Lew is such a fool to risk losing her for the sake of his work, *any* work. Amaris has never wanted kids, not since the abortion that followed her shattered engagement, but now she sees how you can fall hard for them, feel yourself called to their care.

Choden goes to help Tenzin and Dechen. Over the small fire they lean whispering, Choden now with her glasses off, the three faces ambered like archetypes, maiden, hunter, crone. This is not the twenty-first century. This is not even the first century. Smells of methane and clover honey waft from the flames and the smoke collects until a gust of wind steals in from the back, under the canvas, and clears the air.

"Your stomach okay?" Book whispers to Amaris, startling her back to awareness. Now that he mentions it, there is a discomfort, hard to isolate among all her pains—a cramping, low down, though it's too early for her period, thank God.

She sits up. "I'm not sure, why?"

"Mine's a bit off. Always a risk, eating and drinking in a village."

"I don't know if anything ever tasted that good before," she says.

"I know," he says with sudden feeling.

"Those apricots!"

"And that *chang*." He extracts a vial of pills from his kit, shining the penlight on the label and holding it back from his face. He asks, "What's your favourite film?"

The question usually bores her—everyone wants to know what the filmmaker's favourite film is—but she has never been happier to answer: "Weirdly, it's this old Soviet-era documentary, sort of, called *I Am Cuba*."

"'Weirdly' why? It's a great film."

"You've *seen* it?"

"Twice, in Sarajevo."

"No way."

"An MSF fieldworker had a copy there."

"'Weirdly' because it's Soviet agit-prop kitsch—not exactly my staple diet. But it's a gorgeous, gorgeous thing. All that polarized black and white, those long tracking shots . . ."

"You notice the cartoonish *Yanqui* in sunglasses," he says, "in the bar scene?"

"Sure, I've seen the film a dozen times."

"It's Dr. Strangelove. Right down to the shades and the grin." As Amaris pictures the character, Book adds, "That's where Kubrick got him, I'm sure of it"—and he too seems relieved to be talking culture, forgetting nature, the elements around them, his own creaturely fears. She's grateful, sensing he has convened the moment for just this reason.

"Maybe you're right," she says. "Yeah."

"I'd take long odds."

"And Kubrick would have loved *I Am Cuba*," she says. "Those tracking shots, the flow, the linked stories. Wait a minute—didn't they both come out in '64?"

"But couldn't Kubrick have seen the film while making

Strangelove? I heard he kept improvising as he went along, changing characters."

"Hmm, maybe, yeah. I'll have to see it again, both films, when I get, you know. When we get home to the city. Lew, by the way, full disclosure—I overheard a lot of your talk with Sophie. I hope—I mean—I couldn't help overhearing—"

"Voices carry out here."

"—and it's not my business, but I think they're right. You need to go home."

"Including your voice," he says. "Sorry if I shouldn't have heard your own story."

For a moment she's quiet, then says, "I'm okay with that. I guess neither of us are any good at minding our own business, eh?"

He looks down, smiling, then brings a pill of some kind to his mouth and slips it under his tongue, to absorb the medicine faster, she guesses.

"Lew—what are you doing out here, really? I mean, okay, I realize now you're not some mole for the Dalai Lama, but . . . most of the humanitarian types I've known have either been fakes or else trying to compensate for some, uh, some kind of misconduct. You know, moral crusaders who've been on the take, charity fundraisers having serial affairs, whatever. I'm not saying—I mean, mostly you seem really different, but . . ."

The pill under his tongue makes him mumble and speak with text-message brevity: "Wish I could say I've turned down bribes, but no one's offered. As for affairs, no. I loved Nika. Anyway, she'd see through a lie, if I tried, and there'd be no . . . there'd have been no court of appeal. To her, life—it's like that film, all black and white, polarized—to a fault. It's her one real fault."

"I wasn't prying, you know, about . . ."

"You were prying and I'm grateful. Nice to talk about that other life, even so."

"I just sense you'd rather be in, you know, Monaco or Vegas, making a living at the poker tables, not doing crisis postings in Bosnia."

"If you can't bluff your wife about an affair, you'll never make a dime in Vegas."

"Ha, that's a point."

With sudden, untypical shyness—his eyes dodging hers almost bashfully—he says in that drunk's mumble, "Maybe I just really care for people. I mean, I feel *linked* to them, all of them, I always did, and if there's a way I can help them . . ."

"Sure, okay, but . . ."

"Except that's a lie, you're right." He grimaces, gulping down the pill, as if tired of whispering around it. "You're right, in a violent crisis, it's hate as much as love."

"I wasn't thinking so much of *hate*."

"But you should. I hate them, the ones who make these messes. Death squads, governments, fanatical mobs, multinationals. I try to screw them up by getting in their way, depriving them of their body count, bearing witness—all that. Which is why folks like her"—he tilts his head back toward the fire—"they blow me away. The ones who have the best reasons in the world to hate, sometimes just don't. That's as good as a miracle gets."

"Lew, why did you take that pill? Is it—"

"It's just Lomotil, for my gut."

"For a second you looked so angry, I thought, you know. Your heart."

His adamant gaze softens—another quicksilver shift. He looks almost grateful; weary. "Thanks, no, it's Lasya, her pains are starting, pre-labour, at least—can't be worrying about my gut. Tell me if you need one, okay?" He says this gently, as if sensing what she doesn't want him to know: that she'd be embarrassed now to ask him for a pill like that.

Over the wall of dunes, dawn transfuses the icy sky with tropical reds and pinks. Choden stirs a few sleepers awake for tea and food. Book rests his hand on Sophie's shoulder, tells Choden the girl should sleep on. From someone's stomach, a seismic rumble that might be funny at any other time; the Tibetans find it funny anyway and their laughter ripples through the shelter.

Amaris drains her mug and eats a rolled ball of mushy, nutty flour that Choden calls *tsampa*, then curls up in the sand. She spoons with Sophie, pushing her face into the warm, fleecy back of Sophie's hood. The sleeping girl presses back against her for warmth and Amaris slings an arm over her. No fighting this exhaustion. From the border of consciousness, too far gone to return, she registers a faint mosquito whine—maybe a spotter plane, high above them—but this sand is quicksand and she's sinking, nameless.

Pain hauls her awake, tugging and griping. A saffron light glows down through the canvas that ripples and flaps in the wind. Sophie groaning softly beside her. Lew on Amaris's other side, close enough to warm her. She wonders if he knows it. He smells like smoke and some pungent spice, maybe fenugreek. She would like nothing better than to remain here, snugly enveloped, but she has to sit up, clutching her stomach, squinting urgently out into the overexposing glare of sun on sand. Tenzin, with his long rifle, lies just under the lip of the nearest dune, peering over the top, his back turned to the shelter, the hood up on his sheepskin coat. She wriggles free of Sophie and Lew, stands, hobbles quickly outside.

It's like her muscles have been eaten by necrosis. She passes sections of broken wall but wants to get farther away. Hopes the handsome Tenzin won't turn and see her down here and really how can she care about such things now? Hurries through the remains of a wood frame doorway, squats behind a rubbled wall. She can just see the shelter. The sun burning hot, the wind glacial. Checking over her shoulder like a spooked child: just wilderness, the sands giving way to a gravel plain, then the high mountains drowning in cloud.

A scream rips the air, slicing through her. She looks but can't see much in the shadows under the canvas. Lasya must be in labour. Or Norbu is attacking someone—Choden, Lew. She sees that now he's pouncing up, reeling among the others with garbled cries, stepping in the ashes of the fire and staggering out into the light, gripping his child-sized weapon. Could he be looking for Amaris herself? She's already in such distress that the fear seems irrelevant. She clamps her eyes at another spasm. Cold sweat. Now Lew is out there with Norbu, addressing him in soft, coaxing tones. Choden there too. Tenzin gazing down from his lookout, pensively smoking.

Lew and Choden lead Norbu back into the shelter. He seems cooperative. Maybe he was dreaming, hallucinating, maybe he's still asleep, suggestible, not really dangerous to anyone but the Chinese. *You are Chinese.*

Sophie hunches out next, clutching her stomach with both hands, face tipped down so that it's lost in her hoodie. She walks with tight little steps toward Amaris's spot. Amaris in her pain says nothing, then realizes the girl will stumble on her and be startled, terrified. Putting on her sunglasses she calls softly, "Comfort station's over here."

"Hi," Sophie says, hiking her black Tibetan skirts and squatting next to Amaris. The girl fits a note of stoic humour into that *Hi*, even smiling. Impressive.

"Is Norbu . . . ?"

"My dad's talking to him. With Choden and Sonam. Trying to give him a shot of something."

They're silent for some minutes until Amaris says, "Used to worry I spent too much time, back home, taking baths, grooming. Makeup. Dressing to the teeth. And you know what? It was all worth it."

The girl nods, winces. She and Amaris, side by side, unselfconscious in their predicament as if they've been doing this for years.

Amaris, finally: "I think it's incredibly brave what you did, coming after him."

"You really think so?"

"If I say it, I think it."

Pause. "All I hate is that I have to feel *selfish*. Just for wanting him home."

"That's what got you into trouble, isn't it?

"What?"

"With the cops. You wanted to bring him home."

The girl's brow tightens pensively—or in pain. "I still am in trouble. We'll be dealing with it when we go home."

When, she says. Amaris is downgrading her own hopes to *if.* But then Sophie is at an age of residual faith—disillusioned, but still believing the tarnished guardians of her childhood have some protective power. Then again, maybe hers do.

Norbu is wailing now. Tenzin with his rifle lopes and seat-slides down the back of the dune and strides toward the shelter, flinging down his cigarette like a man whose patience has finally caved. Lew and Choden come out to meet him. The three huddle for a few seconds and then duck back under the canvas. There's chaotic movement toward the back of the shelter, a stifled cry. The yak bellows and snorts. A minute later Tenzin emerges into the light with his rifle in one hand and Norbu's machinegun in the other.

Thank God, thinks Amaris.

At five p.m. the fugitives set out, a fiery wall of stormcloud looming ahead above the mountains, the sun already lost behind it. Lew has given Amaris and Sophie pills so they can continue the march. Norbu, still limp from the heavy dose of sedative that Lew shot into him when they seized his gun, is slumped on the yak, though Lasya's pains are worsening and she would seem the obvious passenger. But she walks, she says she wants to, up this sun- and wind-chapped plain rising to a pass between two bare, low, eroded peaks: like a portal to the real mountains beyond. Tenzin, shouldering both guns, hollers them onward, slapping the yak's haunches, glancing back toward the razed monastery and the hours of sand dunes, layers of them undulating like an inland sea.

Hours later as they file into the higher cold—snowflakes starting in the dark—the throbbing drone of a helicopter builds behind them. An incandescent light descends and settles near the ruins where they slept, maybe ten kilometres behind them now. The edge of the sand desert is bathed in its light. Hard to tell the size of the aircraft or how many men are disembarking. Amaris checks her triathlon watch—8:22 p.m.—and the tiny diode display seems fatally conspicuous, like a lit match in a blackout.

Lew calls softly to Choden, "How much farther to the pass? It's Lasya. Her water just broke."

Lawson, Tashi and Jake start up the wall not long after dawn. There is no dawn. Solid cloud swarms the mountain. Snow squalls, shocks of wind. The lens-shaped clouds he saw late yesterday were, as he feared, the forerunners of a massive stormfront billowing southeastward. In the night, as he walked Shiv down the moonlit mountainside, he kept glancing back at that nearing mass, a sierra of icy clouds like a floating replica of the Himalayas. Of course he'd known it was coming—before eight p.m. Kal, patching through calls from base camp, had given the latest weather bulletins. Of course, of course. Just when he'd gotten people interested in his discovery. Though it was not just his discovery, or his emergency escort service for Shiv, that callers wanted to talk about. They rehashed their "ethical" questions. They wanted comments on the rumours about Book's video. They mentioned the weather warnings and asked if Lawson still meant to push on.

How insulated they all were, in every sense.

He and Shiv didn't reach Camp Two till after three a.m.—later than planned—because Lawson had slept through his alarm at eleven thirty. He coughed himself conscious an hour later and tried to rouse the porter, tightly curled in his green bag like a larva. *Come on, come on.* He'd kept a Thermos of water in his own mummy bag so Shiv could have a few mugs of tepid tea before they started down. Amphetamines now seemed a better bet.

At some point, in a half dream, he saw his wristwatch and realized he'd been helping lace poor Shiva's boots and crampons for over fifteen minutes.

He hauled the man out of the cave into the constellations: with the storm approaching, the last of the clear sky seemed violently clear. This was the lower edge of the troposphere, almost outer space. The night's cold was interstellar. Lawson linked the astronaut umbilicus of the rope from his own harness to Shiva's and turned the small, addled man to face downhill, to start him going like a Slinky. Shiv went first so that Lawson could brake him and also watch and dig in if he fell. Though Shiv's arms hung dead at his sides, he kept his legs flopping steadily. Lawson recalled that he had a wife and four children to return to.

"Okay, Shiv, that's it. Nothing but downhill now. You're going to be okay."

Delivering him to Kaljang at Camp Two, Lawson got the verdict at last. The embassy had reached base camp just after eight—Lawson's cut-off time for patched calls—so Kal hadn't radioed up, but the news was in: the video would be appearing that night on a hundred million Chinese TV screens and was already posted on official websites, where Book and the others were being called "terrorists at large." And somehow a leaked version was already logging hits on YouTube—thousands of them.

Lawson's plight has gone viral.

He staggers back up to the snow cave at six a.m., his mind reeling, erratic. The last half-hour, with clouds enveloping the mountain and visibility dropping, he's had to follow the bamboo wands marking the trail. To push on to the summit today would be more than dangerous, and yet to stop, to give up and turn back, would be, for him, suicide. The end of everything. There's a faint glow from inside the cave—Tashi heating water? You just need some hot coffee, he thinks, a short rest. No food. Can't stomach it now. Nothing good left anyway. Maybe just climb the fucking rock alone—others always bring trouble. Word is, the doctor doesn't look coerced on the video. Maybe he *wasn't*. Maybe Amaris was involved, *is* involved, too. They were plotting to abandon the expedition from the first, maybe, just using it, using me, to get up to the pass . . . who knows. *Walk away*. The wind's still light—moderate—and the ropes are there and Murloe's trail is waiting at the top of the wall.

The coffee revives him and briefly clears his head and gutsy Jake says he's ready to climb, though his face, usually on the gaunt side, is puffed up as if from hives or a hockey fight. In comparison, Tashi's bony face, sunburned black but for a milk chocolate ring around the eyes, looks freakishly small. It could be hanging from a headhunter's belt. Yet the beady eyes are clear and sharp: "Ready as always, Sahib—though I hope the monsoon dies first!" As for Jake's knee, it looks no worse than before, and Jake says he can move it, can manage, and he intends to. Getting him to the top will be a challenge but there's no way Lawson will refuse to help a man showing grit and spirit.

The summit team weakly clink their mugs over the hissing stove.

As they set out, with Jake and Tash using oxygen, gusts start to swirl and blow snow. (Should have started at three, four a.m.) His large concession: he will ascend the ropes *with* them, to speed up the assault. Because even now he might have tried soloing, even though Tashi would not have been able to get photos in these conditions and his critics, far below, would have disapproved—disbelieved. So let them. Fuck them. (Dust-devil gusts now, like the loops of his thinking.) Himalaya.net calls him a megalomaniac. *Rock and Ice* calls him a megalomaniac. No one ever talks about *micromaniacs*—the critics, the mild-hearted many, desperate to fit in and keep their heads down, who fail to climb their own mountains. They'll never understand a Lawson. They want champs to root for, but they still feel they can judge mavericks (like a Lawson) for their necessary obsession. (Him first, then Jake, then Tashi, jumaring up in short jerks—too damn slow—toward the clear skies he hopes to find above the wall.) He's mumbling lines he has tacked on the corkboard above his desk, laser-printed in bold 24-point caps, among clippings, photos of himself, and one of Jenn and the dogs. Mumbling fragments, though usually he can quote it all. A worrisome sign. But normal up here. And I feel okay. Getting a bit warm. (He's in his wind suit and down thermal gear over what

Tashi calls his superhero clothes—the Lycra and fleece bodysuit he's trying to patent, hopes to market.) It's not the critic who counts, nor the one who points out how the strong man stumbled, or when the, uh . . . the doer could have done better. The credit belongs to the man in the *arena*, who at worst fails while daring greatly . . . whose place is never with those, uh, cold, cowardly . . . no, cold and *timid* . . . souls who know neither victory nor defeat.

Teddy Roosevelt.

They've stopped again. Jake needs another break. Lawson's breathing slows, his mind clears, goes silent, a vacuum. And as he stares at the wall, insight comes, like a chock dislodged by some ghost climber high above, falling and striking his helmet: his colleagues are not just critics, they climb and risk as well. And Book and Sophie and Amaris—in serious danger of their own. Then he glimpses a second, larger truth that flits out of view like a stone vanishing into the mist below, even as he tries to look away: there's a lie at the heart of every adult life. A buried self-deception that makes it possible to climb on.

He removes his overmitts, finds his sunglasses, holds them to his face in the grey light: his image in the mirrored lens deformed to a big-nosed cartoon. He often uses the lenses to fix his hair or adjust his toque while on a climb, especially before a photo. Now he just stares. A muscle jumps in his jaw. He's out of gum. He's out of *everything*, he recalls, and his mind rockets away into familiar grievances and vindications and his radio starts beeping and he swears and ignores it and he's Wade Lawson again.

They rest briefly on top of the wall by the husk of Murloe's sheepskin coat. The coat remains exposed despite the snowfall— windswept for eighty years. Tashi, on all fours, examines it like a snow leopard sniffing a carcass. Though Jake seemed interested in Murloe last night, he now sits with his back to the remains and to the wind, his legs straight out in front of him as he gapes into cloud. Lawson turns the man's gas regulator higher. He, Lawson, still hopes they'll climb above the storm, soon. This is no place to bivouac, as Murloe must have found out.

When Lawson looks closely into Jake's face—at last catching the man's emptied eye—to ask if he's good to go on, Jake nods slowly, saying something inaudible over the wind and through the mask.

Sunless noon. They inch along the razor ridge, step, pause, step, pause—Lawson leading, using the ferrule of his axe like a cane to test the snow. They might be halfway to the top or more. Wind steady, straight at them, freezing the skin, but it's better like this— side gusts would be deadly, and this headwind helps fill his lungs with the diluted air. Snow still falling and blowing and everything monochrome, the narrow ridge under their crampons, the white-out around them. Treacherous how you can't see the ridge peeling away to either side, though for Jake now that might be helpful. He's in obvious pain, limping, slowing them down, yet if he could see where they actually are up here it might stop him dead.

Then he's down on one knee, waving, pointing at his mask. Shouldn't be out of gas yet. Lawson edges closer—as close as he dares. Jake trying to speak. He pulls down his mask and the words tumble out as if they've bunched up inside. "Just leave me here!"

"Don't be stupid, Jake! If you can't go on, we'll stop. Or Tash'll take you back."

"Go back on my own."

The words blowing away in a streamer behind him with his breath.

"Jake, listen to me! Don't worry, Jake. Uh, we're going to, uhh . . ."

242 ~ STEVEN HEIGHTON

Tashi eyes him through his goggles as if to say, *Well, Sahib?* Lawson tries to think clearly. (If this wind would just *shut the fuck up*.) Send Tash back with Jake? A part of Lawson does want the mountain to himself. And Murloe—if he finds another trace of him, he'd rather, for some reason, find it alone. Then again. (Then again *what?*) Jake doesn't look like he can go another step. (That's it. Right.) He might pull Tash off the mountain with him, on the way back. In fact, it's likely. (Is there another option?) For a moment Lawson stands panting, trying to decide. Static in front of his eyes—his radio beeping again—nothing.

"Build you a cave here, Jake. Side of the ridge. Make you comfortable. Tash'll stay with you. Or maybe come to the top, with me. Then we'll take you down together. Won't be long." Glancing sidelong at Tashi, he realizes that he, Lawson, is waiting for feedback from the kid. Tashi tugs down his mask, says words the wind instantly impounds. Across the burnt Sherpa face, as he stands in the gale on a blade of a ridge thousands of feet in the sky, a wide, impudent grin is creeping. Or it's a grimace. Again Tashi speaks and again Lawson hears only the tone, which to him seems . . . mocking. "Tash!" he shouts. "I mean, *Jake!* Both of you—get your fucking masks back on!" And he reaches around to the side of his pack for the snow shovel.

Lawson radios down to Kaljang to tell him Jake is resting in a snow cave while he and Tash go for the summit. Kal wants to patch through Sophie's mother again. "Not now," Lawson tells him. *Not ever*, he thinks. "Need to save our breath for this last push, Kal." *Need to move fast*, he thinks, trying to coach another dose of adrenaline from his wasted body.

Jake isn't looking his best. Could be simple altitude sickness or something worse—maybe a fast-moving infection from the knee? *Could* that happen, when you were this weak, infection spilling through your system in hours? No, he decides. They mark the cave with wands and leave Jake a Thermos of what is now iced tea. Tashi, who seems to be having trouble with his hands—he hates his clumsy overmitts and sheds them too often—leaves Jake his half-used oxygen cylinder, plus his extra. "Just in case Sahib and me are delayed," he says, insisting he can finish the climb without gas. This act surprises Lawson, moves him. Maybe he has underestimated the kid. (But is it a good idea?) Lawson's radio again. Don't answer. He instructs Jake not to talk to anyone on his own radio except Kaljang. "Including your own relatives, Jake—okay? They might get the wrong impression. About your, uh . . . your condition now. By how your voice sounds. Don't worry, man—back for you soon."

Lawson means it.

They leave Jake in his windless den, stretched in his long mummy bag, nothing showing but the snout of his oxygen mask. By the cave mouth they rest a few more minutes, Tashi now breathing hard. Chafing his hands together. That's definitely a wince, not a grin. No more chatter. He's learning to be serious. Tough climbs can do that.

"Let's rope up," Lawson calls.

As they struggle back onto the ridge, something gnaws at him, as if he has forgotten some minor but mandatory task. Jenn needs him to pick up one of the dogs at the vet's. Faintly he hears the beeper on Jake's handset going. Lawson has turned off his own.

On the ridge some time later there's a sound like a cackle, a burst of raucous, mocking laughter, and he turns his head, ready to brace with his axe. He's alone. A brief, sharp tug on his harness and he throws himself down and digs in with the pick, bracing hard. Nothing. He looks around. The rope from him to Tashi trails down the sheer ridge's northeast face and vanishes, not far below, into the whiteout. With the dullness, the drugged calm of his exhaustion, he reels it in, hand over hand. Its end comes jiggling up the slope. He holds it to his face, and for a while he stares and stares stupidly. Like a senile man trying to lace up his shoes and not finishing the job, Tashi didn't tie in properly. He needed that gas—and his hands were bad, Sherpas hardly ever complain and he was slapping his hands and grimacing and Lawson recalls that he'd *noticed* that and was about to speak up, but then his mind had strayed.

He checks his own fastening, as if it matters now. As if a Lawson could blow it that simply. He's not thinking either. He too relegated to dementia.

He must be near the peak, keeps thinking he's reached it in the whiteout, but it keeps receding as he shuffles on, testing the corniced snow with his axe. He can't seem to turn back. Gusts colder, scudding through his skeleton. Three p.m. The light fainter. There is no light, no dark either, just static grey. A Lawson doesn't quit. He stops to pant, hunched over the cane of his axe, decades older. His shivering calms. Maybe this is it. At times a man feels closer to ghosts, a long-dead climber, a brother, a dead baby, than to the living. No expectations . . . no reproach . . . ghosts are easier to love, like dogs.

Hell, I'm not just going to disappear! I can do fourteen one-arm chin-ups!

The ridge levels off, falls away, and it's the peak, he believes— then he dimly sees the slope continuing upward on the far side of a kind of notch in the ridge. Doesn't seem to belong here. He climbs down snow-covered rocks and there's a cave in the far wall of the notch, creamy stalactites of blue ice almost blocking its mouth, and maybe, his mind whispers, this is death, this silent gap in the journey, with soft powder snow falling slowly, shyly around him.

There in the cave, as he kneels on the threshold, he finds Murloe.

At midnight the refugees reach the pass. It's marked by another cairn of flat, piled stones. A few dozen ravaged prayer flags, on ropes radiating from the top of the cairn to the ground, thrash in the icy wind. The Tibetans pause and add stones to the cairn— Diki contributing a pebble— while the monks and nuns mutter monotone chants. Sophie solemnly adds a stone and Book has to look away. Amaris doesn't participate in the simple ceremony but she watches with respect, it seems, as if it's the funeral of a stranger. When everyone has passed, Book adds a stone of his own.

They descend onto a plain lapped in by low, steep, snowless mountains that grow larger toward the plain's western end. Beyond it, Kyatruk and the higher Himalayas must be lost behind that huge, moonlit firewall of cloud. By two a.m. they come alongside a lake, which must have filled the whole plain at one time; its wave-torn waters are lit in flashes, the moon beaming down through shreds of fast-moving cloud that bring occasional squalls of snow and hail. Book walks on one side of Lasya, her husband on the other, Choden beside Book to translate. Book can't make out if the stolid Lasya is in true labour yet, and this is no place to stop for a cervical exam, assuming they'd let him do it, which he doubts. Through Choden, Tenzin says they will climb another pass on the far side of the plain, above which there's a little pine forest in a valley where they can rest. Tenzin keeps repeating a heavily stressed phrase, which Choden now gently translates: "Mr. Lodi would like us to speed up a little. He fears we'll not be sure to reach the pine valley by dawn if we don't speed up."

In fact they're slowing down. The yak, with Norbu still slumped face down on its spine, a blanket bound over him, seems tired as well. Now and then Lasya will stop and hunch over slightly, her eyes closed, lips compressed. Like Amaris, she has a strong chin, a slight underbite that somehow completes her beauty. Skin so clear and smooth it seems stretched like a drum-skin over her bones. Her mate Sonam watches her with grave concern. He could be her father now—his greying hair and sparse whiskers seem greyer, his puckish, laugh-lined eyes stricken and grim.

Book keeps glancing back to check on Sophie—she and Amaris holding Diki's hands on either side—and to scan the horizon for signs of dawn and pursuit. Just before five, light starts infiltrating the landscape and their route becomes clear: up ahead, the lake and the plain end, meeting a high crag like a large decaying dam. Cutting down into the crag is a broad notch that a waterfall must once have carved. From the floor of the plain to the base of the notch, a trail seems to zigzag up a fanning ramp of sand or scree.

A light appears by the lake, off to their right, but it's faint in this twilight and Book asks Choden if she can see it too. "I'm afraid I'm the last one to ask about that, Lewis," she says. She calls to Tenzin, who replies in his thin, lispy tenor, a cigarette wagging in his lips. Choden says, "He believes it's the hut of a nomad family, Lewis. There still are some in this part of Tibet, where nobody ever comes."

"Can we stop there? Give Lasya a rest?"

"We can't, alas. We'd be welcome, of course, but Mr. Lodi

makes the point that if the Chinese learn the nomads have helped us . . ."

"I'm not thinking straight," Book says, angry at himself.

They turn away from shore to swing wide around the light—a butter lamp, he sees now, in the doorway of a yurtlike dome, a number of animals staked around it, small yaks or ponies. Better to leave the lake anyway. It's torture to drag along beside it and know the water is undrinkable, salty, Choden explains, like all these desert lakes.

The sun below the skyline behind them now casts its red light high onto the clouds crowding the Himalayas to the west. As the fugitives veer back toward the lake, completing their detour, two squat men wearing yakskin robes emerge from the receding yurt as if stumbling out of a quantum wormhole. One slowly lifts a hand high and there it stays.

Lasya is deep in labour now. Waves of pain squeeze moans out through her tight-closed lips. She's shuffling, trying not to stop. Norbu soon wakens on the yak and looks wildly around. Roughly Tenzin helps him down and points ahead and then up: the high crag is almost on top of them now. They lean into a fan-shaped slope of scree. Switchbacks climb it to the base of the notch, where a few small, sentry-like pines stand waiting. Zapa looks too big for this trace of a path but his hooves pick their way nimbly, almost daintily, Dechen hanging onto his tail with one hand, bent double as he half tows her upward.

The echoing roar of an aircraft fills the plain. It comes scooting low over the shore, a glass bubble body and damselfly tail—a small recon helicopter, not the arc-lit monster that landed last night by the ruins. Tenzin yells in a high, cracked voice; Choden calls, "He means *faster!*" The exhausted climbers now find a grotesque, spasmodic energy, lunging up and around the hooks of the trail, Book behind Lasya, glancing back to check on Sophie, who's pulling Diki by the hand, Amaris following. Diki makes little hiccupping sobs as her short legs chug upward.

They've climbed into pink, descending sunlight—now maybe the wine-red of the nuns' and monks' cloaks won't flag them all against the grey of the scree. So far the helicopter doesn't seem to see them. Banking steeply it buzzes the nomads' tent and there's a megaphonic blaring, not "Ride of the Valkyries" but a bombardment of distorted, staccato words. Lasya has sagged to one knee, groaning low in her throat. Book's hand is on the small of her back, pressing—"It's okay, we're there, come on!"—while half the party jams up behind them. One of the monks panics, shortcuts up across the hook, loosing a small slide of gravel and sand. Book is about to tell Sophie to shortcut, too, but now Lasya is up again, moving. He squints back across the plain—the helicopter trying to land as the pilot fights to keep the nose up, the air too thin here even for this small craft. Must be over 15,000 feet. Book panting, pushing Lasya gently from behind. His guts are churning. He needs another pill. Down on the plain, a hatch opens and two tiny forms in camouflage gear duck out and run toward the yurt. Now he picks out movement beyond the yurt, on the east side. Several figures—from here he can't be sure how many, three, four?—are already fleeing on their ponies, galloping away along the salt lake, dust rising. Sophie bumps into Book from behind and he grabs her hand and pulls her and pushes Lasya with the other. The receiving line of small trees stands just above. The older nun, Dolma, is wheezing and flushed. "Go, go!" Book hears himself, pushing Lasya harder. Tenzin is near the top, hauling the yak by its nose-ring lead. Book glances back downward: the two soldiers emerging from inside the yurt and hunching low as they run back to the helicopter. They will either fly after the escaping nomads or come for the refugees that they must be aware of by now, exposed on this wall with the sun brightening.

Tenzin stands between two dwarf pines, the weapons over his shoulder, reaching his long arm down to help people over the top. He grips Book by the shoulder of the Tibetan coat and Book can feel his strength. Tenzin hauls Sophie, too, then sweeps up Diki and plunks her down behind a boulder. A different world up here: stunted pines receding up a long, narrow ravine, like a high valley in the Rockies. Down on the plain the helicopter is trying to take off, nose lifting but then dipping too far as it lurches forward, almost scraping the ground. It banks toward shore, using the gradual downslope to gain height. Over the lake it climbs, Book urging it to turn away, disappear, but now it tilts and wheels around steadily and flies right at them. "Everyone down!" he says just as Tenzin shouts something, unslings the guns from either shoulder, then gapes down at the machinegun as if stunned to find he's been carrying it. Everyone falling back into the trees—"Farther!" shouts Book—and crouching under the boughs.

The yak is a problem. Tenzin prods it with the rifle and it trots a few steps along the faint trail into the pines but then stalls, glancing over its shoulder, conspicuous as a Jeep. The helicopter comes barnstorming out of the sun. It will barely clear the notch. Book crouches between Lasya and Sophie and he pushes down on Sophie's nape until she's prone on the needle carpet under the trees. Seen through branches, that bubble of glass hurtles toward them, not thirty feet above, and he gets a flash of a woman in a pilot's cap, gripping the stick—a fortyish face, rigid with attention or terror.

The pea-green belly and tail streak overhead.

"Did they see us, Papa?"

"Not sure. Don't worry, love. They can't land in here."

In a winded voice Amaris snaps, "They've *seen* us, Lew—Jesus, they've seen the yak, you think they'll think he's a stray?"

Tenzin thumbs a long cartridge into his rifle—a bolt-action hunting rifle, old but cared for, the breech sleek with oil. Ducked down in the trees, no one can see the helicopter but they hear it juddering back toward them, the sound murderously amplified by the walls of the ravine. Book glances at Lasya, now on her hands and knees, head down, panting, her many long braids hanging to the ground. Sonam at her side. This stand of little Christmas trees, filled with orange light, will be her maternity ward. Book has helped deliver babies in even worse conditions, in Kigali, in Pristina, though he can't recall ever feeling so exhausted.

"Lewis!" Choden beside him, raising her voice as the helicopter nears. "I've brought your kit."

"Thanks—right." *Wake up.*

Choden cups a hand around her mouth and shouts in his ear, "Mr. Lodi would ask you to take the small gun! I do hope you won't."

"I'm delivering a baby."

"Sure he doesn't want Norbu to hold it, but Norbu is, ah—what's the word—he does demand it." Book looks back: the tall man and the smaller one standing on the trail behind the yak, their arguing drowned out by the helicopter's roaring.

"I don't want it," Book shouts, "and Norbu can't have it. He'll fire on the copter and they'll shoot back."

"Tell them to get down!" Amaris calls.

Tenzin lifts a knee—his hands hold the two guns—and kicks with his lanky leg. The gumboot topples Norbu down into the small pines. Tenzin turns and runs to the lip of the notch and crouches behind the boulder there.

The helicopter snarls overhead, back into the sun above the plain.

"Lew, let me help now!"—Amaris crawling over—"just lying here's impossible!"

"If you could just keep Diki clear. The baby's coming fast."

"Papa, they're flying back!"

"What . . . ? Don't worry, love, they can't land up here. They won't shoot."

"Why are they going so slow?"

Book bends to study Lasya's face. "Choden? Ask her if she—"

A pine cone above Lasya's back explodes like a small, silent grenade. The earth in front of Sophie's face erupts with little geysers of needles and dirt. Then the sounds—a stitching of shots. Book leaves Lasya and flings himself down on his side, blocking Sophie's head. Amaris has thrown herself over Diki and now tucks the child's exposed, squirming arm beneath her. Book glances over his shoulder, through the pines. The copter is turned broadside, edging along the lip of the notch, two men firing through the open hatchway, and Book sees that most of the shots are lopping boughs and chipping bark around the yak. They're trying to kill Zapa, to slow the escape, but the copter is wobbling badly, bullets spraying everywhere. Tenzin replies with one shot; it sounds like the crag has split open. Norbu is up, still drunk on Diazepam, weaving toward the boulder, and now he yelps and falls on his face as if he's tripped over a root. He doesn't stir. Needles and twigs and cones rain down on the huddled fugitives. Book curls closer around Sophie. Useless—a bullet would pass right through him.

He's up and running stooped through the low trees on pumping, anaesthetized legs and he tucks in behind the boulder next to Tenzin, who fires again. The helicopter floats there, the sun behind it filling the clear bubble with red light. Someone in the hatchway is down but there's more wild shooting. Tenzin grunts

something, coolly reloads. Book watches his own hands pick up
the machinegun and the steel is black and cold as a bone-saw. In
stop-motion he flicks what must be the safety, cocks the handle,
lifts the muzzle. The gun convulses in his hands. He sprays wildly,
blinded by the sun, and he keeps on firing till the violent palpita-
tions cease and Tenzin cracks the air with a last shot and Book can
hear and see again: the sky emptied except for the sun, the helicopter crumpled down there at the base of the crag, its tail rotor
gently turning. No explosion. He blinks away tears of rage and
grief, looking urgently for any sign of life below them, besides the
far-off, receding dust trail of the nomads. The rotor slows to a
stop. The rising sun has lit up strandlines around the lake—con-
centric rings tracing the lake's shrinkage over time, from full and
fresh to salt-bitter.

Sophie sits in lotus position with her back against a pine tree,
deeper in the grove, Diki slumped in her lap, asleep. She's trying
not to move and wake the child up. She's too stunned and numb
to move, though now and then a hand, a foot, a shoulder twitches.
In the dappled light her father kneels by his open medical kit, rubbing an antiseptic wipe between his hands. His eyes don't blink or
shift or seem to know she is there as they peer through glasses at
the pine duff around his knees. He goes on rubbing his hands,
absently, almost violently, as if trying to stop the shaking. Now he
removes his glasses, swabs his face, cleaning off flecks of Norbu's
blood that could pass for his own blood, his own wounds.

The birth seems almost a small thing now. Not much for him
to do. Lasya is still strong and things go quickly. She squats, her
chuba and apron hiked up around her waist, her arms extended,
one of them around the trunk of a pine, the other over the

shoulder of her husband, who kneels beside her and whispers in her tiny, scarlet ear and doesn't react now as she snaps back at him. Sophie, a dozen steps off through the trees, can tell she's biting back her louder cries, as if the soldiers are close enough to hear. Her cheeks and her exposed, blue-necklaced throat flush red under the brown skin and the flush deepens in waves with her moans and now the top of the baby's head shows like a large, bloody egg. Sophie has never seen a birth except in a high school video, yet she's numb to this one. A death, a birth, another death. In her shock she seems unshockable. Norbu, struck in the chest, lies maybe twenty steps away, his face and torso covered with his baggy parka. His legs in the loose skateboarder jeans and basketball shoes stick out like after a gang shooting. Before coming to Lasya her father tried to save him, swearing as he stanched and clamped the wound, and Sophie had to look away, knowing it was too late, even for her father, he would fail, fail, fail, blood seeping with each desperate chest compression, leaking during the mouth-to-mouth. She's trembling unstoppably. Diki doesn't wake. Dolma and the monks chant in their throats around Norbu's body—*Om mani padme hum*—and Choden tends a small fire, heating water. Amaris furiously, rapidly snaps sticks for the fire, her lips quivering. Tenzin, out of sight through the trees, stands guard behind the bullet-chipped boulder at the top of the notch.

Her father still looks stunned. He won't be able to act if needed. But when the baby's smeared, elongated face emerges with the worm-blue cord looped around the throat, he hooks a finger in to loosen it and receives the baby as it slithers out in a purple clump. Silence but for the funeral murmur of that chanting. Her father, moving fast now, hunkers between Sophie and the baby, doing something, and she thinks, *Another death*, what could be more natural—then a high wail needles through her head from ear to ear.

A few moments and her father backs away on his knees: Lasya lying on her open coat with the baby, wrapped in a grey blanket, crying on her chest. The cord still runs between them like a rope between climbers. Lasya's *chuba* and apron remain hiked up. Between her spread legs she looks wounded and raw, but even this view can't make the dazed Sophie flinch, though she does seem to be sobbing, without tears. Choden bustles over with cloths and a too-small bowl of steaming water and her father glances back at Sophie. "A boy," he mouths, trying to smile with his glassy red eyes, as if hoping to comfort her.

Diki's head, in the black felt cap, lifts and droops again.

Poor Zapa has been hit, but the only sign of the bullets lodged in his heavy rump is his thirst—he's been drinking and drinking from the small pool a little deeper in the grove. Sophie can see him through the trees. Light flaring off the water. She should be longing to drink and rinse her face in that same cold water (she assumes it's cold) and now feels herself doing it, over and over and over and over, clear Georgian Bay water, a scent of warm resin, and she wakes up, lifts her head, her instincts tingling. Her father, Choden and Amaris talking softly behind her. Lasya's *chuba* is down now, covering her. Her husband and Dechen sit with her and the baby, its weirdly thick black hair spiking out around the blanket.

"I'll be half an hour," her father is saying. "I'm just going down to the copter."

"You're not *thinking*, Lew." Amaris's voice has gone parched and small, as if she's old and dragging an oxygen tank. "They must be dead. And if they're not, they'll shoot you. They already tried, remember?"

"Might be someone I can help, till the soldiers come. They'll be coming soon."

"Another reason not to go."

In her sensible, melodic voice Choden says, "If another helicopter arrives, Lewis, or an aeroplane, you'll not have time to get back up the . . . the slope there."

"I won't let you go down there without me," Sophie cuts in.

"Sophie!" He sounds surprised, caught out. "You okay? There's tea now. You want some tea?"

"If you're going down, I'm going too."

"Let's not go through this again," he says. "You've got Diki to care for."

"If you're going off again, I'm going with you!"

"Sophana, listen . . . God*damn* it." He comes out from behind the tree and glares down at her, then squats with a low grunt. A sunbeam floods his dark face, shrinking his pupils, yellowing the spoked green around them, so the lenses seem foreign, probed to the roots, nothing solid showing beneath. Where is he? She's losing him, or he has lost himself. He should never have picked up that gun. He told her once that he last held a gun as a teenager—his dad's "vermin Cooey," whatever that was, for foxes and groundhogs at the farm. He never meant to use another gun on anything.

"I followed you before and I'll do it again," she says through jittering teeth, weak to the core, but committed.

"She's got you, Lew. You can't leave us."

"Will you stay *out* of this?"

"What, you think this is a *private* matter," Amaris cries, "a nuclear family thing? There's nothing private now! Forget it. That's over. We're like a . . . we're a *group* here, Lew, okay? No one's separate. You'll endanger the whole group if you go get yourself captured, or killed." She stops and coughs hard and Sophie thinks, *Just shut up. You're right, but just shut up and let me do this.*

In a softer, hoarser voice Amaris adds, "We don't want to lose you too, okay?" and now Sophie sees deeper into her father's eyes: he's hoping somehow to revive the helicopter crew, the ones he helped kill—to *un*kill them—and maybe return to who and what he was before he picked up the gun. And it hits her with a cruel spasm under the breastbone: there's no returning, no bridges back.

Tenzin yells something from the boulder in a shaky voice. Sophie looks up. For the first time the healthy colour drains from Choden's cheeks, and her father sees that too.

"You're right," he mutters, as if talking to himself. "You're both right again. I'm not thinking clearly. Can't do the triage." He looks up over Sophie's head to where Amaris and Choden stand. "Choden, how long do we have?"

Tenzin's stressed voice comes again and Choden listens with her bristly head cocked to the side and a hand raised for quiet. In the near-silence before Choden translates, Sophie hears a droning, like the sound of a distant generator, brought by the wind.

"Mr. Lodi says . . . it's a very large object flying at us. A large aeroplane. He thinks it means to land on the, on the plain, beside the lake. And he thinks there may be also vehicles of some kind on the far pass, coming down into the plain."

Her father growls something under his breath.

"Mr. Lodi says they can be up here within two hours."

"We'll have to start once the placenta comes," her father says, standing suddenly, as if revived by the latest crisis, as he *would* be—that's how he has lived his life away from his family, from Sophie, hasn't he, thriving on crisis? Maybe that's his fuel, his drug, even more than lively social events are. "Should be any time. She'll have to walk somehow. I doubt the yak can carry anyone now."

"You know how much farther it is?" Sophie asks Choden.

"Mr. Lodi hasn't travelled this route for some years, but he thinks a day or two."

"We should all go fill up with the water," her father says. "And the skins—they'll probably freeze, but fill them anyway."

Amaris has said nothing since hearing that she's right, as if she thrives too much on conflict to know what to do with agreement. Maybe that's *her* drug, Sophie thinks, getting a flash-vision of a world of oblivious adults, all with clashing addictions.

Amaris hunkers down beside Sophie and her face crimps with pain. In her damaged voice she tells Sophie, "Here, let me hold her now. You go to the pool first."

"Could we go together?" Sophie asks. "Dechen wants to hold her," she adds, giving the child a light squeeze. "I don't want to go anywhere alone right now."

There's stormy-looking cloud right overhead, but out of the clear skies to the southeast the sun still burns and by the pool among the trees its rays are hot. The air is cold. The pool has the warm, turquoise hue of a cove in a tropical holiday brochure. Into its icy water they slide their morgue-white feet—Sophie's long and thin, like the rest of her, Amaris's stumpy, the toes impacted, as if they've been bound since childhood. She never liked them. A scent of smoke comes through the bitter pines. Each summer Phil and Naomi would take her camping near Whistler and she always hated it, missing the city and her friends, but she'd give a lot to be camping there now, a child again, fed and protected. They'll be losing the sun before long, fleeing deeper into the mountains. She stands up, quickly strips down while the injured yak watches through its black bangs from the far side and then drops its head to lap at the pool with its giant lunchmeat tongue.

"You're going *in*?" Sophie says.

"You too," Amaris insists, and this reassertion of her orderly habits, this bathing in a battle zone, must be a good sign. Surely if you don't expect to survive, you don't bother. Sophie wades in after her, but she clambers out fast and turns away, shy, of all things, even here and now, after what they've gone through, while Amaris stays hunched and aching in the pool, sucking air through her teeth, chafing her body with both hands for warmth and also to scrub away this place, this journey, her fear of dying.

She gets out, drying her skin with quick, gingerly dabs of her balled up T-shirt, as if somehow to soak up the water and yet keep the fabric dry. Through chattering teeth she says, "What'll you eat first—first night back in the city?"

"You mean Kathmandu?"

"No—back home."

"Spaghetti," the girl says in a reverent murmur. She's still turned away, shivering, the fine braids twitching over the back of the turquoise necklace as she wraps the *chuba* around her. "In olive oil. With a spicy tofu tomato sauce. Tons of Asiago grated on top and melting."

"Tofu? Something Asian after this? Not Greek?"

"And my *yiayia*'s feta salad. And a huge slab of *galactoboureko*."

"What's that?"

"Custard in phyllo pastry."

Sophie turns to face Amaris, who's still dabbing, trying to hurry. Sophie says, "And in another year or two I'll have my own little place downtown, and cook for myself and my friends and drive around on a Vespa and write songs and graphic novels. And I'll work at a food bank, and wait on tables, and I'll start some courses at OCA and maybe go full-time the year after. And I'll visit home for dinner, like, once a week and we'll have big noisy

Greek dinners the way we used to all the time, and we'll all be there." Her blue eyes shine out of deep, bruised pockets, under straight, strong black brows. This is the longest stretch of personal information she has offered in Amaris's hearing. Not information, though—invocation, a spell cast on the future.

Pulling on her tights, Amaris says, "You'll have to come to my place sometime. I hate cooking—we'll order in. It's a small place but the ceilings are high, and the light . . . it's fantastic in the fall. And the bathroom is *huge*."

"I'd love to," Sophie says earnestly, as if she has forgotten where they are and what's happening. "I mean, just to talk to someone older who's actually an *artist*."

Across the pool, two of the young monks are kneeling to drink and fill water skins. Amaris suspects they've been watching her and the girl, though their eyes are averted right now. She couldn't care less.

"You must miss your camera," Sophie says.

"I keep thinking how much less dangerous this would all look through a lens."

Sophie's hopeful look deflates and Amaris is angry at herself for breaking the spell. It's her professional reflex—force people to face cruel truths. Young innocents especially. She's sick of her reflexes. Still, the girl recovers fast, lifting her hood into place, pulling on her parka and zipping it up with a determined expression. She looks older than when Amaris first met her in Kathmandu, but that change is nothing compared to how much older she acts.

"If I ever had a kid, a girl," Amaris says quickly, "I think I'd give her your name. I love your full name. It's Greek, right, 'Sophana'?"

"Khmer, actually."

"Khmer? It doesn't . . ."

"My dad heard it when he was working with refugee kids on the Thai border, a few months before I was born."

Pause. "Did he get back in time for your birth?"

"He was on his way. I was, like, three weeks early. Bad timing's just been our luck."

The soft-footed Choden appears without warning, a ghost in glasses. "We'll have to set out quite shortly," she says. "Lasya is ready now. And the soldiers . . . Really, you two, bathing in water like this surely isn't safe! Please, be careful. My tutor, he was always wanting to bathe, even in cold water, and he caught ill and he had to go home."

As Amaris and Sophie follow her back, they exchange a stunned glance: an army is coming for them and Choden has just warned them of the dangers of a cold dip. She leads them through the raking boughs and needles of the pine grove, avoiding the faint trail where Norbu's body lies. In the sun-stippled clearing the party is gathering, Lasya already on her feet, her striped apron scooped up above her waist and tied somehow at breast level, creating a womb of wool where the baby nestles. Lasya looks only a little drawn, a touch pale, as if after a long day of housework.

Tenzin shouts something from his lookout. Amaris's eyes—the only real lenses she has left—impel her toward that spot and she ducks through the thinning, shrinking pines while Lew, behind her, calls her name. She speeds up. As she nears the lookout, Tenzin rises, turns and starts toward her, wearing aviator shades, his strained, handsome face speaking, but she points ahead: "I have to see what's there, okay? I have to look." He seems to get it. He turns again, an armed chaperone, and walks the few steps back with her. From the pocket of his sheepskin coat he takes a pair of tiny, ancient binoculars, almost like opera glasses, and hands them to her.

In the middle of the plain, some distance away, a big-bellied army-green propeller aircraft sits, windowless except for the cockpit. It must have brought the soldiers who are now trotting toward the base of the crag, where the helicopter lies, sending up a long coil of char-brown smoke. The soldiers are spread out like a patrol, maybe fifty strong, maybe a kilometre short of the helicopter and the base of the zigzag path that will lead them up here. By the salt shore, the yurt is a gusher of flame with oily purple fumes coursing up. Beside it, a pile of something burns in that same furious way, and with a surge of nausea she thinks *bodies*—human, animal?—gasoline or something has been poured over everything and now beyond the flames, distorted by the heat, more soldiers appear, running back toward the main body of men. Now is when she needs the camera. As they burn the evidence. "Don't worry," Lew startles her—he has come up from behind her, his hand lightly bracing the small of her back—"the people got away. But the soldiers must think they helped us. We heard them shooting the animals. They must have lost it, seeing the helicopter." She doesn't reply; her voice seems shattered. She nods her head, even surer now that he was *right* to act, almost glad for the brass hulls of the casings glittering around her boots, the twisted debris of the helicopter there below them.

In the distance beyond the airplane, coming fast, a motorized convoy, a dozen Jeeps or maybe ATVs trailing a wake of grey dust.

"Let's get out of here," Tenzin says in Tibetan. She understands him fluently now. As the situation gets more extreme, the range of things anyone might be saying contracts to a few urgent universals, like on the inside flap of a pocket phrasebook. Help. Fire. I'm lost. I'm ill. Get the doctor. Hurry. Please.

~

They file up a path through the dwindling pines, the walls of the ravine closing in as if they're climbing into a trap. From high above, somewhere in the clouds, an aircraft's muted snarl. The ravine ends at another heartbreaking, dam-like slope with a faint path slaloming upward. Before starting up, Book glances back: near the base of the ravine, where Lasya had her baby, charcoal haze rises like a mist in the trees, with little flares and fingers of orange light. For a moment he thinks somehow he's seeing the fires down on the plain beyond—the burning yurt and the pyre of animal corpses—then understands, the small forest is burning, and with it Norbu's shallow, pine-duff grave. No smell of smoke; the west wind is sweeping it out over the plain. Book catches the eye of Tenzin, who is bringing up the rear, his thumb hooked under the strap of his shouldered rifle, a cigarette in his tight lips. Tired eyes, almost swollen shut. He plucks the cigarette from his mouth and tosses it down on the scree as if to show Book how he ignited the fire.

Book lets him pass, then stoops and picks up the butt and hungrily inhales.

From the top of this latest slope they stand panting, watching the fire chew its way slowly up the ravine. Choden seems close to losing her superhuman composure. Her watching face stays impassive, but a tear flows out from under her glasses and down her plump red cheek. Besides the poplars and the fruit trees of Tyamtso, these burning evergreens, who knows how old, are the only trees they have seen in this desert. And their shelter saved the fugitives. Sophie weeps openly. Lasya squats, her eyes tightly closed, arms folded over the still bundle on her belly and chest. Again the hum of a surveillance plane, though there's no sign of the pursuing troops, who must be staying back, out of the smoke. But the forest is sparse and the fire won't last.

Everyone adds a stone to the meagre, prayer-flagged cairn, even Amaris in her sunglasses.

They follow an ancient stream bed curving to the northwest and on through a much broader, deeper valley walled in by prodigious peaks, their frozen upper reaches merging into cloud. A few icy pellets of snow spatter down. No more trees, no sun, nothing growing here, it's as if they've journeyed a few thousand miles north in an hour, into the Arctic. The Tibetan survivors, in their heavy skin coats, with brown, stoic, bone-stretched faces, look more than ever like their distant cousins, the Inuit.

Nobody speaks, every face folded low out of the wind. Book walks behind Sophie and Amaris. He's struck by how well Dechen and Lasya are keeping up, then decides it's just that the rest of them are slowing badly. The yak is limping, favouring its right hind leg. Diki, slumped on her father's shoulders, keeps coughing herself awake. That line from somewhere about the solid, unkillable children of the very poor—whose is it? In Book's experience poor children are consummately killable, by any number of things.

They rest for half an hour in the lee of a boulder that must once have smashed its way down the ice and gravel flank of the mountain above them. Strings of prayer flags run from the top of the boulder to the ground, but the flags are in tatters, their dyes washed out to a sameness of grey, the inscriptions scoured clear by the snows and the sandpaper wind.

Next to him Sophie says softly, though not so carefully that others can't hear, "I love you, Papa." The *Papa* comes out garbled. Her lips are too numb. He doesn't dare try out the words himself—he will break down—but just squeezes her hand and looks away.

He creaks over to Lasya, trying to hide his condition, and through Choden he asks her how she feels. Deep shadows now under Lasya's liquid eyes. Somehow they make her more beautiful, like a saint after a long solo vigil, or visionary fever.

Choden translates her two or three sentence answer as, "Pretty well."

"And the baby?"

Lasya looks expressively at Book as she speaks with halting effort—her lips and chin, like Sophie's, must be numb—then turns to Choden as the nun translates, louder: "Nursing already, sleeping and nursing."

"Good, good."

"But, Lewis . . . how are you, yourself?"

"What do you mean?"

He knows exactly what she means.

"It isn't in your nature, Lewis, what you're after doing—what you did back there. You're a healer, in your heart. But I'm sure you must have thought you must."

"I didn't think at all," he says heavily. "You don't think I had to?"

She studies him through lenses that seem like magnifying glasses, burning into him. Those enlarged eyes—the whites so clear and unpolluted—make him feel old and disgraced at one glance and like an ignorant child the next. Lasya eyes him as well, then there's a muffled mew and gurgle and she looks down and rocks her hidden baby.

"Mr. Lodi has been hunting since a boy," Choden says. "His father taught him to shoot—his father, who fought against the Chinese? Now Mr. Lodi, he's quite boastful for a Tibetan man, he says that he's an excellent shot and I believe him. And yet he was one fighter alone, with a weaker gun. On the whole, Lewis, I think you did as you had to—but honestly, I don't know quite how to think. It's so troubling. I really don't hate the Chinese, not even their government, and yet His Holiness has said one does have a . . . a duty to self-protect."

"I guess I don't regret it. I just wish it hadn't had to be me."

"Of course, you must." She blows on her bare, steepled hands, as if keeping an ember alive between them. "There's a story His Holiness tells, Lewis. About a Bodhisatva—a wandering holy man?—who finds himself in a boat with some travellers and a sort of, ah . . . a serial killer. The Bodhisatva recognizes this killer and he takes him aside as night falls and he whispers, 'I know who you are, and I must ask you not to harm the other passengers.' The man says, 'Ah, but I mean to kill them all, one by one!' 'Please, you must not,' the Bodhisatva says, but the killer won't agree, he keeps insisting he *must* kill. So they debate through the whole night and the passengers are so tired, they just sleep in the boat. Dawn comes and the killer says the debate is over, and he takes out a long knife. And Lewis, what do you suppose the Bodhisatva does?"

Book shrugs, barely. "Maybe says, 'Kill me instead'?"

Her kind eyes harden with a prosecutorial glitter that startles Book fully alert. She leans closer. "But then the man would just go on to kill the others! This would be a coward's path for the Bodhisatva, just sparing himself a view of the violence! No. Here is what he does. He seizes the knife from the killer and he cuts the man's throat from ear to ear and casts the dead body over the side. Of course, you are surprised! But Lewis, the Bodhisatva had to act. He did try everything else. So now he saves the passengers, but also he saves the *killer* from this deed—the awful weight it would lay on his soul. It's compassion he acts with, no hatred of the killer, no lust for revenge. Only the pure of heart can do that. To be honest, I doubt that I could, now. I really might be too afraid."

"I'd be angry."

"You didn't do it out of anger, I don't think—what you did."

"Or compassion either." He draws air through his chattering teeth. "And what keeps eating at me is—we helped *make* this mess."

"We? You mean this group of us?"

"The West. Bullying China for over a century. It's how new bullies get made."

She nods thoughtfully. "We call that—but you must know the term."

"Karma? Sophie uses the word. I still say cause and effect."

"The terms don't matter, Lewis."

"The pilot was a woman," he says, and he sees again the grey, rigid face through the windshield.

"Yes, Mr. Lodi said so. He seems troubled too. Lewis, do you feel ready to walk on?"

They climb deeper into the mountains as the grey daylight fades. Behind them in the distance some animal howls. He glances around. No one else seems to hear. He doesn't hear it again. The wind has died. No one speaks for what seems hours and darkness condenses around them without a moon or stars.

If only history were ever history.

"Papa?" Sophie calls, like a child in a car's back seat, "how much farther?"

"Not much farther. Do you want me to . . ." *Carry you on my shoulders*, he almost says. He's slipping. A Halloween maybe eleven years ago, Sophie on his shoulders pointing up at the moon in a haze: *Look, Papa, the moon is glowing for its costume!*

Book wakes himself with a stifled cry. Amaris is there. They're walking together in a cold mist. Her gloved hand on his forearm. "Lew?"

"Fell asleep on my feet. Hasn't happened since residency."

"Were you dreaming?"

He shakes his head as if saying *no*. In fact, he's trying to dislodge the dream, shake free of it. From the front doors of Dawson College, where he gave a talk on the ethics of borderless medicine a year before the school shooting there, his son emerges holding a long-barrelled revolver, like the one Book's father owned. It's Pavlos and yet it isn't—the face and the Red Bull cap and baggy parka and sloppy jeans and wallet chain are Norbu's. Smoke billows from the gun's muzzle like an overdone stage effect. Screams from inside the school. As Book watches, the boy feeds the long barrel into his mouth and thumbs back the hammer. Unable to shout, his feet cemented into the pavement, Book with his whole being strains toward his son, whose voice, unimpeded by the barrel, is a clear, slow, robotic monotone: *I'm sorry, Papa. I just got so hungry.*

"Yeah, so . . . sorry," Amaris says faintly, as if echoing the dream.

"What? What is it? Did I—"

"You said back there I was right, so I should admit I was wrong, before. Starting with how you should never have crossed the border. I mean, I was *filming*—they might have grabbed me anyway. Plus, you felt you had no choice. Which you didn't. Anyway, I get it now. I was wrong about you, Lew."

"Maybe you're wrong about you, too," he says softly.

"Let's keep this about *you*, okay?" The liver line between her eyes deepens. "Sorry. It's just . . . I hate when people act like they know me better than me. I dumped the one shrink I ever saw after one session. They made me go when I was Sophie's age."

"They wanted Sophie to go this fall," he says, thinking, *And I brought her here instead.*

"Plus, I said you put finding her above the rest of our safety. But you were right to—to put her first."

"Amaris, thanks, but you don't need. . . . You've been great up here. Strong. I mean, it's hard enough knowing how to act at sea level, on a full stomach."

The slow crunch of their boots, deafening in the dark.

"Never knew it was possible," she says, "to feel like this, and still be, you know."

"On your feet?"

"Alive. I did an Ironman, six years ago. Thought that was the worst."

"We're almost there," he says. "One more night."

He smells her sweat, a slight, good bitterness, like cracked pepper, and a memory comes back to him like something suppressed for years: as he lay next to Amaris in the ruins of the monastery he got a stubborn erection.

They shuffle on through the darkness and Book decides he has to ask again after Lasya and the baby, and just then Lasya stumbles, falling hard on her hip and elbow. She has twisted her body just in time to protect the baby. Sonam, Choden and Book kneel beside her and Book says that they all have to rest now, no matter what.

Behind a broad, squared boulder the size of a suburban bungalow Tenzin and Choden build a small fire of pine twigs and yak dung. Once the kettle is on, Tenzin stands and picks up his rifle and speaks, looming over the sprawled refugees, a wiry giant, his face weirdly animated by the firelight from below. Then he turns and walks lopingly downhill into the dark. Choden explains that he means to keep watch ten minutes down the valley, so that the others can sleep. She's very sorry, she tells Book, but she must pass along Tenzin's request about the other gun, in case anything happens to him while he's keeping watch: it's in one of the saddlebags. They should start again by three or four in the morning, she says, unless the soldiers begin to catch up.

Book nods yes, as if in a dream. A moment later he's dozing, sitting up. Choden wakes him with a mug of smoky, lukewarm tea, stinking richly of rotten butter, and he chugs it back and gets to his feet and joins her and makes his rounds of the ward: Pema, Lasya, the baby. All holding their own. Sophie and the others are hungrily gnawing on frozen apricots. Dechen kneels beside Diki, stroking her hair, singing hoarsely, her pipe stuck in the side of her mouth. Her ancient throat sounds scraped and scabbed. The words are Tibetan, but that tune—what is it?

This apricot like a fruit Popsicle from his childhood, worlds away.

There's no wind, but out of the higher peaks a bitterly cold draught funnels downvalley. They're all compassed close around the fire, the monks in a tight clump on the north edge, the nuns across from them. On the east side, the widow Dechen huddles with the family, a family of five now, where last night they were only three. A crisis always generates these small miracles and reparations. On the west side Sophie sleeps closest to the dying fire, Amaris behind her, then Book, who feels the night's cold through the layers of wool and sheepskin over his spine. He's wearing the Tibetan earflap hat. It would be cold enough tonight in a polar-proof mummy bag, inside a tent; the refugees have only their coats and a few wool blankets. Still, everyone else seems to be sleeping hard.

"Lew, can you get a bit closer?" Amaris whispers, after a time. "I'm frozen."

"I'll try."

He spoons with her, chastely, draping his arm across her shoulder, to Sophie's shoulder. He doesn't want Amaris to feel his painful erection—aching, like a nocturnal hard-on in adolescence.

She turns to him. "Lew."

Her breath like tart apricots, bitter tea. In the light of the embers, the faintest down of hair at the corners of her lips, which she must usually wax.

"I know," he whispers.

"Here."

Hard to say who kisses whom, their lips locked, forming a conduit of heat, a closed circuit between them in the deep freeze.

He says, "We can't."

"You're right. We're wearing *gloves*. And you're in earflaps."

She muffles a desperate laugh as they grope.

"No, I mean . . ."

"I know, Lew."

He kisses her hard, in love with that small, insurgent laugh. A brave gift.

"This won't work," she whispers thickly. "Here . . . let me turn."

She rolls away, pushing her backside against him.

"Jesus," he groans. "But . . . not with her there."

"I know. Okay." But she's reaching back for him. His bare hand under her parka.

"She'd feel betrayed," he says. "Her . . . Amaris . . ."

"But this could be it—the end."

" . . . her hopes."

"We'll stop."

"If it were anywhere else," he says.

"*What* anywhere? I mean, come on, Lew, what's . . . there's no . . ."

"I know. If only. God, I'm dying."

She goes still. Her rapid, shallow breaths tapering off. He doesn't dare move.

"Okay, Lew. You're right."

What do you mean I'm right? he wants to howl.

"Selfish of me," she whispers. "It's my specialty."

"No. I feel just the same, Amaris. But . . ."

"I can tell."

"No, I mean it," he says.

"I *know* you do."

"And you're not," he whispers, "selfish."

"I will be again, soon. Can't wait."

He pushes closer and she pushes back and they lie still, his arm again draped over her shoulder, reaching to Sophie's shoulder, and for a moment Sophie seems to be lying *too* still—then her arm flutters slightly and her breathing resumes its deep rhythm. Against Amaris's small body his erection won't subside, he's aching with lonely desire and it's a struggle not to move against her and he has no idea how he'll ever find sleep, but then he wakes in the same position and his body is warm and calm against hers and his spine is icy cold and the night has cleared and opened: the Milky Way like a Silk Road flowing across the dark.

When he wakes again, the stars are dying, Choden hunkered over the fire, stirring it with a pine twig, the glowing coals mirrored in her glasses. Her bare hands tremble. Tenzin's tiny binoculars now hang around her neck, and that's odd—shouldn't Tenzin have them himself? Book doesn't move and the nun doesn't glance over, yet after a moment, still watching the coals, she says, "I'm afraid we'll have to depart quite soon, Lewis. The soldiers' flashlights seem to be coming up the valley."

What a Wonderful World: that's what Dechen was singing, with Tibetan words.

In the ice blue atrium of the cave, Lawson sits out the storm, hearing his quick pulse thudding inside his skull and seemingly outside it, around him, dully amplified by the cave walls. With his flashlight he examines Albert Murloe: a wilted mummy in a heavy Shetland turtleneck, khaki wool trousers, thick wool socks spackled with ice crystals and grains of gravel. No boots. He stepped out of his boots somewhere between the top of the wall and the cave, Lawson decides. Near the top of Everest, decades of extreme solar radiation bleached George Mallory's exposed shoulders to white marble, but here in this freezer, Murloe's face has darkened like a bog man's—or is Lawson seeing the residue of the walnut juice the man used to dye his skin? He's lying on his side, balled up as if he's still cold, his knees tucked high, elbows pressed to his ribs, bare, shrivelled fists scrunched in front of his face like a boxer. The gutted eye sockets stare toward the mouth of the cave, which is fanged with large icicles.

The shock of finding the body has defibrillated Lawson's brain—it seems to function now and he knows, he thinks he knows, that this moment is *real*, though he keeps feeling himself lapsing back into those trippy regions on the edge of sleep. The summit can't be far. He and Murloe must be just below it. Murloe may well have made the summit, though on the whole it's more likely that he got this far and fell just short. He'd have been hypo-thermic, his feet dead as stumps. Probably caught in a bad squall. Not that Lawson *minds* if Murloe got up there first. He no longer sees him and himself as truly separate and is touched by the lone-liness of his death—Murloe's death. Lawson isn't dying. But he needs to nap. Just an hour or two. Wait out the worst. The summit can't be far and he means to get up there, even if going back down into the world to claim credit, later, seems impossible. The fresh blame. The death, or deaths. He tries radioing Jake. No response—static—the faint, pan-frying crackle of the solar wind. He should crawl back outside and try again, in a few minutes, and he will, he will. But first. (First what . . . ?) Amaris and Book and Sophie waving from the distance far down there in Tibet, taunting him, maybe, for needing rest.

Each time he half wakes beside Murloe his instinct is to sit up and turn on the flashlight and check for life signs, but he feels too drowsy, heavy—his limbs glowing with a gentle warmth, a lush numbness, as if he's drunk half a dozen hot buttered rums—and he slips back under, curled up, almost spooning with the corpse. It's okay. He's not scared. Jenn was scared sleeping with the three smaller toes on his right foot that turned black from frostbite after Mount Logan—they had to wait until the flesh finished dying so the surgeons would know how much to cut off. Perfectly normal, they explained. There were maggots at work, and a bit of a smell, though not as much of a smell as you might think. Still, he guesses things like that must strain a marriage.

He wakes to a sound in the cave mouth and sits up, surprisingly refreshed. Grey daylight. A pair of unblinking yellow eyes the size of marbles peer in between the icicles. He has seen jaegers high in these mountains, though never much above 6,000 metres, and never close up. The bird's auburn feathers are iced. It stamps its black feet like a man in snowy boots preparing to enter a house. *Gorak*, that was the Sherpa word. He guesses it has come for *his* eyes now. He reaches with his mittened hand and the bird makes a short, rattling caw and retreats, puffing out its feathers, displaying great, totemic wings.

No, it's okay. Don't be scared. Don't go.

He reaches farther, to the mouth of the cave.

Please.

There's an aerial thumping, a flash of feathers, and the bird is gone, out of view.

Beyond the cave mouth, the snow has all but stopped. Lawson's strong heart is beating almost normally, as at sea level. In a calm trance he abandons the handset radio, the flashlight, his backpack containing the camera and his sponsor's flag. It's clear to him now that these things are irrelevant. Clear that what's irrelevant is unreal. He drags Murloe's mummy out through the cave mouth into the daylight and the Shetland sweater seems to hook on something on the cave floor. He pulls gently and it comes free. How little Murloe weighs. Lawson's tired arms register no strain as he hefts the husk and carries it back up the side of the notch onto the ridge. Like carrying a small child. Even a baby. Zero gravity. The peak can't be far. Let me help now. Couldn't help the dead baby or Clyde or that other dying climber with his face stillborn, gentian blue. Most ways of loving are lonely, but there are other ways. He has seen them. Sensed them. You wanted to get what you didn't give. There is still time. Still overcast but the snow has stopped and the wind is calmer and the ceiling barely half a pitch above. Clouds lifting to reveal two sides of the pyramid, all but converging. His view downward to either side exploding—lesser peaks, range on range under fresh-fallen snow, jutting up through lower tiers of cloud like a polar archipelago. Sun through the haze like a moon. Murloe's husk weighs something after all. Lawson's arms tremble and he kneels and hefts the mummy over his shoulder in a fireman's carry.

They near the shrouded peak and the last clouds back away. Lawson climbs with small steps, panting, inhaling odours of lanolin and woodsmoke from the Shetland wool Velcroed to his stubble. The summit pyramid is weirdly perfect, as if drawn with a combination square. A template of a summit. All others, botched replicas!

We're almost there.

Never realized I was this close, Murloe replies, his voice muffled from behind Lawson's back. The enunciation is upper-class
Yankee, the tone clipped but affable. He sounds a bit like a Kennedy.

So there was a storm? Lawson asks.

There certainly was a storm. I wasn't in my proper mind by
then. Ought to have turned back.

That's not our style, though, is it, says Lawson.

Well, I suppose it isn't.

We'll get there together. I think we're there.

The slope levels out and falls away in all four directions. It's
dead calm. They can go no higher. Over the far side of the mountain, the Himalayas recede, wave on wave like ocean swells in a
spindrift of lower cloud. The vertigo here is thrilling. From here
you could howl in God's face.

He lays down his burden, kneels and props up the stiff husk in
a seated posture.

Ah, a sky burial! says Murloe. Splendid. I attended several in
Tibet.

I think I read about them, Lawson says.

They leave your remains, you see, and the birds come for you.
Of course, the elevation here is too extreme for any bird.

I must have been dreaming, says Lawson.

Yes, it's the air up here. Healthy for the lungs, I believe, but
hard on the grey matter. Then again, an oxygen-fast, now and
then, might be as wholesome as any other. Splendid view, isn't it?

You earned it. I'm going to leave you here.

Well, that would be fine! That's awfully good of you!

But there's nothing I can leave *with* you.

Such as foodstuffs? I've gone beyond that, my friend. Years
beyond!

Right. Of course.

It's awfully good of you to do this, you know.

I guess I'll be going down now, Lawson says.

Fine! Thank you so much!

It's really nothing. I'm glad I could help.

He gets back to the cave and somehow a full day has gone by, it's dusk and he crawls inside and pillows his head on his pack, it's lonely without Murloe's remains and there's the handset radio, so on a whim he crawls back out with it and tries to stand but he's dizzy and lies sprawled there and turns it on and at some point, then or some time later, it beeps. The cloud ceiling is gone. A few harbinger stars shining down. He has never felt as deeply peaceful as he does now—nowhere close. There's nothing left to prove. There never was.

"Come in!"

"Wade Lawson, is it you? Over?"

"Kal! It's good to hear another human voice! How are you down there? How is Shiva?"

"Pardon? Oh, improving very well! There's a Nepali doctor here now, and others here also. How are you? Where are you now?"

"I'm good, good. We're near the summit. Uh . . . actually Murloe's still up there."

"Who is, pardon, who's up there? Jake Kravchuk? Tashi Sherpa?"

"Jake? No, *Murloe*. Right, though—thanks for the reminder—I need to go check on Jake. Maybe he's still asleep. I'll go join him there. And I'll explain to you all about Tash, soon. I'm finding it hard to remember right now. It's kind of strange. But you know what Tash is like. He might just be playing a joke on us. Sure *you* haven't seen him?"

There's an interlude of static.

"——are you now, exactly, Wade Lawson? Come in? We can't get the GPS reading."

"Come in, Kal?"

"Are you really a——not need help now? It would—— exactly where? Over."

"I told you, Kal. We made it. We're near the top. And I feel good. I'm pumped. Kal? Come in?"

"——let people know you did the summit, then?"

"Oh, sure. If you feel like it."

"Pardon? Come——like yourself, Wade——please to climb lower now——oxygen and——over!"

"Don't worry, I'll explain everything when I come down."

"You are coming down?"

"I don't think so."

A spree of static like the ovation of a massive, distant crowd, then Kaljang says, "——wife is on the satellite dish again. Over."

"Book's ex-wife?"

"No! Your ex-wife——call again."

"Jenn? She's on the phone?"

"——patch her through now?"

"Yes," he cries, "now!"

There's a click and he hears Kaljang's scratchy voice say, "Please talk now!"—then Jennifer, halfway through a sentence, speaking in her soft lowland burr. The static vanishes completely, as if Lawson's will to hear every word is keeping it at bay.

"——still there, Way? It's Jenny. What's happened, Way? Where are you?"

"We made it to the summit. I'm near the summit of Kyatruk. Really good to hear you, Jenn. You sound so damn *clear*. Where are you?"

"What's that? Are you starting down now?" (She says the word like *dune*.) "What time is it there?"

"I'm not sure."

"Where's your *watch*, Way?"

"Don't seem to be wearing it now. It's dark out here."

"What?"

"More stars by the minute."

"You're outside, then? Why are you not—"

"I was wondering if you'd call . . ."

"Of course I would call, Way."

" . . . when all that stuff first started happening."

"I was camping, with Michael and, uh . . . and the baby. No TV and no mobile. We got home last night and since then I've been ringing you. Way, you need to come *down*. You can, can't you? Physically you're able?"

"Come on, Jenn—you know me."

An annoyed-sounding pause. "Way . . . what's happening up there?"

"I feel *good* up here, Jenn. It's hard to explain. Like, it's not even me feeling good up here. It's like I'm . . . six miles above myself. Like I forgot myself somewhere and if I come down, I'll just have to step back into my skin. Yeah, and now I've got your voice in my ear, even—so that's the whole package. I'm good now."

"Way . . ."

"Hey, know what I've found out? Heaven isn't the place you think it is."

There's a pause: no static, just perfectly distilled silence.

"But you cannot just sit up there and let yourself die!"

"I'm already dead," he tells her, "and it's fantastic."

"Way, if this . . . if it's some twisted form of revenge you're. . . . I'm sorry, Way, but I had to get on with my life!"

"Jenn, no, listen! I'm *happy* now!" (But. Except——) "My only concern now is Jake and Tash. I mean, I can't figure out what's happened to them. It's like I've set them down somewhere and lost them. Lost the map. I'd really like for them to experience this high, too."

"Way, you need help."

"They may have snuck off, though," he says. "If they decide to lay low, you know who'll get blamed, eh? That's the problem."

"It's going to be fine, Way, I promise, but you *have* to come *down*."

"But, Jenn, Jenny, this really feels like My Rock."

"Oh, you! You and your—if it hadn't been for you and your bloody *rocks*—"

"Don't say that."

Ten thousand miles away she's crying.

"I mean, it was our son, Jenn . . . right? He took the marriage with him."

"It isn't right to blame a wee boy. At least he tried to survive!"

The signal disintegrates, then recovers. In the lull, he seems to hear a third voice, a faint signal interjecting in a whisper, *She's right, she's right—she loved you, and* you *loved you*. A love-triangle travesty.

"——want you to come down, and not————like the baby."

"What? Jenn? Come in—please!—come in?"

"——down and get on with————stand to think of you dying alone!"

A satellite flows across the night sky like a ship, a trawler, seen from below, up there on the surface of the world, towing the drift-net of static that ripples between him and the only non–blood relation he has ever been able, almost, to love. For a moment he sees it. The failure to love is the only failure. Then he seems to lose focus, a lapse of static behind the eyes. When he wakes he is in the ice cave, sitting like a Buddhist monk, facing a cave mouth now almost sealed by a portcullis of icicles. Through the opening that remains, the *gorak* peers in at him: yellow eyes the exact shade of October aspens in a high valley.

You've come for my eyes, he says, extending his bare hand to the bird.

THE LIGHTS COME BOBBING UP the dark valley like the torches of that army he read about in Darjeeling—a medieval army that perished in a snowstorm crossing a high pass as it marched on Lhasa. Now and then, faint sounds of crunching boots, clinking steel. They might be here in an hour. In the darkness he waits shivering, the small machinegun slung over his shoulder and the medical kit in his hand. His mouth is too dry for the pre-dawn ration of soda crackers and dried apricots. The water is frozen in the skins—no time to thaw and boil it for tea. He does get an icy gobbet of meat into him, some kind of tinned luncheon stuff. He pockets the two remaining crackers for later, or for Sophie.

The others prepare behind him. When he turns around, Amaris, a few steps away, more than meets his eyes, so that what happened last night—the dreamlike kiss, their whispered dialogue and close-nestled sleep—is verified, given a passport into their real, waking lives, such as they are right now. It does help. Desire is a narrative that keeps you moving forward, even at a crawl, needing to find out. Sonam loads blankets and the frozen water skins onto the yak, who's snorting steam, trembling under his heavy, frosted coat. As Sonam hoists his coughing daughter onto the animal, it stamps and brays, sweeping its massive head back at him, grazing him with its horn. Sonam takes Diki back onto his own shoulders, but Sophie, beside him, says "Wait—let me help," pointing at the child and then, with both mittened hands, at her own shoulders. Book's heart surges with pride and love. Sonam with his feisty, gap-toothed smile—he's lost a tooth at some point in the last few days—wags his hand toward the head of the valley and repeats some word, maybe "later," then *thu-je che*, "thank you."

The faint swishing of Choden's robes approaching. "Ready, Lewis!" she whispers. "Please be careful with that."

"Right, sorry. You do know the way?"

"Mr. Lodi said to me, from here, it's a sure thing." She recites carefully, "Climb until the little pass at 6,500 metres, on Kyatruk's shoulder, which is the border, then south along the border, down to the glacier and the main pass, where I believe your base camp is."

He nods. "It does sound close. We must be at 6,000 now."

"Kyatruk is just ahead, sure, we should see it when the trail turns a little, but it is a mountain. It takes days for pilgrims to walk all around Mount Kailash—the mountain that's holy to us?"

"You don't mean it's going to take us days?"

"I think we'll be there by dark, Lewis."

"Thank God," he whispers—a phrase he hasn't used in years, since before Rwanda. After a moment he asks her, "Did you ever do that pilgrimage, around Kailash?"

"Alas," she says, matter-of-factly. "Now I never shall."

They turn and start after the others, Tenzin not among them. Over the fire before the others woke, Choden told him that Tenzin had come back from his post an hour earlier to wake her—she was already awake, tending the fire—and warn her that the Chinese were coming. He'd handed her his binoculars. He'd told her he would climb the far side of the valley and snipe at the soldiers from the mountainside to draw their fire and slow them down. If he stayed with the refugees, he feared, he might bring the soldiers' fire on *them*, while his own shots, farther up the valley, might cause an avalanche. This way, once the refugees were safe, he could disappear into the high passes and try to make his way slowly home.

"Does he think he has a chance?" Book asked. "Did he ever think so?"

Choden took off her glasses, adjusted the strap and polished the lenses with the sleeve of her over-robe. "He hoped, but he wasn't hopeful." She strapped the glasses back on, regarding Book calmly in the firelight. "It's just my opinion, but I believe Mr. Lodi really did want to lead us here, and now to fight with the Chinese, in the guerrilla way, like his father. I can see how you feel, Lewis, but he makes the choice in his own pride of heart."

The anonymous massif to their left will hide the sun for most of today, maybe all day, but the twilight is rising. Sonam, with Diki on his shoulders, leads the groaning yak by its rope and nose ring instead of slapping its wounded haunches. Dechen walks bent double, using a pine bough for a cane, her other, bare hand twirling a prayer wheel. The young monks still move in a bobbing cluster like one being. Sophie and Amaris support Lasya between them; she's stiffer, wearier today, but insists on carrying the baby, still swaddled tight to her chest. The burly nun Dolma keeps wandering off-trail, her hands stretched out and groping, as if she has been struck blind. She's the last of the party Book would have expected to give out. He guides her back onto the trail. He keeps glancing behind them. When those flashlights are no longer visible, there'll be enough light in the valley for the soldiers to see their quarry, not far ahead.

The muffled wail of the baby, then the mother's lullaby, tender and terrified. They're approaching the snowline, the sky a deep, freezing indigo over the white pyramid that's massing into view—Kyatruk, finally, it must be—while a heavy subsystem of snow clouds billows downvalley toward them, not a thousand feet above the trail. Beside the trail now a few bones glow in the twilight, then a long rift of sooty grey snow. One by one the refugees dodder off course and scoop up handfuls. The snow is hard, sharp-grained, seeming to cut the inside of Book's mouth and tongue as he sucks it.

A harsh, tearing shot rolls out across the valley. Sophie and Amaris, ahead of Book, halt and turn their opened faces, while Lasya, singing softly between them, her head bowed toward her son, doesn't look back. As Book turns, there's a flash from high up on the north side of the valley, above the snowline. He counts by seconds and hits five before the thunderclap—Tenzin's second shot. Now the valley's dim floor is lighting up with small red flashes, like gas flares in an oilfield, and soon after comes the squiblike clatter of automatic weapons firing.

Sonam shouts something and sweeps his arm overhead to point upvalley. The party creaks back into motion. Book stands frozen, watching the firefight, his squinted eyes beginning to pick out tiny figures crouched on the valley floor, far out of range of his own weapon with its final ammunition clip. On the snowy slope high above the distant toy troops, a small crag, a scattering of black boulders. Tenzin must be up there somewhere.

A hand on Book's shoulder. He turns, somehow expecting Amaris.

"Papa, *please*, would you hurry?" She says it as if she's twelve and they're in a mall and he's wasting time, making small talk with another adult. But her white, hooded face is solemn and haunted: no rolling of the eyes. No girl her age should have to look like this.

"The shots, could they reach us?"

"We're a long way out of range," he says, exaggerating slightly. "Don't worry, love—they want to capture us, not shoot at us." But he isn't sure they don't want to shoot the Tibetans, and the girl is dressed like one. He's glad she's still wearing her hoodie, at least. He always disliked it—it makes her look sullen, concave, hungry, as if she or her friends have ever known hunger, except by choice—but up here it's a slight marker of difference.

"Could they get Tenzin from there?"

"It'd have to be a really lucky shot. He'll be all right, love."

He takes her hand as they walk, glad the machinegun is slung on his other side.

"We're almost there, right?"

"From what Choden says, almost."

"You saw the animal bones back there?"

"I did, yeah." He doesn't tell her what he knew at a glance: they were human. A fibula, several ribs, a few vertebrae. Maybe she suspects it herself. They could have been there for anywhere from five to fifty years, maybe longer.

"Papa?"

"Yes, love."

"About last night."

He looks at her quickly. There's plenty of light in the valley now. Too much light.

"You were awake," he says, "weren't you?"

"I just want you to know something."

"Damn it," he says, "I'm sorry."

"No, listen."

"Nothing happened, okay?"

"Would you *listen* to me?"

His felt boots are quiet, but he hears his steps clearly. "Go ahead, love."

"If it were anywhere else, I might—I'd probably be upset, but up here everything's so different, you know?"

He nods. "It sure is."

"So I want you to know—I can live with it, if you, like, feel something for each other. I mean, I know you do."

"Sophie," he says, moved but not wanting to crush her hope of a parental reunion, though he sees now it's too late, it always was, "you know it might just be the, the situation, throwing us together? I mean, not together, but . . ."

"Why do guys never see this stuff," she mutters.

"You mean, what women feel about them?"

"No," she says, "what they feel them*selves*."

Even at this altitude he's not stupid enough to try answering.

"Papa, you're sweet, to be worrying how I'd feel. But I realized up here, the last day or so—I just want to see you happy. Whatever that means"—her voice is strained now, fading out—"when we get home."

He lifts a gloved hand to his eyes. The ozone smell of blood. How did she suddenly become the adult, helping *him* up the valley? Maybe we're meant to live in a state of permanent crisis, no time for small talk, nothing taken for granted, people doing and saying now what they're afraid of leaving undone or unsaid, everyone stripped to the soul—the weak of character unable to hide the truth and con you, the flawed transcending themselves, and the strong, like his daughter, stronger by the moment.

The hard crash of Tenzin's rifle. As the echoes dissolve, there's a far-off drone of engines and he and Sophie look up. In the brightening sky high over the valley—above the icy ridges hackling on either side—a spotter plane and its frozen contrail catch the sun.

The fugitives pause at the snowline, where the scattered plots of snow consolidate into a deepening white field and cover the trail. Ahead and above, low blue clouds are filling the valley, shrouding Kyatruk. Choden trots back to Book and Sophie and says they must allow Zapa to rest briefly, to eat the last of his fodder—from this point, he will have to make a trail for them through the snow. Sophie sinks into the snow and flops onto her back with her arms out, eyes shut, as if making an angel. She doesn't move.

No shots have been fired for several minutes. He asks Choden for the delicate binoculars. The eyepieces freeze the skin around his eyes. As he trains the lenses on the north side of the valley, the Chinese resume firing and after a few seconds he finds Tenzin—puny at this range—hunched and loping between boulders, trying to move west up the valley. As he runs, he hits a snowdrift and vanishes in a spray of powder and re-emerges covered with snow, as if he's run through a plaster wall. He keeps going but he gets bogged down in deeper stuff and takes cover behind another rock.

Book sweeps the good lenses down the slope and finds the Chinese pinned down on the valley floor. Some of them are crouched behind boulders, firing upward toward Tenzin. They're in desert camouflage gear, helmets, heavy vests—down vests or Kevlar—and they wear backpacks. Behind one boulder several men crouch, two firing over the top, another holding something to the side of his face, probably a radio phone, while a kneeling medic works on a man who lies on his side on the ground—the only visible casualty. Yet something's wrong. Book counts only a dozen, maybe fifteen men. He scans around. Behind another rock he finds a blurred heap of camouflaged objects and he sucks in a breath—a pile of bodies?—then brings them into focus: the backpacks of the missing men.

Lowering the binoculars, he scans upvalley: movement in the nearer distance. He seats the eyepieces back in place: about thirty men, their submachineguns held across their chests, coming up the trail at a forced march. Jets of breath fusing, dissolving above them.

"We have to go right now."

Now he notices one of the soldiers in the middle of the group—
a bandage crossing his face diagonally, covering an ear and an
eye, vanishing into a helmet that's too big for him. He's visibly
struggling, weaving. "My God," Book whispers. "It's Palden."
There's a small detonation of gravel to the left of the soldiers.
Seconds later, the crump of a rifle. Tenzin wasn't lying about his
aim. He must be half a mile from the soldiers and has barely
missed. The men all duck and slow down and then, still hunched
over, speed up again.

"Did you say Palden Jangbu?" Choden asks.

Book lowers the binoculars, shaking his head as if to say no,
but saying, "Yes."

"I thought this might happen," Choden says—Sophie listening
from the snow, Amaris approaching. "They'd much prefer to have
Tibetan troops take us, if possible, you see."

Amaris says sharply, "Better optics, sure."

"They might send him ahead," Choden adds, "to catch us up.
They've done such things before. Him or other Tibetans, if
they've any."

A sound comes like the splitting crash of the rifle but painfully
sustained and growing louder so that the fugitives, strewn in the
snow, flatten themselves, some covering their ears. A silver, spur-
like object flies up the valley at the altitude of the fugitives and
directly toward them, though still a few miles off. A jet fighter. It
banks in a quick, stiff manner, like a radio-controlled toy, rocket-
ing toward the north side of the valley. In profile it's much larger
than expected. On its tail, the blur of a red star. Two missiles streak
from its wings, trailing comet tails of pillowy white smoke, then
plunge into the mountainside below the rock where Tenzin was
hiding. There's a piercing flash and a ballooning fireball. A creo-
sote cloud scudding away. The jet veers back upvalley, toward the

fugitives. Book crouches beside Sophie and sets a hand on her shoulder to keep her down. He glances back, finds Amaris on her knees beside Diki, her arm around the crying child's shoulders, speaking softly to her. "Don't worry!" he yells, but the clap of the explosion buries his words. The jet zips over them, shredding into the low clouds and then, half a minute later, blowing back into view much higher above, skimming in the opposite direction down the valley. In seconds it's a glittering speck in the open skies to the northeast.

A pitted crater of scorched snow and gravel where Tenzin was before. Now a frothing surf seems to break downward over that hole: the avalanche, small but sufficient, blitzes on down the mountainside, past the snowline, into the valley bottom, its long, mounting rumble now audible—but the momentum of those tons of snow exhausts itself far short of the pinned-down soldiers, who are already beginning to stand up and edge out from behind the rocks where they were crouching.

"We set out now," Choden calls. Sonam is driving the bawling yak up the snowy valley, whacking its haunches with a switch of pine. Book needs both arms to haul Sophie upright. "Go on," he tells her, pointing up the trail, and she says, "What do you mean, what are you doing—let's go!" and he growls at her, "Give me a second here," and she says, "Why?" and he says, "Hurry up!" and she cries, "You are not staying back here like some hero in *300*!" and he says, "No, I promise you—go *on*," and she, "Only when you do!"

He gives up, shakes his head, thumbs off the safety catch. "Cover your ears," he tells her, and squeezes off a burst, flinching as the gun bucks in his freezing hands, shooting into the clouds. He lifts the binoculars to his eyes. It was more of a burst than he intended but it has the intended effect: as the men hear the shots, the leader lifts his hand and the men all freeze and drop to one knee, their helmets tucked down.

He pushes Sophie ahead and starts after her. "Go, go on!"

"I'm *trying*."

Light snowfall starting. Might give them a little cover, and the pursuing soldiers seem rigged out for speed, not a winter storm—they've left their heavier gear behind in that pile of backpacks. He pauses to let Sophie get ahead. Choden lags back to join him and now in silence she and Book plod along. Choden never looks behind, Book looks back all the time: the snow picking up, screening their retreat like a creeping barrage, starting to fill in the trail they're breaking for the soldiers. There's still hope. Again Dolma strays off-trail and sags to a praying position and Book and Choden start toward her, but she picks herself up, muttering, dusting herself off and reeling onward, her white sneakers lost in the snow.

Choden's small red sneakers flash clearly as she pads along.

"Your feet all right?" he asks. "Can you feel them?"

"All too well, Lewis. Thank you."

"What was she saying?"

"She isn't making much sense, but I believe she means she won't be captured. She won't go back to the jail in Lhasa, or a prison. Come to think of it, Lewis, neither will I."

Her voice is unchanged—mellow, measured—but her cheeks have lost their incandescence and the lively dimples have vanished. She doesn't look at him as she speaks: "The jail where I met you, that was different. Officer Zhao said that Lasya and I wouldn't be harmed—I think he sensed my feeling—and he kept to his word. At the jail in Lhasa, they weren't like that. One said to me they meant to prove that a nun's training couldn't prevent us from calling out in pain, and so they did. They did prove it. They hit us with tubes of rubber filled with sand. It's surprising how good a weapon that is. Then they changed to a, another, uh . . . the electronic batons." She says it like *battens*. "I believe you call them cow prods. I do hope they aren't used on cows anymore. The guards, men and women, they used them in quite a few ways. They thought I learned to speak English so as to contact the foreign medias, or to explain our story to tourists from the West. It's partly true, for sure, but . . . it angered them some deeper way that we're nuns, I think . . . never making connections with men . . ."

He shakes his head, as if surprised—as if he hasn't heard similar tales many times before.

"They don't do such acts with their own persons, though. They use the prods."

"I thought you meant that."

"So, Dolma won't hear of being captured again."

"I'm really sorry, Choden."

"Don't mention it," she tells him.

A shot rings out in the distance, beyond the snow cloud they're walking in. After some moments, a second, confirming shot. The piercing pitch is unmistakable. It's Tenzin. The fugitives slow down, gape at each other and squint around them, as if their guardian, back from the dead, will emerge out of the snows at any time.

Minutes later the jet fighter howls back up the valley.

Amaris and Sophie, with Lasya and the baby between them, glance back as the sound of the fighter mounts. Nothing to see beyond the snow's interference. Everything is white or grey except for the plum-red Buddhist robes. Now all around the party, a yellow flash, like sheet lightning somewhere in the clouds. Seconds later, the air strike's blast shatters the valley and leaves Amaris's ears thrumming. This time, she numbly assumes, they got him.

"Keep moving!" Lew yells and she can see him now, he and Choden nearing, herding the group in front of them. Life assigns such unthinkable scripts: Lew Book, humanitarian doctor, swaying along with a machinegun hung over his shoulder like the bloodied, macho hero of an action flick. It doesn't make him more attractive—she goes for rogues, not Rambos, and his skin is mottled with soot and dirt and blood, his green eyes flashing in the dark face with a cornered urgency—yet last night she wanted him as fiercely as she ever wanted a man. She still does. He meets her stare and she hears herself blurt at him, who knows why, "Maybe you could help break the trail a bit now?" The yak is leading, they'd be helpless without it, but the first few who follow— Sonam, carrying the child; the clumped trio of monks; the tiny widow—are still doing more to trample a path than Lew and Choden. Then Amaris sees how the glow in Choden's cheeks has burned out, how there's a fog on her thick glasses that must leave her almost blind but she's doing nothing to clear them.

Lew doesn't answer Amaris. His brow is knotted—he's either trying to figure out the meaning of her simple phrase or he's angry about it.

"He wants to be at the back," Sophie says, stating the obvious, "with the gun."

"I know, forget it. Don't listen to me."

The wind rising, throwing the dry, phoney-looking snow into their faces and eyes—burning soapflakes. Amaris draws the hood of her warm parka on over her toque while the wind keeps razoring through her tights. She hears Lew speaking to Choden and now Choden shouts hard into the wind so that her voice sounds stressed and much older. Sonam, without looking back, hollers a reply and slaps the yak with the switch. It hurries for a few steps, lowing mournfully, then its hindquarters buckle and it's kneeling on the trail, gusts of breath chuffing back between its horns. Sonam swings Diki down off his shoulders and lifts the switch and torques his arm far back, pausing with obvious reluctance before each blow. At each blow, Sophie cringes. "Don't!" she cries. Diki makes throbbing wails, Dechen shakes her prayer wheel instead of spinning it and howls what must be curses at the enveloping cloud and the horizontal snow, Dolma staggers, flaps her mittens in front of her closed eyes, as if the stinging flakes are a hail of hornets. The monks brace themselves around the yak's slumped hindquarters like men trying to push a van out of a snowbank. Amaris can foresee the group going to pieces; it terrifies her and snaps her alert.

"Unload it—him!" she calls, then turns around to see Choden and Lew just as they pass her and Sophie on either side. "Lew, Choden! Dump the blankets and the water and everything—we just have to go for it."

"Right," Lew says, and Choden says, "We will," and calls out to Sonam as she and Lew stride forward. Sonam drops the switch and grapples with the panniers. Lew wades through the drifting, knee-deep snow beside the yak and disappears behind its head. For a moment she wonders if there's something in his medical kit he can use on the animal—would an EpiPen help now, adrenaline for an hour or two? She leaves Lasya with Sophie and gets around the shrieking Dechen, stepping left off the narrow trail so she can see Lew. Icy flakes cut into her eyes like ground glass. The monks readying for another push, two of the three turned away from the yak, squatting low with their backs braced to its haunches. Lew is feeding it something. The long, jaundiced tongue unscrolls. Sonam gives a shout and the young monks grunt in chorus. The yak's hindquarters lift and instantly it trots forward and the two back-ward-facing monks fall seat first in the snow. They glance at each other, startled, and for the span of a few breaths they laugh silently.

Sonam hands out paper packets to the fugitives, one each, bowing his crumpled face and repeating something as he sets the packets firmly in their hands. Cookies of some kind. He won't meet anyone's eyes, as if ashamed to be giving so little. Amaris nods thanks, though she can't think of swallowing anything now except water. They gimp back into motion, stepping over the strewn blankets and panniers and frozen water skins, even Lew's medical kit, its mouth gawped open like something dead; she guesses he has stowed whatever he can carry in his pockets.

As he heads for the back of the line again, he stops to check on Lasya and there's a quick sign-language exchange, then Sophie asks him, "What did you give Zapa?"

"I thought crackers might help him—the salt. He loved the salt."

"I have a few more saved," the girl says.

"Keep them."

"But If Zapa needs them . . ."

His eyes are a plexus of burst blood vessels but now, at the corners, they crinkle slightly and Amaris senses he's touched and amused by how the girl respectfully keeps using the name *Zapa*. "Okay, love."

"Lew—should we help Dolma instead, for a bit?"

"No, she won't let anyone touch her," he says, and he's gone, and Amaris realizes he has given her arm a firm squeeze.

"You save any food?" Sophie asks Amaris, her voice like a small child's.

"A few crackers and a piece of that meat. But I'm not giving them to the yak." In fact, she's been saving the food for Sophie and Diki.

"I was saving mine for him," Sophie says, nodding back toward her father.

When Amaris looks again at her watch, a half-hour has passed. She's too weak to warn Lasya, beside her, and Sophie, on the farther side, that she has to stop. It doesn't matter—as she stops, so do they. No one alone has the strength to keep the others going, but any one of them can stop them all. Amaris folds over as her stomach convulses. She brings up nothing, not even spit. She puts a little snow into her mouth and they shamble on, side by side, a grotesque chorus line. She's too tired to look back in fear, too tired even to look up, but now she does look up and all of them, even the hulking, black-haired yak, are merging into the blizzard. The florid red of the Buddhist over-robes has dulled to a faint fax of the original, like Choden's dimmed face. When everything is snuffed to versions of grey, she guesses, it'll be over.

She finds herself gaping at Sophie. "You hear that?"

The girl nods from inside her hood, her face ghastly white from the cold, purple around the eyes. The Tibetans jabber in low, emphatic tones. They've heard it, too—another distant shot, as if Tenzin's ghost is still covering them, shadowing them up the valley. Silence falls, except for the wind, and she knows they're all listening for another shot, but instead, over the storm's white noise, they hear their pursuers—a faint exchange of voices, an order, a shouted reply. Maybe a soldier is lost in the snow. Maybe Palden. It's a search! (Maybe we should help, Amaris thinks. This is all a misunderstanding.) She's aware, in thin fits of clarity, that her mind is working bizarrely again. Lasya looks hugely pregnant with the baby under her layers and for a second Amaris is perplexed, recalling the birth. There's a faint mewing and Lasya adjusts her burden and the mewing ends. She's nursing as she walks. They straggle onward. Amaris looks back: Choden steering

Dolma from behind, the two nuns' robes nearly white now. If they were ten metres farther back, they'd be invisible. She can barely pick out Lew, a few steps behind Choden, his head down against the pelting snow. Actually, there's somebody else behind him, a shadow in the storm, which is odd—who could be back there? One of their party must have fallen back, taken over as rearguard. She looks ahead, does a body count, but the primary school math defeats her, she has to start from scratch.

Wait a minute.

She spins around, jostling Lasya, and yells *"Lew!"* He looks up, his face dark, eyes probing, then pivots to face behind him. For a moment nothing happens—that following shadow closing in on him—then there's a flare of pink light like a car's tail lights flashing in fog, and the harsh stammer of a machine gun.

"Papa!"

"Go on, go *on!*" he shouts, still turned away. His voice has a choked, chesty sound. He's stumbling toward them, his upper body twisted around to keep the gun aimed behind. A dark shape lies back there on the trail. Choden pushing, shoving Dolma ahead of her. Lasya bolts clear of the stunned Amaris and Sophie, and now they turn and follow her up the trail; she seems to be hugging herself with cold as she braces the baby and tries to run, passing her husband, who grips a handful of the braids that hang over the back of her coat to keep her from rushing into the drifts, wading past Zapa. He murmurs to her, puts his brow to her temple, an arm around her waist, and they're walking. One of the monks has Diki on his back. Amaris feels her heart rate maxing, the grade worsening, now of all times, *you can do it you can do it* she chants in her mind, that clichéd, can-do mantra that has been the rhythm track of her existence since film school, self-coaching, cajoling her on. It's why she understood Wade without ever really liking him. She gets him even better now.

She and Sophie lean into the slope and the gale and for a long time who knows if there's anyone ahead or in back of them or anything besides this killing climb and this ice-barbed wind that feels as bitterly personal as it's impersonal. *Fuck off fuck off fuck off*—her other mantra. Then it seems she must be dreaming. The climb has grown less difficult. Finally she twigs: the headwind has died and the trail has flattened out. Sonam's face turns, his whiskers a frozen waterfall from nostrils to chin, his eyes flared open, and he's pointing feverishly and can't restrain a cry, though he looks as if he knows he should. Something off to the right of their trail—an igloo with a row of rags above it crusted with ice like socks and dishcloths hung out on a line. She stares dumbly, then sees: it's a snow-buried cairn, lines of frozen prayer flags. They've reached the high pass on the flank of Kyatruk. The border.

"Choden!" Amaris calls. "Is there a Nepali flag here? A Chinese flag?"

Choden is trying to get Dolma to her feet.

"Keep going!" Lew says. "We can't stop!"

"Hard to say," Choden says in a strained voice, then adds something inaudible.

"What? This is the border, right? I mean, will the Chinese . . ."

"I doubt it," she says.

"What? Doubt they'll follow us?"

"Go, Amaris, please," Lew tells her, kneeling beside Dolma. "We'll be right behind you."

"Doubt there are *flags*," Choden almost snaps. "It isn't a true crossing, unless one climbs straight up Kyatruk and over the top. We turn, left. Our route follows the, the border, down to the glacier." She says something in Tibetan to Dolma. Amaris looks back at the cairn. Just past it through the falling snow, a steep wall—Kyatruk—blocks their line of flight, forcing them on a new one. It's possible Wade is right above them now, barely a kilometre off, close enough to hear the shots.

Sonam is driving Zapa to the left, downhill, and Diki now rides on another monk's back, though Amaris hasn't seen them switch her. Dechen and the other two monks, chanting low in their throats, all place small stones on the top of the snowy cairn. Amaris wonders where the stones are from—dug from under the drifts? From their pockets? She would happily add one, no scoffing. Anything, anything now.

She and Sophie have caught up to Lasya and walk with her again as the party turns and starts down a gentle grade along the flank of the mountain. Amaris could weep with relief. It's still freezing and she's trembling as if a blue-cold voltage is running through her, but the snow is falling almost softly now, straight down. To their right, Kyatruk, to their left, another, less blatant slope rising and vanishing into the mist and snow. They're in a ravine or canyon—a clear route down, but also a trap.

"I just heard Tenzin"—Sophie jolting her out of another brief coma—"a shot again."

"Didn't hear it," Amaris says, then asks Lasya, who doesn't speak English, "Did *you* hear it?"

"What? Yeah," Sophie says vaguely. "I heard it."

Lasya seems to be nursing again, weeping as she nurses. Amaris thinks to look behind them, for the others. The visibility slightly better now. No one is there. (How long has it been since we started downhill?) She remembers now—Lew and Choden trying to get Dolma to her feet. She thinks of calling his name. No, don't, she thinks, for Sophie's sake—if he's gone, if Lew is gone, you'll have to get the girl down to base camp yourself.

"Keep walking with Lasya," she tells Sophie. "I have to pee."

"What . . . ? No," Sophie says, "we'll wait."

"Just go. I'll just be a sec." She detaches herself from Lasya and turns back, up the trail. Sophie is stuck now—she won't want to leave Lasya and the baby. The girl peers over her shoulder and says, "No, just . . . wait, where *are* they?"

"Just stay with Lasya."

"*Amaris!*"

"I'll be back."

Amaris sets out fast and within seconds she realizes she has miscalculated. Uphill is no longer an option. The downhill stretch has conned her. She can no longer be of help. She has to help and only Sophie's gaze, presumably still on her back, keeps her moving. When she can't shuffle another step, she looks back down through the snow: no sign of the girl. She grinds out another ten, twenty paces, has to stop, stands on what's left of the trail, gulping this impoverished air, watching the flakes start to cover her state of the art boots—grey laces untied on the right foot, black grommets, mauve tongue and upper. Her breathing starts to relax. She can't focus her mind. The snow's silent voiceover, white flakes over dark boots and garish label, absorbs her, CREST CRUISER. Shoot it in freckly black and white, hand-held and sped-up, like Maddin. Maybe Super-8. These boots are performers, as she was told. Two forty-nine on sale at Peak Stuff. The sales guy young, blond, balding, an anabolic physique. Crudely flirtatious. Whoa—you're going climbing with *him?* You should let me take you instead! His T-shirt was mocha and said EVERLAST. She forgets what she's here for. She has been abandoned here, hours ago or years ago, a lifetime, but it's all right. She no longer feels any grudge. Solo is how it always ends, so why pretend we're roped together in any real way? They slash the only real cord at birth.

"Amaris."

Lew and Choden materializing out of the void, Dolma between them, seeming to walk with little assistance, though her eyes are shut fast, snow pasting her lids and lashes. Lew's stubble also holds the snow; the white has aged him a decade. The cold little eye of the machinegun peeps up at her. He's too spacey to aim it away, and seeing him and Choden, she's too relieved, or something deeper, to object.

She says, "Came looking for you," and tears burn into her eyes like acid and spill over. She can't talk. It has been years since this sort of thing, at least publicly.

Leaving Dolma with Choden, Lew steps toward Amaris, puts his hands on her shoulders, looks her in the eye. A tremor in his hands, a tear in his eye. "Let's go, okay? Before it fills in."

"Where *were* you? Isn't someone . . . I thought I saw someone behind you. No—wait. That was before. Okay."

"We were just helping Dolma up."

"Okay."

He turns her around on the trail, walks beside her. Their steps are so quiet in this snow. With every step down she regains a fraction of clarity.

"Lew. The men behind us. Are they far?"

"Closer than they realize. We heard them when we were back there. But I think they're in trouble—they're not dressed for this at all."

"You shot one," she states, as if trying to convince herself, and him, of the fact.

"The snow was in his eyes. When you shouted, he looked up but he couldn't see. Then he did. . . . They must have sent him ahead. He looked *cold*." He adds, just audibly, "You might have saved our lives. Is this the trail or is that it?"

"Here," she says, but then, not fully certain, calls, "Sophie?"

"I'm here!" Sophie's voice comes. "Is he there?"

"Yes!"

"Better not shout so," Choden says.

They come down the trail and Sophie—standing tensed, her mittens fisted—resolves out of the snow. At the sight of her, Amaris chokes up again, then wonders about Lasya.

"She went ahead," Sophie says before Amaris can ask. "She wouldn't wait. But *I* had to. Didn't know whether to go after her or come after all of *you*. I was just about to. Papa—what happened?"

"Let's hurry," he says. "Let's go, love."

The girl fires a wild look at him. "But you *promised* you wouldn't—"

"But all's well now," Choden interrupts in a clipped, conclusive way, settling the matter.

He sees that Choden must sense Amaris is struggling; the nun now walks ahead and fills in to the left of Lasya. Book and Amaris follow, twenty steps behind. He takes her hand, or she takes his hand. Numb and weak from shock and adrenaline rebound, he stumps along like a patient in therapy trying to regain use of his legs.

The soldier he killed wasn't Palden Jangbu, but he looked Tibetan. Fiery red cheeks were all Book could really see of the face. The eyes with snow-caked eyebrows and lashes were down-turned as the man cocked and raised his weapon in a spasm of fumbling. He was too cold. Book was cold as well, but he had the drop on the man. He's glad not to have seen the face—he'd rather not know the age, rather not wonder if he, the good doctor, has really joined the huge army of "adults" who constantly betray and injure the young.

In a world without adults, every child is a refugee.

"Lew," she whispers suddenly, "are you afraid?"

He nods.

"Funny, I'm not now. Not anymore."

"Good—being scared doesn't help."

She seems to squeeze his hand. It might just be another stint of shivering. Shivering is good; she's not hypothermic yet.

He says, "Harder to judge Lawson now, isn't it?"

"What?"

"Nothing. I'm talking to myself. Let's hurry."

Disorienting pauses delay each winded response, like on a satellite phone.

"You mean, like, leaving someone for dead?" she says. "But you didn't. You did the right thing—with Dolma, with that soldier."

His nod has a sick man's economy of motion; he can't really be sure that the soldier was dead. Twenty or thirty more steps and he says, "Choden thinks you had to come back here, you know. To Asia. She thinks this was all meant to happen, in some way. That's not how I look at life—I wish I did—but I figured it might be some comfort, now."

"Whatever you got," she says.

The others are slipping ahead, almost disappearing as Choden forces the pace, Sophie now seeming to labour to hold on. He can see that she'll do it. He thought that he knew the girl, but she is so much tougher than his version of her—deep through the heart, as folks used to say of gutsy horses, like the ones she loved as a child.

"Excuse me!" a mild voice says, close behind them. He and Amaris wrench their linked hands free and spin around as if they're not exhausted. Book fidgets for the safety catch, flicks it, lifts the gun. Palden stands wobbling on the trail about twenty steps away, aiming a quivering little gun of the same make. His helmet and flak jacket are sheathed in snow and he has epaulettes of snow on his shoulders, which are bunched high, shuddering. He's panting. The dressing across his eye has oozed through. With his other eye he stares imploringly, not like a soldier come to arrest them but like a wilderness survivor seeking help.

"Palden!" Book says, stalling. He's vividly aware that the snow has eased off. Between him and Palden, each separate flake seems to loft down with a precise and crucial slowness.

"Hello, Lewis and Am-am-amaris. . . . Please drop that now."

"Palden, please—your hand. It's trembling. Careful, please."

"P-please, Lewis . . . d-don't . . . "

Book shoves Amaris with his left hand, meaning to push her well clear of himself. He's so enfeebled that she goes nowhere, simply deflates and folds up by his boots.

"Lew!" The huff of her breath bearing his name drifts up and past his ear with fantastic languor. In slow motion she is trying to rise.

"Please, now, Lewis. I d-don't want to . . . I must not fail again!"

"We'll help you, Palden. Come with us—please."

Amaris is up. Palden thrusts the little gun way out in front of him, as if hoping it will do something that he can't.

"I must arrest you! P-p-please!"

"Lew, turn and walk."

"What?"

She clasps his arm, the one supporting the snub muzzle, and slowly draws him backward. Right—she's right. He says, "We're going to keep going, Palden. You can come with us, but we have to keep going."

They turn away from him and walk, gravity guiding them stiffly downward. Book's legs are dead as prostheses. Their hands, though equally numb, join up again.

"Stop, Dr. Lewis—I'm warning, please! Last w-warning . . . !"

A palpitating burst of fire. Amaris shrieks softly and Book sucks air through his teeth and they both dip down in mid-step, but their knees hold—they're still going.

"P-p-*please*!"

They sleepwalk on, five, six steps. Another burst of shots, a faint clatter and a thud. Book and Amaris turn. Palden lies on his back on the trail with one leg straight out, the other twisted sideways at the knee. His arms are lax at his sides, his head tilted back so the face is hidden. The smoking muzzle of the gun rests on the front of his flak jacket, pointing toward his chin. And the slurry of blood and brains on the snow—Book has seen far too much blood in his forty-four years, but never blood as red as this, a wrenching anomaly in the heart of this dove-coloured world.

They stare for only a few seconds, then turn and start back down the trail. Amaris says nothing. Book can say nothing. After a minute that might be an hour, they catch up to Sophie, Choden, Lasya, who are stopped on the trail, Sophie gaping, Choden wearily resigned, watching for whatever's about to loom out of the storm. Without meeting anyone's eyes, Book mutters, "Had to fire a bit more. Try to slow them down."

Sophie exhales and lets her head fall. Through half-misted glasses Choden studies Book for a few seconds, then turns and calls an explanation ahead to the others, barely visible down the trail. And they all stagger on.

This last, bizarre showdown has tapped out Book's reserves: full adrenal collapse, with marked hypoxia. He struggles to keep his boots on the narrow track, keep his mind working, work matters through—what the soldiers are likely to assume, and do next, when they stumble on poor Palden. Think. Shouldn't be so hard to work out, but in his mind the variables keep mutating and dissolving. His gasping frontal lobe throws up its hands. He frowns at his watch, trying to make sense of the digits. Still a few hours of light, if you can call this light.

From behind them a faint prattle of yelling voices seems to morph into gunfire. For a moment he doesn't get it. He looks behind them: just cloud. No way the pursuers can see them. A tight, concise fizzing draws his eye upward: snowflakes switching direction as sharply as damselflies. The shooting stops, then resumes. There's no question. The fugitives are clumped together, Book and Amaris herding from the back, and he realizes they've all broken into a loose, slamming trot. The binoculars slap against his chest and he should toss them but he keeps running. The mother and baby joggling between Sophie and Choden, Dechen clinging to one of the monks as if she has pounced on his back and he's running to shake her off. More of that distant shouting. Maybe they're firing high on purpose and yelling warnings, maybe they're delirious, maybe they're afraid of being picked off one at a time.

There's a raw stench and he's trampling over a greenish spoor in the snow and it goes on and on, Zapa hemorrhaging shit, panic's contagion has swept through them all, nobody immune, a rabble of runaways almost all separate except for Lasya and her nameless baby. You could forget your own child, almost. When the Black Death ripped through Florence and other cities, many parents abandoned their dying children. Another far-off burst of shooting. A feeling of déjà vu. The worst were Beirut, Kigali and a small town in the Congo. In the Congo he did simple arithmetic with spines. The human spinal column is a miracle of resilience. A mortar shell smashes a hut and the parents and grandparents and children are atomized, but the spinal columns remain and you tally them one by one to calculate the losses. As if loss could ever be calculated, redeemed as data.

The purr of an airplane somewhere far above. At some point the snowfall has died. The sun must be falling toward the event horizon of the Himalayan ridges, yet daylight is building inside the cloud like an electrical charge. A breeze reaches upvalley into the cloud, which now seems to be moving, shreds of mist gusting by them and increasing the illusion of speed: space and time shuddering past. Another spatter of gunfire, distant now, and he gets a vision of the freezing men shooting not at the refugees but at the storm itself, that solid crypt of cloud. Minutes elapse. There's no more shooting or yelling. *By evening, still short of the pass, all movement ceased among the multitude.* But the soldiers won't have collapsed, helpless, this suddenly—maybe they've given up now, turned back.

The refugees slow to a steady, determined hobble. The sun appears and vanishes, gauzed over with mist, tatters of scutting cloud, then it breaks through fully and he feels its heat and they're out of the cloud, below the storm. The view engulfs him: the ravine descending, fanning open toward its end, where a wide reach of the Khiong glacier is lit up, effervescing in his eyes. They push on, seeming to lean forward precariously, eagerly, the main border crossing rising to meet them, green and grey military tents now clustered around Sophie's favourite outcrop. It looks tiny. Absurd little flags there. "Look, love!" he tells her, his voice clotting in his throat—he can hardly get the words out—as he prods her gently, *Go*. Base camp is still out of view behind Kyatruk's lower slope. They spill onward, Sonam with his hand at the small of Lasya's back, Zapa clipping along through the shallower snow, seeming years younger, as if sensing the end. Book lifts the binoculars: Chinese and Nepali soldiers on the glacier, to either side of the border. Slowly the fugitives come to a stop, transfixed and blinking, Sophie embracing Choden, whose cheeks have regained their dimpled lustre, Amaris hugging Book, who kisses the salty crease between her eyes, then her upturned mouth. He tastes her tears and wonders if tears of joy taste less bitter, like these ones. They just have to keep to the right-hand wall of the ravine, as they're doing—they're already on the Nepali side.

As they near the glacier, base camp comes into view. Next, a party climbing toward them up the ravine. He stops and looks through the binoculars: it's a platoon of Gurkhas, the short, fit-looking troops he saw in tropical Pokhara. Now they wear khaki parkas and maroon toques. They come striding up through the shadows under the west wall of the ravine, dragging stretcher sleds like a first-aid crew on a ski hill. Strange to see people moving so smoothly, athletically. There are non-soldiers carrying what look like medical kits, and a stocky Sherpa in tight jeans, with a self-conscious sway and a cigarette in his mouth, as if he knows he's being watched—by Sophie, thinks Book, amused, jubilant.

"Stretchers, and doctors too," he announces. "And Kaljang's there."

The girl doesn't seem to hear. Book focuses on Kaljang again, to be certain, then sweeps the lenses down onto the glacier and finds the outcrop of boulders, the small border stone, Chinese soldiers milling around. He thought there might be media crews here, on the Nepal side, but the Nepalis must have kept them away. A few Chinese and Nepalis are arguing, one of the Chinese pointing a hand up the slope toward the refugees. Something glints among the boulders where Sophie and Kaljang and Book and the rest of them took cover during the first attack. The light lifts everything to high resolution: soldiers tucked down there like a SWAT unit behind a car, heavy black rifles with long scopes on top. An officer talking into a radio. Book's breathing tightens, but then he thinks, They can't shoot people on this side of the border, not

with the Nepalis watching and the Tibetans unarmed. He senses
a flaw in this thought—like leaning over a *bagh chal* board, smelling danger but unable to pinpoint the threat. He lowers the binoculars, brings them back to his eyes, swings the lenses around,
trying to find the snipers. There. The flaw hits him at the same
moment he sees the muzzle flash, like a neural spark clearing a
synapse. He's not Callum Lewis Book, borderless doctor, with a
G-8 embassy and a prominent NGO to speak for him, he's Tenzin
Lodi or some other poor, dark local who has bloodied the long
trail behind them with corpses.

Now Sophie knows this ravine, remembers gazing up its length
from below, even exploring its lower reaches on a mild, windless
day with Kaljang, in another season, another age. The slope
turned out to be wrong for the snowboard, too gentle, sharp rocks
just under the snow. (She was playing with a *snowboard*.) How
many nights has she been gone? She can count just a few. Four,
five—it seems impossible. They're going to make it. She's going
to get him down. Now base camp comes into view, her own little
tent, Kaljang's tent, Wade's toasty control tent. She shudders so
intensely she pees a little.

She glances over her shoulder at the mist and cloud still filling
the upper part of the ravine. The soldiers must have given up. She
hopes they all make it back. Something catches her eye—the top
of Kyatruk is sheathed by a dark twister of cloud, but between that
high storm and the clouds choking the upper part of the ravine is
a long, white, sunlit slope with a few islands of jagged rock goug-
ing up through the snow. Near the bottom, not far above the
ravine, something red and yellow gleams among the rocks. She
knows that pattern of red and yellow. She stumbles, not watching

her step as she looks back over her shoulder, trying to work it out. Tashi's parka. Tashi, the class clown—it must be—of all people. She can't believe he'd fall. She thinks she must be wrong. She's about to tell her father, who's aiming the binoculars down toward the glacier, when she hears a pulpy thud and his knees crumple and he drops, slumping forward onto his face. She looks at Amaris, at Choden—nobody sees. It's a slow-motion dream where everyone but her is stunned, slow and doesn't react. Her father trying to rise as if he's done a long set of push-ups and is straining for one more. A ragged red hole in the back of the coat. The machinegun has slipped off him and lies in the snow beside his stethoscope. The crash of a shot billows up the valley.

She runs and kneels and rolls him toward her. "Papa!"

Distant cries fill the ravine, and Sophie, fearing another shot, squints down at the glacier and makes out an officer beside the boulders, yelling at several men with large rifles. The sun has moved into its notch between the peaks west of the mountain, its molten light spotlighting the border and the valley as it shines down the glacier at the same angle it shone when she first saw the Tibetans fleeing toward her, five days ago. Five years ago. Others coming to help her now, Amaris, Choden, the monks. Her father's eyelids are clenched shut but he opens them and they're lucid, the pupils huge, the whites no longer inflamed. In a clear voice, subdued but firm, he says, "Just heard the most beautiful sound."

She grips his gloved hand. "Shhh."

"Now I know it. Like when you arrived . . ."

"Don't talk, Papa, they're almost here!"

"The sound of you breathing," he says.

~

Amaris speaks to Kaljang in a whisper, all the voice she has left: "Did he make it?"

"Sophie's father?" Kaljang asks in a sober undertone, as if in a funeral cortege; Amaris wearing sunglasses like the widow. He grips her elbow, helping her down the last gentle stretch to the glacier. Lew lies swaddled in a sled bumping along twenty steps down the trail, Sophie walking next to him, a Gurkha towing him from the front, another braking from behind.

Kaljang says, "Too early to be sure. I hope so."

"I mean Wade," she says. "Lew's going to pull through."

"You mean, he will live?"

"He will. He has to."

"I hope so, for Sophie's sake."

"Wade's gone," she whispers, "isn't he?"

"I'm sorry, Amaris, yes—he must be lost in the storm. A search party will be trying to climb tomorrow, but we probably won't be getting far up in all the snow. His ex-wife did call last evening, to try to talk to him . . ."

Amaris, surprised, turns her tired eyes on Kaljang; Wade gave the impression he never expected to hear from his ex-wife again.

"I did try patching her through to him," Kaljang says, "but alas, no answer! I'm afraid by that time, he was already unconscious or dead."

FOUR

EVERY LOST COUNTRY

This is my simple religion. There is no need for
temples; no need for complicated philosophy.
Our own brain, our own heart is the temple;
the philosophy is kindness.

—THE 14TH DALAI LAMA

December 2006

THE CLIP IS NO MORE THAN FIVE SECONDS, ten or fifteen seconds in slow motion, and you play it again and again, trying to be sure of what you see. Its colour is diluted, as if the scene was shot with a small hand-held device, maybe a mobile phone. Yet the lens doesn't jiggle or recoil despite the violent action sprawling toward it—the struggle of the twinned figures in the foreground; behind them, blurred figures running through a temple courtyard in Lhasa, Tibet; a sense of riotous noise, gunfire, screaming, that was either not recorded or has been muted to subtext under the narrator's weighty baritone. Maybe there's a tripod involved. A more elaborate camera. Yet at no point do the foreground figures give any indication of knowing that their moment—it's sometime in the 1990s—is being recorded. Maybe they're too dazed and frightened to care.

At first you confuse the Scene Select and Forward/Rewind functions on this unfamiliar remote, and this slows down the process of rewinding, replaying. Weakness and impatience make things worse, especially when it comes to coordinating the sequence of commands—pause, play, pause, fast-forward—required to view the clip in slow motion. But the hardest thing is aiming the muzzle of the remote at the stricken faces there and repeatedly squeezing the trigger, point-blank. That's what it feels like. It always will. Your right side is weak enough that you can only hold your arm straight out for a moment, and if your aim isn't true, you have to lower and rest the arm and gasp for breath and try again.

All the things you'd like to rewind and try over.

In the clip, a Chinese soldier in a pea-green helmet too large for him and a tunic with crimson trim, no weapon, stumbles toward the lens, and a face is peeking over his shoulder, somebody on his back. The face sinks out of sight, returns, brushcut skull, swollen eyes, a little Chaplin moustache of blood under the nose. The soldier himself has no moustache, just a slight pubescent fuzz over his lip. A beautiful kid with perfect bones. He could almost be a girl. His stupefied, guileless eyes are searching, his lips open in breathless bewilderment. A few steps short of the lens—this border in time and space that you can never cross—the soldier veers left and the Tibetan monk on his back appears fully, in profile, a tiny, red-robed novice, eleven or twelve years old. Subtract the setting, the outfits, the blood and the shocked, glassy stares and this is a home movie of a kid in junior high giving his little brother a ride. Pause, rewind, pause, play, pause, slow-forward. The child's left arm extends over the soldier's left shoulder and the soldier grips the bare arm with his own left hand. The soldier's right hand, down by his hip, gathers a fistful of the child's robes and holds tight. The two reach the right edge of the frame and almost pass through it and disappear—the camera wheeling, trying to follow—then the soldier swings back and the pair staggers in front of the lens for a last time. The child's eyes keep closing and his head lolls. The soldier's open mouth moves, perhaps speaking, reassuring himself and the child that they must now be headed for safety.

You never know what love is going to require of you; you just hope you'll be equal to the crisis.

Play it at normal speed and the narration concerns "the occupier's atrocities" and you've seen enough evidence of those first-hand, but if this clip is meant to simplify the categories and seal the case—Chinese warrior attacks Tibetan pacifist and drags him off to jail—it doesn't work. See how the child-monk clings. Others have beaten the child with fists and boots and rifle butts and truncheons and who knows what else, but this Chinese soldier is trying to help him. Aim again, fire, pause. She sent you this documentary, the work of a New York colleague of hers, because she knew, you're certain she knew, that you would find this one brief clip and take solace in it, however pained, however partial. You keep it frozen at the last moment before the figures cross through the border of the frame, back into their differently sabotaged lives, paired in this fleeting refuge. Stay.

December 20, 2008

S OPHIE AND HER FATHER SIT playing *bagh chal* and drinking red wine in the kitchen of his small rental apartment. Everything here is mismatched in a stylish, amiable way, as if the place has been furnished from funky yard sales—a vintage Arborite table, stainless steel café chairs, no plate or glass the same but all attractive in their way. This tasteful chaos is not his work, of course; Sophie and her mother, and on one fun occasion Sophie and Amaris, furnished the apartment in preparation for his discharge from the clinic in September. It's a third-floor apartment above a Greek café near the corner of Danforth and Logan, walking distance from the house, where Sophie is staying for the Christmas holidays before returning to Asia. This kitchen has a wide window crowded with light and a generous view west up Danforth to the clustered towers of the downtown.

It's the shortest day of the year but you wouldn't know it. The late light is ample and forgiving, the sun backlighting a Himalaya of cumulous massing to the west of the city, like summer thunderheads. A sort of Chinook thaw has gripped Toronto. The snow has melted and the streets, freed of their drifts, look amazingly, promisingly wide.

She hopes this is the last stage of his convalescence. Two years and three months, less a few days, since their return. When he emerged from his coma in a Kathmandu hospital, they flew him back to Toronto, where he entered a phase of recovery that involved serial setbacks, including some terrifying (to her) return visits to the ICU. He had sustained a certain amount of spinal damage, so that once he was out of bed he wasn't really "back on his feet" at all, but instead working to regain function in his legs— and a few times she had to pram him down aseptic white corridors in a wheelchair, clamping shut the valves of her senses and sentiments to hold it together. Then a sort of nervous breakdown— his—although it was clear he had really been broken since the coma, his mental symptoms overshadowed by his physical struggles. At least four different doctors informed her she was lucky her father was alive. He himself never said he felt lucky to be alive, not for a long time, and that alarmed her—though now, as she sits across from him in this small, warm kitchen, playing *bagh chal*, he seems to feel it again, finally. His chin and jawline are fresh-shaved, blue-grey, smelling of soap, and it's nice to see him dressed in something other than a bathrobe and pyjamas: overdyed black jeans, a new belt with a complicated pewter buckle, a crisply ironed maroon shirt. His long-lashed eyes are once again his own, no longer the low-battery, evasive, impostor's eyes that for over a year frightened her and at times *enraged* her in the clinic when she visited, on her two returns from Asia, where she has been working in refugee camps in India and Nepal.

They're sharing a bottle of Chilean red while they play. The slanting, luscious sunlight, like eight p.m. light in July, gilds the little brass tigers and goats and projects a dense, creeping weft of shadows across the board, which makes the game's visuals even more appealing but also makes it harder to play—hard to see exactly what's going on. Her father, playing tigers, is en route to an easy victory and she is delighted. In the clinic she was able to beat him with zero exertion, and when she actually *tried* to lose to him—so as to encourage him, convince him he was improving—it didn't help at all, he lost anyway, and that upset her very much. Now he has regained his sharpness, his pleasure in the game. Through the fall, he has been tapering off the clinic drugs and now is free of them at last. He's bantering, almost as pleased when Sophie makes a surprise move and zoos up his southwest tiger as when, now, he leaps another of her exposed goats, inflicting a mortal wound on the herd.

"Your goats are curry, love."

"Hold off on the dinner invites," she tells him. "You've just lost a tiger."

"When Kaljang used to get me where I've got you, he'd urge me to resign. You need a top up?"

"That's just in chess, isn't it? Shouldn't we save some for Amaris?"

"There's another bottle," he says. "Portuguese. And she'll probably bring one too."

"She'll bring gin and olives and a *shaker*," Sophie replies, a touch too fast, she knows, overselling the line, like a bit player trying to steal a scene, milk extra laughs from a middling quip. But she is so relieved to have him back—so eager to keep him upbeat.

"You heard from Kaljang lately?" he asks. "Like, in the last few hours?"

"Maybe." She can feel a smile betraying her, spreading over her face like a blush. Kaljang emails almost every day while she's over here. She has been seeing him on and off in Pokhara, Nepal, where she has been volunteering some of the time and where he is now based as a climbing guide. Through him and Choden Lhamu, she gets occasional reports on the others who were with them in Tibet. Choden herself is working toward her *geshe* at the Dolma Ling nunnery near Dharamsala, and she writes actual letters—on yellow newsprint, in an ornately flowing cursive you'd think she learned in a distant century—to Sophie and to her father and Amaris as well. *Ani* Dolma is at the same nunnery, and she likes it there, though unfortunately she is often unwell these days with bronchitis and pneumonia. Dechen has been reunited with her children in the Kathmandu Valley. Sonam, Lasya, Diki and the baby—they named him Norbu Tenzin—spent four months in a refugee camp in Nepal before travelling on to Dharamsala to join the growing Tibetan exile community. The three young monks are also in Dharamsala, at the new Nechung monastery.

Her father's Asian Tiger, as he calls it, easily jumps a fifth goat to end the match. They switch pieces, set up the board again. The light grows richer and moodier by the moment, darkening the wine, seeming to deepen the flavour, which is growing on her, though on the whole she'd still prefer a sweet white, a lemonady rosé or an Indian lager. Her father's Greek pasta sauce, simmering on the stove (tomato pureé, heaps of finely diced garlic and onion, basil, tuna, feta cheese) smells amazing, one of the scents of her childhood. Homemade garlic bread in foil wrap on the counter, ready for the oven.

She still doesn't take any of this for granted—being enfolded in this sunset, these aromas, the plentiful food, loving company— though she guesses she might be taking it for granted, by now, if it weren't for her work in Asia. (Why is it so much easier to maintain grievances than gratitude?) Not that she's forgotten those five days in Tibet, and what followed—her collapse after the flight home, her mono-like exhaustion, convulsive nightmares even during the day when she tried to nap (she had to nap constantly), the intense diplomatic inquiry and media attention and anonymous hate-email and rape and death threats along with all the confusing fanmail, her YouTube celebrity (1.8 million hits and counting for her video of the Khiong Glacier Shootings), her mother's dizzying shifts between incredulous rage and smothering care, Pavlos's pivots from untypical affection to mute tantrums of envy over her "fame," the therapy her mother insisted on and that she felt too tired for, the aftermath of the bungled heist, which meant community service the court now agreed to defer, and her father, of course, suddenly childlike—which made her feel responsible far beyond her present capacities, which angered her, yet again, their roles *again* reversed years too soon.

And Amaris? Who's on her way over here now, twenty minutes late, but then Sophie senses that's normal for her, she's always overbooked, editing video on her laptop or writing emails till the last minute and slightly beyond, then leaping up and dressing fast (yet smoothly, as if she's planned her evening outfit earlier in the day, *knowing* she'll be running late), daubing on a little makeup in her nice bathroom (Sophie has visited several times), her mouth a beautiful O as she hurries on the lipstick, eyes widened with a sense of urgency and irritation at being late yet *again*. She has been working hard to finish her new film, a short documentary she won't say much about, except that it's set on the Mexican-American border and there's no dialogue or voiceover, just a few framing titles and music. She has done nothing yet, she says, with all the footage she downloaded onto her laptop at base camp, before being captured. Friends and colleagues all tell her it's a diamond mine waiting to be dug—think of it, a feature doc about Wade Lawson's last climb, combined with her recollections of the ordeal in Tibet! In fact, several big producers have approached her, but she still isn't ready to go back to the material. Besides, her starring role in the crisis has brought her enough attention, both good and bad, that for now she's under no pressure to do anything lucrative. She also feels (and she looks surprised to hear herself tell it, the exclamatory crease between her eyebrows deepening) *sorry* for

Wade, dying up there completely alone, and she doesn't want to exploit that and make a film until she is certain she can do it in the right way.

In fact, it isn't clear that Wade died alone—he might have died with Jake, even with Tashi, whose body is the only one of the three that has been found. The immediate rescue mission, including Kaljang, quickly recovered the young Sherpa's body, but then had to turn back short of the Lawson Wall, as it's now called by the media. The next June, a German-Nepali expedition set out for the peak—hoping also to locate Wade's and Jake's remains and determine if they'd summited—but they had to retreat from the wall not once but three times, in whiteout conditions. A German filmmaker who went along on that climb is said to be working on a documentary about the search for Lawson and about his controversial career. Last time Sophie heard, the man was trying to mount a new expedition but was having trouble getting permits from the Nepali government—and even more trouble finding sponsors. After all, it has been two years, and how long do stories, even big ones, stay in the news these days? So her father says. Like Sophie herself, he seems relieved that their story is receding into smaller and smaller font.

Still, she occasionally surfs news sites or simply googles keywords to follow up on the aftermath in China, and around Tyamtso, where the villagers created for her a fleeting paradise at the possible cost, to themselves, of a lasting hell. Hell didn't happen, it seems. The authorities, probably fearing an image-management disaster in the run-up to the summer Olympics, decided to make a PR exhibit out of Tyamtso, releasing video clips of PLA military engineers helping the villagers to rebuild their bridge. (In one of the clips Tenzin Lodi, distinctively lanky, long-haired, a cigarette in the corner of his mouth, can be seen repointing the mortar on one of the cairn-like piers.) The wounded refugees left behind in the village—Lhundup and the nun Pema—were quietly arrested, then conspicuously freed. Norbu Dawa, killed by the helicopter crew before their accidental crash (as it has been officially declared) has been branded chief culprit in the jailbreak shootings; the authorities maintain that the death of this "Splittist assassin" has closed the case and satisfied The People's need for justice. Meanwhile, Lieutenant Zhao has largely recuperated from his wounds, received a promotion and returned to his family in Beijing, where he holds an administrative post. As Sophie's father comments, the authorities had a choice between punishing him for failing, and thus admitting a failure, or else celebrating his heroic wounding. Trying to make the best of a fiasco that provided them with few heroes, they chose to turn Zhao into one.

And what of Palden Jangbu, the Tibetan PLA corporal she met only briefly in Tyamtso? Sophana now knows what happened to him—several times in the clinic her father told her, speaking in a halting, haunted voice, so that she wasn't sure if it was a true memory or a delirious vision. But since his recovery he has confirmed the story, as has Amaris—and while Amaris seems willing to talk more about it, to study and reframe the event from different angles and try to understand, her father has made it clear he doesn't want to talk about it again. *Taking the Hippocratic oath*, he told her one time in the clinic—another odd segue—*it's a perjury. You swear to do no harm, but you do your share.*

Seems no one wants to talk about Palden. There's no mention of him anywhere on official Chinese news sites. Feed his name into any search engine and all that pops up are a few references to Palden Jangbus who can't be him: a Tibetan guerrilla chief executed near Gyantse in 1961, a lawyer for refugee rights in New Delhi, the Facebooking owner of a Tibetan café in Amsterdam.

It's odd to think of anyone these days suffering total digital obliv-ion—as if dying alone in a remote, cold place, your body buried under the snows, were not enough of an erasure. And this haunts Sophana. Which is why she keeps making sketches of Palden, based on her limited memories. When she gets a few images that seem right—face-on, profile, three-quarter—she'll run them past Amaris, and then start working up a short, speculative graphic tale, trying to lend Palden some sort of prehistory and, at the same time, a narrative afterlife.

She guesses that by now he must have had a "sky burial." The snows in that ravine must have melted enough by the next summer that his body would have been unblanketed and the scavenger birds and birds of prey would have moved in, till only his bones remained. And somehow this reminds her of another of the rituals Choden has mentioned in her letters: she has been learning to col-laborate on a sand mandala, a composition of differently dyed sands that a group of nuns arrange, over a number of long, silent days, into an elaborate, exquisite pattern. When the mandala is finished, the nuns promptly destroy it, raking and blending the sands back to a sort of nebular chaos, as if to say that no complete thing—a body, a nunnery, a relationship, a country, the universe itself—can hold its form for long.

Amaris McRae's new short film, *Bordercam Near Vamori*, is com-posed entirely of surveillance video, some of it slightly doctored (tinted, sped up into time-lapse, slowed down) taken from a webcam mounted on a new border fence in the Sonoran Desert near Vamori, Arizona. The webcam belongs not to Amaris but to U.S. border security services now outsourcing some of their surveillance work to "virtual border patrol deputies"—thousands of them. Apparently there are too few state and federal agents to monitor the twenty-four-hour video coming in from a growing network of webcams along the Mexican border. Early last year, in an online article, Amaris read about a Maori security guard, working nights in an industrial park in Auckland, New Zealand, who now spent hours every week staring at sweeping, low-res feeds of a newly fenced stretch of desert southwest of Yuma. He had a password and logged on every night. If he observed suspicious activity along the fence—either refugees or drug runners attempting to climb or cut through or tunnel underneath—he was supposed to email tips to border security headquarters. Officials wouldn't say if he had sent them any useful tips so far.

For the six months that Amaris watched and downloaded webcam feeds onto her laptop—logging on for a couple of hours a day and sometimes at night—she saw little and yet so much. The fish-eye webcam turned 200 degrees and back again every two minutes, giving a grainy black-and-white vista of the fenceline and southern horizon from the west to the east: a featureless, hot tundra with a few saguaro cacti to the south and, off to the southwest, a lonely mesa and a range of snowless peaks. Sun setting just to the left of the fenceline. Unclear forms loping out of the distance, defining themselves now as wild dogs trotting east along the fence, glancing through it into Arizona (maybe a hare or an antelope on the other side?), eagles, buzzards, vultures gingerly alighting on the razor wire topping the fence, tumbleweeds ploughing into it and piling up there in a southwest gale, storm-blown dust and sand at times subtracting visibility to a few metres. On two occasions a security crew of some kind drove up on the U.S. side, approaching from the west in a dusty black Jeep with official insignia on the hood, maybe checking to see if the fence was intact. On the second occasion they parked close under the webcam and two officers got out and stared up and conferred, maybe wondering if they should examine the camera, while the lens veered indifferently away from them. Two minutes later it swung back. They stood face to face now, smoking, laughing about something, two bearded, thickset, genial-looking men.

The next time the lens swivelled back, they and their Jeep were gone and the desert was desert again.

She was greatly relieved that she never saw anyone trying to cross the border. How could she have been certain what they were—refugees of poverty or of drug violence, or actual drug runners? Gun runners? The smugglers she would have reported, refugees she could not have. *Bordercam Near Vamori* is twenty-one minutes of lyrically intercut footage showing the weeks and the weather passing over and through the porous border, silent days flowing across the earth, big storms, a wild dog chasing a buzzard off a tiny carcass and then gnawing on the carcass, burying the remains. The two guards standing on the desert floor, peering up at the webcam, until, by the third pass, there's nothing. Finally a storm, late December, two a.m., snowflakes blowing like a gale of shooting stars across the dark screen while the credits silently roll. Sophana Book, Dr. Lewis Book, Choden Lhamu and her adoptive parents are among the people Amaris thanks. *This film is dedicated to my birth parents in Vietnam, whoever they were.*

October 2006

*The air of those high mountains turns anyone into a mystic, and the
depths of a convalescence can do the same: even wearing an oxygen
mask, the patient drifts in his mind through a trackless delirium. "The
patient." Who, you wonder remotely, is the patient? Here there is no I,
not yet—the ego remains an extravagance that takes too much fuel—
here there is only* him, *or* you. *In the wintry chrysalis of the sheets, as
respiration slowly proceeds, you see him, isolated yet unalone, people
slipping in or out of the room, and often, it seems, they keep vigil,
though it's hard to distinguish night from day, your children, Nika,
and, on a few occasions, Amaris, too, a feeling of peace and bliss at
times expanding through your body like drip-fed morphine.*

Gratitude for the gift of each connection. Each new moment.

*Toward the end of this twilight, a recurring dream. It belongs in
a class with those dreams where you discover a formerly unknown
room in a house that you've inhabited for years. In this version, you
realize that you have a child you've somehow forgotten. You have
left him or her somewhere and forgotten and now you learn that the
child has been discovered and is flying home to you and that
certainty explodes into your heart with excruciating joy—a sort of
coronary of euphoric pain. For some seconds there's no limit to this
returning joy. To be happy, see yourself as entitled to nothing.
Breathing without the mask, you crest a pass in your mind's eye:
there's nothing up here but prayer flags.*

NOTES & ACKNOWLEDGMENTS

My gratitude goes to the following people, whether for expert advice, editorial acumen, or other forms of help and support:

—Editor Michael Schellenberg and Production Editorial Assistant Amanda Lewis. Also Marion Garner, Deirdre Molina, Michelle MacAleese and Adria Iwasutiak of Random House Canada

—Anne McDermid, Martha Magor and Monica Pacheco of Anne McDermid and Associates

—Mary Huggard, Elena Heighton, Pelly Heighton, Tara Heighton, Esme Varvis and John and Christina Heighton

—Edna Alford, Jeff Balderson, Jared Bland, Judith Cowan, Richard Cumyn, Elisabeth Harvor, Jenny Haysom, Michael Holmes, Bruce & Peggy Horne, Michael Hurley, Reena Kukreja, Alvin Lee, David McDonald, Shane Neilson, Michael Newman, Alec Ross, Douglas Roy, Ingrid Ruthig, Alexander Scala, Mark Sinnett, Sue Sumeraj and Dasey Wangkhang-Silva

A winter 2009 writer-in-residence stint at the University of Ottawa was helpful in various ways, as was a brief residency at McArthur College, Queen's University, in 2007. I'm thankful to both institutions, as well as to the Canada Council and the Ontario Arts

Council for its support. I also want to thank the Yaddo Foundation for giving me an ideal place to begin the novel, in February 2007.

One reference work I found indispensible was Peter Hopkirk's excellent *Trespassers on the Roof of the World*. Martin Windrow's *The Last Valley: Dien Bien Phu and the French Defeat in Vietnam* provided, via Richard Cumyn, one piece of essential information. A version of the story of the Bodhisatva and the murderer is recounted in *Emotional Awareness: A Conversation Between the Dalai Lama & Paul Ekman, Ph.D.* The phrase that Lewis Book tries to remember, and misquotes, on page 263 of this novel is from a poem by Ezra Pound.

This book is for Mary, who was there.

—S.H.
Kingston, Ontario
November 2009

STEVEN HEIGHTON is the author of the novel *Afterlands,* which has appeared in six countries; was a *New York Times Book Review* Editors' Choice along with a best book of the year selection in ten publications in Canada, the U.S. and the U.K.; and has been optioned for film. He is also the author of *The Shadow Boxer,* a Canadian bestseller and a *Publishers Weekly* Book of the Year. His work has been translated into ten languages, and his poems and stories have appeared in *London Review of Books, Poetry, Tin House, The Walrus, Europe, Agni, Poetry London, Brick, Best English Stories* and many others. Heighton has won several awards, including three golds for fiction and poetry in the National Magazine Awards, and has been nominated for the Governor General's Literary Award, the Trillium Award, a Pushcart Prize, the Journey Prize and Britain's W.H. Smith Award.